Susan LEWIS

Last Resort

arrow books

Published by Arrow Books 2009

8 10 9 7

First published in Great Britain in 1996 by
William Heinemann
Random House, 20 Vauxhall Bridge Road,
London SW1V 2SA

www.randomhouse.co.uk

Addresses for companies within The Random House Group Limited can be
found at: www.randomhouse.co.uk/offices.htm

The Random House Group Limited Reg. No. 954009

A CIP catalogue record for this book
is available from the British Library

ISBN 9780099534334

Penguin Random House is committed to a sustainable future for
our business, our readers and our planet. This book is made from
Forest Stewardship Council® certified paper.

Printed and bound in Great Britain by Clays Ltd, St Ives plc

Acknowledgements

First and foremost my thanks must go to Hilary King for sharing so generously her experience of the magazine world as well as her wealth of contacts around the globe. This book as it stands wouldn't have been possible without Hilary's input and for that as well as her friendship I shall always be deeply indebted.

In Hong Kong my sincere thanks go to Julie Ammann of the Mandarin Oriental Hotel and Justin Strachan for the unforgettable experience of a night in Mongkok. I thank Tom Andrews too for his help. Sheri and Rob Dorfman and Teresa Norton Bobertz I thank with all my heart for smoothing the way and making my stay in Hong Kong so memorable and pleasurable.

Also I thank John and Hilary Andrews for the doors they opened in Manila, one of which led to Barry Riddell, a remarkable man whose knowledge of all things Filipino and whose enthusiasm for the book added such richness to the story. Of those in Manila who spared me so much of their valuable time I would like to thank Atty Ramsey L Ocampo, Police Chief Superintendent, PNP Narcotics Command; Miguel G Coronel, Police Chief Superintendent, PNP Director for Operations; Crescencio Maralit, Police Chief Superintendent, Antipolo.

And on the idyllic retreat of Pamalican which is home to the Amanpulo I thank Madeleine and Belle – and Alison Frew and Trina Dingler Ebert for organizing the trip.

Chapter 1

'What do you mean, you don't know where you are!'

'What I said: I don't know where I am.' The plaintive voice echoed down the line, along with the muted honking of horns and alien street bustle.

'But how the hell can you not know where you are? How did you get there?'

'By plane – I think.'

Penny Moon closed her eyes briefly, opened them again and looked impatiently at her watch. This was something she could do without at the best of times; today it was about as welcome as a Dear John. 'OK,' she said, holding on to her exasperation, 'just tell me the name of the country and we'll work from there.'

'But that's just it, I don't know which country I'm in.'

'Jesus Christ,' Penny muttered, thinking only her scatty kid sister could do this to her on such a morning. 'Well, look around you – what colour are the people?' That might give them a fighting chance.

'They seem to be, well, sort of black, I suppose,' the answer came after a pause.

'What language are they speaking?'

'I don't know. I don't understand it.'

Penny took a deep breath. 'Is it hot or cold?'

'Hot. Very hot.'

This line of questioning was proving about as productive as a lottery ticket. Thinking of which, 'Do you have

1

any money?' Penny said.

'Not a bean. I might have been robbed, because I'm sure I did have some the last time I looked.'

Penny looked out of the smeary, casement window to where south London was basking in yet another dismal, rainy start to a day. She gave a short, impatient sigh. There were times, like now, when she wished she could be as capricious as Sammy and not give a damn where she was or where the next sou was coming from. Except, of course, Sammy did care, otherwise she wouldn't be calling. 'Look,' she said, realizing she was going to be late, 'get yourself to the nearest police station and call me from there. I'll be at the office within an hour.'

'But how am I supposed to know where the police station is,' Sammy pointed out.

'You'll find it,' Penny told her and, slamming down the phone, she snatched up her briefcase, pulled on her raincoat and ran out of the door. A few seconds later she was back, puffing from the sprint up the stairs, to collect her umbrella. She was definitely going to miss the bus now and the chances of finding a taxi in Wandsworth on a morning like this were about as good as rooting out a workable European policy.

'Any chance of borrowing your car?' she cried, bursting into her flatmate's bedroom.

'What?' Peter grunted, prising open a bleary eye.

'Your car,' Penny said. 'I'm going to be late otherwise and I can't be, not today.'

'Just pay for the parking tickets,' he told her and, rolling over, went promptly back to sleep.

Ten minutes later, having drenched Monica, her neighbour, in making a rally-like swerve to the kerb to scoop her from the depressing clutch at the bus stop, Penny was swearing in time to the pulse and swish of the windscreen wipers as, up ahead, the lights changed from red to green and back to red with nothing moving. She loved London, absolutely adored it, except on mornings like this when it

2

seemed the entire world's mood was as filthy as the weather and when it was debatable which was going to boil over first, her frustration or the radiator of Peter's ancient Mini.

Looking at her watch, she groaned aloud and only just resisted the temptation to slam her hand on the horn and keep it there, as though the noise might transform itself into a giant prong that could slide beneath all the other cars and flick them into the Thames. Of course, being late wasn't going to change anything, the decision on her promotion would already have been taken, but if only, just this once, she could show her boss that she was capable of arriving somewhere on time . . .

'OK,' Monica declared, attempting to lurch forward within the confines of her seat belt to stuff the newspaper she'd been reading into her bag.

'Did they run it?' Penny asked, throwing her a quick glance.

'Nope,' Monica responded shortly.

For a moment Penny wondered if the lingering drops of rain on Monica's freckled cheeks were, in fact, tears, and when Monica turned an unsteady smile in her direction she was left in little doubt.

'What was the article on?' Penny asked.

'I can't remember,' Monica replied dismally. 'The only thing I seem able to retain these days,' she added, gazing glumly down at her thighs, 'is water.'

Smiling, Penny reached over to squeeze her hand. This had been happening to Monica for several weeks now and, though it had never happened to Penny, as a fellow journalist she had no problem understanding Monica's depression. To have one's articles consistently dropped and for no apparent reason was both humiliating and frightening. She could sense the dilemma going on inside Monica as keenly as she could if it were her own predicament: was it that she was losing it, could no longer report events in a way that was informative,

3

readable and insightful; or was it that Monica's boss, the editor of the newspaper for which she worked, was trying to edge her out now that he had dumped Monica in favour of the home affairs correspondent?

'Have you thought about striking out on your own, going freelance?' Penny asked, inching the car forward.

Monica nodded. 'I think about it all the time, but I've got a mortgage to pay – and if . . . Well, if I am losing it . . .'

'You're *not* losing it,' Penny told her firmly.

Monica turned to look at her and this time her smile held more assurance, a glint even of laughter and not a little affection. 'Being around you always does me good, Penny Moon,' she chuckled, 'but please, spare me the positive thinking. I'm not up for it this morning.'

Penny grimaced as her stomach clenched with a lively spasm of nerves. 'No, me neither,' she said.

'Oh God, I'd forgotten,' Monica groaned. 'Today's the day, isn't it?'

'Today's the day,' Penny confirmed.

'So, do you think you've got it?'

Penny shrugged.

Monica turned to look out of the window. 'I think you have,' she said, trying to keep the envy from her voice. It wasn't that she would begrudge Penny her promotion to features editor on *Starke*, it was simply that Penny's life seemed to have a golden halo of luck around it and when compared with Monica's life right now Penny's seemed so insufferably charmed and cosy that Monica would have bartered her very soul for a boss like Sylvia Starke.

'You'd make a terrific editor, you know,' Monica said generously. It was true, in a lot of ways Penny would, and a little flattery at this point might not go amiss, especially as it was very likely she'd be looking for a new job pretty soon. Magazines weren't really her cup of tea – she preferred the cut-and-thrust and impossible deadlines of daily newspaper journalism – but beggars and choosers and all that.

4

Penny laughed. 'I don't think Linda Kidman would agree with you,' she said, to a chorus of angry horns as she shot through a set of red lights at World's End. 'In fact, she's pretty damned certain she's got the job, if for no other reason than she's much more experienced than I am. She's been with *Starke* at least twice as long and she's proved herself over and over.'

'So have you,' Monica pointed out. 'And Sylvia's just crazy about you, everyone knows that.'

'But she's fair,' Penny said. 'She's announcing the results herself, by the way.'

Monica gave a snort of laughter. 'Well, that's that, then, isn't it?' she declared. 'She wants to be the one to tell you that you've finally achieved what she's been grooming you for ever since she plucked you out of knitting patterns and napkin-folding on that happily long-forgotten little rag you started on.'

'It might be that she just wants to let me down gently,' Penny countered, hoping to God it wasn't true. If it were and Linda Kidman was going to be her boss, then she didn't see that she'd have any choice but to leave *Starke*, for the very idea of having to suffer Linda's supercilious adjuncts to triumph was about as palatable as having to kiss Linda's backside, which she would unquestionably be expected to do. In truth, it was the prospect of having Linda as her editor that had added several sticks of dynamite to her own ambition – an ambition that had, of late, become something of an obsession. And, in turn, the obsession had prompted some hilarious self-mockery as well as laconic outbursts of theatrical woe that had had the rest of her colleagues convulsed with laughter.

'You don't think thirty is too young to be a features editor, do you?' Penny asked. 'I mean, it might be my age that—'

'Your age will have nothing to do with it,' Monica interrupted. 'I told you before, it's your ability that counts.' A part of her would have liked to go further and remind Penny of the recognition she had achieved on both sides of the Atlantic for some of the intuitive, witty and occasionally highly controversial interviews she had produced for *Starke*, the fortnightly news/gossip/features magazine that had a circulation of over half a million, but with her own confidence on the rocks she wasn't in much of a mood to rub her own nose in someone else's brilliance – especially when that someone was almost ten years her junior. Which just went to show what a nasty, niggardly and sour old spinster she was turning into, she thought glumly; for there was no way in the world that Penny would ever be so churlish or mean-spirited, no matter how down on her own luck she might be. But then, they all be Penny Moons, could they? For not everyone had been blessed with such an irresistible and charitable nature and nor was it everyone who had been offered a job in New York after writing an article on Graham Greene's antipathy towards Americans which, with its beautifully scripted irony, had even had the Americans laughing. Nor could many boast Penny's gift for knowing all the right buttons to push when it came to interviewing. Everyone, from under-secretaries to undertakers, from prime ministers to pimps or megastars to media moguls, seemed almost eager to confide their secrets in Penny Moon, probably, Monica reflected, because of Penny Moon's unique and enviable knack of making them forget they were being interviewed. Monica knew that Penny attributed her remarkable talent to the lack of excitement and adventure in her own life, insisting she got her thrills and spills vicariously, through her interviewees. But that was a load of old hogwash, if Monica'd ever heard any, for if she had just a fraction of Penny Moon's social life she'd be actively fighting off the social diarists, as Penny's was the phone that never stopped ringing, Penny's was the liveliness and wit that everyone wanted at their table, or their ball, or their opening night, just like Penny's was the ear that was always willing to listen. And, Monica guessed, it was Penny's popularity in London that had been behind her reason for turning down *Vanity Fair*. Everyone knew how much Penny adored London – and who could blame her when she seemed to have the whole damned town at her feet? Besides, there wasn't a Sylvia Starke in New York and mentors like that didn't come along with the no. 14 bus, did they?

'Do you mind?' Penny said, picking up the headset of her Walkman. 'It's an interview I did weeks ago now and I've got to have it written up by the end of the day.'

Monica waved a hand for her to continue. It was quite typical of Penny to cut blithely through the London traffic with a Walkman plugged into her ears without any regard for danger.

It was true to say that were Penny and Linda Kidman competing for an appearance on the front cover of *Starke*, then Linda would win hands down, but Penny was not without her physical attributes either. She wasn't particularly tall – about five foot four, Monica reckoned – neither was she particularly slim – she enjoyed her food and wine too much to be that – but she was curvaceous rather than overweight. Even so, Monica couldn't help hoping that Penny had at least as many dimples in her thighs as she had in her cheeks; it seemed only fair. She was a natural blonde with a thick, glossy bob that either swung around her collar or, as now, was tumbling heedlessly out of an elastic band. Her eyes were as blue as a midsummer sky and as sunny, her cheeks were silky smooth and permanently pink, and her mouth, whilst not large, was most definitely verging upon it and often looked, Monica thought bitchily, as though she had just given someone the blow job of his life. Her smile was as infectious as her humour and her ubiquitous air of recklessness and chaos was, if anything, what would lose her the job of features editor. For, intellect and ability aside, Penny was impulsive, hectic and impossibly emotional.

And, if there were any justice in this world, that fall she had been riding for these past two years must surely be just around the corner.

They were by now crawling past Peter Jones in the drizzle and as Penny removed her headphones she was muttering palatable profanities at a cab driver who was studiously ignoring her as she tried to edge her way in front of him. Winning the battle and wincing at the deafening blast of his horn, she gave him a jaunty little wave and plunged into the bedlam heading towards Eaton Square.

'Did you read that piece in the *Spectator* about Lord Lucan?' Penny asked, as they approached Lower Belgrave Street, where the dastardly deed had taken place. 'Oh shit! I don't believe it! Is there some kind of contest going on as to which borough can dig up the most roads in rush hour? It's like bloody open-heart surgery around here. Where shall I drop you, by the way? Will the corner of Grosvenor be OK?'

'That'll be great. What time's your meeting with Sylvia?'

Penny glanced at her watch. 'Five minutes ago,' she winced.

'Will you call me, let me know how it goes?'

'Sure,' Penny grinned, 'if you feel up to dealing with a self-pitying—'

'No, no, don't say it,' Monica cut in. 'The job's yours and we both know it. Just call me when it's confirmed and I'll grab a cab and come help you celebrate.'

A few minutes later, after abandoning the Mini by an out-of-order parking meter, Penny made a quick dash through the rain and in through the revolving front doors of *Starke* magazine. Greeting the receptionists and security staff she headed on past them towards the lifts, hoping they wouldn't notice that she was as nervous as a witch on a stake. She so desperately, *desperately*, wanted this job. She knew that everyone was rooting for her, that they, like her, didn't relish the prospect of working under such a coldly efficient fish as Linda Kidman, but what everyone else wanted wouldn't necessarily hold too much sway with Sylvia – in fact, knowing Sylvia, it wouldn't hold any sway at all. And maybe the run of luck that had gone on for almost two years now, the virtual Midas touch that could so easily have gone to her head for the recognition it had brought her, was about to do a rainbow on her.

With an unruly shudder of nerves she stepped out of the lift, fighting the lack of self-confidence she tried always to keep carefully hidden. No doubt for the most idiotic of reasons, she was suddenly believing that the decision on her promotion was still in the balance and that it was her appearance here, at the final hurdle, that was going to let her down. She hadn't done her hair properly, she'd simply pulled a long, shapeless sweater on over a scruffy pair of leggings and her boots were quite shamelessly in need of a clean. Oh God, why did she never think about these things until it was too late?

'Ah, there you are,' Rebecca, Sylvia's secretary, said with a chuckle as Penny came haring across the office, apologizing for being late and inadvertently knocking things off desks as she passed them with her heavy bags.

'I'll be right there,' Penny called, stopping at a secretary's desk and dumping her Walkman on the top of the in-tray while begging Gemma, the secretary, to give the transcription priority.

'You can go straight in,' Rebecca told her when Penny finally presented herself, grinning and breathless.

Penny turned to look at her colleagues who had stopped what they were doing to give her surreptitious winks and discreet fingers-crossed, not wanting to offend Linda, who was successfully feigning nonchalance at her desk over by the window and still awaiting her summons.

Taking a deep breath, Penny treated them all to a comical face, dropped her briefcase and umbrella where she was standing and pushed open Sylvia's door.

'Ah, Penny,' Sylvia smiled, swivelling away from her computer terminal. 'My, you look flustered. Bad journey in?'

'You could say that,' Penny answered, stripping off her fake Barbour and glancing anxiously at the coat stand, where Sylvia's silk number was hanging.

'Go ahead,' Sylvia said, getting up from her desk and walking across the rose-coloured carpet to a tray where fresh coffee was percolating. She was so elegant with her short, silvery hair framing her elfin face, her tall, slender body and exquisitely tailored black suit that Penny could have groaned aloud at her own sartorial fiasco.

'This is the first time I've seen you to congratulate you on the Frederick Lacosta interview,' Sylvia remarked, her Swiss-French accent as enchanting as the sparkling humour and urbanity in her soft, grey eyes. 'I know how much you enjoy giving coverage to the oddball characters of the world, though I must confess I found your choice in this instance somewhat startling. But then I had forgotten that sometimes there's an amusing side to death, which, may I say, you handled with admirable sensitivity. I was afraid, to begin with, that you were about to trawl the depths of sentimentality, but I should have had more faith. It was an excellent piece, Penny, dignified, compassionate, informative and funny – and, no doubt, it will have turned Mr Lacosta's Knightsbridge funeral parlour into one of the busiest terminals between here and the Elysian Fields. Coffee?' she added, starting to pour into the exquisite bone-china set her secretary laid out all sparklingly clean and ludicrously dainty each morning.

'I'll have six of those,' Penny said, referring to the oversized thimble Sylvia was holding up as she sank into a deep leather sofa. 'God, I hate London,' she sighed, tearing the elastic band from her hair.

Sylvia looked surprised. 'But I thought it was your great passion,' she said.

Through the vertical blinds at the vast picture windows Penny could see the familiar glimpses of Victoria's glistening rooftops and the gloomy oppressiveness of the February sky. 'It is,' she said. 'I just hate the dreary weather – and the traffic.'

'Mmm,' Sylvia commented, seeming, somewhat bewilderingly, to approve of this response. 'Well,' she went on, sitting on the sofa opposite Penny and crossing her ankles, 'it could be that the news I have for you is going to come as something of a pleasant surprise, then.'

Penny's heart skipped. She'd got the job! God only knew what it had to do with the weather, but who the hell cared as long as she'd got it? 'I won't let you down,' she vowed passionately, sitting forward and wanting to squeeze Sylvia with all the might of her gratitude. 'You won't regret this decision. I know you've had your reservations about my age, I know there's still a lot for me to learn, but I've got what it takes, Sylvia, I just know it.'

Sylvia smiled and looked down at her cup. 'Yes,' she said, 'you do have what it takes, I won't argue with that, but your euphoria as well as your promises are a little, how shall we say, premature?'

Penny looked as though she'd been struck. What did she mean, premature? Hadn't she just said that she'd got the job? Well, OK, not in so many words, but what other good news could there be? There wasn't anything else she wanted.

'You're aware, I'm sure,' Sylvia went on, smiling into Penny's watchful eyes, 'that we have recently acquired Fieldstone Publishing.'

'I had heard,' Penny said warily, not knowing anything about Fieldstone other than the fact she'd never even heard of any of their publications.

11

'Well,' Sylvia continued, 'I've decided that I would like you to edit one of the magazines in that group.'

'Edit? You mean, full-blown editor?' Penny said cautiously.

'Yes, full-blown editor. You have just the sort of energy and enterprise needed to get this particular magazine off its knees and back into the marketplace.'

Penny wasn't thrilled. 'Which particular magazine are we talking about?' she asked, feeling a dread of the answer start to burgeon.

'*The Coast*,' Sylvia answered, looking at her through lowered lashes and bracing herself for the response.

'Oh my God, you're sending me to Bournemouth!' Penny cried in horror.

'No, not Bournemouth,' Sylvia smiled. 'The South of France.'

Penny's mouth dropped open.

'*The Coast* is a magazine that caters for the English-speaking community on the French Riviera,' Sylvia explained.

'I don't believe this,' Penny mumbled, trying not to panic. 'Are you telling me that you're sending me to the South of France?'

Sylvia nodded.

'Oh my God, this is terrible,' Penny declared, getting to her feet. 'What did I do?' she challenged. 'Why are you banishing me? I thought you were happy with my work?'

'More than happy,' Sylvia assured her, 'which is why I have set you this task. You are quite capable of getting that magazine up and running and turning it into something you are going to be extremely proud of.'

'But I loathe the South of France!' Penny exclaimed rashly.

'Have you ever been?'

'Of course I have. And I hate it.'

Sylvia was baffled. 'Most people would jump at the

chance to go and live in the South of France,' she commented.

'Yes, people who are planning retirement or rip-offs,' Penny said cuttingly. 'In other words, vegies and villains. Well, thanks, but no thanks.'

'The alternative is to carry on here under Linda Kidman,' Sylvia pointed out.

'Oh my God,' Penny groaned, clapping a hand to her head and slumping back on to the sofa.

'And,' Sylvia went on, 'your French, I believe, is virtually fluent.'

'No!' Penny lied, shaking her head. 'I don't know a word of French except pasta.'

'That's Italian,' Sylvia said, her eyes brimming with laughter.

'You see,' Penny cried, throwing up her hands. 'I can't speak a word of French.'

'It says here that you can,' Sylvia said, opening up Penny's personnel file, which was lying on the cushion beside her.

'I lied,' Penny said, catching a glimpse of her application form.

Laughing, Sylvia said, 'I might have believed you were it not for the interview you did with Madame Mitterand entirely in French just a few weeks ago.'

Penny looked crestfallen. 'Why are you doing this to me?' she wailed. 'Why couldn't you just have made me features editor here?'

'Because I want you in the South of France. It'll be good experience for you . . .'

'Sylvia, we're talking about a readership of nine geriatrics and a poodle and an exposure of such limited proportions I'll be one of the geriatrics before I make it.'

Sylvia laughed again. 'You're in too much of a hurry, young lady,' she said. 'Your time will come, make no mistake about that and if you do turn that magazine into a success then who can say what kind of opportunities will open up for you as a result?'

OK, Penny, she said to herself, straightening up, *time to resign*. She took a breath, but now that the moment had come the words for some reason wouldn't. She'd never find another Sylvia and, much as she abhorred the idea of leaving London, to refuse this offer might just turn out to be one of the biggest mistakes of her life. On the other hand, so might accepting it. 'How long are you intending to send me over there for?' she asked miserably.

'A year, maybe two.'

Penny collapsed over her knees in dismay. She was on the point of raising another objection, when Rebecca popped her head round the door.

'Sorry to interrupt,' she said, 'but your sister's on the phone, Penny. She says she's been arrested.'

Penny's arms circled her head as she gave a wretched groan. Well, at least one thing was for sure: today couldn't get any worse. 'Do you mind?' she asked Sylvia, who answered by waving her to the phone.

'Did she say where she was?' she asked Rebecca as she crossed the room.

'In a police station,' Rebecca answered prosaically.

Penny shot her a look and picked up the phone. 'Sammy?' she said.

'Ah, Pen, there you are,' came Sammy's chirpy voice.

'What have you done to get arrested?' Penny sighed. 'If it's drugs, I'm going to let them hang you.'

'I haven't been arrested,' Sammy giggled. 'I just said that to make whoever the old sourpuss was go and get you.'

'Ingenious,' Penny muttered. 'So, where are you?'

'You'll never guess.'

'No, you're right, I won't.'

'I'm in Casablanca. You know, that place they made the film about.'

'Yes, I've heard of it. Have you figured out how you got there yet?'

14

'Somebody brought me here on a private jet. He didn't own it, or anything, he's just the pilot. But anyway, it seems like he had to go off again in a bit of a hurry and ended up forgetting about me.'

Refraining from remarking on the pilot's discerning lapse of memory, Penny said, 'So how much is it going to cost me to get you home?'

'Um, I worked it out that if you send me three hundred pounds that should cover my hotel and air fare.'

'OK, give me the bank details,' Penny said, too practised in this now to show any horror at the amount.

'That,' she said to Sylvia, pointing to the phone as she turned back to the sofa, 'is one very good reason why I can't go to the South of France. She's not safe to be left alone. I mean, look what happens when I'm here. I dread to think what she'd do if I weren't.'

'They have telephones in the South of France too,' Sylvia remarked drily. 'But why don't you take her with you?'

'Take Sammy to the South of France! Are you kidding! She'd have us both arrested before you can say Jacques Médecin.'

Sylvia arched an eyebrow. Médecin, the notorious ex-mayor of Nice, was, if memory served her correctly, still facing charges of corruption, so maybe Penny had a point about villains. Still, it wasn't a topic she was going to pursue. 'Take Sammy with you and give her a job,' she said. 'It could be just what she needs. Something to concentrate her mind. A bit of responsibility, a pay packet of her own . . .'

'And whole harbours full of yachts to smuggle herself away on,' Penny added woefully.

'Well, think about it,' Sylvia chuckled as she got to her feet. 'I'm sure you've got a busy day in front of you so take the weekend to think things over and we'll have a spot of lunch together on Monday when you can give me your final decision.'

'Do I have any choice?' Penny enquired.

'Yes, of course you do,' Sylvia answered, opening the door. 'But I think we both already know that you're not going to take either of the alternatives. Incidently, Rebecca here will give you some back copies of *The Coast* to look over.'

'Shit!' Penny muttered under her breath as Sylvia closed the door behind her.

She was too late to pull a mask over her disappointment which meant that as Linda Kidman sailed past for her session with Sylvia Penny had the joyful experience of being gloated at. Resisting the urge to smack her one, Penny took herself to her desk and sat down heavily.

'What's this?' she snapped, pulling a cardboard box towards her. 'Oh God,' she groaned when she saw the range of anti-cellulite creams Claude, the celebrity beautician, had sent her.

'Pen!' someone shouted. 'Yolanda and Maurice want to see you as soon as you're free. They want to know how the piece on that Italian judge is coming along. I think they're rather keen to run it *before* the Sicilians put Whatever-her-name-is in her concrete boots.'

Penny rolled her eyes. Great, just what she needed right now: the editor and news editor ganging up on her for an interview she'd done in Rome five days ago with Carla Landolfi, the Italian judge whose courage and rectitude in the face of repeated Mafia threats begged any number of mythological metaphors. The entire interview was in Italian and she hadn't even translated it yet. Well, she'd just have to wing it, keep Yolanda and Maurice happy for a couple more days and move like greased lightning all weekend.

'Anyone seen the photographs I left on my desk?' she cried, riffling through the chaos. 'The ones of her Honour?'

'Frank came up for them earlier,' Philip Collins, the

sub who sat opposite, informed her. 'He left a note . . .'

'Where did this come from?' Penny demanded, picking up a giant hardback book by some obscure writer with an unpronounceable name. The note hooked inside read: 'Thought this was just up your street. A rampantly political Russian romance. Need the review by the end of next week. Any chance? Maybelle.'

Penny slung it to one side and picked up her phone. 'Anyone know the number for the art department?' she yelled.

'4962,' Philip answered. 'So, come on, how did it go in there? Don't keep us all in suspense.'

Having received an engaged signal, Penny replaced the receiver and heaved her briefcase on to her desk. 'How are you doing with that transcript, Gemma?' she called out.

'Another hour and you should have it,' the secretary shouted back.

Knowing they were all watching her, Penny looked up at last and, finding Philip's curious round eyes and fluffy chin in her direct line of vision, she felt a surprising flood of affection for him. He was an ablutophobe who blithely stank out their corner, irritated her to the point of violence and frequently had her reaching jibberingly for the bottle by lunchtime. But suddenly today she loved him, adored him, wanted to sit opposite him for the rest of her days and inhale the glorious odour of his unwashed body. 'If I told you I'd got the job it would make me one of Congreve's first magnitude,' she answered dolefully.

'You're obfuscating, Penny,' he sweetly reprimanded.

'No, I *didn't* get the bloody job!' she seethed. 'And, what's more, I'm leaving.'

A general murmur of surprise and dismay reverberated around the office. Having Linda Kidman as the boss was bad enough, but without Penny there the place was going to be about as much fun as a German resurgence

17

of patriotism.

'You didn't really give your notice in?' Karen Armstrong, one of the assistants, asked incredulously.

Penny shook her head. 'I'm being banished to the fucking French Riviera,' she said wretchedly.

The others exchanged puzzled glances, unable to fathom why Penny should find that such an odious prospect, especially when they learned that Penny was to be given her own magazine.

'Because,' she explained, 'all my contacts are here, all my friends are here, I love London, I love my life and I don't have the remotest desire to end it.' What she didn't add, for modesty forbade, was how ridiculously proud and excited she had been to read about herself in *The Times* just last week when a journalist she didn't even know had advised Lynn Barber and Zoe Heller to sharpen up their acts because 'Penny Moon is fast becoming the most widely read and respected interviewer in the country'. How could Sylvia do this to her? It was like asking a bride on the eve of her wedding to exchange the man of her dreams for a deaf-mute dwarf with the life expectancy of Methuselah and the get-up-and-go of a pork chop.

'You'll be coming back, won't you?' Philip said. 'I mean, *eventually*.'

Penny shrugged. 'Who knows? But even if I do you'll all have moved on to other things by then and all my contacts will be in Linda frigging Kidman's black book. It'll be like starting from scratch all over again.' Slumping forward she rested her chin despondently in her hands. 'Plus,' she added, 'I don't know a single, solitary soul down there.'

'Well, I don't think you'll be short of visitors,' Annie Kaplin, another journalist, grinned, already thinking about her summer holiday.

'When are you going?' Karen asked.

'God knows. I haven't actually said yes yet. Oh shit,

why can't she send Linda? She'd love it down there on the Riviera, strutting her stuff for the seriously brain dead. And what the hell am I going to *look* like down there in all that sun? I won't be able to cover up any of the nasty bits ... Maybe I'd better keep those cellulite creams and try a bit harder. What the hell's all that?' she cried, glaring up at the post boy as he dumped a sack full of mail on the floor beside her.

'Applications for the Declan Hailey talk on nude art,' the post boy informed her. 'I was told to bring them all to you.'

'You left this in Sylvia's office,' Rebecca said, handing Penny the scribbled bank details Sammy had given her.

'Oh yes, thanks,' Penny said, taking them. 'I suppose I'd better do that now or she really will manage to get herself arrested. Anyone fancy the wine bar for lunch? I'm in need of one last binge before I start the next deportation of fat cells.'

Laughing and groaning, they all turned back to their desks. Penny's diets were as legendary as they were unsuccessful – though at times they were almost as good a source of entertainment as her outrageously chaotic love life.

Chapter 2

Early the following afternoon, complete with overnight bag, portable computer and bulging sack of Declan Hailey mail, Penny was unceremoniously deposited by a taxi into the driving rain at the entrance of a secluded and picturesque little harbour just outside Portsmouth. Two neat rows of smart town houses, currently being belaboured by the storm and hazed by low-sailing grey cloud, fringed opposite sides of the harbour, where yachts of all sizes and descriptions bobbed and clanked recklessly on the swelling tide.

As Penny struggled along the narrow towpath with her luggage she was wondering what kind of mood she was going to find Declan in after their phone call the night before when she'd tried to persuade him to come up to London rather than her having to drag all the way to Portsmouth when she was so busy. He'd won the battle, partly because she'd had too much to do to spend the time arguing, but mainly because not having seen him all week she wasn't about to deprive herself any further of the kind of things they enjoyed most.

After almost a year they were still photographed and written about on a fairly regular basis, though nothing like when they'd first got together. It was Penny's revelation that the nude portrait which had catapulted Declan into the media spotlight was indeed of the royal personage rumour claimed it to be. Since one of Declan's trademarks was never quite to reveal the face of his subject – in this instance, the woman concerned was draped languorously across a bed of silk cushions with her face turned shyly into the crook of her arm – no one had been able to say for sure whether or not it really was the mischievous limelight-seeker whose flagrant hedonism was known to provoke many a wince at Her Majesty's breakfast table. After interviewing Declan Penny had been able to put an end to the speculation with the exclusive that he, in an unguarded moment, had given her. Declan had been furious that she had gone to print with what he called 'a royal confidence', and had publicly challenged Penny to print the entire truth of their interview. Penny hadn't, for two reasons: first because *Starke* wasn't the kind of magazine that ran that sort of story; second, because she wasn't proud of the way she had allowed herself to be so easily – and repeatedly – seduced during the weekend it had taken her to interview him. Instead she had written him an apology which had also reminded him that she hadn't revealed the fact that he and the *married* lady concerned had had an affair. Declan had agreed to accept the apology on the condition that she, Penny, sat for him for three whole days the following week at his studio in Portsmouth. As it turned out, they made love for three days, which both had known they would, and ever since then Penny had happily posed for him whenever he asked, but only because of what it led on to, certainly *not* because she hoped to see the end results on public display – which they never were.

As she approached the last house in the terrace, which masterfully concealed an expansive top-floor studio with a panoramic view of the sea, she was desperately hoping that she wasn't going to find him in one of his artistic sulks. She needed to talk and, when in spirits, he was the most level-headed adviser she knew, whose logic, though as peculiarly and poetically Irish as his long, jet-black hair and devilish turquoise-blue eyes, always seemed to contain more basic common sense than most would ever credit him for. But when in a sulk he was totally insufferable and best given the kind of berth one would normally reserve for a kamikaze recruiting agent.

Inserting her key in the lock, she pushed open the door and dropped her bags in the hall.

'Is that you?' Declan called out as the door slammed behind her.

'It's me,' she called back, looking up through the three levels of wrought-iron staircases. She waited a moment, then started to smile as he came to lean on the banisters and look down at her. His dark hair was tied in a ponytail, his lean, handsome face was smeared with paint and he was badly in need of a shave.

'Hi,' she said, thinking that Diane Driscoll, the diarist for one of the seamier tabloids who was more commonly known as the Doyenne of Drivel, was right when she'd written that 'one look at the artist Declan Hailey is enough to electrify the extremities with the desire to be titillated by his masterful brush'.

'Hi,' he said. 'Hungry?'

'Mmm, a bit,' she answered. 'You working?'

'Yeah. Richmond's here.'

'Hi, Richmond,' she shouted.

'How you doing, Pen?' the Olympic gold medallist called back.

'Just fine. I'll leave you to get on with it,' she said to Declan. 'I've got a whole stack of things that need finishing by Monday. Did you pick up the papers this morning?'

'They're on the table,' he told her. 'Got a kiss for your old man?'

Blowing him one, Penny shrugged off her coat, then carried her computer through to the sitting room, where the log fire he'd no doubt built for her was smouldering

22

towards extinction in its black marble niche. The rest of the room was in its normal state of chaos, telling her that he'd had guests the night before and Mrs Pettigrew had once again been too hungover to make an appearance.

Yawning, she pushed her fingers through her hair and started to clear a space for herself on the glass-topped dining table that separated the high-tech kitchen and eclectic bedlam of the sitting room. Then, finding some hot coffee in the percolator, she emptied it into the one remaining clean cup and went to rekindle the fire. Much as she liked Richmond she was hoping he wasn't planning on staying the entire weekend, which most did when they came to Declan's, for people were drawn to him as if he was some kind of messiah. But since Richmond lived just a couple of miles down the road she doubted he'd stay long and as Declan knew she wanted to talk he'd have very likely built some time for them into whatever the weekend schedule was. Meanwhile she had the rest of this Italian interview to translate and with the promise of a couple of hours without interruption she'd do well to get down to it.

The first hour went well, Carla Landolfi having had plenty to say that was both revelatory and unflinchingly courageous, but when it came to adding her own comments to the interview Penny found her mind wandering back to Sylvia's decision to send her to France. Apart from desperately not wanting to go, the thing that was bothering her most about it was why Sylvia had chosen now to send her into exile, when, to be frankly immodest about it, her rising popularity as an interviewer was just what *Starke* needed and, unless she'd totally misread everything, was projecting her towards the position Sylvia had always intended her to occupy. So to banish her now didn't make any sense. It was like nurturing a prize-winning rose then snipping off the bud before it had a chance to blossom.

Getting up from her chair Penny wandered back to the

fire and stacked a couple more logs. As she watched the flames flare up, she bit down hard on the anger that was growing inside her. Her diary was full for weeks ahead, requests were coming in all the time for her to interview celebrities and statesmen, as well as offers to talk from the normally publicity shy, so why the hell would she want to go to France? She'd almost rather take a job on the *Sunday Sport* than leave London now. The trouble was, though, she doubted she had it in her to throw everything back in Sylvia's face by turning her down when Sylvia had done so much for her?

With a quick sigh of impatience she turned to answer the phone. Everything was silent upstairs and, knowing Declan would just let it ring rather than break his muse, she snatched up the receiver and barked, 'Hello!'

'Pen? Is that you?'

'Mally?' Penny cried, breaking instantly into a smile. 'Where the hell are you?'

'London!' Mally yelled ecstatically. 'We just got in. I called your flat. Peter told me where you were.'

'How was the tour?' Penny laughed. 'I read about it. Seems you were—'

'Fan-fuckin'-tastic!' Mally cut in, in a broad Northern accent. 'But what the hell are you doing in Portsmouth? We're only here for the weekend.'

'Then get on a train and come down,' Penny cried. 'There's plenty of room. Declan won't mind.'

'What, all of us?' Mally gasped excitedly. 'D'you hear that, you pissheads?' she called over her shoulder. 'She's inviting us down there.'

Penny laughed at the bawdy cheer of approval from Mally's band. 'Yes, all of you,' she confirmed. 'Get on the next train.'

'Right on, sistuh,' Mally boomed. 'Be there as soon as we can,' and after jotting down the address she rang off.

Still laughing, Penny replaced the receiver and strolled back to her computer. Mally and her rock band were old friends from college days whose rise to fame was beginning to take on meteoric proportions. They'd already had a number one hit and the next was currently zooming up the charts, while their recent tour of the States, from what she had read, had been a total sellout. It would be great to see Mally and the boys, but, damn it, how was she going to get rid of Richmond before they turned up so that she and Declan could talk? She'd told him on the phone about France, but though he hadn't passed any comment at the time he had seemed as keen to discuss it as she'd expected him to be.

Smiling to herself, she sat back down and rested her chin on her hand. The entire world knew how possessive Declan was of her – his public outbursts of jealousy had on one momentous occasion resulted in him challenging a hapless young hack to pistols at dawn and, on another, to emptying a plate of squid over an MP's head, in order to, as he'd put it, 'cool his filthy ardour', because he'd been gazing a touch too lustfully into Penny's eyes. There were countless other incidents too, most of which had found their way into one diary column or another and kept the better part of London, if not the nation, highly entertained with the hot-blooded romance that, at the outset, no one had believed would last.

But it had and Penny smiled to herself as she recalled how only last weekend, which they had spent at his studio in London, he had left a message on his answerphone announcing to the world that he couldn't come to the phone because he was making love to his woman. This was so typically Declan that it had simply made her laugh when she'd found out, and, besides, it was the truth: they'd spent a rare and blissful two days without a single interruption and she could only wish they were similarly occupied right now.

A surprising *frisson* of excitement suddenly passed through her, but it wasn't only at the thought of their love-making, she realized, it was also at the idea of the kind of life they would lead if they did go to France. She was in no doubt that if she went Declan would come with her, if for no other reason than on the couple of occasions they had visited the Riviera he'd talked so wistfully of living there, had waxed so lyrical about the quality of the light, that she'd almost felt guilty at the way her job tied her to London. Once she had attempted, half-heartedly it was true, to persuade him to give in to his longing and take a studio in the artist's village of St. Paul, but the conversation ended pretty quickly as there was no way he was going without her.

So, she asked herself with a sigh, what was there to discuss? Sylvia had made up her mind, Declan would be all for them going, and, she had to confess, now that she'd had a little more time to get used to the idea, the thought of all the parties she and Declan would throw, the endless stream of guests from London and Ireland, as well as the circle of itinerant intelligentsia and slightly barmy indigenous wits he would inevitably attract, was becoming quite appealing.

Damn Richmond, she thought, glancing at her watch. It had only been in the past couple of months that Declan had started to do male nudes and, boy, had she learned a thing or two about male vanity in that time! To see them gazing at Declan's perfect renditions of their beauty was like watching Narcissus catching his reflection in a stream. They couldn't tear themselves away and Declan, loving nothing more than he loved praise, was quite happy for them to ogle his masterpieces for as long as it took him to get bored – which could be anything from an hour to an entire day, depending on the subject's eloquence.

It was rare for her to interrupt him while he was working, but in this instance Penny felt justified in climbing the three flights of stairs to the studio, for she had to let him know that Mally and the boys were arriving. With any luck this would remind him that the time they would have to talk had suddenly become limited – and if she were to let him know how keen she was to remove her own clothes right now, then Richmond would probably be out of the door in even less time than it took to put his trousers back on.

Pausing when she reached the top stair she rested her elbows on the banister, and quietly regarded the scene in the studio. Declan, his shirt unbuttoned and hanging loose over the elastic waistband of the Turkish-style pants that drooped well below his navel, was at his easel, a brush between his lips, a palette on the stool beside him and such a fixed air of concentration about him that Penny felt reluctant to speak. Though his skin was pale, dressed the way he was he had something of the Suleiman about him, and as she noticed the outline of his genitals beneath the flimsy fabric of his pants a spark of lust bit deeply into her.

Richmond was sprawled across an old maple-wood day bed, his perfect, athlete's body gleaming with the oils he had earlier massaged into his ebony skin. One arm was thrown across his eyes, the other hand was resting, Penny noticed with some surprise, beside an almighty erection. She wondered how long he had been in that state and whether it was something Declan had insisted on or was simply a result of Richmond having recently taken a quick dekko at his portrait.

Canvases were stacked all around them, fighting for space with vast, embroidered cushions, a couple of threadbare throne-style chairs, an assortment of three-fold screens and the usual artist's paraphernalia, which cluttered every available surface. The scent of whisky in the warm air was only slightly masked by the turps and tempora, and the dazzling spotlights focused on Richmond's body made it almost impossible to see the colourless seascape beyond the rain-spattered windows.

As she brought her eyes back to Declan she saw him wink, telling her he knew she was there. A minute or two later he removed the brush from his mouth and, sliding a hand into his trousers as though into a pocket, he stood back for a critical view.

'Fucking brilliant,' he said, the obscenity rolling off his Irish tongue like a lover's endearment. Then, removing his hand from his trousers, he planted it on his hip, hooking his shirt out of the way so that Penny could see his partial erection.

Smiling to herself, Penny waited for him to turn and look at her. When he did she allowed her eyes to rest on his for a moment, then dropped them blatantly to his groin. The exhilaration he felt when he'd finished a portrait never failed to manifest itself in the kind of rampancy she had no problem in matching, which was why he always waited until she was around before applying the final strokes.

She was so ready for him that she'd almost forgotten Richmond was there, until he swung his legs from the day bed and stood up. He was the same height as Declan and about the same build – and, she noticed, still as hard as a constable's truncheon.

'Watcha,' he said to Penny, stretching his arms above his head, then running his hands down over his chest. Since he appeared totally oblivious to his erection, or the fact she could see it, Penny found herself becoming increasingly fascinated by the dark beauty of his masculinity. In fact, she could barely tear her eyes away as she watched him pad over to the easel to take a look at Declan's latest *chef-d'oeuvre*.

As they stood side by side, staring wordlessly at the portrait, Penny was struck by how devastatingly attractive a contrast they made, one so white, the other so black. It felt strangely, almost mind-blowingly, erotic watching two such powerfully built men standing in such close proximity when both were sexually aroused. Declan turned to look at her, as though knowing what was going through her mind. She thought for one heart-stopping moment that he was going to invite her to join them and wondered what she would do if he did, but then he turned back to the portrait as though telling her this was a fantasy they would keep for later.

Then suddenly she felt her legs turning to water as Richmond's arm came up to rest across Declan's shoulders. Declan turned his head towards him and as their lips met she saw Declan's tongue move into the darkness of Richmond's mouth.

Shock rooted Penny to the spot as she stared at them with the kind of compulsion she experienced when watching a horror film. The air was charged with their eroticism; she could feel it moving through her with the cutting edge of silk. Richmond's hand was sliding beneath the waistband of Declan's pyjamas. Their mouths were still joined; the dark sweep of their lashes quivered in the mounting intensity. Richmond was holding Declan's fully erect penis, moving his hand back and forth. Then he stepped in closer and as his own penis brushed against Declan's he circled his fingers around both, clamping them together, while with his other hand he began to push Declan's pyjamas down over his hips.

Penny turned quietly away and walked unsteadily down the stairs. When she reached the sitting room she simply stood there, staring blankly into space. The greatest part of the shock, she realized, was not so much what they were doing, but that they had done it in front of her, that Declan had so clearly wanted her to witness his initiation into the world of homosexuality. What was surprising her even more, she realized dully, was her own calmness in the face of such blatant and stupefying infidelity.

Her head went to one side and as she caught her reflection in the mirror she gave a humourless laugh. How the hell was she supposed to handle this? Should she storm out in a fit of prim, Victorian disgust? She didn't much feel like doing that and, besides, how could she when Mally and the boys were already on their way? So did she just sit there and wait for them to finish? It was going to feel pretty weird trying to get on with her work while Declan was upstairs getting laid by a long-distance runner. She guessed she just had to hope he wasn't a long-distance lover.

Walking over to the kitchen, she put more coffee in the percolator, then turned to watch the rain sliding down the windows. It was hard to believe that the man who made love to her so tenderly and boisterously and so damned regularly was upstairs now playing the woman for another man. She felt herself starting to turn hot, then slightly dizzy with the fear of what it really meant. It was as if the past two days had descended on her world with all the vengeance of Nemesis, tearing out the roots of her career and shattering all the trust and belief she had had in Declan. And as the images of what they might be doing to each other began to flash hideously through her mind she knew that she was never going to be able to bring herself to make love with him again after this. The betrayal was absolute and irrevocable. The hurt and the shame was unforgivable.

Suddenly she was shaking with fury. The bastard! How could he spring this on her now when he knew how vulnerable she was feeling about her job and knew too that since her mother had died and Sammy had gone off travelling he was the only person she felt close to, the only one she ever turned to in times of need. This was one of those times and what was he doing? He was up there literally getting his ass screwed off by another man, while she was down here feeling like a superannuated idiot who didn't know whether to put the kettle on or tie the bastard's balls to his ankles with a short string.

The bucket was already under the tap, water cascading into it, as she fumed with a deadly mix of resentment, devastated pride and fury. Hiking the bucket out of the sink she marched up the stairs. As she turned into the studio the light blinded her for an instant; then, seeing them writhing about on the cushions like a negative trying to get processed she dumped the entire contents of the bucket over them, before snatching up a tube of black paint and squirting it all over Richmond's portrait.

'What the fuck . . . ?' Richmond protested as she started to walk out of the studio.

'Be-Jesus, she's angry!' Declan muttered, using the back of his hand to wipe the water from his face. 'Penny! Penny, get back here.'

Penny swung round. 'Oh, I'm not angry, Declan,' she seethed. 'Why should I be angry that you want to play Polo mints with Mr Bassett, here?'

'She calling me a liquorice allsort?' Richmond grunted.

At any other time Penny might have laughed. As it was, she was too hurt and angry to respond. The only thing that brought her a moment of relief was the sight, from the corner of her eye, of a discarded condom wrapper. 'I don't know whether you've just lost your virginity, Declan,' she said scathingly. 'If you have, I hope it hurt like hell. But if you've done this before then I'm making you a promise here and now: if there's the slightest hint of any virus whatsoever in my blood when I go to get it tested, I'll be back here to cut off your dick and shove it so far down your throat you'll be wearing your balls as earrings. Have you got that? Are you receiving me?'

'But Penny, m'darling, you got this all wrong,' he said, smothering his slackening genitals with his hand. 'To be sure, you got this all wrong. I thought this was what you wanted, so I did. You said you wanted two men . . .'

'That was *fantasy*, Declan,' she shouted. 'Don't you know the god-damned difference? And if it *was* what I wanted, it was supposed to be me who had the other man, not *you*!'

Declan grimaced. 'Well, to be sure, I can see there's

31

been some confusion here,' he said. 'But I love you, Pen. I love you with all my fickle heart, so I do.' He grinned roguishly, as though expecting to make her laugh.

'Is this the first time?' she demanded.

His expression was a burlesque of shame.

'Stupid question,' she muttered, contempt adding itself to the anger.

'You know what it's like for me, Pen,' he said mournfully. 'I can't be controlling me hormones now. But it's you who makes me life worth living. It's you who gives me—'

'Save it, Declan,' she snapped. 'I'm getting myself tested – and providing I'm not harbouring some killer disease, you'll never see me again.' She was surprised by how much those words hurt, for she meant them and she loved him and she just didn't want any of this to be happening.

'But, Penny, aren't we to be going to France together?' he asked plaintively.

'In your dreams, Declan,' she cried.

'Oh, now don't be saying things like that,' he protested. 'You know how I've always wanted to go to France.'

'Then go, Declan. Go, and take him with you.'

Realizing he was again being spoken about, Richmond jerked his head round, moving his gaze from the devastated portrait that now showed what he would look like if it really were possible to melt under the burning animosity in Penny's eyes.

'You see, I just like sex,' Declan said, with his unique flair for *non sequiturs*. 'Well, you'll be knowing that, but the best is always with you, so it is. Didn't I say that to you, Richmond: the best is always with Penny.'

'Some people are satisfied with the best,' Penny snapped as Richmond obediently nodded his head.

'And to be sure I am,' Declan assured her. 'But it's like, well, you know how it is, people come in different

32

shapes and sizes and I like to be trying them all. But my heart belongs to you, Penny Moonshine. Everyone knows my heart belongs to you. But sometimes a man needs something else, so he does.'

The absurdity of the situation, a situation only someone like Declan could ever bring about, wasn't by any means passing Penny by, but her normally indomitable humour was blunted by the pain of knowing how much she was going to miss him.

'I'll get myself tested,' she said sharply, 'and I suggest you do the same. How many other women have you slept with? They should be told too.'

'Oh, now, listen to what you're saying, Penny,' he objected. 'You're assuming the worst. I'll not be having AIDS, I promise you that. And the other women, now they won't be reacting the way you are, so they won't.'

Penny's heart twisted. So there were other women too. How ludicrously naïve of her never to have suspected it before. 'Nevertheless, I think you should inform them of your bisexuality, or at least get yourself tested to make sure you're clear,' she said.

'If that's what you're wanting, then take it as done,' he said. 'Just don't be walking out of my life.'

'I'm sorry, Declan,' she said.

'Penny! I'll never sleep with another man,' he cried, leaping to his feet as she started down the stairs. 'I swear it, Penny. Let's go to France, put all this behind us and start over, why not?'

Stopping, she turned back to look at him. 'It's not just the men, Declan,' she said. 'In fact, the strange part is if it weren't for AIDS I could almost forgive that – after all, they can offer you something I can't. But it's not something I can live with, Declan; nor can I with the other women.'

'Monogamy? That's it: you'll be wanting monogamy,' he said decisively, as though this aberration of the female psyche had never occurred to him before. 'I can give you monogamy.'

'No, you can't,' she said. 'I should have realized it before, but I suppose I just didn't want to.' She smiled bleakly. 'We've had some good times together, Declan, some great times, but as of now I'm signing out of the harem.'

He waited until she reached the landing below, then in a voice that was imbued with gentleness he said, 'Penny, if you're going it alone from here, if there's nothing I can say to change your mind, then you take my advice now. Always remember how special you are, that this humble man who has erred still loves you – and if you were maybe to be lose a little bit of weight now, well, I'd be happy to take you back.'

Perfect, Penny was seething to herself as she walked on down the stairs. *Just perfect*. Why could she never think of the devastating exit lines when they were called for? But in truth, despite the hurt, the very rumness of it all was almost making her laugh. Though only, she guessed, because Mally was on her way and, if nothing else, Mally would be able to make her see the funny side of it all. Knowing Mally, she'd even find it funny to discover Penny waiting at the station ready to board the next train back to London. Nothing ever seemed to faze Mally, and ordinarily Penny had to admit that nothing much fazed her either, so the hell was she going to let this be an exception. She had a mountain of work to get through, plenty to occupy her time and her mind; it was just a shame that by Sunday night Mally would be gone and by Monday she, Penny, had to have an answer ready for Sylvia.

Damn Declan! she thought, tears burning her eyes as she gathered up her belongings. Damn him, damn him, damn him, for the idea of going to France without him was making her resist it all the more.

*

'. . . and I'll take the *magret de canard*, thank you,' Sylvia said, closing the menu and handing it back to the waiter.

Penny's blue eyes, though slightly red from all the crying she had done over Declan these past two days, were sparkling with laughter. 'Not very subtle,' she commented.

Sylvia inclined her head questioningly.

'Bringing me to a French restaurant,' Penny clarified.

Laughing, Sylvia raised her glass of light, carefully chilled Provençal *rosé*. 'There's a lot of this, too, where you'll be going,' she said.

'I'm sure there is,' Penny remarked, clinking her glass against Sylvia's.

Sylvia's affection was clear in her eyes as she looked at Penny. 'I'm glad you've agreed to go,' she said, smiling. 'And though you might not think so now, you'll thank me for it in the end. You're too young to be tying yourself to one country, and England, I'm sorry to say, is fast becoming the backwater of Europe. You need to be out there experiencing more of the world and most young women of your age would give a great deal for an opportunity like this.'

'It's OK, I feel ungracious enough as it is, so you don't have to rub it in,' Penny said with the ingenuous bluntness towards her superiors that had warmed Sylvia to her at the very beginning. 'Did you get a chance to look at the memo I left for you this morning?'

Sylvia nodded and with a wry smile said, 'As usual when something is penned by you, *ma chère*, it made rather entertaining reading. However, I have to say that I am in complete agreement with you: the magazine as it stands is . . . Now, let me see, how did you put it?'

'A heap of shit,' Penny provided.

Laughing, Sylvia sat back in her chair. 'As I recall, what you said was that "after diligently excavating this mine of slothful pomposity the odd gem could be found glinting. But, taken in its entirety, it was the apogee of banality expounding more self-congratulatory twaddle than a Labour party press release." '

'I was feeling benevolent at the time.' Penny grinned.

Still laughing, Sylvia said, 'So now I should like to hear any ideas you might have for putting it to rights.'

'Still early days for that,' Penny responded, popping an olive into her mouth. 'That's not to say I don't have ideas, it's just that I would like to do some more homework before I commit myself to paper.'

'Then I would suggest that you make a trip to the South of France and get the lie of the land, see if you want to keep on any of the staff or contributors or even the premises – and while you're at it, you can find somewhere suitable to live. You'll have a generous allowance – as the editor you will be called upon to entertain quite frequently, so I'd advise you to choose a nice villa somewhere.'

Penny had to admit that, on the face of it, it was all sounding pretty irresistible, but taking a deep breath she said, 'Look, I know I've said I'll go, and I will, but there still remains just one tiny little snag – I don't have any experience of actually running a magazine . . .'

'I'm aware of that,' Sylvia answered, 'which is why I have arranged for you to spend as much time as possible with Yolanda before you go. It's also why I have assigned someone to work alongside you.'

Penny's eyes instantly narrowed. 'Oh? Who?' she said warily.

'My godson, David,' Sylvia replied.

Penny's glass hit the table, slopping wine on to the chequered cloth. 'You don't happen to mean David Villers, do you?' she said, horrified. 'No, please tell me you don't mean him!'

'Yes, I mean David Villers,' Sylvia confirmed, as the waiter placed an hors-d'oeuvre in front of her.

'Then, that's it!' Penny declared. 'I'll have to resign now because I wouldn't work with that man if my entire life depended on it. I'd rather be Linda Kidman's lackey.

I'd rather go back to Preston. I'd rather juggle chainsaws than work with David Villers.'

'I had no idea you felt so strongly about him,' Sylvia said, trying hard not to laugh. It wasn't the first time she'd witnessed such a heated response from a female where her godson was concerned and she doubted it would be the last. In fact, knowing Penny as she did, it was highly likely there'd be an endless stream of them coming up over the next few months that would be as colourful as they were entertaining.

'Sylvia, this isn't funny,' Penny said earnestly, her luminous eyes clouding with despair. These had not been an easy few days and so far there was no sign of any let-up. 'I know he's your godson,' she said, 'but, I'm sorry, I can't stand him and I certainly can't work with him. So I'm afraid you'll have to find someone else.'

Sylvia was shaking her head. 'The more I've thought about this, Penny,' she said, 'the more convinced I am that your – how shall we put it? – unique combination of talents is exactly what is needed for the job. Just give yourself a chance . . .'

'But not with David,' Penny implored. 'Please not with him. I'll do it willingly, I'll go and you'll never hear a word of complaint from me, if only you'll say it doesn't have to be with him.'

Sylvia was more bemused than annoyed. 'Why on earth do you dislike him so much?' she asked. 'In fact, I didn't even realize you'd met him – he's so rarely in the country.'

'Oh, I've met him all right,' Penny said tightly as the unsavoury memory flaunted itself brazenly in her mind. 'And he's rude, arrogant, lazy, selfish, spoiled and downright fucking horrible.'

'My, my!' Sylvia chuckled. 'I always knew he had his faults, but what on earth did he do to you?'

Penny looked away. She wasn't about to admit to Sylvia that once, while under the influence of a little too

37

much wine, she'd come on pretty strong to her precious godson. They'd been at a party in one of the plush restaurants on the Embankment at the time and Penny, like every other woman present, had been aware of David Villers from the moment he'd walked in. Being as strikingly good-looking as he was with his long, curly blond hair and strong, well-defined features, it was hardly surprising he'd caused such a stir. But it wasn't only his looks that attracted people to him, for his self-confidence and easy humour had a magnetic allure all their own. He'd been there for almost half an hour by the time Penny plucked up the courage to respond to the interested glances he was casting her way. It wasn't until she had already introduced herself that she'd realized the glances had in fact been directed towards the leggy brunette somewhere behind her. However, with a reck-less, champagne-induced bravado fizzing through her, instead of moving on she had attempted to block his view of the other woman by bobbing around in front of him, snatching his smiles for herself while going into some hideously embarrassing routine designed to impress him. Even now, as she thought of it, she could feel her toes curling. But that was by no means the worst of it, for if she remembered correctly, and sadly she knew she did, every time he'd politely tried to excuse himself she had unflinchingly pressed more of her amus-ing anecdotes upon him while sidling doggedly with him across the room. *Oh God, why do we do these things?* She was cringing inside. It was only after the call of nature had prised her briefly from his side that he had made good his escape and then, coming back down the stairs, she'd overheard him apologizing to the host of the party for sneaking out early but he just had to get away from the 'stumpy little blonde who's coming on to me like some sex-starved Sumo'.

As she looked at Sylvia, still trying to think of an answer, Penny was sunk in the misery of her recaptured disgrace. How could any self-respecting woman have embarrassed herself like that? Unfortunately the answer was 'easily', since if the truth were known she had a bit of a knack for it. But why couldn't David Villers just have stayed in Miami where he belonged? Actually, if she remembered correctly he was a Scot, but he'd lived in the States for ten years or more, or so he'd said, and as far as she was concerned the USA was more than welcome to him. She had no idea what he'd been doing over there and neither did she care. Except now he was back in England, at least she presumed he was, and he was about to discover that his partner in this new venture was none other than the sex-starved Sumo. Wasn't he going to be pleased!

'Does he know yet that it's me who's editing?' Penny asked.

'Yes.'

Penny's eyes opened wide. 'Didn't he object?' she cried indignantly. He could at least have done her that favour.

'To be truthful with you, Penelope, he didn't seem to know who you were.'

Penny felt the colour burn her cheeks. 'Please, don't call me Penelope,' she said.

'But why on earth not? It's such a pretty name.'

'Because it sounds plump. Looking plump is bad enough. I don't want to sound it too.'

Sylvia laughed. 'You really are such a funny thing at times,' she said. 'You've got so much going for you, including a lovely face, and, who knows, maybe a bit of sunshine and exercise will get that body of yours into better shape.'

'Meaning I need it,' Penny bristled.

'Meaning . . .' Sylvia threw out her hands. 'I don't think I can win here so let's get back to the subject of David, shall we? Amongst the lengthy list of superlatives you used to describe him I will challenge only one. He isn't lazy. Regarding the rest, I concede you may well be right. But he has an exceptional flair for business, which is why I have asked him to take on this magazine with you. You will have equal power...'

'How can we when he's your godson?' Penny protested. 'And if, like you say, he's so much more experienced in the world of business than I am?'

'You will have equal power,' Sylvia repeated, 'which is something David is already aware of and hasn't disputed. To all intents and purposes the magazine will be yours, as will the decisions, and he will help out on the finance and business fronts where necessary. So there is no need to concern yourself about some kind of power struggle.'

'What's his title going to be?' Penny enquired loftily.

'He doesn't actually have one,' Sylvia answered. 'Neither has he asked for one. However, *you* are the editor and together you and David will fulfil the role of publisher. Naturally, when you get the magazine back on its feet you will need to increase your staff, and at that point we will review the situation. As it stands, it will be all hands on deck and I imagine everyone, including you and David, will be performing as many menial tasks as you will editorial. However, the budget I am having drawn up for you is more than generous, so you won't be reduced to making the tea just yet.

'Of the staff currently on the magazine,' she continued, barely pausing for breath, 'I would suggest that you retain Marielle Descourts, who has been acting editor since we took over Fieldstone when the previous editor resigned. She is, as her name would suggest, French, and will undoubtedly have an invaluable knowledge of the region as well as some good contacts when it comes to contributors. I took the liberty of speaking to her on the phone this morning to tell her that you will be arriving within the next week or two.'

'What's she like?' Penny asked.

'I'm afraid I don't know her at all,' Sylvia answered. 'But from the sound of her I'd say she's around your age and her English is excellent. Ah, thank you,' she said as the waiter refilled their glasses. 'I suspect, or rather *hope*, that the two of you will become great friends,' she went on, 'and that together with David you will make a formidable team.'

'And what if I feel,' Penny said, knowing that she already did, 'that the entire face of the magazine should change, including the title, distribution, price, frequency of publication et cetera? Will the budget stretch to that?'

'If you can show me good reason for making such drastic changes, then I'm sure we can come to an arrangement,' Sylvia answered. 'The accountants tell me that there is every likelihood we will be operating at a loss for quite some time, but it's what I expected.'

Penny looked at her curiously. 'Why are you so keen for this magazine to work?' she asked. 'I mean, to put it bluntly, it's nothing more than a local rag that's never going to find its feet in the world of giants.'

Sylvia smiled. 'Call it the whim of an old lady,' she chuckled. 'I have a fondness for the Riviera, it's where my husband and I met and spent many holidays over the years.'

Inwardly Penny shrugged. If you were as rich as Sylvia then you could afford that kind of whim, she supposed.

'There is just one other thing,' Sylvia said. 'Initially you probably won't have the time, but I know you have a passion for writing short stories, which I imagine will find their way into the new magazine, and, if they do, I'd like to publish them in *Starke*. I also want to continue to run your interviews where they are relevant for *Starke*. This way we will keep your name in the big league, as it were, and I'd like you to feel free to call upon *Starke*'s resources to add to your material should you feel it necessary.' She laughed at the look that had come over

41

Penny's face. 'Does that help soften the blow of your name being taken out of lights?' she asked. Without waiting for an answer she said, 'It means that, should the new magazine not succeed for any reason, the damage to your career will be as minimal as I can make it. But let's not look on the gloomy side, because I have every confidence in you and in David and I fully expect to see the new version of whatever you choose to call it on the stands by the end of the year.'

'*What!*' Penny gasped. Then, with a mischievous twinkle, she added, 'If you'd drop David, I'd do it single-handedly by August.'

Sylvia smiled. 'Then, *with* David, perhaps you could do it even sooner.'

Penny rolled her eyes. There was obviously no getting rid of him so it was a waste of time trying. 'Just answer me this,' she said: 'if it turns out that for some reason David doesn't want me on the magazine, what happens then?'

Had Sylvia not taken so long deliberating her answer then Penny might have considered it as innocuous at it sounded, but when eventually she said, 'I· foresee no problems on that particular front,' Penny's suspicions were immmediately aroused.

'Meaning you do on other fronts?' she challenged.

'Meaning,' Sylvia responded smoothly, 'that you will find David a hard man to alienate. Now, why don't we eat our lunch and turn our attention to more important matters . . . such as the content of your new magazine.'

Though Penny wasn't yet prepared to commit any of her ideas to paper she needed little encouragement to test them out on Sylvia; so, giving in to the change of subject, she began outlining some of her initial concepts, whilst, for the moment at least, keeping her curiosity in check. Besides, it could be that she was reading too much into Sylvia's last two remarks, for on the face of it they really didn't add up to much. Nevertheless Penny's instincts were telling her that there was something about David's involvement in this new magazine that, for some reason, wasn't being shared with her.

Chapter 3

A week later Penny was gazing down at the vast, snowy peaks of the Alps, which were glistening like great mounds of Lalique glass in the dazzling midday sun. The flight into Nice at any time of year was spectacular, but on a day such as this when there wasn't a cloud in sight and the rugged mountains were cloaked so beautifully in their gleaming white winter coats it was impossible not to be moved by the sheer magnificence of it all. In fact, it was making her think of Declan, for the last time she had taken this flight he had been with her and though on that occasion there had been no snow the compelling beauty of the Alps, much to the amusement and delight of the other passengers, had moved him to song.

He'd called her several times during the ten days or so since she'd left him, but there was nothing he could say to change her mind and make her go back. His bisexuality just wasn't something she could live with – in fact, it had killed her feelings for him as effectively as if he had taken an eraser to a pencil sketch. Of course the imprint was still there and it was true to say that she was feeling pretty lost without him. But she knew that would pass and the negative results of her blood test meant that she must now put it all behind her and move on.

As the plane began its descent, circling down over the

still, turquoise-blue sea and hugging the coastline into Nice, she was watching the passing land and seascapes and trying to make herself believe that this was soon going to be her home. It didn't seem real, but she wasn't sure whether that was because a very strong part of her still didn't want it to be, or because the shimmering light on the deserted sandy beaches and majestic stucco-fronted buildings lent the place a strangely ephemeral feel.

Her schedule had been frantic right up until the moment she'd left. She, Yolanda and Sylvia had done so much research into the Côte d'Azur and had tossed around so many ideas that, though still in the theory stage, Penny had found herself becoming almost childishly excited by the sheer enormity of the challenge. Now, as the plane skimmed over the sun-spangled sea and glided smoothly on to the runway at Nice airport, she was far more nervous than excited at the prospect of having to begin putting at least some of her ideas into practice. How the hell did she know what anyone wanted down here when she'd only ever visited the place twice?

But she was going to find out, which, of course, was why she was here on this recce and the reason she had asked Marielle to meet her off the plane so that they could get started straight away.

The flight was only half full, so it didn't take long to get through customs and around to the baggage reclaim. It was as she was hauling her suitcase off the carousel that someone touched her arm and asked if she was Penny Moon.

Recognizing the voice as belonging to the person she had been speaking to on the telephone this past week, Penny turned to greet Marielle Descourts. 'Hi,' she said, letting go of her case and lifting her hand. 'It's good of—'. She stopped dead and blinked in amazement as she stared at the woman in front of her. She felt a bit like a magic lamp that had been rubbed and out had popped the delectable, sultry and stupendously beautiful brunette she had always longed to be. '. . . you to come and meet me,' she finished, reasserting her smile.

'It is my pleasure,' Marielle told her, her slanted, expressionless eyes sweeping over Penny's face. She was wearing a short black coat over a tight-fitting black skirt, thick black tights and extremely expensive black pumps. Her hair was a thick, wiry mass of curls that framed her exquisite face and stopped in a harsh line just above her shoulders. Her make-up, though slightly overdone, was immaculate, the shiny splash of red on her wide, full lips adding a striking contrast to the darkness of her skin and clothes. She was the very epitome of French chic and towered over Penny in a way that made Penny feel so uncomfortably dwarfish and dowdy that it was only the brief glimpse of herself in a mirror as Marielle led the way out of the terminal building that reassured her she didn't look quite so bad after all.

Of course she couldn't wear the kind of clothes Marielle was wearing, but her knee-length navy suede jacket that was covering a long, cornflower-blue sweater dress with starched white collar was pretty smart and both were great colours for her hair and eyes. And besides, she wasn't here for either a beauty contest or a fashion parade, she was here to do a job!

As she stepped outside she inhaled deeply and took a brief look around. There was a glorious crispness to the air and a radiance in the light that made the wintry bleakness of England seem like the planet's dungeon by comparison.

Trying to keep control of her trolley as she hurried across the road after Marielle, who was striding on ahead through the swaying palms into the car park, Penny was beginning to feel like some kind of simpleton lady's maid. This wasn't a good start, she was telling herself, but putting Marielle in her place wouldn't be much of one either. There would be plenty of time over the next few days to assert her authority, as subtly as she could, for alienating Marielle was definitely not on her agenda. Having spoken to her frequently this past week, Penny was already aware of how invaluable Marielle's knowledge and contacts were going to be. Her hostility might be a bit of a problem, though, but Penny was pretty certain she'd win her over eventually. Not right away, though, as she hadn't told Marielle yet that she had already taken the decision – with Sylvia's approval – to do away totally with the magazine as it stood, for the format was so bland and so depressingly tradesman-orientated that it wasn't any wonder they'd had to give it away.

'This your car?' Penny smiled, catching up with Marielle, who had stopped beside a sleek little red Japanese number.

Marielle nodded as she pressed a button on her key ring unlocking the doors. She offered Penny no assistance with heaving her case into the boot; instead, she slid into the driver's seat and waited for Penny to get in beside her.

When Penny came to open the car door she very nearly plonked herself on Marielle's lap.

'You're in France now,' Marielle informed her smoothly.

'Of course!' Penny laughed. 'Force of habit, I'm afraid,' and walking quickly round to the other side she got in and fastened her seat belt.

'So,' she said decisively as they joined the autoroute into Cannes, 'maybe we can go straight to the office. I'm dying to see it.'

Glancing in her rear-view mirror, Marielle pressed her foot down hard and proceeded to eat up the autoroute as if it was a long, slippery string of spaghetti being sucked into a hungry mouth.

'Wow!' Penny muttered, blinking at the passing blur

of scenery; then suddenly she was jamming her feet hard into the floor as Marielle raced up behind a Mercedes and sat inches from its tail. Making a mental note not to travel with Marielle unless absolutely necessary, Penny decided to try a little light conversation.

'Were you born here?' she asked.

'Yes.'

'Actually in Cannes?'

'Yes.'

'It must have been quite something growing up in such a beautiful place,' Penny commented.

Whether it was or wasn't, Marielle obviously wasn't going to let on.

'Your English is excellent,' Penny said, with an ingenuous smile that totally masked the sarcasm, for so far Marielle hadn't managed much beyond yes and no. But Penny knew from their telephone conversations that Marielle was even better at English than she, Penny, was at French. 'Where did you learn?' she asked.

'I have a lot of English and American friends.'

Penny nodded. 'That's nice,' she said. Then, 'Are you married?'

'No.'

Penny waited, but when no reciprocal question was forthcoming she said, 'Me neither.'

The vaguely hoped-for camaraderie of independent, single women was obviously a nonstarter too.

'Are you always this talkative,' Penny enquired after a while, 'or is it just me that you've decided to pour your heart out to?'

Marielle scowled, showing that this time the sarcasm had managed to hit home, but she clearly wasn't going to rise to it.

'Well, if we're going to work together,' Penny said as Marielle threw some coins into the net at the *payage*, 'we're going to have to find some way of communicating. How's your semaphore?'

Penny might just have imagined it, but she thought she'd caught the ghost of a smile twitch those perfect red lips. Well, it was enough to be going on with, for friendship was more of a luxury than a priority and she could tackle it again when the time felt right.

A few minutes later they were turning off the boulevard Carnot on to the *voie rapide*, the road that ran parallel to the coast with the most exclusive part of Cannes sandwiched between. Not that Penny had a clue where they were. All she could see were the backs of tall, mostly slender white buildings on one side with the odd ad for Monoprix or Indian cuisine, and a fringe of extremely grand, almost Florentine-looking, villas interspersed with holiday apartments through the lush tropical foliage on the other. It was in a secluded, palm-studded forecourt outside one of these villas that Marielle brought the car to a halt.

'This is it?' Penny said incredulously, turning to her. 'These are the offices?'

'Yes,' Marielle answered, already getting out of the car.

Penny looked up at the creamy-yellow façade of the villa, at its dark-green shutters, wide, filigree balconies and intricately carved friezes. On both sides of the upper storey were two large, balustraded terraces and reclining on each side of the pointed roof were two happily fat and impudent-looking cherubs. From the outside it appeared more like the home of a minor branch of the Medici family than it did an office, but if this was where she was going to be working she reckoned she could live with it.

The entrance hall was vast, with a high, domed ceiling, art-deco cornices and a dusty marble floor. There was no furniture to speak of and the paint was peeling, but it wasn't hard to imagine what it had looked like in its glory days.

'We don't use the downstairs,' Marielle told her,

already halfway up the balustraded staircase.

'But we will – eventually.' Penny smiled, following on. 'You said on the phone that you have an assistant working with you at the moment. Is she here?'

'Not today,' Marielle answered, offering no explanation as to why.

'But it's been just you two running the shop since the previous editor left?'

'Just us and a few freelancers,' Marielle confirmed, pushing open a heavy white door. 'This is the main office,' she said, standing aside to let Penny through.

Penny stopped on the threshold to look around what might once have been a small, but nevertheless grand, ballroom. All the shutters were open and the sunlight was streaming across the room in wide, misty bands. The walls were cluttered with the usual paraphernalia of a magazine office, though pretty sparsely so, and only one of the half a dozen or so desks had anything on it.

'It's perfect,' Penny murmured, more to herself than to Marielle as her imagination went instantly to work. 'Where are the computers?' she asked.

'There,' Marielle replied, pointing towards an antiquated Compaq that Penny had overlooked.

Penny blinked and, realizing that to ask if it was linked to the internet would be like asking if it was linked to Mars, she saved her breath and tried to remain positive.

'Well, if we get things a little more organized in here,' she said, walking further into the room, 'we can put a production table in the centre and find a use for all these empty desks. I take it they were once occupied?'

'In the early days.'

It was as if Marielle was volunteering just a fraction of what she really wanted to say, as though the rest of it would only be forthcoming on demand. Penny decided to give it a miss for now and wandered over to the high, wide french windows to gaze out on the speeding traffic of the *voie rapide*. With the windows closed the noise wasn't a problem, but no doubt when they were open it would be, which meant they would need to install air-conditioning for the summer.

'What's through there?' Penny asked, pointing towards a half-open door at the far end of the production office.

'That,' Marielle said, going to the door, 'is my office.'

Correction, Penny thought, as she walked into the room: *was* your office. The desk was surprisingly untidy, given the neatness of Marielle's appearance, and the walls were sadly devoid of anything other than a couple of jejune front covers of previous issues. A computer terminal complete with its own compact laser printer was on a side desk and behind the grand, leather swivel chair a set of french windows opened out on to a large, balustraded veranda.

'And in here?' Penny said, pushing open the door to a floor-to-ceiling cubicle in one corner.

'That is a *cuisinette*,' Marielle informed her.

Penny nodded, looking it over and thinking they either needed a cleaner or must change the one they had, since the sink was a bit grimy and the twin hotplates were a touch too grungy for her liking.

'Well,' Penny said, clasping her hands together as she walked back into the production office, 'as I said before, it's perfect. I take it those are more offices over there behind those two doors,' she said, pointing to the windowless, north side of the room.

Marielle nodded. 'They have never been used.'

Well, at least one of them would be now, Penny was thinking with relish, for in her mind she was already assigning whichever one he wanted to David Villers – who, interestingly, hadn't even attempted to make contact yet, and since she had no idea where he was she considered that her own negligence in that area was

51

perfectly excusable.

Looking around again, she felt a momentary depression steal over her as the hollow stillness and lack of human bustle made her feel as though she had been plucked from all the carousing hullabaloo of a circus and deposited in Shirley Valentine's kitchen. London had never felt so dear, nor so far, as it did in that moment.

'OK,' she said, casting aside the gloom and pulling a chair up to one of the empty desks, 'we've a lot to sort out in the next couple of weeks, so let's start by getting someone in to discuss our technical needs.'

Marielle's perfect brows arched as she perched on the edge of her assistant's desk. 'And what exactly would they be?' she enquired in a supercilious tone.

'That's why we need experts,' Penny pointed out. 'Someone who can advise us on everything from air-conditioning to computer graphics.' She picked up her briefcase and flicked it open. 'I have a list here of the kind of equipment and people I thought we might require to get things operational.' She handed a copy to Marielle, who grudgingly took it and treated it to a frosty-eyed glance.

'We are already operational,' she intoned.

Penny took a breath. 'For *The Coast* maybe, but not for the new magazine.' Then, without giving Marielle a chance to respond, she went on: 'I've had a rough blueprint drawn up of what the magazine might look like. The final decision will of course be taken after consultation with you and David, but you will see from this,' she said, handing Marielle a copy of the blueprint, 'what sort of areas I intend to cover. If you know anyone with an interest in any of these fields – fashion, interior design, gardening, cookery, entertainment, et cetera – and who may like to contribute, I'll be happy to see them. There is one stipulation, though. Whoever they are, they must be bilingual because my intention is to make the new magazine bilingual, since to cater just for the English-speaking population imposes unacceptable limitations on the circulation. It will be a community magazine and, as the French make up by far the greater part of the community, it would be insane to cut them out. And here,' she said, delving into her briefcase again, 'is a list of people I would like to meet, the editor of the *Nice-Matin* being the most important. Maybe your assistant, when she next graces us with her presence, can fix up some meetings for me.

'Now, about recruitment . . .' she continued. 'To begin with we shall be quite a small team consisting of myself, David Villers, you, a general assistant, a sales and marketing director, an advertising director and two subs. As well as the deputy editorship I would like you to take on the role of production director.' Not even a glimmer of a response. 'But the most important person at this stage is the designer. I have already recruited someone in London who will come down to oversee everything from the look of the magazine to the launch of it. His name is Jeffrey Silver. He drew up the blueprint you are looking at there and he's had considerable experience in getting new magazines off the ground. On the list of people I would like to meet I've included several advertising agencies. They will handle the actual launch, which I hope will take place at the end of August.'

There was a tightness around Marielle's mouth that told Penny how royally pissed off she was, but she said nothing.

'Uh, before we go any further,' Penny said, looking through more documents she had taken from her briefcase, her mind clearly dealing with several things at once, 'maybe you could hire a team of decorators to come and spruce the place up a bit. Oh yes,' she said, as her eyes alighted on a memo she had sent Sylvia, 'there are two extremely important points here, the first being that the new magazine will be a bimonthly as opposed to a monthly and, second, it will no longer be free. We'll need to discuss the setting of a price with David when he comes.'

'And when will that be?' Marielle asked coldly.

'I've no idea,' Penny answered, continuing to lay things out on the desk. After a while she stopped and looked up at Marielle, who hadn't moved. 'I'm sorry,' Penny said, 'I obviously didn't make myself clear. When I asked if you would sort out the decorators, I meant now.' Then, with a beaming smile. 'There's no point in dragging our heels, is there?'

Marielle's nostrils flared, but, slipping off her coat, she went to sit at her assistant's desk.

'Is there a photocopier?' Penny enquired, glancing around.

'There.' Marielle pointed at a small, desktop job.

'Well, that's not going to get us very far, is it?' Penny remarked. 'Make task number two the hiring of a decent-sized copier, one with all the magical little functions but no tendency to break down. Incidentally, did you manage to contact any estate agents to find me somewhere to rent?'

'Yes. We have a rendezvous with her tomorrow morning.'

Penny nodded. 'Her' wasn't quite what she'd had in mind, for she'd been planning a blitz on house-hunting, but one agent was a start.

It was much later in the day, after Penny had gone through the laborious task of copying virtually everything in her briefcase for Marielle's perusal, that Marielle at last spoke without prompting.

'Your ideas,' she said, fixing Penny with her sharp, green eyes, 'are ambitious, to say the least. I am wondering where so much money is coming from.'

'From the Starke Organization,' Penny answered. 'And as to whether they will all be cost-effective, I can't say yet. Again, we need to speak to David, but before we do that perhaps you'd like to put forward any ideas of your own.'

Marielle looked down at the single sheet of paper she was holding. 'If I have any,' she said eventually, 'I'll let you know.'

Not a particularly satisfactory reply, since brainstorming was something Penny adored. However, it seemed she was going to have to wait until they had a few more people on board for the real fun to begin and, meanwhile, time hadn't been wasted. Several decorators would be arriving over the next few days to give quotes; delivery of a photocopier was promised for the end of the week; a team of boffins from a computer company were eager to explore how best to serve their needs; France Telecom had agreed to come and discuss phones the following week; an office-supply company had already biked round their brochures and an employment agency was lining up security guards, secretaries and cleaners to be interviewed.

Unfortunately, throughout all their endeavours not so much as a crack had appeared in Marielle's polar ice-cap of a demeanour, which, Penny was thinking to herself as she stretched and yawned, was going to become pretty wearing if she didn't break it down soon. But, she reminded herself, she wasn't looking for a bosom pal and since Marielle's efficiency, grudging as it was, had more than helped to get the ball rolling Penny supposed she'd just have to make do with that for now. It would be a whole lot easier, though, if Marielle would come out with some serious opposition to the changes, or if she'd spit out all the resentment she was harbouring and give them the chance to have a thundering good row and clear the air. But maybe that wasn't Marielle's style.

'OK, time to call it a day,' Penny said, stifling another yawn as she hefted her briefcase back on to her desk and began to refill it. 'What time am I meeting the estate agent in the morning?'

'Ten o'clock.'

Penny looked at her, waited, then with a long-suffering sigh said, 'OK. Is she coming to the hotel?'

'Yes.'

'Does she know which hotel?'

'She will by the morning.'

'Fine. Now, if you wouldn't mind dropping me off I'll see what I can do about hiring a car.'

After leaving Penny at the fancy Carlton Hotel, Marielle sped out on to the Croisette and raced furiously off towards Cannes la Bocca and the HLM – council flat – she shared with her mother. She'd known, even before meeting Penny Moon, that she was going to despise her. Now that they had met, she more than despised her, she loathed her, self-opinionated bitch that she was. Oh, sure, she was going to make a success of this glitzy new magazine – how could she fail when she had the backing she had? Well, that was OK by Marielle, she'd always wanted to lift the profile of the magazine, and if having to put up with Penny Moon for a while was the way it had to be done, then so be it. Penny Moon wasn't going to last long, though, Marielle already had assurances on that, but she had to make sure that Penny Moon's personal failure did nothing to damage the magazine, so that when Penny Moon went back to England in disgrace it would be she, Marielle, who was the obvious choice to take things over. She gave a snort of laughter. Just one day in Penny Moon's company had been enough to show Marielle where her Achilles' heel lay, for Penny Moon was, without a doubt, the kind of woman who'd let her heart rule her head. Disastrous! And with the self-esteem problem Marielle had detected the instant they'd met, Marielle didn't see how she could fail. And maybe, now she came to think about it, she was going to enjoy using

Penny Moon's emotions as the weapon that would finish her, and, if all that Marielle had been hearing about David Villers was true, then Marielle could hardly wait to meet him.

The next two weeks sped by and what she, Marielle and Clothilde, the mumsy, smiley assistant of Marielle's, managed to achieve in that time was enough to make Penny's head spin. That she all too often felt like Quentin Tarantino might if he were asked to script *Neighbours* was something she forced herself not to dwell on. Instead, she reminded herself how refreshing it was to find such willingness and enthusiasm in Clothilde, when Marielle's sullen co-operation was beginning to make the telephonists at Electricité de France seem positively helpful. Unfortunately Clothilde could only work part-time, since she had a husband, three children and an ageing father to look after, but what she managed to get through during the hours she was there was enough to convince Penny that, come what may, she was going to keep her on.

The most productive hours of all had been spent with the editor of *Nice-Matin*, who, amazingly, had yielded up a whole wealth of contacts with such disarming readiness and generosity that Penny had almost felt embarrassed. But that was the French for you, she remarked happily to herself: either all – as with the editor and Clothilde – or nothing – as with Marielle.

She had left Marielle in charge of following up on possible contributors that morning while she went off on a last foray into the villa-strewn hills behind Cannes to look for a house before going back to London the next day. She'd visited so many villas and *mas* and private *domaines* that in her mind they were now all starting to blend into one blurry mass of stupendous luxury. But, despite the numerous appealing features and false-start excitements, nothing so far had felt totally right. That was until the agent drove her through the meandering, leafy lanes around Mougins, to a villa that as soon as Penny clapped eyes on she knew she would take.

It was fairy-tale time: a blushing, glowing, riotously fertile Eden of tropical colour and breath-taking splendour. The house, all Moorish arches and gleaming white walls, sprawled across the end of the long, curved drive like a secret haven enticing you to come and share its private view of the sea. The lawns flowed across the hillside like gentle, undulating waves, the palms soared and fanned against the backdrop of a brilliant blue sky: the giant cacti bristled with sturdy pride.

As the agent let herself into the house Penny walked round to the south-facing terrace and let her eyes make the slow, entrancing journey from the turquoise-blue pool with a bubbling jacuzzi at one end and a bougainvillaea-claimed pergola at the other, out to the distant, slumbering red rocks of the Esterel, across the sparkling Mediterranean Sea and on to the pine forest that hugged the boundaries of the property.

As she wandered down the wide, semicircular steps to the edge of the pool she felt like Alice in a wonderland of unbelievable riches. Behind her the agent was pulling open the white slatted shutters to let the bright spring sunshine pour into the house. Penny retraced her steps and followed her from the farmhouse-style kitchen to the vast sitting room with its balustraded mezzanine, ivory grand piano and huge stone fireplace; then on into the two downstairs bedrooms and bathrooms. All the parts of the house were on different levels and each room had its own access on to the sun-dazzled terraces, which were linked by finely mosaiced steps and edged by bougainvillaea-covered balustrades.

Back outside again, the agent showed her the summer-kitchen, the utility room, the barbecue area, all the time keeping up her estate agent's spiel, her voice as crisp as the air and her appearance as neat as the garden beds. Then, leading the way back in through the french windows to the dining area, she stopped as Penny stood on the threshold and marvelled at the seductive elegance of the place. The long, glass dining table for twelve with its brass legs and accompanying high-backed, pale linen-upholstered chairs was on the upper level of the sitting room, and as Penny wandered down the steps, passing over antique silk rugs scattered across the terracotta-tiled floor and ran her hands along the backs of voluminous-cushioned sofas and chairs, she couldn't help wondering why the rental was so low for such a magnificent house.

'Because,' the agent told her, 'the owners will only accept a five-year commitment and they realize that often people want only two years, maybe less.'

'And what if I want to leave before the five years are up?' Penny asked, wandering out into the oak-beamed and stone-flagged entrance hall and making for the stairs.

'They will require a minimum of six months' notice.'

Penny didn't think that would pose much of a problem. 'Where are the owners?' she asked.

'They live in South Africa.'

'Don't they ever come here?'

'No, the house is an investment,' the agent replied. 'As you can see, it is beautifully furnished and cared for.'

'Mmm,' Penny commented, thinking how surprisingly homely it felt despite its rambling spaciousness and air of grandeur.

'And this,' the agent said, pushing open a solid oak door on the first landing and standing aside, 'is the master bedroom.'

As Penny went past her, the agent flicked on the lights, then went to the double french windows to push open the shutters. Beyond was a cosy little veranda with its own view of the sea and a white, wrought-iron table and chairs set slightly back from the jasmine-covered balustrades.

When the agent turned round, she was bewildered to see Penny shaking her head and laughing.

'I'm sorry,' Penny said, 'but it's so fantastic I can hardly believe it,' and bouncing on to the king-sized antique brass bed, which was covered in the same white satin and lace of the drapes that fanned down over the wall behind it, she sat surveying the expensive fitted wardrobes, chests and dressing table that lined the walls.

'And through here is the principal bathroom,' the agent said, going inside and switching on the lights.

Penny was already prepared, but, even so, its luxury made her gasp. Everything, from the long, double-basined vanity unit with its recessed lights, to the bidet and toilet, to the multi-head shower and deep corner bath, was in a soft, ivory-coloured marble with a hint of green vein running through. The palms and ferns were fake, but it was hard to tell even when she touched them, and the plush, cushiony carpet was deep enough to lose her feet in.

'Well,' Penny said, as they walked out of the front door and she gazed up at the quaint, sixteenth-century hilltop village of Mougins, 'I think you can start drawing up the contract. I'm going back to England tomorrow, but anything that needs my signature can always be sent Chronopost. By the way, you did say that the maid and gardeners are paid from the rental, didn't you?'

'That is correct,' the agent confirmed. 'And the pool maintenance. And the security system.'

'Incredible,' Penny murmured. All this for a mere thirty thousand francs a month, which at today's exchange rate was round about three and a half thousand pounds. That was five hundred more than her allowance . . . Still, if she didn't manage to beat the price down she'd make up the shortfall from her own pocket, because this was probably the only chance she'd ever get to live in a place like this. And with one last, disbelieving glance around, she got back into the agent's car, feeling so good about the extraordinary success of these past two weeks that she was almost looking forward to seeing David, if for no other reason than to gloat at what she'd managed to achieve without him. Childish, she knew, but there was already little doubt in her mind that this forced partnership of theirs was, at best, going to be spiked with feisty little battles of one-upmanship. At worst . . . well, that was something she wouldn't dwell upon for now, since she was still pretty convinced that she had yet to get a full picture of his real involvement here.

She'd spent many hours trying to imagine what kind of subterfuge or chicanery might be afoot behind David's appointment, but so far she hadn't been able to come up with a credible scenario, or at least not one that took account of a magazine of such startling insignificance. In fact, she would have put her suspicions down to her own passion for intrigue if it hadn't been for the wall of silence she had come up against on enquiring when exactly David might be planning to grace them with his presence. It wasn't that she wanted to see him – she was experiencing an annoying turbulence in her nervous system at the very prospect – but she had expected to have at least received a telephone call by now.

After finalizing what she could with the agent, Penny thanked her for the lift back and ran up the stairs to the production office. Her spirits were high, not only because of the house, but, perversely, because of the pleasure of knowing she would be back in London by this time tomorrow. In fact she was in such a good mood she was debating with the idea of inviting Marielle to dinner that night to fling a few more shots of friendship

61

at her impenetrable reserve. However, she got no further than pushing open the door before her exuberance was brutally eclipsed by astonishment, which was in turn rapidly displaced by intense irritation. David Villers, in all his manly splendour and proprietorial audacity, was perched on the edge of Marielle's desk at the far end of the office.

Penny remained standing where she was, bristling with resentment, but neither of them seemed to notice and, considering the gluey intimacy of their laughter and the sultry look in Marielle's eyes, it didn't appear they were going to. Penny's blood was rising to the boil. The fact that he had chosen to turn up unannounced like this, as though he was on some kind of checking-up mission, made her want to flatten his appalling, overblown ego for the sheer arrogance of it.

As she continued to stare at them, for the moment unsure how to play this, she could only feel astounded at her own stupidity for not having realized that something like this would happen. Though he had his back to her and though Penny hadn't seen him for over a year, the look on Marielle's face was enough to bring flooding back to Penny's mind just how irresistible he was. His untidy, curly hair, as blond as her own, was a little shorter than the last time she'd seen him, and though he was sitting down it was easy to tell – and she remembered only too well – how tall and slender and nauseatingly muscular he was. Pursing her lips at one corner, Penny tried to swallow the shameful memory that was burgeoning inside her of how he had once described her and she was dreading the moment when he turned round and recognized her.

'Ah, Penny,' Clothilde said, coming out of Penny's office, 'you're back. How was the house? Any good?'

'Perfect,' Penny said, assuming a nonchalance she was far from feeling as she slung her briefcase on a desk and hung her coat on the back of the door.

When she turned back, David was on his feet and watching her with a smile of curiosity in his narrowed blue eyes that Penny found intensely irritating. 'So you're Penny,' he said, coming towards her with a hand held out to shake hers. 'It's good to meet you at last.' His voice held a strange mix of Scottish and American accents and Penny detested it instantly.

'I've been hearing a lot about you,' he told her as she tried to assess whether he was simply pretending not to recognize her or whether his ignorance was, as it appeared to be, genuine. 'Seems you made yourself a lot of fans over in London,' he went on as she reluctantly shook his hand. 'And Marielle here's been telling me how you're racing ahead with the new magazine.'

Patronizing bastard, she was thinking, as, forcing a smile, she said, 'I didn't realize you were intending to turn up today. If I had, I'd have been here to greet you myself.'

He shrugged. 'It's OK,' and turning back to Marielle he added, 'I've been well looked after.'

'You don't say,' Penny muttered, moving on towards her office. 'Maybe you'd like to—'

'I was just acquainting David with the list of possible contributors,' Marielle interrupted, gazing up at David as though no one else was in the room. Actually, Penny was thinking irrelevantly, he was even taller than she remembered, and, since he hadn't bothered to use his charm on her when they'd first met, the brazen quantity of it that was flowing out of his powerfully seductive eyes towards Marielle right now was also something new to her. Still, decidedly unattractive as she found it, it was certainly making a new woman out of Marielle, for this was the first time she'd seen Marielle's teeth. Not that there was anything particularly remarkable about them – she hadn't *really* been expecting fangs – they were just small and white and as perfect as the rest of her, revealed as they were in a smile!

'How have you got on with ringing around?' Penny asked her.

'I was just telling David,' Marielle answered, her eyes still on his as he resumed his position on the edge of her desk.

'Oh good,' Penny said. 'Perhaps you'd like to tell me too.'

'Phone for you, Penny,' Clothilde called over from her desk. 'It's someone from the local English radio station.'

'OK, I'll take it in my office,' Penny said, and with a withering look that was wasted on both David and Marielle she walked into her office and closed the door behind her.

When she came out again a few minutes later, having told the caller that she'd get back to him nearer the time regarding advertising space for the new magazine, it was to find Marielle's and David's heads very close together as they pored over the blueprint of the magazine.

'And here,' Marielle was saying, 'I thought it would be a good idea if we ran a few real-estate pages, complete with photographs, the way they do in the English country magazines.'

'Terrific,' David said, the unmistakable resonance of seduction in his approval.

Penny glared at Marielle in dumbfounded fury, for she had just quoted verbatim what Penny herself had said only a few days ago.

'And on the page following the real estate I thought it would be a good idea to run the column on living in France,' Marielle went on, 'for which I've managed to find both a French and an English expert. It'll be more of a letters column really, with the experts giving advice.'

Unbelievable! Penny was thinking. How the hell did she have the gall to pass all that off as if it were her own when she, Penny, had found the experts courtesy of the editor of *Nice-Matin*? 'David,' she said tightly, 'I think we should get together on costings.'

'Sure,' David said, without looking up, 'we can do that. I'll be right in when Marielle's finished up here.'

Seething with rage, Penny went back to her desk to try to work out the best way to handle this without appearing petty.

Half an hour later, when there was still no sign of him, she once again ventured out to the production office, only to find him putting on his coat.

'I thought we were going to go through some figures,' she snapped.

'Sorry. I don't have time right now,' he grimaced, looking at his watch. 'Things to do, people to see – you know how it is. But I'll take you two ladies for dinner tonight, if you're both free.'

'You mean you're leaving, just like that!' Penny exclaimed, very close to losing her temper.

He looked at her in surprise. 'Why, how else would you like me to leave?' He grinned.

Penny's jaw tightened and, resisting the urge to say 'on a stretcher', she turned back into her office.

Marielle was already proprietorially ensconced in the front passenger seat of the black Saab convertible when David stopped by the Carlton Hotel to pick Penny up at seven-thirty. So, having no choice but to climb in the back when David tilted his seat forward to make way for her, Penny greeted Marielle warmly. She was damned if she was going to let either of them know how much they were getting to her.

The journey up through the hinterlands to the clifftop restaurant at Gourdon – overlooking the spectacular Gorge du Loup, which they might have been able to see if the night hadn't been pitch-black – took over half an hour, during which time Penny might have been more comfortable in purgatory. She caught only snatches of their conversation, but it was clear they weren't talking business and if David looked at Marielle's legs one more time they were all three of them going to hurtle off into the Gorge. Maybe she'd get a taxi back, Penny was thinking to herself as they were shown to a table beside a roaring log fire in *Le Nid d'Aigle* – 'The Eagle's Nest'.

Having come as far inland as they had, Penny had assumed that Marielle had chosen the restaurant, but if that was the case she certainly hadn't had to give David any directions to get there; nor, Penny noticed, had she introduced David to the *maître d'*, who was in the process of greeting David like a long-lost brother. To Penny's immense satisfaction, when David presented Marielle to the *maître d'* he mistakenly called her Marianne, but unfortunately Marielle didn't seem too put out about it. Instead she used the opportunity to put an admonishing, but none the less provocative, hand on David's as she corrected him.

Having recommended various dishes, the *maître d'* left David with the wine list, which Marielle proceeded to peruse with him, managing to make an innocuous label such as Domaine Jean Gros sound as though it were some kind of erotic vintage endorsed by the *Kama Sutra*. Having finally made her choice, she sat back as David turned to Penny to ask if she had a preference.

'Whatever you choose is fine by me,' Penny answered, surprised he'd remembered she was there.

But it turned out to be only a fleeting recall, for he and Marielle then continued getting to know each other while Penny smarted away in silence, wishing she could think of something to say that would cut them both down to size but wouldn't dent her dignity in the process.

Eventually, having borne up throughout the starter, she decided to try swallowing her chagrin along with a succulent piece of lamb and suggested that they might like to discuss whether or not the new magazine should take any sort of political stance.

'Oh, but that can wait,' Marielle protested, screwing up her beautiful little nose. 'We are having such a wonderful time. Why spoil it by talking boring politics?'

Ignoring her, Penny looked to David.

'French or British?' he asked, his dark eyes resting on hers and seeming to emanate a power that Penny felt horribly diminished by.

'I thought European might be more appropriate,' she answered, failing to keep the edge from her voice.

He nodded. 'Of course. Left or right?'

Seeing Marielle's hand snake under the table towards David's thigh, Penny bit down hard on her anger and, deciding to forgo the pleasure of talking politics while they fondled each other, said, 'Perhaps Marielle's right: we should save it for the office.'

'As you like,' David responded, seeming either not to notice Marielle's hand or happy just to enjoy it.

'What were you doing in Miami?' Penny enquired as he turned back to Marielle.

He shrugged. 'Oh, a little of this, a little of that,' he answered. 'Have you ever been to Miami?'

'No.'

But Marielle had and once again Penny was cut out of the conversation.

Penny wasn't sure whether there was any real malice on David's part, maybe, she tried comforting herself, it was just a total oblivion to everything beyond Marielle's figure-hugging dress that clearly defied the wearing of underwear. Her nipples were so prominent that even Penny found her eyes repeatedly drawn to them. Turning away to gaze absently at the other diners and the various knick-knacks on the walls, Penny began asking herself again how she was going to handle this, for as David's so-called equal partner she must not allow herself to be treated like a nonentity.

The situation continued for several more minutes, during which time Penny persevered with the struggle to control her temper. They appeared so impervious to her discomfort and so engrossed in their flirtation that she began to wonder if by some strange quirk of the atmosphere she had managed to become invisible. Their heads were so close together as they murmured and laughed and curled their fingers around each other's that Penny could feel the colour blazing a route to her cheeks. But whatever happened she was determined to hang on to her temper. She wouldn't, *mustn't*, allow herself to make a scene that might be construed as jealousy. She watched Marielle's fingers slide along the back of David's hand and bury themselves inside the sleeve of his thick, navy sweater; then, lifting her eyes to his face, which appeared more handsome than ever as the firelight bathed his skin with a warm glow and made his smile impossibly white, Penny found herself wondering if there was some kind of conspiracy going on here. Were they intentionally trying to put her in her place, to make her feel of such lowly importance that she might just give up and go back to London for good?

Tearing her eyes away, she felt a great swell of resentment rise within her. It was going to take a damned sight more than their sordid flirting to get her to abandon ship now. After all, she was the one who'd put it together so far, so the hell was she going to hand it over to them.

Looking up as the waiter handed her a dessert menu, Penny detected a light of sympathy in his eyes, which was almost too much to bear. But, with a warming smile of reassurance, she said, '*Cogito, ergo sum.*'

'What?' Marielle said, running her eyes down the menu.

'Descartes,' David enlightened her, his eyes laughing as he turned them to Penny's. 'I think, therefore I exist,' he translated.

Marielle appeared none the wiser; nor did she appear to appreciate the way David was regarding Penny. Penny turned haughtily to her menu, made her selection and realized too late that she was the only one taking dessert. This, coupled with the fact that David was again preoccupied with Marielle, didn't do anything to help alleviate the feeling that she was once more the big fat gooseberry.

However, as they waited for the dessert to arrive, David began making a half-hearted attempt to bring her into the conversation . . . until Penny's stony reception caused him to say, 'Hey, come on, lighten up, will you?'

Penny glared at him, speechless with indignation but before she could think of a suitable rejoinder her *tiramisu* arrived and her temper instantly deflated as she regarded it with dismay. It was such an enormous helping she felt sure that everyone was looking at her with disgust.

Closing her eyes, she dug in her spoon and was just lifting the creamy, chocolatey evil to her mouth, when David said, 'You're not actually going to eat that, are you?'

Penny stopped dead and turned to look at him. The sex-starved Sumo remark was screaming through her mind and, looking down at her plate she suddenly saw red!

'Not now, no,' she said through her teeth.

'*Oh, là, là!*' Marielle murmured as Penny landed the dish splat, in David's face.

'Jesus Christ, what did you do that for?' he cried, grabbing a napkin. 'I was only trying to tell you there was silver foil on your spoon.'

As the fury drained from Penny's face, mortification turned her rigid. 'Oh God, I'm sorry,' she mumbled. 'I thought . . .'

'You thought what?' David laughed, attempting to wipe the gooey custard from his face.

'Nothing,' she said. 'I just . . . I just misunderstood, that's all.'

The other diners were all looking in their direction by now and, as David got up to go and clean himself off, Penny wished that the eagle whose nest they were dining in would come back and carry her off to a distant land. Brilliant, she was thinking to herself, just brilliant. After an entire evening of amazingly uncharacteristic restraint you go and blow it all by jamming a damned custard pie in his face. What will you think of as an encore!

They travelled back to Cannes in near silence, except for David's occasional burst of laughter. Penny was in the back seat again, wishing she could flick the little bit of cream off his hair that he'd obviously overlooked. It was a nasty little reminder of what a toe-curling idiot she had made of herself and what was worse was how funny David seemed to find it. She wasn't sure why she minded so much about that, she just did.

When they got back to the Carlton she was tempted to invite him in for a nightcap to try to make amends, but guessing that he and Marielle had other things to do she simply said good night and started to get out of the car.

'Oh by the way,' she said to David as he held the door open for her, 'I'm going back to London tomorrow, so I was wondering where I might be able to get hold of you – should I need to.'

'I'll be staying right down the road here,' he said, waving an arm in the general direction of the Martinez Hotel a few blocks down. 'Some friends of mine have misguidedly handed over the keys to their apartment. I'll call the hotel later and leave a message for you with the phone number.'

'OK,' she said. 'Well, good night and, once again, I'm

sorry about the, uh, misunderstanding.'

'Think no more of it,' he told her with a grin and, getting back into the car, he and Marielle drove away – no doubt, Penny was thinking to herself as she walked into the hotel, to get on with the dastardly deed. Then quite suddenly she started to laugh as the funny side of what had happened finally reached her. He'd deserved nothing less after the way he'd treated her, the bastard, and just wait till she told her friends back in London! The episode would be good for a laugh, if nothing else . . .

Chapter 4

'Here, let me help you with that.'

In mid-stumble through the front door, bags suspended from each shoulder and suitcase dragging on the floor, Penny looked up to find her sister's cheery face grinning down at her.

'Sammy!' she cried, dropping her luggage and wrapping Sammy in her arms. 'When did you get here?'

'Yesterday,' Sammy answered, hugging Penny tightly. 'Peter's gone off skiing with his boyfriend and said I could stay.'

'For how long?' Penny asked, holding Sammy at arm's length and giving her a thorough, motherly-like inspection. 'You look fantastic,' she told her, pulling her into another embrace. 'I can hardly believe you're here.'

Sammy's eyes were suffused with sisterly devotion as she watched Penny give her another critical once-over before turning to haul her suitcase in the door. She was five years younger than Penny, and, like Penny, had such a glowing complexion she could almost have passed for a teenager. At five feet ten she was six inches taller than Penny and slender almost to the point of being skinny. Her hair, unlike Penny's, was extremely fine, several shades darker, and fell from a centre parting to well below her shoulders. But her eyes were a virtually identical cornflower-blue and shone with the same wicked humour and intelligence.

'So what's all this Peter's been telling me about a new job?' she said excitedly, following Penny down the narrow, dark hallway into the spacious sitting room, which, were it not for the dull sky outside, might have been invitingly sunny. 'It's in France, he said. Something to do with a new magazine.'

'Make me a cup of tea and I'll fill you in,' Penny said, shrugging off her coat and hitting the button on the answerphone. 'And don't think you're off the hook over that Casablanca caper,' she called after her, 'because I haven't forgotten.'

Half an hour later, having replayed her dozen or so messages and returned the more urgent calls, Penny slumped on to a tatty sofa and looked at Sammy's bright, eager face. She adored her sister more than anyone else in the world – always had, since the day Sammy was born. So had their father, but sadly he had died before Sammy had reached her eleventh birthday and now, since their mother's death, Penny sometimes felt as though she'd taken on the role of both parents. Meaning that Sammy was an unruly, often unmanageable child, but Penny wouldn't have had her any other way. Actually, she would, for she'd have had Sammy living with her if only she could pin her down, but since Sammy had graduated she'd spent her time roaming the world and getting into more scrapes than the Marquess of Blandford, that Penny was continually obliged to get her out of.

It wasn't long before they were doubled-up with laughter as Penny reached the *tiramisu* part of her story, then gave a long and painful groan at the spectacular childishness of it when she was supposed to be the smart and sophisticated editor of a new magazine aiming to take the South of France by storm.

'I wish I could have seen this David's face!' Sammy laughed, folding her legs in under her. 'What did he say?'

'Would you believe he laughed?' Penny grimaced. 'The bastard actually found it funny, which made me feel even worse, like I was some kind of clown or something.' Laughing again and shaking her head, she said, 'How on earth am I ever going to get him to take me seriously when I go around flinging custard pies in people's faces? Still, that's up to me to sort out. What you have to sort out is whether or not you're going to come with me.'

Sammy's face instantly lit up. 'Me!' she cried incredulously.

'Yes, you. I've got a job all lined up for you, if you want it, that is, and just you wait till you see where we'll be living. It's out of this world.'

'Oh, Penny Moon, I just love you,' Sammy gushed, diving on to Penny and throwing her arms around her. 'I've been wondering what I should do next and I thought it was about time I got myself a job – what is it, by the way?'

Penny grinned. 'Agony Aunt,' she said. 'I want you to take on the problem page and a few other things besides.'

'Are you kidding?' Sammy shrieked. 'My own column?'

'Your own column,' Penny confirmed. 'I'll have to try you out first, obviously, but we both know you can do it standing on your head. I just need to get you past Marielle.'

'Why, if you're the editor?'

'Because I don't want her giving me any more problems than she's already creating,' Penny yawned.

'What's she like?'

'To look at, absolutely stunning. I couldn't work out at first why she wasn't striding the catwalks or brazening it out with other journalists in Paris. But these past couple of weeks have shown me why she's still on the Côte d'Azur.'

'Why?' Sammy prompted.

'Because,' Penny answered pensively, 'she isn't actually all that bright. She certainly thinks she is, but if you ask me she's a bit of a pygmy in the intellect department and her writing is . . .' Her eyes flashed as though daring herself to voice what she really thought. Deciding it was too bitchy she sufficed with: 'barely average. And the way she's throwing herself at David, trying to create a rift between us, just isn't subtle enough to make me think her clever in any way.'

'Can't wait to meet her,' Sammy commented wryly. 'And what about David? What's he like?'

'Oh God,' Penny groaned, 'don't ask me about him! He's your typical right-up-himself playboy type with so much charm it oozes out of him like jam. And why I should be worrying about him taking me seriously when he's done absolutely zilch to get this magazine up and running so far . . . Did I tell you, he's Sylvia's godson? I did. Well, he behaves like he is, because though she's assured me we have equal power he's already parading around like he owns the joint and Marielle is lapping it up.'

'So he's a bit of a looker, is he?' Sammy grinned.

'Oh, yeah, he's that all right.' Penny sighed.

'How old is he?'

Penny shrugged. 'God knows. Mid to late thirties, I suppose.'

Sammy was eyeing her closely. 'You sure you don't fancy him?' she said.

Penny was on the brink of an explosive response, when she pulled herself back. To go that route might appear she was protesting too much. 'Perfectly sure,' she answered calmly.

Sammy started to laugh.

'I am!' Penny said indignantly. 'I've always told you that I'll know instantly when the right man comes along.'

'How will you?'

'Instinct, of course.'

Sammy nodded wisely. 'Like you did with, what was his name? You know, the transvestite?'

'He was *not* a transvestite,' Penny retorted. 'He just liked wearing women's underwear. And I never did say I was in love with him.'

'But you did claim to be in love with Graham,' Sammy reminded her. 'Graham of the wife, three kids, two mistresses and a dog he was so devoted to he couldn't possibly leave his wife.'

'Infatuation,' Penny corrected testily. 'And we're all allowed to make mistakes.'

'Now let me see,' Sammy said, putting her head to one side. 'Then there was Don, wasn't there? The European political correspondent for CNN.'

'There was nothing wrong with Don!'

'I didn't think so,' Sammy agreed, 'but you were going to marry him at one stage, weren't you?'

'He asked me and I said no,' Penny answered. 'OK, it took me a couple of weeks to say no, but I did in the end because I knew he wasn't right for me.'

Sammy gave a quick flick of her eyebrows. 'That doesn't sound particularly instantaneous to me,' she commented. 'Anyway, what happened to Declan? Or are you still seeing him?'

'We broke up just before I went to France,' Penny told her. 'I'll tell you the details later, but I left him because I knew it wasn't right. Just like I know David Villers isn't, so Marielle is welcome to him.'

'Sounds like some good times ahead,' Sammy remarked. 'But you can handle it and with me there too at least you'll have someone on your side. So, when do we go?'

'Good question,' Penny said, pursing her lips thoughtfully. 'I've taken the house from a fortnight on Monday, so perhaps we could find out if we can move in the weekend before. That should give me time to clear up here, see Sylvia and say goodbye to everyone. Did Peter say when he was coming back, by the way?'

'In two weeks,' Sammy answered.

'Well, he shouldn't be a problem,' Penny said. 'He's been wanting to move Larry in for a while now, but was too kind to say so. Anyway, I'm starving, do you fancy going out somewhere for an early dinner?'

'Great,' Sammy replied, springing to her feet. 'Where shall we go?'

'What about The Canteen in Chelsea Harbour? It's one of the in-places right now.'

Sammy's eyes grew round. 'I was reading about that place just before you came in. It said you have to book weeks in advance . . . and it's Saturday night.'

'Stick with me, babe,' Penny said, winking and reaching for the phone. A couple of minutes later the booking was made and Penny was wondering what it was going to be like living in a place where she had nothing like the leverage she took almost for granted in London. The prospect flattened her spirits and Sammy's next remark didn't help either.

'Do you think,' she said gently, 'that before we take off for France we should go up north to visit Mum and Dad's grave?'

As Penny looked away she felt the familiar tightening of grief in her heart. Since the funeral she hadn't been able to bring herself to go to the grave again and she knew she wasn't going to be able to now.

'It's OK,' Sammy told her, 'we don't have to. It was just a thought.'

'I send Mrs Diller money each week to take flowers,' Penny said lamely.

'Don't think less of yourself for not going,' Sammy said, putting a hand on Penny's shoulder. 'After all, she's not there really, she's right here with us.'

Penny smiled and swallowed the lump in her throat. 'She's right here in you,' she said, 'because she was every bit as daft and every bit as adorable.'

*

With so much to do before leaving Penny hardly saw Sammy over the next couple of weeks, though she guessed Sammy had made her own quick trip up North and was spending the rest of the time catching up with her friends. Sylvia was eager to hear about all the new ideas Penny had come up with during her brief stay in France and laughed with such obvious delight when Penny told her what a start she had got off to with David that Penny started to feel rather pleased at what she had done. Sylvia was less reassuring about Marielle, though, saying that she thought Penny ought to keep a close eye on her, because, after all, Penny was going to be on Marielle's territory and it wouldn't be wise to make an enemy out of someone who was clearly so useful. She feigned horror when she saw the rough costings Penny had come up with on her own, but within a few days the budget had been increased by twenty per cent and the extra rental on the house was passed too.

Though there was little time for reflection, Penny was nevertheless slightly dazed by the feeling she was being allowed to write her own ticket. In fact, the whole project was beginning to take on such an air of unreality that she was starting to feel more like a player in a game she couldn't lose than someone who was preparing to battle her way through the minefields of launching a new magazine. Perversely, it was only when Sylvia or Yolanda pronounced some of her ideas to be unworkable that she felt truly comfortable with her new role, but even so she was still finding it hard to see herself as a boss when she really didn't feel like one and nor was she convinced that she actually had what it took to be one. That wasn't to say she was considering backing out – far from it, in fact, she'd already come too far for that, and, besides, she was becoming kind of attached to her new magazine lately. So why doubt herself when Sylvia obviously had total faith in her and when, in her more

78

confident moments, she was sure she would come through?

During the hectic week before her departure, which included a radio phone-in for LBC, a book review for *Time Out* and the handing over of material on interviews she had already set up, she kept trying to round up her friends and colleagues for some kind of farewell bash. But, typical of Londoners, their diaries were always booked weeks in advance and though a couple could make it one night the others couldn't and vice versa. Experiencing intense swings in emotion as the day of departure approached, their unavailability made Penny feel horribly like someone already in the past. She was used to having a full diary herself, but she'd always managed to make room for emergencies. And that was how she saw herself, as an emergency. For this was going to be her last chance to dish out invitations and extract assurances from everyone that they'd stay in touch or come to visit.

However, the night before she was due to leave the surprise was sprung. Sylvia had invited her to dinner at Mossiman's, saying she would send a car to pick Penny up and take her there. But when the driver sailed right on past the restaurant Penny got her first inkling that something was afoot. And what a something it turned out to be. Sylvia had taken over a West End nightclub and it seemed everyone Penny had ever known or inter-viewed was there. The place was bursting with journalists, photographers, celebrities, politicians, activists, sports people, high achievers, New Age heal-ers, designers, novelists, restaurateurs, reviewers, astrologers and any number of the many eccentrics she had interviewed. They were all there to wish her good luck and tell her how sorely she was going to be missed. Penny was so overwhelmed that all she could do was shriek in surprise and joy as she recognized one face after another, after another.

They rocked and bopped the night away, drank the place dry of champagne, then moved on to wine, and devoured a magnificent buffet that had been prepared by a team of Mossiman's students. Sylvia made a speech that got tears flowing and Yolanda presented her with a gold Cartier pen, a red, leather-bound and gold-embossed diary from Smythson's of Bond Street, and a hilarious caricature of herself in a beret with a string of onions around her neck and umpteen scandalous rags and lawsuits fluttering from her hands.

At the end of the evening, as Penny moved tearfully from one embrace to the next, she wished to God that Sylvia hadn't singled her out for this job, because the idea of leaving them all behind was suddenly almost too much to bear. It no longer felt like a game she couldn't lose – quite the reverse, in fact: it felt as if she was being sent straight to jail.

The feeling persisted into the next day, when she and Sammy boarded the plane for Nice and got there to find it cloudy and cold and being thrashed by the mistral. It was only Sammy's rapturous cries as the estate agent took them slowly along the drive towards the wonderful villa that stopped Penny getting on the next plane back.

Fortunately the following day the wind had dropped and though it was still cold it was clear and sunny, so Penny decided that a little exploration of their surroundings was in order. They started by searching out the local *boulangerie*, where a fat, merry old lady with a whiskery chin and floury apron treated them to a hearty Gallic welcome and wanted to know all about what they were doing in France, while wrapping their crusty baguettes in flimsy paper and popping a couple of succulent butter croissants into a bag – on the house. After, they strolled across to the café, which was satisfyingly populated by Gitane-puffing *ouvriers* in black berets and blue serge overalls and, less satisfyingly, a few local yobs. They sat outside sipping piping-hot, thick creamy coffee and soaking up the uniquely French atmosphere.

Later they took a walk through the artist's village of Mougins, which nestled around the peak of the hill overlooking their villa and the sea. Though they were not wildly impressed with the paintings, the village itself was so picturesque that Sammy used up an entire roll of film on shots of the old stone fountain, the quaint little houses fringing the narrow, cobbled streets and of Penny, braving the cold outside one of the chic, overpriced bistros.

After lunch the rain started again, so they drove around in their rented car for a while getting a feel of the densely forested, hilly terrain with its cute little Provençal villages and brief but glorious glimpses of the sea. Finally, tired but a lot happier than she'd been the day before, Penny turned the car for home, while Sammy snored gently in the seat beside her, maps, guidebooks, a new beret and ropes of garlic scattered around her feet.

When they returned to the villa, Penny stood for a while gazing out at the drizzling rain as it rippled the surface of the pool. She was even more nervous than she had expected to be at the prospect of all that lay ahead and, standing here now, she could once again feel herself starting to doubt her ability. However, deciding the only way to beat her nerves was simply to get on with things, she picked up the phone to call Marielle, firstly to let her know she had arrived and, secondly, to ask if Marielle had arranged the meeting Penny had mentioned in one of her faxes.

'Yes, I have called it for tomorrow morning at ten,' Marielle told her.

'I see,' Penny said, failing to keep the tightness from her voice. 'Well, I'm afraid that doesn't suit me, so I'd appreciate it if you could call it for Wednesday, as I asked.'

Marielle was silent.

'I take it that the people I asked you to contact have all

been contacted?' Penny enquired silkily.

'They have.'

'What about David?'

'He says he will come to the meeting if he can. Maybe Wednesday won't be convenient.'

Penny looked up as Sammy walked into the room. 'Thank you, Marielle,' she said, meeting Sammy's eyes. 'I'll see you in the morning.'

Turning over the pages in her address book, Penny found the phone number of David's apartment and dialled it. She let it ring for some time, but there was obviously no one at home so she put the receiver down again, damned if she was going to call Marielle back to find out if she knew where he was.

'Well?' Sammy prompted.

Penny's eyes moved back to hers. 'Well,' she said, 'I think it's high time David Villers and Marielle Descourts found out who the real boss is around here.'

Sammy grinned. 'That's the spirit,' she said. 'But just don't let them become an obsession, OK? No, I know it's still early days, but now's as good a time as any to remind you that there are other things in life that are more important than that magazine.'

'Mmm,' Penny said thoughtfully. Then, giving a sudden shiver, she turned to look at the fireplace. 'It's cold,' she said. 'Do you feel cold? Let's light the fire.'

The digital clock at Nice railway station read 20:55 as Robert Stirling, a short, balding, overweight American in his early fifties, alighted from a second-class carriage to merge with the masses. In his right hand he carried a nondescript briefcase; over his left shoulder he toted a heavy, worn-out holdall. His protruding bottom lip supported a fat cigar; fallen ash dusted a lapel of his belted raincoat.

As he moved unobtrusively through the crowds his small, piercing eyes were searching out the bland faces of his back-up. The weapon he had been handed in Paris was concealed in the briefcase together with a history of David Villers's life.

By the time he reached the exit two dark-suited men were flanking him. One had taken his holdall; the other was speaking to him in low, rapid Italian.

Taking the cigar from his mouth, Stirling stopped to crush the remains underfoot. Then in a gruff, impatient voice, he said, 'Speak English.'

Forty minutes later Stirling was boarding a British-registered, Turkish-built motor yacht at the Port Pierre Canto in Cannes. As his heavy bulk rocked the hull the door of the deck salon opened and Marielle Descourts, in a red, skintight pant suit, came out to greet him.

Early the next morning Esther Delaney, a short, flamboyantly dressed, elderly woman with vivid hazel eyes and a wrinkled complexion, breezed smilingly through customs and started along the walkway towards the arrivals hall of Nice airport. In her long red cape, white fur hat, with matching muff and white leather boots, she caused more than a few heads to turn, which pleased her enormously since she imagined they were probably wondering if she was famous.

Spotting her husband waiting for her in the crowd, she lifted an arm to wave, at the same instant as a tall, distinguished-looking man in his early forties dressed in casual clothes and carrying a large sports bag moved on past her, responding to an unobtrusive signal from a desk clerk in one of the car-hire booths.

From the corner of her eye Esther Delaney watched the man, waited for him to get information from the desk clerk before leaving the airport, then, going to her husband, she raised herself up on tiptoe to kiss him and straighten up his cravat, whispering, 'All clear.'

As they walked to where Wally Delaney had left his car, right outside the terminal building, the casually dressed man was sliding into the back of a limousine. Neither of the Delaneys looked in his direction; nor did they acknowledge the chauffeur as he settled his cap more neatly on his head and got into the driver's seat.

'Everything in order?' Wally asked, as he settled in comfortably behind the wheel of his Mercedes and steered it out through the car-hire parking lot towards the airport exit.

'Absolutely,' Esther confirmed. 'Just a teensy hiccup when we got to Zurich, but it's all sorted out now.' Her eyes were burning brightly with the memory of her trip. 'They were all there,' she told him.

Wally made a sound in the back of his throat as his upper lip twitched his thick, ginger moustache. Then, referring to the man who had got into the limousine, he said, 'How long is he staying?'

'He didn't say, but he wants you to call him tonight. Did you give the chauffeur a mobile phone?'

Wally gave an affirmative grunt; then, propping his cigar in his mouth, he leaned forward to press in the lighter.

They travelled in silence for a while, until Esther lifted her little white leather vanity case on to her lap. 'Think we should stop off at a bank, dear,' she said.

As Wally glanced over at her she opened the case to reveal a wad of 500-franc notes as thick as the Alpes-Maritimes telephone directory. Wally's pale eyes were gleaming as he turned them back to the road.

With a smile of satisfaction, Esther leaned her head back against the head rest and allowed her mind to drift for a while. She hadn't been as happy as this for a long time – not since their son, Billy, had died ten years ago, just before his twenty-third birthday. It was a subject she rarely discussed, but the new friends she had made since leaving the Far East and coming to the Côte d'Azur ar knew that her seemingly boundless energy, cor d with her alarming intake of wine and the heartfelt pleasure she received from the young when they showed up at one of her soirées, was all a result of her childless state. What no one seemed able to get to the bottom of, though, was what she did when she was jetting around the world in search of antiques for Wally's little shop, *Bijou*, in Le Cannet, for she rarely, if ever, came back with anything.

The way the Delaneys had made their fortune was one of the best-kept secrets on the Riviera, for no one believed – at least, it was more interesting not to believe – that Wally's income from the shop, given his astonishing ignorance when it came to antiques, could possibly have provided them with the kind of life style they enjoyed. Esther, while floating around her cocktail parties in outrageously glamorous attire, was extremely fond of telling stories about when they had lived in Singapore, or Malaysia, or Hong Kong – which they evidently had, for she knew far too much about the places for it not to be true – but exactly what line they had been in before this antique racket no one had ever been able to find out. The more generous of their acquaintances were of the opinion that Wally had been an army man, if for no other reason than he looked the part – though no one could give a satisfactory explanation as to why he wouldn't admit to it. The less generous could, however, for they had it on the highest authority – no names mentioned, of course – that Wally had indeed been an army man, but had been court-martialled for offences that ranged from some kind of fifth-columnist activities to being discovered exposing himself behind the women's barracks.

Esther, fortunately, was blissfully unaware of these damning rumours and rather enjoyed the air of mystery she so carefully cultivated, when the truth was that until five years ago Wally had been an executive for a washing-machine company. His incompetence had resulted in them being posted all over the world, until in the end he'd been pensioned off early, though with nothing like as golden a handshake as he had been expecting. So when they had been approached by their current employer, just after arriving on the Riviera, and been offered a situation that provided them with the means to live far more comfortably than they ever had before, they had grabbed it with both hands. Two years on, Wally had at last regained a sense of his own importance and Esther, when she travelled, managed to fulfil all her social-climbing ambitions as well as compensate for her frustrated motherly longings by mixing almost exclusively with the rich and famous. Not when in France, however, because in France, for reasons of security, her employer insisted she keep a much lower profile – which on the whole she did, for she was every bit as discreet as her position required her to be, even though most who knew her would never have credited her with such powers of restraint.

Looking over at Wally, she blinked and smiled. With his red-veined nose, faded brown eyes and widely spaced teeth, he was most certainly not an attractive man. But Esther loved him, wouldn't know how to survive without him, in fact, not after all these years. And Wally's word was law in their house, always had been and always would be, which meant that between them Wally and their employer saw to it that Esther rarely had to take a decision for herself – a fact she was extremely glad of, even though, secretly, she rather admired the modern independent young women she came across nowadays. Though heaven forbid she would ever have to go out into the world and fight for herself the way they did. No, she was very happy with Wally, thank you very much.

Feeling her watching him, Wally reached across to the glove compartment and took out a neatly wrapped little package, which he dropped casually into her lap.

'Oh, gosh,' she cried, her eyes lighting up as she read

the name of an exclusive jeweller on the label. 'What is it this time? Oh my! Wally!' she gasped when she saw the ruby-and-diamond pin that was going to look just perfect on the flouncy new cocktail dress with all those fringes and sequins she had bought herself in Zurich. 'It's lovely,' she told him, pulling down her sun visor to test the colour against her sallow complexion and giving a sigh of pure pleasure.

'Friends?' he said gruffly.

For a moment she looked baffled; then, remembering, she laid a hand on his arm, saying, 'Of course we're friends, dear.'

'Didn't mean it, you know that, don't you?' he said, referring to how he had lost control just before she'd left and shaken her so hard it had made her cry. He'd done it because he'd caught her looking at photographs of their son, Billy.

'Of course, you didn't,' she told him. Then, after a pause, she gave a little laugh and added, 'I'm such a maddening thing at times, I'm sure. I don't blame you at all.'

He sucked several times on his cigar, puffing out dense clouds of smoke, as though to mask himself from the shame he always felt when she blamed herself for his intolerance of her grief. 'So,' he said abruptly, 'he wants me to call him tonight?'

'Yes. I think he wants you to drive some friends of his to Barcelona at the weekend.'

Wally nodded. After a moment he said, 'We had a delivery yesterday.'

Esther turned to look at him and, reading his raised eyebrows, clasped her hands together in delight. 'How splendid!' she cried. 'He will be pleased. He was afraid it wouldn't get here in time. Was everything in order? Photographs, stamps and all those little things I don't understand?'

'Shipshape,' he responded, nodding for her to look out

of the window.

As the chauffeur-driven limousine swept past them Esther turned casually in the opposite direction. 'My, it's a lovely day,' she murmured, gazing out at the sunny hillsides.

Wally's eyes tracked the limousine until it disappeared round a bend in the autoroute. 'By the way, got ourselves some new neighbours,' he said, deciding to put a bit of a sprint on himself.

'Really!' Esther said. 'Who are they? Have you met them?'

Wally's eyes remained on the road ahead. 'Two girls,' he said. 'Sisters.' Then, after a pause: 'One of them's a journalist.'

When Esther didn't speak, he turned to look at her and watched her eyes dilate as he grinned.

'You don't mean . . . ?' she said. 'Oh, Wally, you're not saying it's the girl who's come to take over *The Coast*?'

'Yes,' he nodded, 'I *am* saying.'

'Oh my, oh my!' Esther murmured, clapping a hand to her face. 'And right next door to us. What a perfectly dreadful coincidence.' The feverish excitement that was now burning in her eyes not only totally belied her words but was something Wally could easily have predicted.

'Have you told you-know-who?' Esther asked, mouthing the last three words.

Wally shook his head. 'Not yet,' he answered.

Esther's smile widened. 'I say,' she whispered, 'do you think we might dare to invite her over? Just the once,' she added hastily. 'I'd simply love to meet her. Wouldn't you?'

Wally gave a non-committal shrug, even though it was precisely the response he had hoped for. Meeting and getting to know Penny Moon could put him and Esther right at the centre of things, a place he wouldn't mind being, providing it was clear, just in case things backfired, that it was Esther who had put them there – not him. 'Bit risky, wouldn't you say?' he commented, feeling that this mild little protest would go some way to keeping him on the right side of their employer, were he there to hear it, but at the same time would do nothing to dissuade his wife.

'No one need ever know,' Esther said. 'I mean, after all, she is our neighbour, and how would it look if we didn't invite her over?'

'Actually, I think we're going to have to, old thing,' he answered. 'Gave me a gin and tonic the other night, so got to have her back, wouldn't you say?'

'You've been over there?' Esther cried.

'Had a bit of a problem with one of the outside lights,' he explained. 'Asked if I knew an electrician. Fixed it for her m'self, gave me a gin and tonic to say thanks.'

'Oh, how perfectly splendid,' Esther trilled.

Though Wally's lips didn't move, inwardly he was smiling, for it was pleasing him to be able to offer her this other little jewel – an excuse, albeit tenuous, to meet Penny Moon, who, apart from everything else about her, was most certainly young enough to satisfy Esther's craving for youthful company. 'Could invite her over while I'm in Barcelona,' he suggested offhandedly.

Esther's eyes widened with surprise. 'But don't you want to be there too?' she said.

He shrugged. 'Thought it would give you girls the chance for a bit of a chinwag,' he said, puffing out a few more clouds of smoke. 'Don't want old duffers like me in the way, what?' What he meant, in fact, was that if they were going to invite Penny Moon, a journalist, into their home and their employer somehow got to find out about it, then if he, Wally, wasn't actually there no blame could be attached to him for doing something their employer would find very hard to forgive.

'You're a wonderful man, Wally,' Esther smiled ingenuously, laying a hand on his arm.

'Yes, well, you just be careful what you tell her, old thing. She's a journalist, remember. Probably got a way of getting things out of people they'd rather not tell, what?'

'Oh, I shall be ever so discreet,' Esther assured him.

Wally grunted and sucked noisily on the end of his cigar. During the half-hour he was over at Penny Moon's the other night he hadn't been able to resist dropping the odd hint or two that there were certain things he knew about that might just interest her too. Not that he'd had any intention of telling her, of course, but it was one of his particular pleasures in life, getting people going, stirring up the old curiosity then leaving them high and dry. She hadn't been very quick on the uptake, though; hadn't asked him any questions the way he expected a journalist to. But she had the kind of eyes that looked as though they were seeing right through a chap. He'd left just after noticing that, for the way she was looking at him had made him feel as though she knew a whole lot more about him than he'd ever want anyone to know.

'I do hope she'll come,' Esther said, her eyes clouding with the prospect of rejection. 'She's quite famous, you know, in London. Billy told me.'

Wally's eyes opened wide with alarm and, fumbling his cigar out of his mouth, he said, 'Who told you?'

Esther's eyes fell to her lap. 'I'm sorry,' she whispered. 'I only went the once and it doesn't do any harm, really it doesn't. And it comforts me to be in contact with him.'

Wally jammed the cigar back in his mouth and puffed so hard he could barely see the road ahead. This seance nonsense had to stop before it sent the old girl off her rocker.

'He sends his love,' Esther told him softly, then immediately started to slap him on the back as he began to choke and splutter while struggling to keep the car under control.

Her darling boy had told her a lot of other things too,

90

but she decided that now probably wasn't the time to tell Wally, not when they had just run into the back of the car in front.

Chapter 5

As Penny came to an abrupt halt on the threshold of the production office Sammy and Jeffrey, the designer they had just collected from the airport, collided into each other behind her, then peered over her shoulder to see what had brought her to a standstill.

That the four-metre-long production table had arrived was no surprise, for Penny had known it was coming, however the number of computer screens displaying their access menus to the information superhighways was as unexpected as it was impressive, but for the moment it was the number of people standing and sitting around drinking coffee and idly gossiping as they presumably awaited her arrival that was causing the greatest surprise – in fact, had Penny not spotted Marielle at the other end of the room she might have thought she'd stumbled into the wrong office.

Suddenly galvanized into action, Penny pushed her way through the crowd, and, with no regard for the person Marielle was talking to, said, 'Would you mind telling me who all these people are?'

'Ah, Penny,' Marielle said smoothly, treating her to such a condescending sweep of the eyes that Penny actually felt herself flush. 'Good morning. We were expecting you a little earlier than this.' Turning away, she started to clap her hands for attention.

'*Mesdames, messieurs,*' she said, as everyone turned in

her direction. 'May I introduce you to Penny Moon. She will be conducting the meeting I have called you all here for and if you have any questions, any comments or worthwhile suggestions, please feel free to make them known. First, however, I would like you to introduce yourselves to *Mademoiselle* Moon by telling her your names and what you will be doing for our new magazine. If everyone would take a seat at the table, we will proceed in a clockwise fashion. Clothilde we already know so, Céline, perhaps you would like to begin.'

'*Bonjour, mademoiselle,*' the pleasant-faced woman began as Penny's stupefied gaze came to rest on her. 'I am Céline Minaudière. My speciality is food, so I shall be supplying restaurant critiques and recipes.'

'*Bonjour, mademoiselle,*' the middle-aged man next to Céline said, smiling. '*Et bienvenue en France.* My name is Barnabé Monray and I am a subeditor.'

'*Salut,*' the cheery-faced lad next to him said. 'I'm English, my name's Paul Smith and I'm a freelance hack.'

The next person was on the point of taking breath, when Penny finally pulled herself out of her stupor and, doing her utmost to disguise her anger, held up her hand. 'OK, that's far enough!' she said. 'I'm not entirely sure what's been going on here, but I don't think it's going to take much working out, so before we go any further I'm afraid that whatever promises Marielle has made to any of you are null and void as of this moment, since she does not have the authority to recruit anyone. However, I will be happy to see each of you individually, when we will go through the proper formalities of interview.' Turning on her heel to glare at Marielle, she said, 'In my office now, please.'

She got only as far as the door before Marielle said, '*Monsieur* Villers has approved each—'

'My office,' Penny cut in furiously and, pushing the door open, she stalked inside, shaking with anger.

'Close the door,' she barked as Marielle came in after

her.

With a long-suffering sigh Marielle pushed the door closed and looking every inch the editor in her short-jacketed navy suit and white silk shirt, she sauntered over to Penny's desk, folded her arms and rested her weight on one leg.

'Where is David?' Penny demanded, taking off her coat and dropping it on an armchair. 'And what is all this?' she barked, seeing the untidy piles of paperwork on her desk.

'It's mine of course,' Marielle replied, in a tone that suggested Penny was the usurper here. 'I was here until very late last—'

'Then clear it out and don't use my office again without my permission,' Penny snapped. 'Now, I repeat, where is David?'

'I'm afraid I don't know,' Marielle answered, resting her chin on a perfectly manicured finger.

Penny's eyes flashed. 'Then I suggest you find him, Marielle, and tell him I want to see him before the end of the day. And if you ever try pulling another stunt like that one out there on me again I'll dismiss you on the spot. Do we have that straight?'

Marielle smirked.

Tearing her eyes away and putting her briefcase on her chair, Penny said, 'Right, I'll want to see the CVs, references and published examples of the work of everyone out there, and if they don't have all that with them you can send them home to get it. I'll allot each person twenty minutes, so you can draw up a schedule and those who aren't required immediately can come back later. If they're not available later it'll be up to them to contact me themselves to make another appointment. Now, clear my desk, please.'

Marielle took her time stacking everything into neat little piles, then finally scooped up her work and carried it to the door.

'You will find my sister, Samantha, out there,' Penny told her. 'She has the designer with her. Ask them to come in, please.'

As the door clicked shut behind Marielle, Penny put a hand to her head and closed her eyes. Her temples were throbbing and she was perspiring badly. She was quite unused to speaking to people that way, but then she'd never been in a position of authority before. But how much authority did she have when David bloody Villers was going behind her back like this? Her nostrils flared. And where the hell was he, the god- damned coward?

She looked up as the door opened and Clothilde came in carrying a cup of coffee. It was only then that Penny noticed the fresh paint on the walls, the additional chairs and tables placed in her office and how much larger and lived-in it appeared because of it.

'You're a life-saver,' Penny smiled as Clothilde put the coffee on her desk and Sammy and Jeffrey came in behind her. 'No, stay,' she said, flopping down in her chair as Clothilde made to leave.

Sammy was grinning all over her face. 'What a bitch!' she chuckled. 'Did you fire her?'

'No,' Penny answered. 'But I probably should have. Clothilde, this is Sammy, my sister, and Jeffrey, the designer.'

Jeffrey's eyes, made twice their size by the thick lenses of his wire-rimmed spectacles, softened in a smile as he shook Clothilde's hand.

Penny fought back a smile of her own as she saw the instant adoption in Clothilde's expression, which was transferred to Sammy as Sammy stepped forward to shake her hand too. For a moment Penny was tempted to ask Clothilde to warn her if she ever saw Marielle stepping out of line again, but to start splitting the team into two separate camps at this stage probably wasn't wise.

'Clothilde,' she said, 'do you think there is any chance at all that you might be able to fix me up with a secretary, even just a temporary one, by the end of the morning? I know I should have thought about this sooner, but no doubt I'm about to discover that plenty of other things have slipped through the net too.'

Clothilde's wrinkly face broke into a smile. 'As a matter of fact,' she said, 'I can offer you my niece, Brigitte. She is staying with us at the moment from Nantes. She will be nineteen next week.'

'What qualifications does she have?' Penny asked.

Clothilde grimaced. 'I don't think any,' she answered. 'And, to be truthful, her English isn't very good, but she is a bright girl with a lot of energy and if nothing else she will be able to help out until you find someone else.'

'OK, thank you,' Penny smiled, wishing she could ask Clothilde to take it on, but Clothilde's other commitments wouldn't allow her to work the kind of hours Penny would be putting in over the next few months. 'Maybe you'd like to go and give Marielle a hand in sorting out an interview roster,' she said.

'You're going to interview them all?' Sammy said, sitting down in one of the padded-leather and steel-limbed chairs the other side of Penny's desk.

'It would seem crazy not to,' Penny answered, taking a sip of her coffee. 'After all, they're here, and for all I know they might be perfect. And, if they've come from where I think they have, the chances are a lot of them will be.'

'Why, where do you think they've come from?' Jeffrey asked, shrugging off his tweed jacket to reveal a pair of splendid red braces over a bright yellow shirt.

'I gave Marielle the list of contacts the editor of the *Nice-Matin* was generous enough to give me. He said he was going to make a few more calls on my behalf as well, which I imagine he has and Marielle has worked from that too. Which is fine, but she had no right making any promises or, indeed, hiring a single person without my say-so.'

'Did she have David's?' Sammy said.

'So she claims and I don't imagine she's lying. But that'll be for him and me to sort out – when he decides to show his face. Until such time I need to get these interviews over with and I'd like your help, both of you.'

'Mine?' Jeffrey said. 'But—'

'Yours,' Penny interrupted. 'I'll need a sounding board and someone else's gut instincts, so you two are it.'

By six o'clock that evening, punch-drunk from so many interviews on so many different subjects, Penny had seen fifteen out of the twenty or so people, most of whom she had hired either on a permanent or a freelance basis, with the result that they now had on staff an advertising director, a sales and marketing director, a fashion editor and two subeditors. The advertising and marketing directors, she had learned, were the only ones David had interviewed personally. And their lengthy list of contributors contained experts on everything from French bureaucracy to cryptic crossword puzzles – which, Penny thought wryly to herself, could easily be one and the same thing. But that this small stretch of coast had yielded up so much talent and in such a short space of time was something Penny was finding extremely curious, despite the help of the editor of *Nice-Matin*.

'I get the feeling I'm missing something somewhere, do you?' she remarked to Sammy and Jeffrey when the three of them were once again alone together. 'I mean, it's all been so damned easy. I wasn't expecting to be in this position for at least another month or two and now here I am about to call a full editorial meeting for tomorrow.'

Jeffrey shrugged. 'Well, I wouldn't knock it if I were you, because this means you have every chance of getting launched by the end of August. Incidentally, at the risk of stating the obvious, you still need to find yourself a good printer.'

'Yes, I hadn't forgotten,' Penny told him. 'We'll get on

to it straight after the meeting tomorrow.' Dropping her pen on the pad in front of her, she turned to put her feet on the edge of Sammy's chair beside her. 'You're very quiet,' she remarked.

'Mmm,' Sammy said. 'I was just wondering if maybe Sylvia had been to work down here – you know, calling in old favours, rounding up all the contacts she has ... What do you think?'

'It's certainly possible,' Penny answered, treating herself to a luxurious stretch. 'And if she has, who can blame her? After all, it's her money. Anyway, I don't know about you but I'm in sore need of food and drink before I start getting my act together for the meeting tomorrow. You don't have to stay on, Jeffrey. You must be tired, having only just flown in this morning, and you still haven't checked into your hotel yet, have you?'

'Aren't you staying with us?' Sammy asked, turning to look at him. 'We've got plenty of room.'

Jeffrey smiled. 'Penny did offer, but I've ungraciously turned her down. I'll find myself a little studio apartment somewhere for the duration. Meanwhile, a hotel suits me fine. So, if you're sure you don't need me any more tonight, I'll be off.'

'Give young Brigitte the number of your hotel, will you?' Penny said. 'I might need to call you later. I'll leave a message if you're not there. And, while you're at it, ask her to go and rustle up some kind of takeaway for me and Sammy.'

In fact, feeling the need to move around a bit, Penny followed Jeffrey out of the office and, seeing Marielle sitting at her desk, busying herself with God only knew what, she waited until the door closed behind Brigitte and Jeffrey before asking Marielle if she had managed to contact David yet.

'Yes,' Marielle replied, keeping right on with what she was doing.

'And?' Penny sighed wearily.

'He'll be here for the meeting tomorrow.'

'Where is he now?' Penny asked.

'He didn't say.'

Rolling her eyes in Sammy's direction, Penny said, 'Well, maybe you'd like to give me the phone number you dialled.'

'He called me.'

'I see. And when exactly did he call you?'

'A few hours ago.'

'So why didn't you put him on to me?'

'You were interviewing,' Marielle reminded her.

A few seconds ticked by, then suddenly Penny's hand crashed down on the desk in front of Marielle, making her jump.

'Thank you,' Penny smiled as at last Marielle looked up at her. 'Now, I expect you already know that I have approved most of the people you had here today, but there were two I didn't. The first was the film reviewer, because I have other plans for that column; the second was the Agony Aunt, because Samantha here will be running the problem page.'

Marielle slanted her eyes in Sammy's direction. 'Nepotism?' she said derisively.

'That's it,' Penny confirmed shortly. 'Now, back to the matter of recruitment: I'd like to know how you managed to round up all those remarkably talented people in such a short space of time.'

Marielle shrugged. 'It wasn't difficult. I know a lot of people.'

Penny's eyes bored into hers, but though it was evident that Marielle wasn't going to relinquish the credit she did at least have the grace to blush.

Penny flicked a glance towards Sammy, who was watching them from the doorway; then, making a supreme effort to keep the chill from her voice, she said, 'Maybe, Marielle, you would like to come into my office where we can discuss exactly what it is that you object to so strongly in me.'

Marielle looked at her, and for the second time that day she allowed a condescending sweep of her eyes to speak for her.

'It doesn't need to be this way,' Penny told her, hanging on to her temper. 'I'm perfectly prepared to accept you as an integral part of the team, but in turn you are going to have to accept that I am your boss.'

'Correction,' Marielle said smoothly. 'David is my boss.'

Penny inhaled deeply and closed her eyes for the count of ten. But before she could speak again Marielle said, 'Would you mind telling me what qualifications your sister has to run a problem page?'

Penny looked at Sammy and Sammy gave a brief shake of her head. 'Sammy's qualifications are known to me,' Penny answered, 'and will also be made known to David. All you need to know is that Sylvia Starke is happy with my decision. And quite frankly, Marielle, if you don't buck your ideas up a bit your dismissal will become another of my decisions Sylvia Starke is happy with.'

Marielle rose majestically to her feet, her glassy eyes glittering with malice. She uttered not a word as she started packing up her briefcase, then walked across the office to get her coat. 'That is the second time today you have threatened me,' she said icily. 'I will not be putting you to the trouble again. I resign,' and swinging the door open she stalked out.

'Fuck,' Penny muttered.

'Good riddance,' Sammy added.

Penny turned to her, shaking her head. 'As much as it galls me to admit it,' she said, 'we need her. There's still a hell of a long way to go and her knowledge of the region, as well as her efficiency in getting things together the way she did today, is too valuable for me to let go.'

'So what are you going to do?'

'Right now? I'm going to start preparing for to-morrow's meeting. Then early in the morning I'll swallow my pride and call her.'

After working through until almost midnight the night before, Penny was back at her desk at seven the next morning. Until Clothilde arrived at eight she was alone in the office, having left Sammy at home boning up on pop psychology. During the evening she had found another task for Sammy, that of seeking out all the happening hot-spots along the coast, particularly those around the ports. She had an idea for a column that, if it worked, could be quite a winner.

She was just going over the itinerary of the up-coming meeting again, making sure she'd covered everything and trying to shake off the feeling that actually none of it was in the least bit relevant, when the door to her office opened and David walked in. A bolt of nerves instantly shot through her, but having taken a resolution to be pleasant to him and at least to try to forge a partnership that worked for them both, she plastered a smile of wel-come on her face.

'Hi,' he grinned, seeming to find her warmth as amus-ing as he did surprising. His unruly blond hair was damp from the rain and his fine-boned face was as hand-some and self-assured as ever. Penny wasn't sure whether it was that which irritated her the most or whether it was the domineering power of him that seemed to swamp her authority the moment he walked in the door. He was wearing a faded blue sweater over a pale-blue denim shirt and jeans and managing to look far more relaxed in her office as he pulled up one of her visitor chairs than Penny did. 'So, how you doing?' he asked.

'Fine, thank you,' she answered. 'It's good of you to grace us with your presence today.'

'Think nothing of it,' he told her, waving a dismissive

101

hand. 'As a matter of fact I intended to be here yesterday, but a couple of things cropped up that meant I didn't fly in until late last night.'

'I see,' Penny replied, not bothering to ask where he'd been. 'I spent the day interviewing yesterday,' she said, looking back down at the paperwork in front of her to make a show of being distracted by more important matters than his company, 'and it appears, somewhat incredibly, that we are almost up to full strength already. However, I would appreciate it if you didn't go ahead with such major decisions without me in the future.'

'You got it,' he told her affably.

'And I can't help wondering,' she added, fixing him with boldly sceptical eyes, 'where such an extraordinary amount of talent came from and so quickly.'

Laughing he said, 'From you, who do you think? You were the one who went to see Couval at the *Nice-Matin*, you were the one who charmed him into giving you the list Marielle worked from, and I, well, I guess I just got lucky that the couple of guys I knew were available.'

Penny's eyes were still narrowed, but she quickly looked away as he narrowed his too.

'Seem to be a lot of bees around this place, wouldn't you say?' he remarked, looking up at the ceiling.

Penny frowned. 'What are you talking about?'

'Well, Marielle's got one in her bonnet about you and it seems to me you've got one in yours about me . . .'

'David, I have nothing in my bonnet about you,' she told him with exaggerated patience. 'All I have is a desire to make this magazine work, with or without your help.'

He grinned. 'Hey, you're not about to fire me too, are you?'

'If you're referring to Marielle, I didn't fire her: she resigned.'

'Put it whichever way you like,' he shrugged. 'But if you take my advice you'd do well to try and get along with her, 'cos she's going to be pretty invaluable around here over the next few months.'

Penny's eyes dilated. 'Do I take it from that,' she seethed, 'that you have reinstated her?'

He put his head to one side while he considered the question. 'Yep,' he said, 'I guess you could say that.'

'So you've gone over my head?' Penny said, her voice trembling with rage.

'Uh-uh,' he said, shaking his head. 'All's I did was accept her apology on your behalf.'

Penny was on her feet. 'How dare you!' she cried. 'Just who the hell do you think—'

'Hey, hey,' he laughed, holding up his hands, 'calm down. What I meant was, I accepted her apology for the way she's fucked you around and I felt sure you would too once she offered it. Which she's prepared to do if you're prepared to listen.'

'But you've already reinstated her,' Penny reminded him tersely.

'Yep,' he said, 'but I reckoned you didn't really want her resignation any more than I did. But, if you're dead set against her . . .'

'Don't play around with me!' she snapped. 'I'm as aware as you are how valuable she is and if she's prepared to apologize I want to hear it. In the meantime maybe you'd care to let me know just what your input is going to be around here and just how often we might have the dubious honour of your presence.'

His eyes were alive with laughter as, getting up from the chair and strolling back to the door, he said, 'Dubious, eh?'

As Penny's eyes sparked with impotent rage she was so sorely tempted to fling something at him that had he not ducked as though something were already hurtling through the air, she might have. As it was, her lips gave an involuntary twitch of laughter before, collecting herself quickly, she said, 'If Marielle is already out there I'll see her now, before the meeting starts.'

'Sure,' he said, his expression turning serious for a moment. 'And just a quick word of advice, Pen,' he added, making her start with such a familiar use of her name: 'get yourself straightened out on the man-management front, 'cos it's kind of important.'

Half an hour later, Marielle's churlish apology dealt with, Penny was standing at the head of the production table flicking through her last-minute notes while Clothilde and Brigitte circulated copies of a procedural plan intended as a spring-off point for them all. As the general hum of conversation washed over her, Penny was assuming an air of total concentration while very much hoping that by decking herself out in a smart, black-and-white dog-tooth dress and tying her hair back with a neat velvet-covered slide she was looking much more the editor than she felt. At the same time she was savagely reproaching herself for allowing such petty considerations to matter.

Most of the contributors were there, perched on the high stools around the table; so too were the new staff – and this, Penny imagined, was probably the first and last time they would all get together between now and the launch. After today she'd be dealing with them on an individual basis, while scouting around for more contributors to fill the still-vacant slots.

When Clothilde and Brigitte were finished Penny looked up, feeling as nervous as a gauche young actress on opening night. All eyes were on the agenda in front of them and for one panicked moment Penny wondered if she was going crazy. What on earth was she doing here, on the point of telling all these people what she wanted of them? How could she possibly think she was up to this? She allowed her eyes to rest a moment on David, who was sitting at the other end of the table, an elbow hooked over the back of his chair and a foot balanced on one knee as he waited for her to begin. Marielle was next to him, scribbling something on a pad, and to his other side was a small, rather effete-looking man with large glasses and neatly combed black hair whom Penny had never seen before. He looked vaguely Asian in origin, but on the other hand he could be Italian; she was sure she'd find out soon enough – maybe he'd come with a straitjacket ready to carry her off!

Dropping her eyes back to the agenda she allowed herself a few seconds in which to pull herself together, then with an encompassing smile that totally masked her confidence failure she said, 'OK, before we get started there are a couple of general things I would like to say. The first is that from here-on-in this meeting,' and here she switched into French, 'is going to be conducted in French. If anyone has a problem with that,' she said, looking at David, 'then you shouldn't be on the team.' She paused, belatedly remembering that he had spoken French the night they'd been at the restaurant in Gourdon. When no one else spoke up, which was as she expected, having tested all the non-French the day before, she continued. 'As we take each point at a time I would like those of you concerned to make notes that I will be happy to discuss on a one-to-one basis later. Delving deeply into the content of each subject as we go will only serve to draw the meeting out for much longer than necessary and won't have much relevance at this stage. All we need to do is make everyone aware of what is going into the magazine and what our main aims are. There will, of course, be a question-and-answer session as soon as we have been through the agenda.

'I think you are all by now aware that I am keen for the magazine to be as sharp and, I hope, witty as possible. Intellectual pomposity and stodgy, self-congratulatory reportage are out. We have two excellent subs to help with this and until we get ourselves fully established Paul Smith and I will take on the more serious issues as they come up. And puffs can hit the bin as soon as they come in.'

'Puffs?' David enquired.

'Publicity hand-outs masquerading as editorials,' Penny explained, looking around the table. Satisfied that everyone understood and amazed that no one had yet booed her off, she continued. 'As I told you all yesterday, we will be producing a fortnightly publication of fifty-two pages selling at a price yet to be fixed.'

'Twelve francs,' David interjected.

'Thank you,' Penny said, smiling at him gratefully as she clenched her nervously shaking hands. It was a small contribution on his part, but an important one which showed that he at least was taking her seriously. She glanced down at her notes. 'Ah, yes,' she said, 'just one other little matter: we need a new name for the magazine and we have to come up with one before the end of next month so that Jeffrey here can get to work on it. And I imagine it would be helpful to the advertising agency handling the launch to know what to call us. So, again, any suggestions welcome.' She looked expectantly around the table, but at this stage none was forthcoming.

'All right,' she said, hooking a leg up on to the stool beside her. It was as she attempted to bring the rest of her weight behind it that the stool skidded from under her and to her undying mortification she disappeared beneath the table.

There was a sudden flurry of activity as those closest rushed to help her up and collect together the paperwork she had dropped. Not knowing whether to laugh or cry and desperately wishing she had knocked herself out, Penny got back to her feet and began mumbling an apology for the interruption. When at last she brought herself to look across at David she instantly wished she hadn't, for he was clearly in pain, he was trying so hard not to laugh.

'Regular columns,' she said, her face still crimson and

her voice strained by her own efforts to hold back the laughter. She cleared her throat and mentally thanked God that she had made such precise notes for herself, which she could read from while mentally pulling herself back together. 'We'll start with the problem page, which Samantha Moon, my sister, will be handling. To get her started I'd appreciate some bogus letters containing pertinent problems which we can run in the first issue. Next, I need a nutty reader for the letters column to be introduced in the second issue. By nutty I mean someone who takes an eccentric, if not outrageous, opposing view to my editorials. If any of you feel up to that, or know someone who might be, I'd like to hear about them.' She looked around at the silent, attentive faces, careful this time to avoid David's, for if he was still laughing she knew she would lose it altogether.

'OK, moving on,' she said, hoping she wasn't gabbling and suddenly not at all sure that this agenda was in the right order, 'our experts on the French system, Didier Feron and Elizabeth Robbins, who as an American expat has lived on the Riviera for over twenty years, will, I am sure, have no problem concocting queries for the first issue. The restaurant and hotel critics, along with the local arts reviewer, are faced with no shortage of material. Marie-Christine Gunther, who, as I'm sure some of you already know, has an international bookshop in St. Laurent du Var, will be supplying us with our book reviews. As in all other cases, she will alternate her columns between English and French and I am sure we can all help out from time to time with the reviews. Current issues, particularly those of the European Community, I will mainly be taking on myself.'

'Have you decided what stance we will be taking?' David asked, obviously in control of his mirth now.

'Slightly right of centre,' she answered, half hoping he would challenge her on this, for she was far more comfortable with a debate situation than she was with this garbled soliloquy. But David simply nodded, so, looking back at her notes, Penny continued. 'I will also be handling the celebrity interviews,' she said, waiting for Marielle to bristle, which she did most satisfyingly.

'Now let me see,' she said, scanning the page again and hoping no one realized that she'd lost her thread. 'Ah yes, gossip. This is something that will come into later issues, after I have been to Los Angeles to check out a couple of ideas I've had. We will also take our film reviews straight from LA and hang on to them until such time as the films are released in France. Having heard a local American reviewer on the radio here recently giving her critique of the film *Shadowlands* in which she referred to C. S. Lewis as C. W. Lewis and then proceeded to say that the story wasn't believable, when most of us know it is a true story, has convinced me that we'd do better with a more educated reviewer and, considering the fact that *Shadowlands* was, to the best of my knowledge, released in France over six months ago, I think getting our information straight from Hollywood will serve us best.'

Receiving no objection to that, she turned over a page and waited for everyone else to do so. 'The Health and Beauty spot is yet to be filled,' she said. 'The same goes for the entertainment guide, interior design and sport and leisure, of which there must be a wealth of material around here. I shall be speaking to several cartoonists around Europe over the next few weeks in the hope that they will be willing to supply us, and the matter of competitions, free gifts, sponsorship et cetera will be something I will take up with David in due course. Short stories by those of you wanting to try your hand will all get read and some of them I hope will be published. Our Mediterranean gardening expert can't be with us today, but there's very little to say on that since he's the expert, and a motoring column is something we will run as and when it is felt relevant. Special features will be handled either by me, Marielle or a freelancer, and fashion, both male and female, is the exclusive territory of Babette Longchamps, our fashion editor, whose name some of you might know from her time at *Elle*. She will be keeping a close eye on what is going on around the world, but on the whole she will be concentrating on the region and what is available here, looking at everything from supermarket fashion to the more exclusive boutiques of Cannes and Monte Carlo.'

She stopped, took a fortifying sip of the coffee Clothilde had just put beside her, then continued. 'I'd like to run a yachtie page that has nothing to do with the technical aspects of yachting, since that is already well covered by the specialist magazines. What I'm thinking of is a kind of sail-and-regale page that gives a sneaky look at what the mega-rich get up to on their yachts. I'm sure the ports down here are rife with gossip, but it isn't my intention to name names. It'll simply be a light-hearted look at life on the ocean wave, with perhaps the odd innuendo that gives a tantalizing hint as to whom we might be referring, but not if it risks offending or gets us entangled in a lawsuit. My sister Samantha will be scouring the ports, but if any of you already know someone who'd be willing to oversee this for us, even if he or she can't write, please let me know.'

Skipping quickly over the next few paragraphs on freelance photographers, printers, distribution and sales – all matters she would be taking up with Marielle and David later – she came to a subject that brought a smile to everyone's face.

'Aperitifs,' she said. 'I intend the magazine to host a monthly aperitif evening to which all contributors, advertisers and selected readers will be invited.' She waited for the murmurs of approval to die down, then said, 'On that note I suggest you all help yourselves to a coffee from the tray Clothilde has prepared over there, before we get into any discussions on the points I can already see several of you are bursting to make.'

As she closed up her file she couldn't stop herself glancing over at David, who was regarding her with arched eyebrows as if to tell her that so far he was pretty impressed, even if she had made a right charlie of herself by falling off her chair. Penny turned away, refusing to be irritated by him, since despite the reassurance she felt at his approval it wasn't his place to dish it out.

An hour and a half later, after a great deal of productive and extremely entertaining exchanges that went a long way towards settling Penny's nerves and gave her the surprising and slightly heady feeling that she really might make it as an editor after all, she spotted a few surreptitious glances at the clock. It was almost one-thirty and in France pretty well everything stopped at twelve-thirty, if not twelve. So, making a mental note to inform those on staff that two-and-a-half-hour lunch breaks were only to be taken when entertaining, she called the meeting to a close.

'Ah!' she said, as if suddenly remembering something, and turning back to the table she looked across at David. 'Unless, of course, David has anything to add.'

Assuming he was totally unprepared, she waited for him to look floored. But he simply allowed his eyebrows to shoot up as though surprised she'd remembered he was there.

'Well, as a matter of fact,' he said, when everyone was looking at him, 'I don't have much to add at this stage. Except,' he said, turning to the man beside him, 'I'd like to introduce Pierre Clemence here. Pierre will be working closely with me and will be available during the times I'm not.' He paused, but as Penny started to turn away he continued with a concise summing-up of the way he intended to allocate budgets, followed by some astonishingly ambitious ideas for distribution, a mind-numbingly impressive list of probable advertisers, who ranged from Renault to Marlboro to Möet et Chandon, the name of the legal and accountancy firms who'd be acting for them, and finished up with a suggestion that whoever came up with a title for the magazine should be awarded a prize.

'Any suggestions?' Penny said, covering her pique with a generous smile. How the hell had he managed to get all that together in the space of a fortnight, she wanted to know.

'How about,' he answered, putting his head to one side, 'a slap-up meal at the Palme d'Or in Cannes with our illustrious editor? But, whoever wins, I give a word of warning: keep her off the desserts.'

The colour instantly flared in Penny's cheeks, since everyone present would probably assume he was alluding to her weight. 'I imagine whoever wins would prefer a companion of their own choosing,' she said chillingly, and with a quick 'bon appetit!' she walked back into her office, followed by Sammy, who had slipped in halfway through the meeting.

'Don't laugh,' Penny told her, actually trying not to herself.

'I'm sorry,' Sammy said, 'but I think you just got a right old dollop of egg on the face to pay you back for the tiramisu.'

'Yes, well,' Penny said with a reluctant smile. 'But what did you think of him?'

Sammy shrugged. 'Well, he's certainly hormonally disturbing, I'll give him that, with those wicked, come-to-bed eyes and that hugely promising bulge in his jeans.' Then, laughing as Penny threw her a look, she said, 'He seems an OK kind of guy to me. And what a speech, eh? Short, to the point and, by God, does he have things under control! I wonder where he found Pierre Clemence?'

'I don't know and I don't particularly care, as long as Clemence knows what he's doing,' Penny responded, sifting through the paperwork on her desk. 'Ah, here it

111

is. Some problems for you to be going on with before the other test ones come in. And maybe you'd like to think about what you're going to call yourself,' she added, turning to the computer.

'Aren't you going to have any lunch?' Sammy wailed. 'I'm starving.'

'I don't have time,' Penny answered, feeling her stomach protest even as she said it. 'Get me a coffee, will you?'

It was the middle of the afternoon by the time she heard the half dozen or so staff returning, the contributors having now taken themselves off home to await a call from Penny to discuss their particular ideas and problems. She picked up a document that had just finished printing and took it out to Brigitte.

'This is a preliminary list of the newspapers and magazines I'd like to subscribe to,' she told Brigitte. 'If you're not sure how to go about it, it can wait until Clothilde comes in on Thursday.'

'It's all right,' Brigitte assured her with an eager smile, 'I'll find out how to do it.'

'You're a star,' Penny said, patting her shoulder; then, glancing at Marielle's empty desk, she went over to talk to Mario, the advertising director. It wasn't that she didn't believe David's claims that he'd managed to get so many big names interested in their humble little periodical, it was simply that she wanted to hear it again, and, perhaps, find out how he'd managed to do it.

Just a few minutes with Mario was enough to confirm what she already suspected: that David had been working on setting up the business side of this magazine long before Sylvia had approached her. And, boy, had he been working, for the list of advertisers who had made provisional bookings was even more stupendous than he'd outlined.

Hearing the door open, Penny looked up from Mario's desk to see Pierre Clemence standing awkwardly in front of the door, his briefcase clutched in both hands, as if unsure where to go or to whom to address himself.

'Ah, Pierre!' Penny said, reading his dilemma instantly. 'I imagine you're wondering where your office is.'

Pierre gave a grateful, if somewhat embarrassed, smile.

'We haven't been properly introduced, have we?' she said, going to him and extending a hand. 'I'm Penny Moon, as you've no doubt already gathered, and I'm pleased to meet you.'

'The pleasure is mine,' Pierre assured her, enclosing her hand in his short, bony fingers.

'Now let me see,' Penny said, turning to survey the office where Paul Smith, the bright young spark of a free-lancer, was availing himself of the telephones, Babette, the fashion editor, was receiving a word-processing lesson from Brigitte and Mario and Barnabé, the subeditor, were debating the various merits of some football team or other. 'Would you like to be out here?' she said to Pierre, 'or would you prefer somewhere a little more private? There are two offices there,' she went on, pointing to the two closed doors. 'I believe David's been using the one on the right, so if you'd like to take the other . . .'

'I'll use David's,' Pierre answered. 'He doesn't normally like to have an office of his own, he just squats in mine.'

'OK,' Penny responded, telling herself that it was David's business how he worked and leading the way into the small, sparsely furnished room with a neat little marble fireplace across one corner she went to open the shutters. The desk contained nothing more than the itinerary for that morning's meeting and the shelves along one wall were completely empty.

'I was hoping to go over a few things with David this afternoon,' she said as Pierre placed his briefcase on the desk. 'Is he coming back?'

113

'Uh, I don't think so,' Pierre answered, not quite meeting her eyes. With Marielle missing too, Penny quickly put two and two together and came up with 'siesta'. Was this something she was going to tolerate, she asked herself, or was it something she should confront right now and run the risk of a showdown with David?

'Maybe I can be of some assistance,' Pierre offered.

Penny looked at him for a moment, liking him but somehow knowing that it was going to be impossible to get close to him. 'Yes, maybe you can,' she said. 'Would you like to come over to my office?'

She waited until they were both settled either side of her desk, then, folding her arms in front of her she said, 'I was wondering, exactly how long have you been working for David?'

'Just over eight years,' he answered.

Penny's expressive blue eyes showed more interest than surprise. 'So you came with him from the States?'

'Yes,' Pierre confirmed.

'I see. And, if you don't mind me asking, what were you doing over there?'

'Generally fixing things for David.'

She frowned. 'What sort of things?'

'Whatever David throws my way.'

'For example?'

'It's hard to generalize,' Pierre answered; 'with David, it's always something new. And please excuse me if I sound rude when I say this, but if you wish to know about David's background I think you should ask him.'

'Yes, yes, of course,' Penny said, colouring. 'But just tell me this, am I right in thinking that this isn't the first time he's launched a magazine?'

'To the best of my knowledge, it is the first time,' Pierre responded.

'Then how long exactly has he been setting this one up?'

'Since the middle of last year.'

'Really?' Penny said, the corners of her mouth tightening. 'But that was long before Sylvia acquired Fieldstone Publishing, of which this magazine is, or was, a part, since we're all now under *Starke*.'

'But these things don't happen overnight,' Pierre explained, 'and Sylvia had her eye on Fieldstone for some time.'

'And all these amazing contacts David has made have presumably come through Sylvia?'

'David knows a lot of people,' Pierre said blandly.

'Evidently,' she murmured. 'And would one of those people, by any chance, be Monsieur Couval of the *Nice-Matin*?'

'I'm afraid you'll have to ask David that question,' Pierre replied.

Penny nodded and, finally conceding that she wasn't going to get any more out of Pierre, asked him if he would care to discuss the finding of a suitable printer with her.

'If you will excuse me for a moment,' Pierre said, getting up, 'I have been doing some homework on that very matter and have made a short list which is in my briefcase.'

Dealing with Pierre, as she found out over the next hour or so, was like taking a lesson in robotic self-control. He allowed himself no particular expressions of emotion, neither was he in the least bit fazed by anything she threw at him, no matter how outlandish or convoluted. He had a cool, logical approach to every situation and, she was fast discovering, a quite exceptional brain that seemed never to consider anything a problem. She guessed that he knew she was testing him, but he didn't appear in the least put out by it; if anything, he seemed to welcome it. It took her a while, but eventually the penny dropped as she realized that he was showing her that she could totally depend on him in David's absence and that in fact it would probably be him she'd be dealing with far more frequently than it

115

would David.

How interesting, she was reflecting to herself as Pierre left her office. She couldn't say it had come as any particular surprise to discover that she was probably going to be deprived of David's presence on a fairly regular basis, but it certainly added a considerable amount of fuel to her speculation about what David's role really was here. However, pushing it to one side for the moment, she picked up the phone and dialled David's number. Whatever *his* plans might be, *she* had a magazine to get on the road here – and since there were certain things for which she needed Marielle's presence and she was in a position to demand it, that was precisely what she was going to do.

As she listened to the ringing tone at the other end and swivelled her chair round to gaze out at the holiday apartments across the road, which looked more dismal than they did inviting on this gloomy day, she was wondering if she really had the courage, or even the right, to do this. But hell, why shouldn't she? She was the editor after all.

'*Oui?*' David's sleepy voice came down the line.

'David, it's Penny,' she said crisply. 'If Marielle is there with you, then I'd like you to send her back to the office now, please. We have a lot to get through.'

'Sure thing,' he responded, as if it were the most natural thing in the world for him to be at home availing himself of the delights of the deputy editor in the middle of the afternoon.

Replacing the receiver Penny turned to her computer, intending to feed in all the notes she had made that morning, but instead she found herself thinking about David. She was partly amused and partly annoyed by the way he had so casually admitted to Marielle being with him, though she couldn't help wondering if their relationship really was going to cause her problems. On the face of it she couldn't see why it should, but it was still early days and she had to ask herself what was the real reason she had summoned Marielle to the office now, when what they needed to discuss could in truth have waited until the morning. However, Marielle herself provided the answer to that as, half an hour later, Penny watched her saunter breezily across the office towards her. Once again Penny needed to assert her authority and once again she was going to do it.

Silently holding her door open for Marielle to pass through and feeling horribly like a headmistress, Penny walked to the other side of her desk and waited for Marielle to sit down.

'What you do in your own time, Marielle,' she said pleasantly, mindful of David's swipe at her regarding man-management, 'is of course entirely your business. But I would appreciate it if it didn't happen on company time.'

Marielle simply looked at her, her beautiful face as calm and serene as a midsummer sea with all the deadly perils secreted beneath the surface.

Penny turned to her computer. 'OK, the entertainment guide,' she said. 'I notice there haven't been any—'

'I shall be doing it,' Marielle broke in.

Penny shook her head. 'You will have other things to do and with so many towns to cover along the coast it has to be assigned to at least half a dozen people. But, of course, if you wish to collate the information when it comes in . . .'

'That's what I meant,' Marielle told her with a disdainful lift of her eyebrows.

'Then I'm sorry, I misunderstood,' Penny said. 'I thought you were intending to be out there scouting around yourself.' She took a breath. 'OK, well now that we've established who is going to present the guide, perhaps we can discuss finding the right people to feed us the information.'

'I'll have a list on your desk by the morning,' Marielle

said.

Penny sighed. Everything was lists with Marielle, there was never any kind of verbal exchange in which they could get excited about a project.

'OK, do it your way,' Penny told her.

Marielle got up and walked to the door, but before opening it she said, 'If David wishes me to work from home with him in the afternoons, then it is my duty to do so.'

Penny's eyebrows shot up. 'Euphemisms like "work" and "duty" are lost on me, Marielle,' she said tartly. 'If you want to get your ass screwed off in the middle of the day, then I suggest you get yourself a job cruising the Croisette. In the meantime, as long as you're on this pay-roll you'll limit the callings of your libido to outside company hours. That's my final word, I don't want to discuss it any further, but should you wish to take it up with David please go right ahead and do so.'

'Be assured that I will,' Marielle retorted.

As the door closed behind her Penny immediately picked up the phone to call David. 'I think you and I should have dinner this evening,' she said, looking at her watch.

'Sure,' he said. 'I'll clear the decks. Where do you want to go?'

Penny thought for a moment; then, deciding that there was every chance they wouldn't get through the evening without some kind of scene, she said, 'I'd like you to come to my place.'

'Sounds good to me,' he said, a smile in his voice. 'Just give me the address and time and I'll be there.'

After giving him both, Penny said, 'Before you ring off, there's just one other thing. I imagine Marielle will be on the phone to you as soon as we've finished and I'd like you to back me up on what I've just told her.'

'Which was?'

'That screwing on company time is not acceptable and

that as the deputy editor she is answerable to me not to you.'

'OK, you got it on both counts,' he said with a laugh and rang off.

Penny sat staring at the phone, a puzzled frown creasing her brow. It was uncanny, she was thinking to herself, that no matter what it was she wanted she always seemed to get it.

Chapter 6

As Penny pulled up in front of the villa later, the outside lights were all on and Sammy was coming out to greet her.

'Look what I've found,' she cried, nursing a fat, fluffy black puppy. 'He was here when I got back earlier, just sitting there on the front steps like he owned the place. Isn't he adorable?'

Smiling, Penny ruffled his cute little head and received an affectionate bite in return. 'He must have come from next door,' she said. 'I saw a whole litter of them when I went over there to ask old What's-his-name about the light the other day.' Then, giving in to the urge to hold the puppy, she dropped her briefcase on the gravel and turned him upside down in her arms. 'Aren't you just gorgeous,' she laughed, tickling his belly.

'Do you think we could keep him – I mean, if they're prepared to let him go?'

'Oh, Sam,' Penny groaned, 'you know that's not a good idea. I haven't got a clue how long we'll be staying and neither of us knows the first thing about dogs. But I have to confess, it's tempting,' she added as the puppy nestled his face in the crook of her arm and gazed rapturously up at her. 'No,' she said reluctantly, 'you'd better take him home. Then you can come and help me prepare dinner for David.'

Sammy grinned. 'Dinner for David, eh?' she said.

'Don't get smart,' Penny told her. 'I just thought it would be safer here than in a restaurant, given how skilfully he manages to get under my skin. Are you doing anything this evening, or would you like to join us?'

'Far be it from me to get in the way,' Sammy said mischievously, earning herself a quick clout on the arm.

Though Penny was laughing, she quite suddenly felt the need to clear this up. 'He's honestly not my type, Sam,' she said truthfully. 'And neither am I his. Besides which, as you know, he and Marielle have got something going. However, that's not to say that I don't think I could come to like him, because I think, given time, that I could. More important, though, is the fact that we appear to be batting on the same team – meaning that it's only Marielle who's out on a limb. But that'll settle down when she realizes that she isn't going to get the better of me through David. And as far as anything else goes where David and I are concerned, you're totally wrong.'

'I was just teasing,' Sammy said, her eyes bright with laughter at the unnecessarily lengthy justification. 'Anyway, I'd better get this little chappie back to his mother – and the answer to your question is that I'm going out tonight. Céline, the restaurant critic, is taking me to where all the happening people hang out in Antibes.'

By the time Sammy came back Penny had poured herself a large glass of wine, put on some soothing music and was staring dejectedly into the fridge.

'Colonel Blimp just collared me,' Sammy said, referring to Wally Delaney. 'He wants to know if we're free for drinks tomorrow evening.'

'I hope you told him no,' Penny said distractedly. 'We haven't got any food, Sammy,' she complained. 'Didn't you do any shopping today?'

'Sorry, I forgot,' Sammy winced. 'Why don't you send out for a couple of pizzas? I found a card in the mail box this morning – they deliver to the door.'

121

'Good idea,' Penny said. 'But that doesn't let you off the hook on the shopping. Get some tomorrow, will you? And have you done anything about finding me a car yet?'

'Give me a chance!' Sammy cried. 'You haven't even told me how much you want to spend yet or what kind of car you want.'

'Not much. An old convertible something. Where's that number for the pizzas?'

'On the desk in the sitting room, along with my first efforts for the agony column. I think you'll like them.'

An hour later, with Sammy gone and the pizzas keeping warm in the oven, Penny, having changed into a pair of leggings and a baggy sweater, was curled up on one of the sofas, laughing out loud at Sammy's responses to the problems Penny herself had set. They were so hysterically funny and in some cases so grotesquely outrageous that it was almost a pity they'd never be able to print them.

Hearing the buzzer announcing David's arrival, she popped a couple more peanuts in her mouth and, having checked on the intercom it was him, she pushed the release button for the gates and opened the front door.

As he entered, the security lights came on along the drive and by the time he got to the house Penny was leaning against the door frame with her arms folded and an irrepressible light of laughter in her eyes. 'What happened to the Saab?' she asked, grinning as he finished weaving a precarious path on a Honda *mobilette* and brought it to a halt in front of her.

'Problem with the fuel injection,' he told her, removing his helmet and hooking it over the handlebars. 'Fancy coming for a spin later?'

Rolling her eyes, Penny walked back into the house. 'I sent out for pizzas,' she told him as he came in after her. 'I hope that's OK with you.'

'Sure. I'll just take a half, though,' he added, patting

his stomach. 'I overdid it a bit at lunch.'

Penny groaned inwardly. That meant she could only have half herself and she was absolutely starving.

'This is quite some place you've got here,' he commented, looking around as he followed her into the sitting room. 'How did you find it?'

'Through an agent.'

She watched him taking it all in and rather liked the feeling his presence seemed to have added. He was quite an enigma, she was thinking, with his air of frivolity that never quite masked the depths of a character she was intrigued to know better.

'Like some wine?' she offered, tucking the hair that had fallen from her ponytail behind an ear.

'Great,' he nodded, opening up the piano and giving it a quick tinkle. 'Do you play?' he asked.

'Not at all,' she answered. 'Do you?'

'Only when under the influence.'

'Red or white?' she said, going into the kitchen.

'Whatever's open. Yeah, this really is a great place,' he said, leaping on to one of the sofas and stretching out. 'I could kind of get to like it here.'

Deciding to ignore the remark, Penny poured him a glass of wine and took it back to the sitting room.

'To you,' he said, raising his glass, 'and whatever we're going to call this magazine of ours.'

'To all three of us,' she said with a smile, touching her glass to his.

'We got off to a pretty good start today, don't you agree?' he said after taking a generous sip. 'Well, some of us got off to a flying start, but ... Sorry, sorry, I couldn't resist it,' he grinned as she flashed him a warning look. 'But I've got to hand it to you, Pen, you sure are getting things together.'

'Thank you,' she said, going to sit down. 'But most of the credit belongs to you and Marielle. You certainly don't waste any time, either of you.'

'Except in the afternoons,' he remarked drily.

Penny slanted her eyes as she looked at him. 'I hope I made myself clear about that,' she said. 'It's not on, David. It's unprofessional and—'

'OK, OK,' he laughed. 'We just got carried away. It won't happen again, I swear.'

'At least not in the afternoons,' she muttered.

His grin widened and, despite herself, Penny laughed. The uneasy moments since asking him to order Marielle back to the office had continued throughout the afternoon as she'd wondered if a part of her had done it out of some kind of misguided jealousy. But sitting here looking at him now, as attractive as he was, she no longer feared that to be the case.

'Incidentally,' he said, 'I like your idea of getting the gossip and reviews straight from LA. When do you intend to go?'

'I'm not sure,' she answered. 'Probably just after the launch.'

'You don't want it in the first issue?'

'I do, but I don't think I'll have the time to go between now and then.'

He shrugged. 'Well, it shouldn't be too much of a problem. I'll make some calls if you like, see if we can get something to cover before you go out there. And when you do go I'll give you some contacts.'

'Thank you,' she said, her head to one side. 'How come you know so many people?' she asked, curiously.

He grimaced. 'I guess I've just been around.'

'Doing what?'

'You name it.'

'No, why don't you?'

'Hey, come on,' he laughed, 'what are you asking for here, my CV?'

'Yes, I suppose that's about the measure of it. I'd like to know who I'm working with.'

'Is that so?' he remarked, with a suggestive lift of his

124

eyebrows.

Scowling, Penny got to her feet and headed back to the kitchen. 'Are you trying to hide something or do you just get off on irritating me?' she called out to him.

'Now, why would I want to irritate you?' he said, from the doorway.

'Why would you want to avoid the question?' she challenged. 'Do you mind if we eat here?' she added, putting the pizzas on the kitchen table.

'Not a bit,' he answered. 'And I'm not avoiding anything. Neither do I have anything to hide, but I'm afraid if you want to know about me you're going to have to ask someone else 'cos I'm a pretty modest sort of chap at heart.'

'OK, I'll do that,' she said, thinking she'd give Sylvia a call in the morning while wishing that suitable putdowns didn't always come to her when it was too late. 'But, tell me, how committed are you to making this magazine work?'

He seemed surprised by the question. 'I'd say about a hundred per cent,' he answered.

Penny's eyes came up to his. 'Why?'

He smiled. 'Why not?'

'I wish you'd stop answering questions with questions,' she snapped.

'OK. I want to see it work because you want it to work,' he said, sitting down at the table.

'Oh, for heaven's sake!' she cried. 'You're not dealing with one of your stupid little airheads here, so stop treating me like one.'

'And what would you know about the way I treat them?' he grinned.

'David stop it!' she shouted. 'I want us to build a good working relationship, but you're making it impossible.'

'I am?' he said, tucking into his pizza. 'Then tell me what you want me to do.'

'I want you to be straight with me.'

'OK.' He thought about it for a minute, then said, 'Well, I reckon what you're really aiming to find out is how come we've managed to get so far so fast? Am I right?'

'You are.'

'Then that's easy,' he told her. 'I put Pierre to work on finding out about *The Coast* as soon as Sylvia told me she was interested in Fieldstone. So your suspicions are correct that I've been involved in this a lot longer than you, and they're also correct where the editor of the *Nice-Matin* is concerned,' he added, thereby confirming that Pierre had reported his conversation with her.

'So the contacts Monsieur Couval gave me actually came from you?' Penny said curtly.

'Not really. They came from him originally, but the list was a lot longer then and by the time you came along I'd already narrowed it down to those I considered to be the best.'

Penny's anger was making it hard for her to swallow. 'So in other words,' she said, 'I was duped into believing that I had managed, as you put it, to charm the contacts out of Monsieur Couval myself?'

'That's right,' he answered, completely unabashed.

'Then I don't see how we can possibly continue working together,' Penny said coldly.

'Why?'

'What do you mean, why?' she cried. 'Because you're doing things your way without even so much as consulting me and you're deceiving me into the bargain.'

'You are in charge, Penny,' he assured her. 'I just used what little know-how I have to get things moving. And I'm sorry about not being straight with you from the start.'

Penny was silent for a while, finding all this as difficult to digest as the pizza now that he'd managed to rob her of her appetite by making her see that in truth she was working *for* him, rather than *with* him.

'Not true,' he said when she challenged him. 'We both

work for Sylvia. We've got equal power, which I think she told you and,' he said, starting to grin, 'you look great when you're confused.'

Penny's eyes flashed with temper. 'It doesn't work with me, David,' she told him angrily. 'I'm as unmoved by your charm as I'm upset by your deceit.'

Swallowing a mouthful of pizza, he picked up his wine. 'Deceit's a pretty strong word,' he said. 'The way I see it is that I just did what Sylvia asked me to do and when you came along I didn't want you to think I was trying to run off with all the glory when we're a fifty-fifty partnership. So that's why I didn't tell you right off about the editor of the *Nice-Matin,* or that I'd been working on setting things up for so long.'

'Did you seriously think I'd be so stupid that I wouldn't see through it?' Penny demanded.

'As a matter of fact, I thought you might be,' he answered frankly. 'But now I know you I have rather a different opinion, which is why I'm no longer trying to deny it. In fact I'd have told you sooner if I'd been able to get over to London during the couple of weeks you went back, but I had to go over to the States to wrap a few things up there. And I reckon the worst you can accuse me of here is patronizing you, which I readily hold my hands up to and swear it won't happen again.'

'So why me?' Penny said after a pause. 'Why do you need me when you're obviously perfectly capable of running the magazine without me and could take all the power if you installed Marielle as editor?'

'Two reasons,' he answered. 'First, it's not me who makes the decisions, it's Sylvia. Second, Marielle doesn't have what it takes and Sylvia's convinced you do.'

Tearing her eyes away from him, Penny got up to go and get more wine from the fridge.

'Hey, come on,' he said, watching her go. 'I'm really sorry I've made you feel so bad. It wasn't my intention, honest. I mean, I don't suppose I thought about it one

way or the other before we met, I was just doing a job . . .
But now we've met, well, I'm kind of looking forward to
working with you. So, what do you say we put this
behind us and start over?'

'You've made me feel such a fool,' Penny told him
bluntly as she refilled their glasses.

'If anyone's a fool around here,' he said, 'it's me, for
insulting your intelligence. It won't happen again.'

For some reason the dark intensity of his eyes and the
convincing concern that had deepened his voice made
Penny smile. 'It had just better not,' she said.

He took a mouthful of food and continued watching
her as he chewed it; then, following it with a sip of wine,
he said, 'Look, I know you're telling yourself you don't
like me very much, but it's still early days and I reckon
you might find that I'm not so bad when it comes right
down to it. And,' he went on, giving her a mischievous
wink, 'I can tell already that you're finding it pretty hard
to resist m—'

'That's it!' she cried, jumping to her feet. 'You've gone
too far now and I've had just about all I can take from
you for one day.'

His smile vanished as he looked up at her in profound
astonishment. 'What have I said now?' he cried.

'It's what you were about to say!' she seethed.

'That you can't resist my jokes?' he said, starting to
grin as he belatedly realized what she'd thought he
was going to say.

Penny looked away as the blood came rushing to her
cheeks.

'Hey, you're not telling me you fancy me, are you?' he
teased. Then, as her eyes came furiously back to his, 'Oh
shit, I feel a *tiramisu* heading my way.'

With one arm pointing towards the door she glared
down at him, determined not to show how very close to
laughing she was despite her anger.

'I reckon you're kicking me out,' he said, faking

amazement.

'How very astute of you.'

'But I haven't finished my pizza,' he pointed out. 'And I'm kind of enjoying myself.'

Giving herself a moment to get both her laughter and her frustration under control, she said, 'If you stay I don't want to discuss anything other than the magazine. Is that clear?'

'Perfectly. Do you have any hot sauce?'

'No.'

They ate in silence for a while. Then, leaning back in his chair and picking up his wine, he said, 'So where do you hail from, Penny Moon? Somewhere up north I can tell by that little trace of an accent. Let me guess . . . No? Oh shit, I forgot, the magazine.' He took a sip of his wine. 'Got any ideas for a title yet? If you do, you might just end up winning a dinner with yourself.'

Rolling her eyes, Penny put down her knife and fork and dabbed her mouth with a napkin.

'You could fling a *tiramisu* in your own face at the end,' he suggested helpfully.

'Stop it,' Penny laughed. 'You're really milking that one now.'

'I swear, I'll never mention it again,' he vowed, hand on heart. 'So what do you want to talk about?'

'Distribution,' she answered.

'OK, what do you want to know?'

At first, as he filled her in on his initial plans for distribution, Penny almost regretted asking, for it was such a complicated business and one he so clearly had under control that it was only highlighting her ignorance. However, she soon found that she was enjoying listening to him and was gaining a great deal of pleasure from the way her own editorial plans, outlined just that morning, were about to effect so many changes in his plans. There was no question about it, Sylvia was right: he really did have a head for business and when it came to ambition

129

he almost took Penny's breath away. He appeared to have no conception of what it was to be conservative and there was no doubt at all that big business and high finance were nothing new to him – in fact Penny had the distinct impression they were much closer to being second nature. It made her wonder again what he had been doing in the States, but as he talked her on through the ever-expanding circle of a European-wide distribution, of what she'd be required to put into the magazine to make it all cost-effective, she could only listen and marvel at how effortless he made it all sound. As effortless as changing the subject and getting her to talk about herself, and to discover that they had nothing at all in common besides the magazine. They enjoyed neither the same music nor the same literature, were diametrically opposed in both politics and philosophy, and were so irreconcilably at odds over, of all things, the ethics and origins of humour that it was some time before Penny realized he was teasing her.

'OK, you win –' she laughed '– the basic amoral principle stands, but if you think you're getting away with Dante's *Commedia* as being the first serious literature ever to make you laugh, then—'

'I didn't say it was the first.' He grinned. 'What I said was that these days it generally comes to mind first. But if you want to go right back, I have to confess to having had a murky pubescent passion for Henry Miller.'

'Show me a schoolboy who hasn't,' Penny commented wryly. 'And I thought we were discussing first laughs, not first erections.'

'Ah,' he said. 'Well, it might surprise you to learn that my first erection had nothing to do with Miller and everything to do with—'

'No, no, spare me!' Penny laughed. 'I know you're going to say something outrageous like Beatrix Potter or—'

'You too?' he cried incredulously. 'It was that damned

Peter Rabbit – got me every time. I thought I was gay until I worked out he was an animal; then I knew I was really in trouble.'

Laughing and shaking her head, Penny looked at him across the table and felt oddly as if she'd known him for a very long time. There was such an easiness between them now, sitting there in the soft, flickering light with the gentle heat of the Aga warming them. Sylvia was right again: he was a hard man to alienate and even harder to stay mad at. Come to think of it, she couldn't quite remember why she was mad at him, but no doubt it would come back to her in the fullness of time. As would the moments when she had got up to light the candles and open the second bottle of wine.

'Well, I guess it's time I was on my way,' he said, gazing deep into her eyes.

When he made no attempt to move, Penny's eyes dropped to his hands, which were resting on the table between them. Her heartbeat was quickening as the heady effect of the wine swirled through her senses and she looked at his fingers. They were long and powerful, and so very close to her own. A warm burn of desire drew itself slowly through her body and, lifting her eyes back to his, she was already taking breath to ask him to stay, when the madness of the situation suddenly reached her and she stopped.

But it was too late . . . He had obviously read her mind, had sensed the extent of his power over her, and his eyes were gently mocking her.

Penny got to her feet, appalled that she had allowed herself to be so taken in by his charm. Even worse was the feeling that if she had asked him to stay he'd have turned her down, for why would he want to spend the night with someone like her when there was Marielle, who was very likely warming his bed even now.

Not trusting herself to speak, Penny led the way to the door. Her head was perfectly clear now and her anger at the way she had almost humiliated herself was directed solely at him. He had known what he was doing, had set out to seduce her to the point he had, and she could only thank God that she had had the self-control to pull back when she did. At least the words had not passed her lips, even if her eyes had betrayed her.

'By the way,' he said as they reached the front door, 'I meant to say this before; if you find yourself being approached by any dubious characters asking dubious questions, put them on to me, OK? I'll deal with it.'

A quick fury sparked in Penny's eyes. 'Would you like to be a little more explicit about that?' she said tightly.

He frowned, thought about it for a moment, then said, 'No, I reckon you can work it out,' and tossing his keys in the air, he caught them, and tripped lightly down the steps to kick-start his moped.

Penny was on the point of closing the door, when something brushed against her leg and, looking down, she saw that the puppy from next door was back. Scooping him up in her arms she cuddled him against her face and watching David ride out through the gates, she whispered, 'Well, I might not have any problem in the future resisting *him*, but I think I might well have one with you, you silly little thing.'

In reply the puppy licked her cheek and peed on her shoulder.

After changing her sweater, Penny put on her coat and carried him back down the drive and along the few yards of lane to the secluded villa next door. There was no sound coming from within the house, but two Mercedes were parked in the car port and slivers of light were showing through the cracks in the shutters.

Placing the puppy gingerly on the grass with its siblings Penny crept quietly back into the lane. So far she had managed to avoid actually meeting Colonel Blimp's wife, even though the woman had phoned three or four times to invite Sammy and her for dinner or drinks. It

wasn't that Penny wanted to offend them, but the idea o
exchanging her London social life for canapés and dou
ble gins with the expatriate haw-haw brigade mos
certainly did not appeal. Especially having met Wall
Delaney, who was as much of a bore as he was ai
anachronistic joke and who had irritated her beyonc
words by trying to arouse her interest in him witl
cryptic allusions to his antique shop not being quite wha
it appeared to be.

Still, she thought, as she walked back into the house
she'd have to go over there sooner or later, if for no othe
reason than she was running out of excuses not to. Anc
maybe it was worth looking into that antique shop of his
for if he was using it as some kind of cover for somethin
there was a chance she might get a story out of it.

Chapter 7

Yes!' Penny cheered, springing up from the chair in triumph.

'You cheated!' David cried.

'Rubbish! Did I cheat?' she demanded, looking around at the rest of the team who were grouped round the computer with them.

'He's just a bad loser,' Paul Smith, the freelancer, grinned at David.

'You're going to have to face it, David,' Penny told him, her cheeks flushed with laughter: 'I'm better at these games than you are. That's the third time I've won . . .'

'Because you cheated!' he declared.

'How did I cheat?'

'I don't know, but I'll work it out.'

'Poor David!' Babette laughed, walking back to her desk. 'You bring in all these CD-Rom things and never yet have you beaten her.'

'Come on, Smithy,' David challenged, 'sit down here and get yourself thrashed.'

'Penny, Agence Méditerranée on the line for you,' Brigitte called out.

'Great!' Penny cried. 'I'll take it in my office. Kill him, Smithy,' she shot back over her shoulder as he and David started to battle it out.

Still chuckling to herself, Penny flopped down in her

134

chair and picked up the phone to speak to the advertising agency David had recently signed up to handle the launch.

It was hard to believe that more than a month had sped by since she'd moved into the villa and taken over the reins of the magazine. She had worked harder in that time than she ever had in her life, but the kick she was getting out of seeing it all starting to come together was worth all the missed lunches and dinners, the frustrations of dealing with Marielle and even the sleepless nights courtesy of David whose appearances in the office were proving even more disruptive than they were erratic, for no one ever seemed to get any work done while he was there, including her.

She was over the embarrassment of the evening he had spent at the villa now, but all the same she was constantly on the alert to make sure that nothing like it ever happened again. It was only during the crazy hours when he'd turn up with some new computer game or other and challenge her to battle it out with him, while whoever happened to be in the office at the time yelled and cheered them on, that she let down the barriers. When they were alone together she was careful that they never discussed anything other than the magazine, and though she longed to ask him where he went when he wasn't there she never did. She didn't want to mislead him into thinking that her interest in him was anything other than professional. The teasing and banter and extravagant practical jokes – of which she was every bit as guilty as he – were just something they did and since it was helping to form a strong and loyal bond throughout the team she was happy to go along with it. The only person who ever showed any reluctance to join in the fun was Marielle, though she did deign, on the odd occasion, to join them all over at Legends, the Mexican café/wine bar across the road, when they all reached a point of such tiredness that things started getting even sillier than usual. Marielle's relationship with David was still very much on, but since it didn't appear to be affecting his judgement in any way Penny could find no reason to object to it.

Now the lighter nights were upon them and the heavy rains had passed, Penny was discovering a very real affection for the Côte d'Azur and its people. So many doors were thrown open to her, so much help and advice was forthcoming, that she was beginning to think that the horror of French bureaucracy was just a myth. She raced around in her five-year-old Peugeot convertible, employing tactics worthy of the most heroic French driver in order to get to a lunch in Eze, or a *vernissage* in Menton, or over to Monte Carlo for a show or a charity gala or, on one splendid occasion, to win 3,000 francs at the Casino. The International TV Festival in Cannes was now over, the mayor of Cannes himself had issued her with a pass, and she had been one of his honoured guests at a dinner he'd hosted for a couple of the French networks. The Film Festival was coming up and, to Penny's amazement and delight, the organizers had invited her to the ceremony for the awarding of the Palme d'Or and she was currently debating whether or not to ask David to escort her. It could be that he wouldn't deem her glamorous enough to be seen with at such a star-studded event, but if that was the case he knew what he could do with himself!

In fact, despite the fun they had together and the so far indisputable success of their working relationship, David was the only real black spot on the horizon. It wasn't that the occasional erotic dream she had about him bothered her particularly, for the truth of her fantasies had nothing to do with David and everything to do with the fact that until now she'd always had a fairly active sex life. However, other than that momentary lapse with David, she'd had very little time to concentrate on affairs of the heart, though something she was managing to find time for was a growing curiosity about David's frequent disappearances and his unerring ability to make things happen whether he was there or not. Of course, there was no question that Pierre was a prodigious deputy, but it was undoubtedly David's influence that got things moving and David's business prowess that was responsible for the unbelievable advances they had made without so much as a hiccup. It wasn't that Penny wanted things to go wrong, it was simply that the total absence of banana skins and the astonishing readiness of all concerned to take on the impossible was making her slightly uneasy. It was patently obvious to her by now that there was a great deal more to David than met the eye, but if he was hiding something shady, which she strongly suspected he was, then the question she had to ask herself was whether she really wanted to know what it was. Well, actually the answer to that was easy, of course she wanted to know, but she was damned if she was going to give him the pleasure of being asked when he knew that he had her curiosity aroused and was so obviously enjoying it that she could have quite happily hit him.

However, at the end of the following week, during most of which David had been absent, Penny decided to call Sylvia. All she wanted to know was something about David's past, something that would perhaps shed a little light on whether or not she was imagining some kind of hidden agenda or whether she was correct in at least one of her suspicions.

As she waited to be connected she shifted the fan around a little to cool herself off, then glanced through the pile of paperwork in front of her that Pierre had just sent in. Seeing what it was, she gave a sigh of exasperation. Marielle, who appeared to regard her position as David's mistress as being far superior to that of being David's partner, was becoming excessively trying with her constant referrals to Pierre on matters that should have been coming to Penny.

At last Sylvia's voice came down the line and Penny turned in her chair towards the open window.

'Penny, *chérie*,' Sylvia cried, 'I've been meaning to call, but time has just run away with me. So, tell me, how are you getting along over there?'

'Just fine,' Penny answered, thinking that that was another thing she found somewhat peculiar, that Sylvia hadn't been in touch over these past six weeks. 'Marielle Descourts continues to be a pain in the neck,' she said, grimacing, 'but one I'm having to live with. Needless to say, David is the main cause of the friction between us.'

'Oh?'

'I'm sure you know what I'm talking about,' Penny told her.

Sylvia was laughing. 'I think so,' she answered. 'David always did have an eye for the ladies – it's what's causing the problems in his marriage.'

Penny's smile collapsed. 'Marriage?' she said.

'He didn't tell you he was married? Well, no, I don't suppose he would. They broke up a year or so ago. He only sees her now when he sees the children.'

'Children?' Penny echoed.

'He has two boys. They're, let me see, they must be four and six by now. Little monsters, the pair of them, but quite adorable.'

'Where are they?' Penny asked, aware that she was starting to lose focus.

'In Florida, with their mother.'

'Oh, I see,' Penny said distantly. Then, quickly pulling herself together, she said, 'Well, good for him or whatever I'm supposed to say to that. Anyway, it's about him that I'm calling.' She stopped. Now that she was on the point of asking she couldn't quite work out how to phrase her questions without sounding petty. 'I was wondering,' she began, 'how you came to be his godmother . . .' Why worry about sounding petty when you

138

could always sound ridiculous, she cringed inwardly.

'His mother and I were at finishing school together,' Sylvia answered, a smile evident in her voice. 'Why do you ask?'

Finishing school, Penny was thinking in disgust. Of course: didn't everyone go to finishing school? 'Well, I suppose I have to come right out with it,' she said.

'You usually do.'

'Yes, well, what I was really wondering was how he knows so many people.' Terrific, Penny, she congratulated herself. Why don't you just ask now how he manages the miraculous feat of walking without crutches when he doesn't have a broken leg?

'How does David know so many people?' Sylvia repeated, obviously baffled by the question. 'Well, I imagine because he's travelled such a lot. Why does it bother you?'

'It doesn't. I mean, what bothers me is that he seems able to pull on so many influential people at the drop of a hat. And then when I ask him how he knows all these people he just says he's too modest to tell me.' Arrogant bastard, she added silently.

Sylvia was laughing. 'Modesty is a new feature in David's repertoire,' she said. 'I'd like to see it.'

'So you haven't seen him lately, then?'

'No. Should I have?'

'No. I just wondered where he was when he was supposed to be here.'

'Why don't you ask him?'

'I'd rather lasso my tongue to a galloping horse than give him the satisfaction.' She suffered Sylvia's laughter until she was sure Sylvia was listening again, then said, 'Basically, I want to know what qualifications he has . . .' Qualifications? What was she saying, for God's sake? 'What businesses has he been involved in before?' she said decisively.

'Oh now, let me see. Well, I guess the easy answer to

139

that is: you name it, he's done it. As I told you before, he has an excellent head for business, which is how he came to be such a wealthy man.'

'I didn't know he was wealthy,' Penny said, feeling her face start to freeze. Again she waited, realizing that Sylvia was enjoying herself immensely at the other end of the line. 'So,' she went on, when Sylvia had finished laughing, 'if he's so wealthy, what is he doing down here playing around with this hick magazine?'

'It won't be hick by the time the two of you have finished with it.'

'That doesn't answer my question.'

'It doesn't? I rather thought it did.'

Penny blinked. As someone who normally prided herself on her ability to ask all the right questions, she could hardly believe what a total mess she was making of this. 'But it doesn't tell me what kind of things he's been involved in up to now,' she said, 'and, for all I know, still is,' she added quickly. She was thinking now of the dubious characters he had mentioned, who hadn't as yet made contact, and she was half afraid that she had made a prize idiot of herself by taking him seriously.

'Well, to answer your question accurately I need to make a few phone calls first. He was in the States for a long time and I'm not entirely *au fait* with everything he was doing there. But, in a nutshell: I know he closed several big deals with shipping agents, getting them to use companies in which he had anything from a minimal to a controlling share; the same with a couple of the big computer companies and I think, but don't quote me, with one of the major record companies. A couple of years ago he won the contract for I can't remember how many government-run trade fairs and, as far as I know, he's still one of the major stockholders in some kind of housing project in Miami. There's probably more, but, like I said, I'd have to make a few calls to find out precisely what.'

140

'I don't think that'll be necessary,' Penny said crisply, and when the perfunctory goodbyes were over she rang off.

The call left her feeling unaccountably depressed. Well, not entirely unaccountably: for hearing all that about him had more or less confirmed her suspicions that he and not Sylvia was her boss. But if he was, then why wouldn't he admit it? Maybe she should try trapping him into it, for she'd had enough experience of him to know that a direct line of questioning would get her nowhere.

Deciding to leave the plotting of tactics until later, she turned back to the paperwork on her desk. Today's major decision, now that David had struck a stupendous deal with a printer in Toulon, concerned the artwork for everything from the front cover of the magazine itself to the snazzy little logo on their letterheads. Marielle and David had already flagged their preferences, which, surprise, surprise, happened to coincide, and Penny wondered how David would respond if she disagreed. She imagined he'd be willing to discuss it, but what if she chose the worst of the bunch, a title that obviously wouldn't work, and put up a show of sticking to her guns? What would he do then? Overrule her? It would be interesting to find out and maybe this was a way to get him to admit that they were no more a fifty-fifty partnership than Jacques Chirac and Noddy.

Looking up as someone knocked on the door, she called 'Entrez!' and when Smithy's cheeky face peered round the door she broke instantly into a smile.

'Smithy!' she cried, getting to her feet. 'I had no idea you were coming in today.'

'Just passing,' he said, kissing her on both cheeks. 'You're looking a bit snowed under,' he commented, glancing at her desk. 'And harassed,' he added, rumpling her already dishevelled hair.

'Spot on with both,' she told him. 'But you're just the

141

person I want to see. See this letter here,' she said, holding it up. 'It's taken eleven days to reach me from the UK. *Eleven* days.'

'Yes?' he said, going to help himself to a coffee from her percolator.

'I want you to organize a comparative analysis of postal systems around Europe,' she told him. 'Set it in motion now and we'll run it just before Christmas. God knows whether it'll shake the French into doing something to improve their act, but we can try.' She put a hand to her head. 'Now let me see, there was something else I had for you ... Ah yes, I know what it was. Somebody tipped me off the other night about a new theatre group starting up down here. I'd like you to look into it. I've got the contact numbers. It might be something we could get into sponsoring. Or maybe I should give that to Marielle,' she added, looking confused. 'Yes, I think that one should go to Marielle and you can take on the French presidential profile we discussed the other day.'

'Anything else?' he grinned, sitting down.

'Did you speak to Brigitte on your way through?' she asked, returning to her own chair.

'She was on the phone.'

'Then see her on the way out. I gave her a list this morning of things I want you to take on. There's a lot, so you'll probably need to rustle up a couple of worthy French hacks to give you a hand – and you could find yourself in Brussels a good deal more than here. Is that OK with you?'

'Sounds great to me,' he said. 'And that leads me rather neatly on to what I've come to see you about. A mate of mine in Paris files a column every fortnight to one of the British tabloids, a kind of offbeat look at life in Paris. He's a bit of a wag so I thought you might be interested in running it too.'

'I'll certainly take a look,' Penny said. 'Get him to fax

me some of his articles and where to get in touch with him.'

'I'll do that,' he said, his freckly face breaking into a roguish grin.

Penny waited, sensing that there was more to come and that whatever it was was probably going to be embellished with the usual Smithy flair for the bizarre. 'Well, come on, out with it,' she prompted when he simply continued to grin.

'I was just wondering,' he said, his jug ears turning pink with some kind of devilish delight, 'if you're going to do it?'

Penny frowned. 'Do what?'

His grin widened. 'You mean David hasn't told you?'

'Told me what?' she asked warily.

'About the bungee jump he signed you up for.'

'*What!*' she cried. 'David Villers signed me up for a bungee jump! Well, you can tell him from me that if he thinks I'm going to jump out of . . .' She started to laugh. 'You're winding me up,' she said.

'No, scout's honour,' he saluted. 'He's put your name down for a bungee jump over at Théoule the Sunday after next. It's for charity.'

Penny's eyes were dancing. 'I couldn't care less who it's for, there's no way in the world I'm doing a bungee jump,' she said. 'Tell *him* to do it.'

Smithy chuckled. 'OK, I'd better come clean,' he said. 'He did put your name down, but then he saw there was parasailing too, so he's put you down for that instead. And guess who's going to be driving the boat!'

'I don't care who's driving,' Penny cried. 'There's no way I'm allowing myself to be dragged out to sea on a parachute.' She looked at him, watching his tawny eyes sparkle with mischief. 'OK,' she sighed. 'Who's driving the boat?'

'David and yours truly.' He beamed. 'So you'll be in safe hands and you can't back out now because we've already got you some sponsors and the publicity's about to start.'

'Paul Smith, if you think my feet are going as much as one inch off the ground with you two in control you've got to be out of your tiny mind. You'll cut me loose or something and I'll end up in a tree on Corsica.'

'Would we do that to you?' he cried in horror.

'Yes! You would! Besides, I've never done it before *and neither*,' she said forcefully as he made to interrupt, 'do I want to.'

'Oh, come on, Pen, be a sport. It'll be a laugh.'

'For you maybe,' she cried. 'But I've got a better idea. Why don't one of you go up and let me drive the boat?'

'Oh, there's no fun in that,' he scoffed.

Despite the sheer absurdity of the idea Penny had to confess that there was a little part of her that wouldn't mind giving it a go. But with David and Smithy at the helm? 'I'll think about it,' she told him, wondering what the hell she could wear when she was already dying at the very idea of exposing her thighs in public. But she could always kit herself out in knee-length leggings or something. 'When did you say it was?' she asked.

'A week on Sunday. Everyone's going to be there trying their hand at stuff they haven't done before . . .'

'I bet you anything David's driven a boat before,' she cut in. 'So what's he signed up for that he's never done? And it'd better be something life-threatening.'

'I put him down for a song,' Smithy told her. 'He's got to do a solo of—'

'A song!' she cried in disgust. 'Not good enough, I'm afraid. Where's the list? *I'll* choose something for him.'

'If you'd heard him sing you'd know it's life-threatening,' Smithy assured her. 'He's that bad they'll lynch him.'

Laughing, Penny said, 'If I don't get to him first. Where is he now, do you know?'

'Right now, not a clue. Haven't seen him since the

weekend. He's back, though, 'cos he called me last night.'

Penny started to speak, then thought better of it. She'd been on the point of asking him if he knew any of David's friends or associates along the coast, but since David had adopted Smithy as some kind of kid brother she strongly suspected that her enquiries would get back to David.

'Well, if there's nothing else,' he said, looking at his watch, 'I'd better push off. Got a date over in Monte Carlo. Fancy having dinner with me one night, by any chance?'

'No, what I want is to have some parasailing lessons before I go out there and make a total idiot of myself. Can you fix them up for me?'

'You don't need lessons,' he scoffed. 'It's easy.'

'Yes, well, we'll see about that,' she said, getting to her feet. 'Come on, let's go and see Brigitte and get that list.'

After Smithy had gone Penny wandered over to Pierre's office to ask him to get hold of David and tell him she wanted to see him that night in her office.

The rest of the team had either gone home or taken themselves off to Legends by the time David arrived. Penny was at her computer, with the various samples of artwork for the magazine spread out on her desk, and having spent the past hour running through in her mind exactly how she was going to handle this she believed herself to be as ready for him as she'd ever be. Even so, as he walked through the door looking very much in need of a shave and regarded her with that habitual lazy humour in his dark blue eyes she felt herself momentarily waver – and the sight of a radiant and deeply infatuated Marielle coming in behind him didn't help matters much either.

As the colour rose in Penny's cheeks, she lowered her eyes for fear that David would read what she was thinking. That he and Marielle had come fresh from indulging themselves in the pleasures of each other's beautiful bodies was so obvious that Penny almost felt like a voyeur. Worse, she felt a total mess and wished she'd thought to wipe away her smudged mascara and tidy up her hair. With a quick and silent reprimand she pulled herself together. What the hell did she care what she looked like? That wasn't what this evening was about.

'Since we're discussing the artwork, Marielle felt she should be at the meeting too,' David said, stretching his long legs out in front of him as he perched on the window ledge.

Penny turned steely eyes on Marielle. It was on the tip of her tongue to dismiss her, but she didn't want to have to suffer the humiliation of David overruling her. So, moving a hand over the artwork in front of her, she picked up the one she had chosen and handed it to David. It was terrible. God only knew who'd come up with the idea, or indeed how it had managed to get as far as a proof – with any luck it might have come from Marielle – but the suggestion for the title of the magazine was JUMP and the logo was a frog. It was so banal it wasn't even funny, which was precisely why she had chosen it.

David looked at it for some time, sucking in his bottom lip as he clearly considered how he should respond. Penny waited. Marielle walked over to him, looked down at the artwork and could hold neither the triumph nor the contempt from her eyes as she turned them in Penny's direction.

'What is it in particular that grabs you about this?' David asked.

'I think it has substance,' Penny responded, inwardly cringing.

He nodded and looked down at it again. 'Substance,' he repeated. 'Can I ask what you thought of the ones I flagged?'

146

Penny shrugged. 'They were OK, but they didn't exactly speak to me.'

'And this one does?'

'Yes.'

'Would you like to share with me what it's saying exactly?'

'It's saying happy, fun, bouncy.'

Marielle looked at David, waiting for him to respond. In the end, unable to contain herself any longer she said, 'It is really the worst idea for a title and for a logo I have ever seen. And to be frank with you, Penny, I am amazed you can call yourself an editor when your judgement is so out of sync with what we are supposed to be doing here.'

Penny swallowed what she would really like to say to that and turned her eyes back to David.

At last he looked up. 'Marielle, would you leave us, please?' he said quietly.

Marielle's eyes widened as she started to protest.

'On your way, Marielle,' Penny prompted, still holding David's eyes.

David waited until the door was closed, then throwing the artwork back on the desk, he said, 'OK, we both know it's shit, so what's this all about?'

'As a matter of fact, I think it's good. As I have already said, I think it's the one we should go with.'

'In that case I think we should throw it out to the rest of the team and get their views on it.'

'Why?'

'Let's just call it democracy, shall we?'

'Why don't we call it, "David wants his own way"? Anyway, it has to be with the printer first thing in the morning. So the decision has to be made tonight.'

'We can always delay the printer, but I don't think we should delay what's really going on here. So, let's have it.'

Penny was aware that she was rapidly losing ground,

for she hadn't expected him to see through her quite as easily as this. But now she really thought about it she couldn't imagine what had possessed her to take him on this way when he was obviously so used to power games that her own feeble efforts seemed suddenly so excruciatingly embarrassing that a parasail in front of the entire world's press with no clothes on at all would be infinitely preferable to what she had got herself into here. However, it seemed that the demon inside her hadn't finished yet. 'What's going on here,' she said smoothly, 'is the choosing of artwork. I have made my choice known. So have you. Unfortunately, we are not in agreement. I have no intention of backing down. I think *Jump* is a great title and I like the frolicking frogs.'

He let what seemed like an eternity go by, then said, 'OK, then we run with it.'

Penny blinked. Her hands were suddenly clammy and her heart was thudding as she began to feel as ridiculous as the frolicking frogs. He wasn't supposed to say that. He was supposed to overrule her so that she could force him into admitting that he was running the show. She wished to God she'd given herself more time to think about this instead of acting on some half-cocked impulse. All she wanted was that he play straight with her and stop pretending that he was as much an employee as she was. But he was damned well going along with what she wanted and she had no choice now but to back down.

'I can't do this,' she said wearily.

'I'm sorry?'

'I said I can't do this. I can't play whatever games you're playing. I'm not equipped for them and neither do I wish to be. I entered into this project with total faith in those I was working with and now I find that I'm being double-crossed all over the place and constantly made to look a fool.'

'Someone's double-crossing you?' he said mildly.

Her head snapped up. 'Yes, you!' she seethed.

148

'How so?'

'Because this magazine is yours not Sylvia's and we both know it.'

His grin was slow in coming, but when it came Penny knew that she had never detested anyone more than she detested him in that moment.

'I'm glad you find it funny,' she said waspishly. 'I'm all for everyone having a good laugh at my expense.'

'Well,' he said, getting up and sliding his hands into his pockets, 'that's what happens when you don't think your strategy through.'

'Is that supposed to make me feel better?' she retorted sharply.

'Not at all. You got yourself into this, you can get yourself out of it.'

'Well, that's easily done. I resign.'

He looked at her for some time, thoughtfully nodding his head. Then, with a vague lift of his eyebrows he said, 'OK.'

Penny's insides jolted. She hadn't expected that. Then, seeing that he was trying very hard not to laugh, she realized that once again he had successfully called her bluff.

Feeling totally wretched, but determined this time to carry it through no matter how miserable it made her, she said, 'When would you like me to go?'

He took a deep breath and let it out slowly. 'Well, I guess Marielle can take over with effect from tomorrow, so if you want to pack up your things now . . .'

Dully she nodded her head and picking up her briefcase she started to slot things inside.

'Oh, for Christ's sake, Penny!' he laughed. 'So, you called a bluff and lost. It won't be the first time, I'm sure, and it won't be the last. So come on, act like a big girl: eat the humble pie and forget it.'

'Don't patronize me!' she snapped.

His hands came up as though to defend himself. 'OK,

OK, I could have put that a bit better. But we both know you don't want to give up now . . .'

'Don't tell me what I do and don't want.'

'Look, why don't we start this over? You show me the artwork you prefer and we'll take it from there.'

'I'm not seeking your approval for my decisions. I came here in the belief that I was the editor and you the business manager, but now I find that *you* are the boss and *I* am no more running this operation than Sammy is.'

'*I'm* the boss?' he said. 'Now what makes you think that?'

'Oh, nothing in particular, just the fact that you own half the fucking world according to Sylvia, so don't try telling me that you're here as a worker when we both know you're lying.'

'No, Pen, I'm not lying,' he said calmly. 'Sylvia is the majority stockholder in the group. As such, she is your boss.'

'But right here on the ground, where it counts, *you* are the one with ultimate control. In other words you lied to me, both of you. I was told that we would have equal power . . .'

'Which we do.'

'Don't be fatuous. How can I possibly have the same power as you when you're who you are?'

'Have I ever done anything to make you think that we are not on an equal footing around here?'

'You're doing it now.'

'What I'm doing now is trying to prevent you from flouncing off in some childish fit of pride and persuade you to behave like a professional.'

'I can't work for you,' she cried, stuffing more papers into her briefcase.

'You're not working *for* me, you're working *with* me.'

'But I can't fail, can I, with all your millions behind me?'

'Oh, I see, it's failure you're after. I obviously misunderstood the situation.'

'Why don't you just fuck off,' she muttered.

Laughing, he said, 'You know what you need, Penny Moon? You need a good man in your bed.'

Her eyes came up to his, blazing with outrage. 'I hope to God you're not offering,' she spat.

His eyes narrowed. 'No, not on this occasion,' he said.

'Why don't you just get out of here, because, quite frankly, the very sight of you is making me dangerous.'

He gave a shout of laughter. 'Penny, you're going to have to learn when is the right and when is the wrong time to quit,' he told her. 'Right now is a wrong time. Sylvia gave you this chance and if you let your pride screw it now it's only you who's going to get hurt. It makes no odds to me who edits this magazine, just so long as whoever it is is good. And you're good, Penny. I've seen you in action and, believe you me, if I hadn't been impressed there is no way I'd have put a single cent behind you. Neither would Sylvia. Yeah, yeah, I know how that sounds: like I am your boss. Well, OK, I guess I am in a manner of speaking. I think that's what you wanted to hear, so there you have it. Now, give yourself a break and stop trying to make an enemy out of me and get on with what you really came here for.'

'Why does every word that comes out of your mouth make me want to scream?'

'I don't know, it sure beats the hell out of me. I'm on your side and you seem dead set on resisting me all the way.'

'Because I can't stand you.'

He grinned. 'Is that so?'

He ducked as a brochure flew across the room, narrowly missing his head. 'Yes, it is so!' she seethed.

'Penny, just give me the title and artwork you really prefer,' he laughed, 'and then we can call it a day.'

Glaring at him, she pulled her choice from the top

drawer and thrust it at him. 'There!' she spat.

He looked down at it, arched an ironic eyebrow, then raised his eyes back to hers. '*Nuance*,' he said. 'Great choice. And unless I'm mistaken, I reckon Marielle just won herself a dinner with you at the Palme d'Or.'

Penny's eyes flashed as her finger came up to point at him. 'One word,' she warned, 'just one word about a *tiramisu . . .*' but she got no further because, to her unutterable frustration, she was starting to laugh too. 'One of these days, David Villers . . .' she said.

'Yes?' he prompted.

'I don't know yet,' she grudgingly admitted, 'but, never fear, I'll think of something – and it'll be even more merciless than a bungee jump or a parasail.'

'I take it Smithy told you,' he laughed.

'Smithy told me.'

'So, you going to do it?'

'I might,' she answered. 'But first I'd like to know what you've put Marielle down for.'

'Marielle?' he repeated in surprise. 'I didn't invite her.'

'Oh,' Penny said, feeling rather pleased.

'But I did invite the *Nice-Matin*,' he told her and giving her a quick wink he rapidly left the room.

Chapter 8

The smart, though unostentatious, cabin cruiser was pulling gently at its moorings at the far end of the Port Pierre Canto in Cannes, its highly varnished decks winking in the afternoon sun as Marielle stretched her long, perfect legs across the bench seat and reached out for her cocktail. The three glittering triangles of her bikini weren't much bigger than the jaunty little paper umbrella in her drink and the thick coconut oil she had coated herself in made her olivey skin shimmer. With the sun beginning to summon its summer might it was already too hot for Robert Stirling, who had a while ago gone inside to take a shower.

Early tourists were meandering along the harbour, wheeling pushchairs, clicking cameras and gazing enviously up at the demigods whose fortunes and life style appeared so close and yet were so many worlds away. Marielle gazed up at the perfect blue sky, revelling in the fact that she herself was generating every bit as much interest and admiration as the yacht – a body like hers belonged on these decks: they were empty, incomplete, without the decoration of a beautiful woman.

The boat rocked gently in the water as Robert Stirling stepped out on to the deck. He was carrying a neat bourbon in one hand, a portable phone in the other.

'So where were we?' he said, flopping down in a cushioned wicker chair and squinting against the dazzling light.

'We were,' Marielle reminded him, lifting one leg and casting a critical eye over the flawless skin, 'about to discuss your friend David Villers.'

Stirling sighed and with a grimace as he scratched his fingers through the mass of wiry grey hair on his chest he said, 'So what's new? Did he get rid of the joke of an editor yet?'

'Not yet,' Marielle answered, sipping her cocktail. 'But he will.'

Stirling cocked a cynical eyebrow. 'You seem pretty sure about that.'

'It's simply a matter of time.' Marielle smiled. 'In fact, he accepted her resignation the other night.'

'So why's she still there?'

'Because Sylvia Starke wants her there. And David isn't about to argue with that, not when he needs dear Sylvia on his side.'

Stirling pinched his bottom lip between his fingers, pulling it in and out. 'And it's your opinion that this editor doesn't know what's really going on there?'

'She doesn't have a clue.' Marielle turned her head to look at him and fixed him with penetratingly seductive eyes. 'So what you have to do, *mon chéri*,' she told him, 'is get me into her position.'

'Correction, *chérie*, what *you* have to do is get yourself into her position.'

Marielle put her drink down; then, swinging her legs to the floor, she placed a hand on each of his knees and looked him full in the face. 'All I want here,' she said, in a persuasively throaty whisper, 'is that magazine. Cannes is my home. I have no desire to live or work anywhere but here. Compared with yours, Bobby, that is a small ambition. So, you get me that magazine, then I could be in a position to get you what you want.'

Stirling smirked. 'Villers is smart enough to see through you, babe.'

'Don't you believe it.'

'Oh, but I do. I've known that man a long time. I know how he works.'

'So why don't you have him where you want him?'

'Because, like I said, he's smart.'

'Get me that magazine and I'll hand him to you on a plate.'

Stirling laughed long and hard at that. 'Marielle, I sure am glad you're not sharing the sack with me.'

'But you know I would,' she murmured, sliding her hands along his thighs.

'Sure, I know you would. And the next thing it'd be my balls on a plate for David Villers to carve up.'

Behind her sunglasses Marielle's eyes darkened. All she wanted was that stupid little magazine, an oracle, a vehicle to make her a celebrity, a voice, an influence right here on the coast. What did she care about the rest of the world? All that mattered to her was this little pocket of paradise where the rich and famous had created a private world of exclusivity and privilege. She wanted to be a part of that, wanted to hold it in her hands and have them pander to her favour as the woman who could as easily make them a laughing stock as she could build their images as icons of power and wealth. Both David Villers and Robert Stirling had it in their power to give her what she wanted, but as things stood they were prepared to let Penny Moon, that hideously overfed English bitch, take the reins.

But maybe, if Penny knew what David's real intentions for the magazine were, if she were told that she was nothing more than a pawn in a game that was rife with danger, she'd go of her own accord. Unfortunately, though, there was no guarantee of that and since it wasn't a gamble Marielle was prepared to take she turned her attention back to Stirling and tried another approach.

'I don't see why you won't do me this one little favour of getting rid of Penny Moon,' she said petulantly. 'After all, I've kept my end of the bargain, I'm sleeping with David.'

'And that's all you're doing, Marielle,' he reminded her. 'You got nothing to show me, nothing to tell me; you got zilch, Marielle.'

Marielle threw out her hands in exasperation. 'How many times do I have to tell you?' she cried. 'I need to get closer. I need that editorship if I'm ever going to be able to tell you anything.'

'Which means I could be wise to throw in my lot with Penny Moon,' Stirling commented.

'You'd be a fool if you did,' Marielle sneered. 'She won't give you what you want and you know it, or you'd have approached her by now.'

Stirling looked impressed. 'Didn't know you had such a thing as powers of deduction, Marielle,' he smirked.

Marielle looked at him nastily, nevertheless she was pleased to hear that she was correct. Then, deciding to change tactics again, she warmed her expression, moistened her full, rosy lips and shaped them into a sultry pout. 'You'd be surprised what I have, Bobby,' she purred, unfastening her bikini top and letting it fall to the floor. 'And, after all, what's Penny Moon to you?'

Stirling looked at her; then, yawning, he put his hands behind his head and closed his eyes. 'Tell me something, Marielle,' he said. 'Exactly what are you expecting me to do to get rid of Penny Moon?'

'I'm sure you know the answer to that better than I,' Marielle said huskily.

'No, no, come on, I'm interested. Exactly what is it you're proposing I do here? Send her back to London, or did you have something a little more, how shall we put it, incapacitating, in mind?'

'It's your choice, Bobby,' Marielle replied, smiling as she trailed her fingers over his legs.

Stirling gave a snort of laughter. 'You been watching too many movies, Marielle,' he said. 'People like me don't go round incapacitating people unless they need incapacitating. And by my reckoning Penny Moon don't need it.'

'But David Villers does, or so you tell me.'

'Ah, now Villers is a different matter.' He yawned again. 'But stick around, Marielle – you never know, you might get what you want.'

'Is that a promise?' she challenged, her eyes glowing.

'Shit,' he groaned. 'Did it sound like one?'

She shook her head.

'Just leave Penny Moon's address on the way out,' he sighed. 'I think I know someone who might be interested.'

'And if they're not?'

'Don't push, Marielle,' he told her.

'And these here,' Esther Delaney said, turning another page in her enormous photograph album to reveal several more shots of major Hollywood stars, 'were taken just after the Oscar ceremony last year. That's me, there,' she said, pointing to a frothy-frocked figure standing between Valentino Petralia, who had directed the winning film, and his wife, Claudia, who had starred in it. 'And there I am with John Montana,' she smiled fondly, tucking the capacious sleeve of her long, ivory silk evening gown out of the way. 'Dear boy, he was awfully disappointed not to get best supporting actor – and, we all agreed, he really should have.'

'This is a very impressive collection,' Penny commented, meaning it, but also saying it because she sensed how much it would please this extraordinary old lady whose mode of dress was about as subtle as Dame Edna's and was so seriously at odds with her Vera Duckworth face that it was the very eccentricity of it, Penny realized, that was warming her to the woman.

Indeed, Esther Delaney beamed. 'It's my pride and joy,' she said, laying the album down and picking up her

157

glass of red wine from the coffee table. Though she didn't appear to be drinking much, her speech was slightly slurred and the stain on her lips told Penny that she'd probably been at it for quite some time before Penny had arrived.

'I hope you don't mind me asking,' Penny said, 'but how do you come to know all these people?'

For a moment Esther seemed perplexed, then out in the kitchen the cooker gave a timely buzz and she jumped to her feet. 'Dinner's ready,' she said. 'I do hope you like salmon. It's a little recipe of my own, you know.'

'Can I do something to help?' Penny offered.

'No, no. You just stay right where you are and finish your drink. Everything's under control.'

Left alone in the sitting room, where a cooling evening breeze was drifting in through the open windows, Penny looked around at the fake-Victoriana that cluttered the surfaces. On closer inspection, however, she thought that maybe some of them were the genuine article. It would make sense, seeing Wally was into antiques – though she was sure he'd mentioned something about oriental crafts. Still, that aside, what really didn't make much sense was all this hobnobbing Esther Delaney was doing with the rich and famous. Unless, of course, she was supplying them with antiques. Penny grimaced. It didn't feel like a particularly satisfactory explanation, but all things being equal it might just have sufficed had Wally not tried so hard to rouse her curiosity the night he'd come over to repair the light.

That was weeks ago now and since Esther's bombardment of invitations had ceased after a few weeks, with so much else on her mind Penny had all but forgotten about her neighbours. She'd also forgotten, she now realized, exactly what Wally had said about his antique business, but now she had met Esther she was reminded of how he had made some kind of derogatory remark about his wife in an attempt to make himself look big. Penny had never had any time for men who did that and was of the opinion that it was only those who knew that their wives had a lot more going for them than they did who indulged in such repugnant disloyalty. And added to that, as Sammy had said, there was something, apart from the physical, that was fundamentally unpleasant about the man.

However, a chance meeting with Esther at the gates a couple of mornings ago, when Esther had been all decked out in a Rita Hayworth-style peignoir and fluffy white mules, not to mention a diamond necklace, had produced another invitation, and hearing that Wally was away Penny had accepted. And now she was glad she had come, even though she'd been dreading it all day, since it was giving Esther such obvious pleasure to have her here.

As Esther came bustling in with the meal Penny got up to help her, taking Esther's matches from the table to light the candles.

'Oh gosh, silly me, I forgot about them,' Esther chuckled. 'Such a good girl. Now, you sit here at the head of the table and I shall sit here next to you. Would you like some more wine? Yes, yes, of course you would.' She giggled. 'I've plundered Wally's cellar for something special,' she confided, 'but shush, not to tell him.'

'My lips are sealed,' Penny smiled. 'Incidentally, where are all the puppies? I didn't notice them when I came in.'

'Oh dear,' Esther said, looking suddenly downcast. 'Wally took them to the Zoo Market in Villeneuve-Loubet. Said we couldn't keep them. Too many, you know.'

As Esther's head went down Penny wondered if she was crying and sure enough as she searched for something appropriate to say Esther pulled a white, lace-edged handkerchief from her sleeve and gave her nose a delicate little blow.

'Said he took them to the Zoo Market,' she went on brokenly. 'But they were mongrels. No one wants mongrels. Afraid he's had them all put down.' Then, lifting her head, she plastered a sunny smile to her face and said, 'But we don't want to talk about those sort of things, do we? Let's talk about you. I'm sure you must have a very interesting life.'

With Esther being such an appreciative audience Penny found herself doing most of the talking as they ate, entering into the kind of name-drop routine that normally repelled her, but doing it because it was so clearly what Esther wanted to hear. It was uncanny, she was thinking, when Esther finally got up to make coffee, this desire she had to please the old lady, and she wondered if it had something to do with trying in some way to make up for the way Wally treated her. Not that she had much evidence of ill-treatment – perhaps oppression was a better word – it was just something she sensed and it was making her feel quite protective towards Esther. Nevertheless, she wasn't much inclined to make these cosy little evenings a regular event, for it wasn't hard to see how easily Esther could become attached to her and, like her as she did, Penny didn't particularly relish the idea of playing surrogate daughter to a woman whose childless state was so obviously at the root of her desire to befriend her – as well as what was turning her to the bottle.

'Where did you say Wally was?' she asked, as Esther set a tray of coffee on the ornate table between the sofa and armchairs.

'Oh, he's in Toulouse,' Esther answered, going over to the little bar to fetch a bottle of Courvoisier and two balloon glasses.

'Not for me, thanks,' Penny said with a smile, as Esther started to pour. 'I have to work tomorrow. When's he coming back?'

'On Wednesday. Oh, that's the telephone!' she said, as

160

though needing to explain what the noise was. 'Do excuse me, dear. I won't be long.'

When she came back she poured herself a large measure of brandy; then, perching on the edge of an armchair, she said, 'So, you're going to the *vernissage* the baron is holding for his latest protégé? How perfectly splendid for you. You know, everyone who's anyone will be there. It really is quite the invitation to have.'

'Will you be there?' Penny asked, taking a sip of coffee.

'Me! Heavens above, no!' she laughed. 'I only socialize with the old duffers. Nice bunch, of course, but not very exciting.'

'Unlike the people you mix with when you travel,' Penny responded, glancing at the photograph album that was still on the table.

Esther's eyes widened, as though realizing she had said something she perhaps ought not to have. In fact, she really ought not to have shown Penny the album at all, but she hadn't been able to resist it, not when she so very much wanted Penny to know that she was a little bit more than just the silly old woman who lived next door.

Her lips formed a tremulous smile as she looked into Penny's eyes. 'You won't tell Wally I showed you the album, will you?' she said.

'Not if you don't want me to,' Penny answered. 'But why wouldn't you want him to know?'

Esther looked momentarily baffled. Then her eyes lit up as she seemed to find an answer. 'He gets cross when I show people,' she said. 'Says it's showing off.' She glanced off to one side; then, bringing her eyes back to Penny's, she smiled again. 'This has been such a splendid evening,' she said brightly. 'I do hope we can do it more often. I don't get much opportunity to spend time with young people since Billy died. Well, why would anyone want to spend time with me? I'm such a silly old thing. Probably drive everyone mad, what?'

Penny smiled. 'Who's Billy?' she asked gently.

Esther's eyes darted about the room as a hand went to her throat. 'Billy was my son,' she answered, seeming to sink in on herself. 'Died, ten years ago. Silly thing. Got a tumour in the brain. Would have been thirty-three next week. Still, we won't talk about that. Wally doesn't like it. Says I should be over it by now. Still hurts, though. Miss him a lot. No one young to talk to now. No one except—'

She stopped and, as her eyes shot to Penny's, Penny realized that she had been on the point of revealing something she either couldn't, or didn't want to, reveal.

Intrigued as she was Penny decided not to push it, for she could sense how much it would confuse and upset the old lady if she tried. Besides, there was every chance she'd find out what it was sooner or later, if for no other reason than both Esther and Wally, in their own different ways, were absolutely bursting to share their secret with someone. She considered herself a strange choice of confidante, if indeed they did end up choosing her, for as a journalist she would surely be the very person they'd want to steer clear of if they were involved in something crooked – which she more than half-suspected they were. Some kind of art fraud was the most obvious choice and considering the number of celebrities Esther Delaney had managed to get herself photographed with over the past couple of years the story, if indeed there was one, might prove quite a scoop for *Nuance*.

'You're going to think this frightfully presumptuous of me,' Esther said, puffing inexpertly on a cigarette, 'but do you think . . . ? well, do you think you might possibly see your way to gracing one of my little soirées one evening? It would be such a *coup* for me having someone like you here and everyone's just dying to meet you. Do feel free to say no, of course. I know it won't be much fun for you mixing with all us old codgers . . .'

'I'd be delighted to come,' Penny interrupted. 'And

maybe I'll bring my boss, David, along too.' If she had to suffer it, then she didn't see why he shouldn't too. And it was high time they both made an effort to mix a little more with the expats.

'Oh, no, no! I couldn't possibly impose on him too,' Esther cried, blanching at the very idea of taking up the time of such an important person as Penny's boss. 'I'm sure he's far too busy to be bothering with people like us.'

'We'll see,' Penny said, getting to her feet. 'I'm afraid I really must be going now, though. It's been a lovely evening and the salmon was absolutely delicious.'

Esther glowed. 'I'm sorry your sister couldn't make it,' she said. 'Maybe next time?'

'I'm sure,' Penny said, picking up her bag.

'And not a word about the photographs, mm?' Esther whispered as they walked to the door.

'Not a word,' Penny promised, feeling like a complete heel when she knew that if there *was* a scandal involving so many celebrities to be uncovered here she was most definitely going to go for it.

A few nights later, Penny was laughing at the way Sammy was overdoing her ecstasy as she sipped champagne cocktails in such exalted company at the eighteenth-century château of Baron von Bergenhausen on the outskirts of Vence. Esther Delaney was right, everyone who was anyone was there: all the resident celebrities, aristocracy, political high-fliers and patrons of the arts were swarming around the château's recently renovated ballroom on the occasion of this spectacular *vernissage*.

The young artist whose works were adorning the newly plastered walls and being admired with the usual intellectual pomposity and claptrap such private views invariably induced, was, in Penny's opinion, exhibiting more awe at finding himself in such celebrated company than he was talent in his monumental eyesores. He'd disappeared into the crowd some time ago now, having been introduced to Penny by the baron himself, who, until this evening, had been playing cat-and-mouse with Penny since receiving her request to interview him for *Nuance*. However, having checked out her credentials with 'unnamed sources in London', he had tonight informed her that he would be happy to throw open the doors of his château to a photographer while availing himself of the pleasure of being interviewed by such 'a highly esteemed and attractive young lady'.

Recognizing him for the lech he was, Penny had smiled winsomely, stiffening slightly as he'd patted her bottom, then had excused herself, saying that she would be in touch soon to fix a date. Moving on around the room she began talking to those she knew from her time on *Starke* and availing herself of the opportunity to be introduced to others who might prove suitable subjects for the future. David should have been with her tonight, but he had backed out at the last minute, saying he had to fly over to London for a few days. Which was how Sammy came to be there with her, all togged out in a skintight, sequinned little number from one of the boutiques on the rue d'Antibes and only just resisting the urge to get out her autograph book.

'I had no idea you knew so many illustrious people,' she said, holding her glass steady as a waiter refilled it.

'It goes with the job,' Penny answered, blushing slightly as she looked away from the man who had just turned and caught her watching him. She had no idea who he was, but it wasn't the first time this evening that their eyes had met and though neither of them had smiled, or gone any way towards acknowledging the other, Penny felt sure that he was as aware of her presence as she was of his.

Like all the other men there he was dressed in black tie and with his rather unruly dark hair and unshaven chin he was, to Penny's mind, extremely attractive. Not handsome, she thought, as her heart tripped on the excitement and anticipation she always felt on these occasions, at least not in the conventional sense of the word; he simply had that indefinable quality about him that made him stand out from the crowd.

'Shame about the rain,' Sammy was saying, looking out through the tall, old-fashioned french windows on to the beautifully terraced gardens with their view of the valley and, Penny guessed, on a good day to the sea in the distance.

'Mmm,' Penny murmured, sure that she was still being watched, but not quite daring to look. 'What time did you want to be in Nice, by the way?' she asked, glancing at her watch.

'Not for ages yet,' Sammy answered, flicking her hair back over her shoulder. 'But listen, you don't have to drive me there. I can take a taxi or bum a lift from someone who's going that way.'

Penny smiled. 'I forgot to ask, what's his name?'

Sammy grinned. 'Stefan.'

'And what does Stefan—?' She stopped, frowning, as she spotted a familiar figure over by the bar.

'What is it?' Sammy said, following her eyes.

'It's the old lady from next door,' Penny said incredulously. 'Now what on earth would she be doing here when she specifically said that she hadn't been invited?'

Sammy shrugged. 'Does it matter?' she said.

Penny shook her head slowly. 'I don't know,' she answered. Then, as Esther Delaney's canary-yellow suit and matching pillbox hat disappeared into the crowd, she felt herself being watched again and unable to stop them her eyes moved back to the man who was standing with a group of other men near the centre of the room. But he wasn't watching her at all, and to her surprise the disappointment she felt was almost as profound as the sudden embarrassment that overcame her as he turned, caught her eye and raised an ironic eyebrow.

'Who *is* that man?' Sammy asked, seeing Penny's cheeks flood with colour. 'He's been watching you all night. Do you know him?'

'Never seen him before in my life,' Penny answered, trying to sound nonchalant, while failing to stop her eyes moving back to his. He was talking to another man, but though he was no longer looking at her Penny had the distinct impression that he knew she was watching him. Suddenly he laughed and Penny almost groaned aloud as her pulses quickened and other parts of her body started to respond. 'I've got to tell you,' she murmured to Sammy, 'that if there's such a thing as lust at first sight, then this is it, because what I wouldn't do to that man given half the chance . . .'

'Why don't you get someone to introduce you?' Sammy suggested.

'Some of us aren't quite as forward as others,' Penny remarked drily. 'Oh God, here comes the baron again. Don't leave me alone with him whatever you do.'

Fortunately the baron was on a mission to introduce her to a few livelier and less lecherous people than himself, some of whom were friends of Sylvia's, she discovered. Not surprisingly, for a while the conversation revolved around their mutual acquaintance – who, they were all wholeheartedly agreed, had done a marvellous job since taking over the reins of *Starke* after the death of her husband.

As they all seemed to know Sylvia quite well, Penny was trying to think of a way of steering the conversation round to Sylvia's godson, when, to her astonishment, she noticed Esther Delaney talking to the man who'd been watching her. In fact, they were both looking in her direction now, and, unless Penny was greatly mistaken, they were talking about her too.

Seeing Penny looking, Esther gave her a jolly little wave, but Penny barely noticed, for the intensity of the man's eyes and the half smile hovering around his lips were turning her hot inside and sending such shivers of excitement through her that she knew, come what may, she had to meet him.

'Think you've just found your introduction,' Sammy whispered in her ear.

'I think I might have found more than that,' Penny responded under her breath, not too clear herself whether she meant she had found an important link in the international art scam she had managed to convince herself the Delaneys were involved in, or whether, considering this irrational heightening of her senses, she had found something of a much more personal nature.

With the continual ebb and flow of people it was half an hour or more before Penny finally managed to corner Esther, by which time the man was over by the door and looking as though he was about to depart.

'How are you, Esther?' she said, kissing the old lady on both cheeks as Sammy joined them. 'I wasn't expecting to see you here.'

'Oh my! I know. Isn't it a surprise? Such an honour. Came right at the last minute. Wasn't expecting it at all.'

'Have you met my sister, Sammy?' Penny said.

'Briefly,' Esther answered, taking Sammy warmly by the hand. 'Just briefly. How are you, my dear? You're looking quite splendid. You both are.'

'Thank you,' Sammy smiled. 'So are you.' Then, deciding not to beat about the bush, she went straight to work on Penny's behalf: 'I've noticed you talking to quite a lot of people here tonight, but, tell me, who's the man over there by the door? I feel I should know him, but I can't quite place him.'

Esther's diminutive frame expanded with pride. 'That,' she said in a whisper, 'is Christian Mureau.'

Penny and Sammy exchanged glances, neither any the wiser for knowing his name, though sensing, from the way Esther had pronounced it, that they should be.

'What does he do?' Penny asked.

'You mean you don't *know* Christian Mureau?' Esther gasped.

'I don't think so,' Penny answered, experiencing an irrational flutter of nerves. 'Should I?'

'Oh, silly me!' Esther giggled. 'Of course, he's much better known in America than he is here. Well, that's why he's here, of course. But, shh, we mustn't talk about that.'

'About what?' Sammy said.

'No, no. We mustn't talk about it,' Esther said, giving her a little slap on the wrist.

'How do you know him?' Penny asked, watching him as he listened intently to the man who was talking to him.

'Shh!' Esther said, putting a finger to her lips. 'He's my employer.'

Penny's eyes narrowed. 'What does he do?' she repeated.

Again Esther giggled. 'You really mustn't ask me things like that,' she said. 'I'm not allowed to tell. You see, he's a *wanted* man.'

Both Sammy and Penny blinked. 'You mean wanted as in criminal?' Penny said, feeling her heart start to race.

'Oh my! I shouldn't have told you that,' Esther cried, clapping her hands to her cheeks, apparently appalled by her indiscretion.

'Don't worry, I won't breathe a word,' Penny reassured her. 'But tell me, what did he do?'

'And how come—?' Sammy stopped as Penny put a hand on her arm. One question at a time was enough for Esther.

'What did he do?' Penny prompted.

'I really can't tell you that,' Esther said forlornly.

'Was he the one who introduced you to all those famous people in the photographs?' Penny asked carefully.

168

'Yes,' Esther answered, brightening. 'And he said I could come tonight. He knew I wanted to and he really does spoil me, you know. But usually he doesn't like me to mix with the same people he does, not here in France. You see, not many of them know that he is wanted by the Dr—' She stopped; then, wagging a finger at Penny, she said, 'Naughty, naughty, you almost got it out of me then.'

'I'd like very much to meet him,' Penny said. 'Do you think you could introduce me?'

Esther looked doubtful. 'I'd like to,' she said, 'but . . .'

'But what?' Sammy asked.

'You see, he asked me who you were just now, Penny dear, and when I told him . . .'

'When you told him?' Penny prompted.

'He knows you're a journalist and . . . Well, you see, in his position . . . Can't take any risks, what?'

Penny shot a glance at Sammy in the hope that her sister would be quicker to see a way round this impasse, since her own mind was somewhat clouded by the intensity of the attraction she was feeling towards the man.

'I think Penny's more interested in meeting him as a woman than as a journalist,' Sammy said bluntly.

Wanting to kick her even though it was true, Penny was about to speak when Esther got in first.

'Oh, I think he'd like to meet you too, dear,' she assured Penny. 'He said he did. But, you see, things are just a teensy bit complicated and I'm— Oh! Heavens! He's looking over here.'

Penny turned to see his dark eyes looking in their direction and, though it was hard to tell from this distance, she felt sure they were laughing. Somewhat brazenly for her, she held his gaze until, with a lazy lift of his eyebrows that gave her the clear impression that he knew what Esther Delaney had told her, he left.

Penny turned back to Esther, feeling a horrible dampening of her spirits now he had gone and not a little

169

frustration. 'Does he live around—?' She stopped, realizing that Esther was no longer there, was in fact beetling through the crowd in an effort to save herself from more indiscretions.

'Well,' she sighed, turning to Sammy, 'what do you make of all that?'

Sammy pulled a thoughtful face. 'What I reckon,' she said, 'is that if you want to meet the man, which you obviously do, then you're going to have to do some more work on the old girl. She's your only link at the moment and from a professional standpoint, if he is a wanted man, you'd be crazy not to follow it up.' A grin spread across her face. 'And from a personal standpoint you'd be certifiably insane.'

Later that evening, having left Sammy with a couple of Sylvia's friends who had offered to drive her into Nice, Penny was winding her way through the pitch-darkness of the back roads between Vence and Valbonne, trying to recall what was on her agenda the following day. It was a task that was proving impossible, for she was unable to get Christian Mureau out of her mind. To tell herself that all she wanted from him was a scoop for *Nuance* – which, of course, he was going to hand her on plate, wasn't he? – was like saying that all she ever wanted from a jeweller's was a look in the window.

Christ, she wished the man behind would get off her tail! Why did the French always have to drive like that? Speeding up a bit, she took a bend far too fast, then decided to hell with it, he'd just have to go at her pace until he found somewhere to pass. Where was she? Oh yes, she hadn't spoken a single word to Christian Mureau, didn't, now she came to think about it, even know what nationality he was, yet already, in her mind, she had them engrossed in a full-blooded affair. Her heart jumped at the thought of it and she knew that somehow, no matter what it took, she was going to meet that man. God-damnit! Why didn't the jerk behind just

170

overtake? There was plenty of room now . . .

Slowing to a mere forty kilometres an hour she waited for the car to overtake. But, to her surprise, it slowed down too and continued hugging her bumper and dazzling her with its headlights. Feeling a spark of unease pass through her, she reach behind her and pressed down the button to lock the car door. The night was so black out here and the forests so dense that she was beginning to wish she'd taken the longer route home via the motorway.

By the time she drove into the brightly lit main street of Roquefort-les-Pins her hands were gripping the wheel tightly and her heart was thudding. Psychopaths were a rarity in France, but certainly not unheard of. For no accountable reason she thought of David and wished desperately that he was with her.

As she approached the red lights in the middle of the village she pulled her car over to the side of the road, in the hope that this time whoever it was would pass. To her alarm he pulled in behind her.

Penny sat where she was, fear pulsing through her as she tried to think what to do. The headlights behind were on full beam so she couldn't see into the car; nor did she think it a good idea to get out. There was no one around and by the time she reached one of the houses anything could happen.

Then, to her horror, she saw two men step out of either side of the car and start walking towards her. Instantly she jammed her foot on the accelerator, but her legs were so weak with fear she let go of the clutch too soon and the engine stalled.

She watched, wide-eyed with terror, her heartbeat thundering in her ears, as one of them came to stand beside her door and the other perched on the bonnet. Both had greased-back hair; the one at her door had a hand inside his leather jacket. A knife, she was thinking. He's got a knife! And as the panic welled up inside her she slammed her hand on the horn.

But the engine was off. The horn didn't work. The man on the bonnet grinned. Her head spun back to the other one as he tapped on the window, then motioned for her to roll the window down.

Hardly knowing what she was doing, she opened it a crack and stared up at him.

'Tell Villers,' he said, his black eyes boring into hers, 'that he won't get away with it. He's got to pay, just like everyone else.'

Then, before the words had even begun to register with her, the men were gone. She looked in the mirror and watched as they did a three-point turn and sped off in the direction from which they had come.

Still shaking, Penny switched on her engine and drove slowly through the traffic lights, down towards the roundabout where she would turn off for Valbonne. From there it was a reasonably short drive to Mougins and home. Thank God she had stopped where she had, for the very idea she might have led them to her villa was enough to set her off panicking again. Of course there was no doubt that they were the dubious characters David had warned her about, but what did they mean, he had to pay like everyone else? Just what was he up to that led that kind of low life to threaten him in this way? She felt strangely protective for a moment, wishing that she had told them to drop dead or go find another bank. Then, quite suddenly, she was angry. How dare he get her involved in his sordid business, whatever it was? And why the hell should she put up with it when she'd come here to do a job, not to be terrified out of her wits by hoodlums on his account?

She was still fuming silently to herself when she let herself into the villa some twenty minutes later. But when she played back the messages on her answerphone and heard a strange, accented voice telling her that he was Christian Mureau, everything else fled from her mind.

Pressing urgently on the rewind button she listened intently as the message replayed.

'Hello,' he said, 'it's Christian Mureau. I think we should meet.'

That was it! Not when, or where or even how she could get in touch with him, just that they should meet.

It was just after four on Wednesday afternoon. The production office was like a three-ringed circus as phones and faxes rang, printers pumped out reams of edited copy and Marielle and Mario, the ad director, haggled over space and position on the flat plans. The air-conditioning engineers were getting under everyone's feet and a bureaucractic bloodhound from the Cannes Chamber of Commerce had decided to pay them a visit today. Pierre was handling him. Penny was at her desk with the door closed as she read through the endless material that was coming her way all the time now as every man jack and his dog tried his hand at something or other. Actually, some of the stuff wasn't too bad, but most of it was heading straight for the bin. Sammy had really come up trumps with a seaman, though, whose tales of shenanigans on board the luxury liners of the rich and famous were going to form the basis for *Nautical Nuances*. Whoever the guy was, he didn't have much of a gift with words, but the subs would sort that – it was the material that was so fascinating.

She had a meeting at five with the team from the ad agency that was handling the launch; she just hoped Jeffrey, the designer, was going to make it back from Toulon in time. She was also in the middle of an editorial that she wanted finished by the end of the day and she still had to speak to the English/French experts on the dryness of their 'life in France' column. Crazy as it all felt, for the moment things were more or less on schedule; but, even so, nothing short of seeing the magazine on the stands was going to convince Penny that they'd hit the deadline.

The precious lunch hour had passed her by again, but a few minutes ago Brigitte had brought in half a baguette stuffed with a rich, creamy pâté and fat, crunchy gherkins. As she ate, Penny was looking down at the newspaper photographs of her parasailing adventure the previous weekend and thanking God that she didn't look even half as ridiculous – or fat – as she'd thought she would. In truth it had been a fantastic, exhilarating experience soaring high above the waves and feeling, just for that short while, the total freedom of a bird. In fact the entire day had been terrific and David's glowing praise of her success when she'd finally sunk, almost gracefully, into the sea and he'd circled the boat round to get her had for once managed to warm him to her rather than irritate her. And watching him sing 'Thank heavens for little girls' on a platform specially erected for the solo performers of the day had made her laugh so much as tomatoes and peaches and all kinds of soft fruit were flung at him while he continued to caterwaul at the top of his voice, that it was only when he and Smithy grabbed her arms and ran her, fully clothed, towards the sea that she promised to stop. That was one of the pictures in the paper: Penny pleading with the two of them to put her down while the rest of the team spurred them on to dunk her. And the other picture was just of David and her, soaked to the skin as they waded back to the shore.

It had been a perfect day right up to the moment Marielle showed up. At that point, David had promptly ceased to notice Penny's existence and switched his attentions exclusively to Marielle. Sammy had accused her of being jealous and in a way Sammy was right, but not in the way Sammy thought she was right, for Penny wasn't in the habit of lying to herself about her feelings. She'd never denied that David was an attractive man and history had proved that she wasn't immune to his charm, but if there were any poor, deluded little hormones within her that were in an unhappy state of falling for him she would most definitely know about them. So no, it wasn't some unrequited passion for David that had made her feel so wretched when Marielle had arrived; it was quite simply that Marielle had looked so sumptuously sexy and exotic in a simple little white dress that had leeched itself so immodestly to her perfect figure that, damp, sand-stained and in serious need of a hairbrush, Penny had felt like Bertha the bag lady.

Not surprisingly, she and David had ended up falling out quite soon after Marielle's arrival, and though Penny couldn't remember exactly what had caused it now she did recall the way he had treated the whole thing – her in particular – as a great big joke. If only once, just *once*, she thought angrily as she stuffed the last piece of baguette into her mouth, she could appear as cool and dignified as her position required.

It was too much baguette for one mouthful, far too much, but it was something she could easily have coped with in the privacy of her office had David – damn his eyes! – not chosen that very moment to come strolling in through the door.

Penny looked at him, unable to do anything about the great wodge of food bulging in her cheek. It was so large she couldn't even move it around and neither, to her dismay, could she speak through it.

David's grin widened by the second as he watched her cheeks fill with colour. 'Take your time,' he offered generously.

Penny's jaw was straining, unable to stretch any wider to dislodge the bread from between her back teeth. There was only one thing for it, she had to open her mouth, but how could she do that with him standing there grinning at her like a Hallowe'en pumpkin?

He sat down, put his feet on her desk, shoved his

hands behind his head and kept right on looking at her. Penny glared back and, to her fury, he started to laugh.

'I wish you could see yourself,' he told her.

An incoherent grunt along with a few soggy crumbs issued from her lips as she attempted to tell him to piss off.

'Sorry?' he said. 'I didn't quite catch that.'

The bulge in her cheek felt like an inflating balloon.

In the end she dived into the kitchenette, sorted herself out, then came furiously back into the office. 'Don't you ever knock?' she demanded.

'From time to time,' he answered. 'So, what's all the urgency?'

'The urgency,' she retorted, 'began on Saturday evening. It is now Wednesday afternoon. Where have you been?'

'Saturday evening?' he said in surprise. 'But I saw you on Sunday.'

Penny felt herself flush. 'Yes, well, I forgot about it then,' she said, feeling ridiculous.

'So what's the problem?' he said. 'Why didn't you speak to Pierre?'

'Because you expressly said that you wanted to deal with the "dubious characters", as you called them, who, as you predicted they would, approached me on Saturday evening. So, who are they? And just what is going on?'

It seemed nothing could budge that appalling grin of his as he said, 'Congratulations, Penny. You know you've arrived on the Côte d'Azur now.'

'What the hell are you talking about?'

'You mean you haven't worked out for yourself who they are?'

'If I had I wouldn't need to be asking you.'

'They were, my little pudding, the Mafia.'

'Don't you dare call me that!' she flared. 'And what do you mean, they were the Mafia? What are you up to that the Mafia should be paying me visits?'

'They control magazine distribution in these parts,' he answered calmly. 'We have to pay, just like anyone else. So what did they say to you?' he asked.

'That you have to pay,' she answered, irritated that he had already said it and suddenly wishing it had been a death threat. 'Now, what is going on, David? And I don't want any of your smart-aleck answers, I want the truth, because if you're involved in some sort of criminal activity I'm on the next plane back to London.' Like hell she would be, she was thinking to herself, for if he was involved in anything to do with the Mafia she wanted to know about it!

'Penny, Penny, Penny,' he said, shaking his head. 'Don't you know that the Mafia have their fingers in every pie down here? They want protection money. A share in the profits. Commissions, call it what you like, but you, we, aren't going anywhere with this magazine unless we play ball. But don't let it concern you. Like I said before, I'll handle it.'

'You're not seriously telling me you're going to pay them?' she cried.

'That is precisely what I'm telling you,' he answered. 'Unless you have a better idea.'

'Tell them to go to hell!'

He nodded, apparently turning it over in his mind. 'Yeah, I guess that could get them running. Yeah, I reckon they'll be sure to back off if I tell them Penny Moon said go to hell.'

'Don't mock me. Are these people dangerous?'

'Have you never heard of the Mafia?'

'Of course I have, you idiot.'

'Then why ask me such a daft question? Now, like I said, leave it with me, I'll sort it. Are you sure they didn't say anything else?'

'What they said was enough to give me two sleepless nights and a serious case of the jitters,' she responded.

'Which is nothing compared with what I'm going to suffer now I know who they are.'

'They'll leave you alone as soon as I strike a deal with them.'

'Then why come to me in the first place and not to you?'

'To be honest, I thought they would come to me. I simply warned you on the off chance they might find their way to you instead. Of course, I'm presuming it was the Mafia,' he added, eyebrows raised.

Penny threw up her hands. 'Oh, this is just great! It might be one of the world's most dangerous gangster organizations, but, there again, it might just be someone else. How many more are there, David? I mean, why don't we throw a party and invite them all? Why don't we just give them their own chequebooks? Why not just hand over to them now?'

'They're not after the company. Just a cut in the profits,' he answered mildly.

'Presuming, of course, that it was the Mafia.'

'Presuming,' he agreed.

'*So*, who else could it be?'

'Search me,' he answered, getting up from his chair. 'But don't let them scare you, Penny. It's not your chastity they're after.'

'Don't you dare walk out that door,' she seethed. 'I want to know what I should do if they approach me again. Better still, I want to know exactly who I'm dealing with.'

'I'll get to the bottom of it,' he told her. 'I doubt they'll come to you again,' and he was gone.

Penny was tempted to go after him, but she didn't want a showdown in the office and she seriously doubted she was going to get any more out of him than she already had. The strange thing was, though she had reacted a touch hysterically with him, his casual acceptance of it all had, in a way, calmed her. Of course she knew that the Mafia were here on the Coast, everyone did, it was just that she hadn't expected them to come knocking on her door. Well, who did? The likes of David Villers, of course. But, as he said, it was part and parcel of running a business down here and, just so long as she wasn't the one who had to deal with them, it might be as well to turn a blind eye to the fact that gangsters were creaming off their profits. After all, ultimately it was his money, so what was it to her if he gave it to the Mafia?

'I'm not sure what it is to you,' Sammy said later that night. 'I mean, like you said, it's probably nothing for you to worry about, but you are involved with him and to be honest with you, Pen . . .'

'What?' Penny snapped when Sammy paused.

'Well, don't go biting my head off, but until Christian Mureau came on the scene I – and a lot of others, I have to tell you – thought that something might be developing between you and David.'

'Why on earth would you think that when everyone knows he's involved with Marielle?' Penny cried.

'I don't know,' Sammy shrugged. 'I suppose it's just the way you make each other laugh and the way you get so mad at him . . . I don't *know*! It's just what we thought.'

'Well, you're wrong,' Penny told her. 'And not just because of Christian Mureau.'

'Have you talked to Esther Delaney again?' Sammy asked carefully.

'No.'

'Why not?'

'Because,' Penny said through her teeth, 'she's not there. And I'm on a pretty short fuse right now, so don't bug me any more, OK? We're six weeks away from the launch and I'm strung out enough without you, David or anyone else—'

'All right, all right,' Sammy cried, holding up her

hands. 'I just told you what I thought, that's all.'

Had Penny not been in such a bad mood she might have confided more in Sammy, but since she was so tired and didn't know what the hell she was really feeling anyway she didn't see the point in trying. It was true to say that David had her at sixes and sevens, but apart from him – and *Nuance*, of course – what she was becoming increasingly more concerned and frustrated about lately was how she was going to meet Christian Mureau.

After contacting a few journalist friends in the United States she now had quite a collection of cuttings about him that, instead of quelling her interest, which, at least on a personal level, it should have done, had only served to excite it further. But that was something she certainly wasn't going to tell Sammy, not when the crime he was wanted for had nothing at all to do with art and everything to do with drugs. Just thank God it was only marijuana, she had repeatedly told herself since reading the cuttings, for had it been anything stronger she knew she'd never be able to justify her attraction to him, even to herself. The trouble was she had become more intrigued with him than ever after reading how he had netted himself over a hundred million dollars smuggling vast container-loads of marijuana out of Hong Kong and the Philippines over to the States, and had done it with such style that he had made something of a hero of himself with the press, as well as making the Drug Enforcement Administration look like half-wits with some of the methods he had used to outsmart them.

Though Penny was trying hard to remain professional about this, it took little more than a glimpse of his face in the cuttings to make her heart tighten with the anticipation of what might happen between them were they to meet. The pull she felt towards him seemed to grow stronger by the day and the fact that he had been pho-

180

tographed with several people she knew – rock stars, actors and writers – fuelled the flame of fascination. But though she was sorely tempted to call one or two of them to find out more about him, she was refusing to give in to it. The last thing she wanted was any of them telling him she was making enquiries about him; if they did, he would naturally assume she was on the hunt for a story – which she was, or at least in her saner moments she was. But there were all too many other moments when the romance and intrigue that surrounded him, coupled with the memory of his eyes across the room and his voice on the answerphone, seemed to encourage her suspicion that, should she ever get to meet this French-Canadian drug smuggler, he was going to be a great deal more important in her life than a mere subject for *Nuance*.

When it came to faking orgasms Marielle Descourts was pretty damned impressive, David was thinking, as he detached himself from her and rolled on to his back. If he'd cared he might have done something about it, but already his mind was moving on to other things. Raising an arm, he looked up at his watch, turning it to the silvery glow of moonlight coming in through the slatted blind at the window. Just after midnight: not even Penny would be at the office now. Sliding out of bed he walked across the master suite of his apartment and into the bathroom. It took him only a few minutes to shower, then, going back into the bedroom, he looked down at Marielle, who was still lying naked on her back, assuming the role of a sleepily satiated vamp.

'Penny tells me our friends along the coast have paid her a visit,' he said, knowing that Marielle would have no difficulty understanding the euphemism.

Her eyes narrowed. 'Oh?' she said, trailing a finger along his thigh towards his groin.

'Oh,' he repeated, catching her hand and removing it.

'Why her and not you?' she asked.

'Good question. Any ideas?'

She shrugged. 'How would I know?'

He kept his eyes on her a moment or two longer, then turning away he started to dress.

'Are you going somewhere?' she asked from the bed.

'No, but you are,' he answered. 'I want you to go to the office and check out the phones.'

'What do you mean, check out the phones?' she hissed. 'What do you think I am, a fucking telephone engineer?'

'Check them for bugs,' he said. 'Especially mine, Pierre's and Penny's.'

'What kind of bugs?'

'Lice, roaches, beetles. *Electronic* bugs, sweetheart. Listening devices.'

She looked at him as though he was losing his mind. 'Why on earth would there be bugs on our phones?' she cried.

His eyebrows came up, as though impressed. 'Another good question, Marielle,' he complimented her. 'No ideas on that score either, I suppose?'

'I don't know what you're talking about. Why would I know anything about bugs in telephones? I don't even know what they look like.'

'You will when you see them,' he answered, throwing her clothes on to the bed. 'Now, no more discussions, there's a good girl. Just go do as you're told and come back.'

When she had gone, he stood on the balcony looking down at the late strollers on the Croisette until she emerged from the apartment block and walked to the middle island, where her car was parked.

Smiling to himself, he turned back inside. The hell she didn't know what a bug looked like! His guess was she'd put the damned things there herself. Pierre had found them the day before and, under David's instructions, had left them in place. It was going to be interesting to see what story Marielle came back with. Bugs or no bugs. Time now, though, to check his own phone before putting in a trans-Atlantic call to his wife.

Chapter 9

'Don't you ever leave this boat?' Marielle asked, curling her fingers over Stirling's balding pate as she sauntered lazily past him.

"Course I leave the fucking boat,' he snapped, jamming a cap on his head and closing his bloodshot eyes to the blinding rays of the sun. 'What do you think, I'm fucking Popeye or something?' He shifted in his deck chair, unable to get comfortable, perspiring profusely in the heat.

'Why don't you come to the launch party?' she teased.

'You're not funny, Marielle,' he muttered.

'But I'm sure David would love to see you,' she baited.

'Yeah, I just bet he would,' Stirling said sourly. Then, after a pause. 'Tell me, did he deal with the boys from Nice yet?'

'I don't know. He won't tell me what's happening there.'

Stirling opened one eye to look at her. She had great tits, he'd give her that, all oiled up for the sun, nipples standing out like freshly popped claret corks. She had great legs too, but shit, was she one dumb broad. 'You must be losing your touch, Marielle,' he remarked maliciously.

'I don't think so,' she purred, winding her arms around his neck and sitting into his lap.

'Save it for Villers,' he rasped, pushing her off as he

broke into a coughing fit.

Marielle wandered across the deck and gazed out at the palm-lined sweep of the Croisette. 'Was it the Mafia?' she asked, with a sideways glance.

'Quit bugging me, Marielle,' he wheezed. 'I'm not in the mood.'

'You know,' she said, putting a slender finger to her chin and gazing thoughtfully up at the sky, 'I could always tell him you're here.'

'If you don't think he's figured that out yet,' Stirling responded, wiping his mouth with a handkerchief, 'then you're even stupider than you look.'

Marielle turned to look at him, a great beached whale in a Chicago Bears cap and khaki shorts frying in the sun. She could take his insults, welcomed them in fact, for the perverse truth of it was they actually turned her on.

'What'd you tell him about the bugs, by the way?' Stirling asked.

'What you told me to tell him. That they were there.' She waited for him to comment, when he didn't she said, 'I asked him if he thought the Mafia had done it.'

'What'd he say?'

'He didn't answer. He's had them removed.'

'Sure he's had them removed, what d'you expect?'

Marielle sauntered back across the deck and curled up at his feet. 'There are ways, you know, of stopping that magazine going to press. Would you like that?' she added when he didn't respond.

'Marielle,' he sighed, 'it don't matter shit to me whether or not that magazine hits the stands. All's I want is Villers right where I want him. The bastard owes me and, boy, am I gonna collect.' He paused for a moment, then peering down at her he said, 'And what good would it do you if that magazine didn't go to press?'

'None,' she answered. 'But I thought it might be what you wanted.'

'Altruism!' Stirling chuckled. 'That's a new one for

185

you, Marielle.'

'I've told you before, there are a lot of things I'd do for you, Bobby,' she purred, stroking her fingers over his fat knees.

'Is that so?' he said. 'Well, it could just be that I don't need diddly from you.'

'You want David Villers, don't you?'

'Face it, you're out of your league, honey. You're a fucking bongo player in this orchestra.'

'If you don't think I can give you what you want, why did you approach me in the first place?'

'I didn't know what kind of show he was going to stage then, did I? But I do now and I can wait.'

'And meanwhile, what about me?'

'What the fuck about you?'

'I want that magazine.'

'Shit, woman, you're like a stuck record. Lay off it, will you.'

'You said last time that you were going to help me get rid of Penny Moon,' she reminded him.

'I did?'

'You know you did,' she said petulantly.

It was a while before Stirling answered, savouring the brush of her nipples against his shins. Keep her sweet, she might just carry on doing it. 'Where's Penny the Moon now?' he asked.

'She went off somewhere with David this morning.'

Stirling's mouth twitched. 'You don't reckon there's something going on there?' he said gleefully, knowing it'd put that cute little nose of hers out of joint.

'You have to be joking,' Marielle responded. 'She's definitely not his type.'

'Mm, she looks all right, what I've seen of her.'

Marielle's head came up. 'You've seen her?' she said.

'Sure I've seen her. You think I go about with my fucking eyes shut?'

'Maybe,' Marielle said a while later as she snaked her

fingers over his thigh and slid them into his shorts, 'David's in a better position to give me the magazine.'

'Maybe he is at that,' Stirling yawned. 'But it seems to me he wants Penny the Moon to have it. And you, Marielle, better make up your mind which ball park you're playing on, here, 'cos by the time I've finished with Villers he ain't gonna be in no position to give you a rag to wipe your butt with, never mind one to put on a newsstand. Now, since you seem mighty keen to be giving me a blow job down there, why don't you get on with it? Perhaps it'll shut you up for five minutes.'

'I reckon now is as good a time as any,' David said as he steered the Saab from the autoroute and headed left up towards Mougins, 'to tell you what a really great job you're doing, Pen. You've pulled a terrific team together, you're on top of everything and despite your occasional lapses into hysteria with me, I reckon you handle yourself pretty well.'

'Well, you don't have to sound so surprised,' Penny retorted, 'and you could have left out the dig. Nevertheless, thank you for the compliment.'

Smiling, he threw her a quick look, then returned his eyes to the road. 'Are you intending to let Sylvia take a look at the proofs?' he asked.

'She hasn't asked to, but I'll courier them over if you think I should.'

'Your decision.'

Penny turned to look out at the villa-studded hillsides, smiling happily to herself as the wind rushing through her hair brought a merciful respite from the cloying heat of the day. She was in a great mood today and not even David had managed to dent it. On the contrary, in fact: he had behaved impeccably all day long. Well, let's not overdo it, Penny, she scolded herself. He hadn't been able to resist the odd jibe here and there and he'd made a total prat of himself along with the other men at the printers over some blonde parading past with next to nothing on. Why did men have to do that? Didn't they realize what gorillas they looked? Still, on the whole, David had been almost bearable, providing she was prepared to overlook the uncomfortable moment at lunch when he'd fixed her with those insufferable eyes of his and asked if, by any chance, she'd been having wickedly lustful dreams about him. Conceited bastard! But for once she hadn't risen to it. Instead she had told him, quite calmly, that should this unlikely event ever occur she would be sure to check into the nearest psychiatric ward, and if he'd asked the question because he was having them about her, then he could just dream on.

They were only three weeks away from publication now and with things still running along suspiciously well-oiled tracks Penny could see no cause for disaster. Nevertheless, it was only the fact that publicity was now gaining momentum, invitations to the launch were out and the first three issues were more or less ready for the printer that was allaying her fears that she might just be designing the Emperor's new clothes. That, and the reason behind their visit to the printer today.

They'd gone to discuss a last-minute change to the first issue that involved a complete reworking of the front cover and the replacement of a celebrity interview. It was going to be tight, the printer had told them, but as long as Penny got the substitute interview to him by the end of the week he would go so far as to confidently predict that they might make it. Smiling at his rare attempt at humour Penny had assured him that it wouldn't be a problem. She could only hope now that it wouldn't be.

This eleventh-hour exclusive, arranged courtesy of David, of course, was going to provide them with the launch of all launches, for the American actress Pauline Fields, who was flying into Nice to begin her summer vacation on Cap d'Ail the following day, had agreed to be interviewed. It was such an amazing *coup* that Penny was still reeling from the shock, for it would be the first time that Fields had spoken to anyone from the press since the untimely death of her husband six months ago in a tragic accident that had almost killed their daughter too. Such an exclusive couldn't fail to put them on the map since Fields's popularity was second only to her fame.

'So,' David said, interrupting Penny's reverie as they turned into the welcome shade of the winding, leafy lane that climbed to the gates of the villa, 'you managed to find yourself a boyfriend yet?'

Rolling her eyes, Penny turned to look at him. 'Why don't you mind your own business?' she said with an affable smile.

'But you are my business,' he objected.

'Now, just how did you manage to work that one out?' she enquired.

'I've got a lot of money invested in you,' he answered. 'I reckon that makes you my business.'

'During working hours maybe; out of working hours, you can just keep your big nose out of things. OK?'

'OK,' he shrugged. Then, after a pause: 'So, have you?'

'Have I what?'

'Found yourself a boyfriend?'

'David, drop dead,' she said sweetly and reached into her bag for the gate control.

'You going to invite me in for a drink?' he asked as they came to a stop at the front door.

'I wasn't planning to,' she answered.

'Well, plans can always be changed,' he grinned, throwing open his door and getting out. 'Maybe we could take a swim first, then I can fill you in on some of Pauline Fields's background over a glass or two.'

After the long, sticky drive back from Toulon there was nothing Penny would have liked more than to plunge into the refreshing depths of the pool, but there was no way in the world she was going to let David see her in one of her skimpy swimsuits. She'd managed to lose a bit of weight these past few months, but she was still a mighty long way from perfect and she didn't trust him not to point it out.

'Actually,' she said, 'I don't want to appear rude, but this evening isn't convenient.'

David's eyebrows shot up. 'So there is someone?' he said, not seeming to like it too much.

'Why don't you just put a sock in it, David?' she responded. 'I've told you already: my personal life is none of your business.'

'Is he the reason for the diet?' he asked.

To her annoyance, Penny felt herself starting to blush. 'The reason for the diet, as you call it,' she answered through her teeth, 'is hard work and not enough time to eat. Now, if you want to take a swim, be my guest. I'll join you on the terrace in half an hour for *one* drink. After that I'm afraid I'll have to throw you out.'

As she wandered off to her bedroom to shower and change Penny was berating herself for turning down this chance to discuss Pauline Fields. It was unprofessional and she knew it. But there was always tomorrow and tonight was the first opportunity she'd had to see Esther Delaney, who'd returned home two days ago – three weeks later than Wally had expected her. Penny had called her from the office late yesterday to invite her over for a drink this evening, which had delighted the old lady almost as much as it had Penny to hear that Wally wasn't available. So she wasn't going to pass up what she hoped would be an opportunity to chat about Christian Mureau when it might ultimately lead to a scoop that could prove even greater than the Pauline Fields exclusive. At least, that was what she was telling herself in what she actually knew to be a self-deluding effort to remain professional about this.

A while later, just before going downstairs to join

David on the terrace, Penny stepped out on to the balcony of her bedroom to look at the magnificent view of the sea. By then she'd all but forgotten that David was still there, so it gave her something of a start to see him beside the pool towelling himself off.

She watched him for a moment, rather liking being in the position of seeing yet not being seen. It seemed to put her at an advantage, something she rarely was with David. That was until he dropped his towel and turned for his clothes. He was, to Penny's dismay, exposing a body that was so breathtakingly beautiful, so hard and tanned, that Penny simply couldn't take her eyes away. His long, muscular legs and the coarse, dark hair of his groin almost made her groan aloud. How easy it was to picture him making love, to imagine the endless pleasure a body like that could give. Dear God – she grimaced as she started to turn back inside – this involuntary abstinence of hers was starting to have seriously adverse effects on her judgement.

She had just reached the door when she suddenly stiffened as she heard him call out, 'Hi, there!'

'Hi,' she heard Sammy call back and Penny almost collapsed with relief. The very last thing in the world she wanted was for David to know that she'd been standing there admiring his body. She'd never hear the end of it!

Walking on to the terrace a few minutes later, she felt the beginnings of a blush creep into her cheeks as David looked up. His damnable eyes flooded with laughter, as if he knew she was still carrying the image of his nudity in her mind, and when he complimented her on the way she looked, to her dismay she found herself ludicrously tongue-tied.

'Don't mind me,' Sammy grinned, looking from one to the other. 'I can tell when I'm not wanted.'

'What's that supposed to mean?' Penny snapped, aware that David with his arm hooked across the back of the chair beside him, was highly amused at her discomfort.

'What it means,' Sammy said, 'is that I'm off out. I just came back to shower and change . . .'

'Where are you going?' Penny called as Sammy headed into the house. 'I haven't seen you for days.'

'I've been staying with Stefan,' Sammy called back.

'And who,' David asked when Sammy had disappeared, 'is Stefan?'

Penny smiled. 'The latest love of her life. He's got this little dinghy that he motors around the harbours selling ice creams to the yachties.'

'He's offered me a job, by the way,' Sammy said, popping her head back round the door.

'You've already got a job,' Penny reminded her.

'Yes, but it isn't full-time, and it's kind of fun zooming around all those luxury boats. You should try it some time. It might loosen you up a bit.'

Penny looked at David and could have quite happily slapped him.

'I didn't say a word,' he protested, holding up his hands.

'You don't have to,' she said shortly. 'You managed to find yourself a drink, I see.'

'Sammy got it for me. So,' he sighed a moment or two later as he gazed out over the garden, towards the sea, 'here we are.'

'What do you mean, here we are?' she demanded indignantly.

David laughed. 'Exactly what did you think I meant?' he asked.

'Don't get tricky,' she said irritably. 'I'm not in the mood.'

He shook his head as though trying to clear it. 'Tell me, did I miss something?' he asked.

Penny frowned.

'Well, you sure weren't this antsy before you went upstairs,' he said. 'In fact, I was kind of getting to like you . . .'

192

'Let's change the subject,' she suggested.

'Fine by me,' he said, tipping his head back as he put the beer bottle to his mouth. 'By the way, I hope you don't mind but I used the phone while you were upstairs.'

'No, I don't mind,' she said, wishing she could shake this sudden bad mood.

'I called Marielle,' he went on. 'She wasn't there so I left a message. I thought someone had better break the news about Pauline Fields to her and I didn't imagine you'd have much of a problem with that someone being me.'

'None whatsoever,' she answered, knowing that Marielle was going to turn green with envy and black with fury that she wasn't doing the interview. 'I wish you luck.'

There was a lengthy pause after that, during which only the cicadas and the calming trickle of the fountain could be heard. It wasn't a silence Penny was particularly comfortable with, but she couldn't think of anything to fill it. Unless of course she brought up the subject of Pauline Fields again. But she didn't want to do that: it would be a long conversation and she was expecting Esther Delaney in fifteen minutes.

She stole a quick look at David, who gave every appearance of being perfectly at ease with the silence. Come to think of it, she'd never seen him anything other than totally relaxed. How wonderful it must be to feel so confident, so at ease with yourself, she thought. But then, looking like him, being as rich as him, and so blessed with charm and all those other detestable qualities he had, who wouldn't feel pleased with themselves?

'Tell me, David,' she said, 'doesn't anything ever get to you?'

'In what way?' he asked.

She shrugged, already sensing she was going to regret

getting into this. 'Well, don't you ever get really wound up about something?' she said.

'Sure I do,' he answered. 'But only things that matter.'

Penny nodded. 'What sort of things matter?' she asked, trying to sound offhand.

'Depends.'

'On what?'

He regarded her closely for a moment, then said, 'There are plenty of things that get to me, Penny Moon, you don't want to worry about that.'

'I wasn't worried,' she told him sharply.

'Good. So, tell me about your neighbours. Have you met any of them yet?'

'Only the ones immediately next door. There's a house just through those trees over there,' she added, pointing.

'French?' he asked.

'No. English.'

'What do they do?'

'They're in antiques,' she answered. 'The oriental kind, I think.'

He nodded as his eyes narrowed thoughtfully. 'Must be doing pretty well for them to afford a place out here,' he remarked.

'Mmm,' she said.

Again there was a silence. For some unaccountable reason she really wished she could read what was going on in his mind. The trouble with David was you *never* knew and, she supposed, that was why she found it so easy to be angry with him.

'Ah well,' he said, putting down his empty glass, 'time I was on my way.'

Penny walked with him to his car. 'Are you serious about your relationship with Marielle?' she asked as he got in.

She saw his smile even before he raised his face to look up at her and braced herself for his mocking eyes. But, to her surprise, whatever quip he was about to make never materialized as the usual humour retreated from his eyes and he said, 'At this moment in time there's only one woman I'm serious about, and it sure as hell isn't Marielle. But,' he added, with a wink, 'things can always change,' and starting up the engine, he circled the car around the forecourt and drove off.

Trying to pin Esther Delaney down to the subject of Christian Mureau was proving much harder than Penny had anticipated. The two of them had been sitting on the terrace for almost two hours, the sun had gone down and Esther's tongue did not, for the moment at least, appear to be loosening with the liberal oiling of alcohol. When she had arrived Penny had had to turn away to smother a smile at the knee-length red silk pleated skirt, black fishnet tights and black silk wrap-around top. Funnier still were the high-heeled shoes, with which the old lady clearly had a balancing problem.

But Penny's humour had quickly died when she'd found that any attempt she made to bring Mureau into the conversation was met with one of the old lady's irritatingly staccato little laughs and a flurry of hands about her face and throat. What Penny had managed to learn, though, was that wherever Wally was right now he was with Christian and that Esther's recent trip to the United States had been made alone. That didn't surprise Penny, however, for Christian Mureau was hardly in a position to cross American shores when he was currently at number five on the FBI's hit parade. But what Esther Delaney had been doing in the States for the past three weeks was something Penny was no closer to finding out now than she was before Esther arrived.

In fact, under any other circumstances Penny might have admired Esther's surprising ability to dodge questions she didn't want to answer. But, as she chuntered on about her time in Malaysia, seeming more and more on edge as each minute passed, as though she knew that

Penny wasn't going to let her off the hook, Penny decided she had let her witter on long enough, and pouring more wine into both their glasses, she took control of the conversation.

'Did Christian tell you that he left a message on my answerphone the night of the *vernissage*?' she asked bluntly.

Esther's eyes instantly glazed.

'Did he tell you?' Penny said firmly.

'Uh, um, yes, you know, I think he might have,' Esther answered, taking a gulp of wine.

'Did he tell you what he said? He said he thought we should meet.'

'Mmm, yes, mmm,' Esther responded, looking anywhere but at Penny.

'Has he changed his mind?' Penny asked.

'No! Um, yes. Yes, he changed his mind,' Esther finished decisively.

She was a very poor liar, Penny thought. 'Maybe, since I don't know how to get hold of him myself, you would give him a message for me,' she said.

'Oh dear,' Esther said, appearing more agitated than ever.

'Surely it won't hurt to give him a message,' Penny responded, disguising her irritation with a smile. 'Maybe you could tell him that I am not looking for a story unless, of course, he wants to give it.'

'No, no! Doesn't want to give a story,' Esther replied, sounding quite definite. 'Wants to meet you, but not for a story.'

Penny was heartened to hear that and refrained from reminding the old lady that only moments ago she had said he'd changed his mind about wanting to meet her. 'Then if you give him my assurance that I am not on the lookout for a story, perhaps he will call me again,' she said. 'Where is he now?'

'Lawyers,' Esther mumbled. 'Talking to his lawyers.

Wally drove him there.'

'Where?'

'Paris.'

Penny nodded, then with no prompting at all, Esther said, 'He's giving himself up.'

Penny's face froze and her heart began to pound. 'Giving himself up?' she repeated, appalled by how close she was to panicking.

Esther nodded. 'Got to strike the right deal with the District Attorney's office first. Then he's giving himself up.'

'How long will the deal take to arrange?' Penny asked, unable to accept the idea that he was about to disappear for good when she hadn't even met him. Esther shook her head and suddenly looked so unbearably sad that Penny said softly, 'You're very fond of him, aren't you?'

'Fine boy,' Esther answered staring down at her drink. 'Damn fine boy. Going to miss him if he goes.'

Penny waited for several moments to pass, then said, 'If he's intending to give himself up, there doesn't seem any harm in us meeting, does there?'

'Not definite yet,' Esther replied. 'Destined to meet, though, I know that. Billy told me.'

Penny blinked and wondered if she had heard correctly. 'Billy?' she repeated.

'Yes, Billy. I talk to him, you know. Through a medium, of course. He tells me things.'

Penny took a moment to digest this. Spiritualism wasn't normally something she put a lot of store by, but under the circumstances she wouldn't mind hearing a bit more. So, leaning her head to one side as a ploy to encourage the old lady's eyes back to hers, she said, 'What sort of things?'

Esther's mouth opened and her lips trembled for a moment before she seemed suddenly to deflate. 'Wally doesn't like me to talk about it,' she answered.

'But Wally's not here, is he?' Penny said. 'And I'd like

to know.'

Esther's face twitched, then to Penny's surprise she seemed to relax a little. 'You're a dear girl,' she said, reaching over to pat Penny's hand. 'A dear girl. All a bit complicated, though. Can't tell you anything unless given the all clear. Won't get it, though. He won't give it, I know that.'

Penny forced herself to smile. 'I already know,' she said carefully, 'about the drugs.'

Instead of the chaos she'd expected this to throw Esther into, Esther simply nodded and said, 'Thought you might. Never did any harm to anyone, though. He's a good man. Bit of a rascal,' she chuckled, 'but he has a good heart. Always good to me. Wants to meet you, but Wally says no.'

'Wally?' Penny repeated, unable to believe that Wally Delaney would have any influence over a man like Mureau.

'Too risky for him,' Esther answered.

Penny pursed her lips thoughtfully for a while, then said, 'I can understand Wally's objections to us meeting, but, tell me, do you object to it too?'

Esther's eyes fell to her glass. 'Have to do what Wally says,' she answered bleakly.

'But do you personally have any objections?' Penny pressed.

Esther shook her head. 'Busy man, but lonely since his wife left him,' she said, almost in a whisper.

Penny's eyebrows went up as she saw now what she should have seen before: that to appeal to the romantic side of Esther Delaney would be a better approach. 'How did he get my phone number?' she asked. 'Did you give it to him?'

Esther's blush was answer enough.

'Can I ask what he said about me?' she said.

'No, don't think I can repeat that. Wally wouldn't like it.'

Damn Wally to hell, Penny thought angrily. 'Would it surprise you,' she said calmly, 'if I told you that I found him very attractive?'

'No, wouldn't surprise me. He said the same about you,' Esther confided.

Penny's heart skipped. Then an extraordinarily rash idea suddenly occurred to her. If Christian Mureau could go to *vernissages*, then what was there to stop him going to launch parties? But almost as soon as she thought it she dismissed it, for getting Esther to go behind Wally's back to issue the invitation would be next to impossible. Not only that: if Christian did come, Wally would accuse Esther of having had a hand in it. But what if she, Penny, somehow managed to issue the invitation herself . . . ?

Sighing, she sat back in her chair and picked up her glass of wine. 'You know, this is very frustrating for me,' she said. 'I very much want to meet him and in your heart I think that's what you want too. But unless I can persuade you to give him a message from me I don't see how that's ever going to happen.'

Esther simply looked at her.

'All I want is for you to ask him to call me again,' Penny said gently.

To Penny's unutterable frustration the old woman shook her head. 'He won't call,' she said. 'Wally's told him not to.'

Only just managing to hang on to her temper, while having no problem imagining Wally describing her as some kind of unscrupulous hack prepared to employ every trick in the book to get her story, Penny said, 'Why is Wally so set against us meeting? I mean, what possible harm can it do Wally?'

'Have to talk to Wally about that,' Esther answered. 'He knows more than I do. Lot of people involved, though . . . all very complicated.'

'I understand that,' Penny said snappishly, 'but since

you gave Christian my number, without my permission, I think you should at least give me his in return.'

Esther's eyes rounded with anguish.

'I'm determined to get my own way over this,' Penny said tersely, not at all proud of resorting to bullying tactics, even if they were probably all that would work on Esther Delaney. 'So either you give me the number or I shall let it be known where Christian Mureau can be found.'

The old woman's papery face turned white. 'Mustn't do that,' she gasped, obviously not realizing that Penny was hardly in a position to when she didn't know whereabouts in Paris he was. 'No, no, mustn't do that.'

'Then give me his number.'

'I'll take the message,' Esther replied.

'And you won't tell Wally?'

'No, no, mustn't mention it to Wally.'

Half an hour later Esther Delaney was walking unsteadily down the drive. When she reached the gates she looked back, to see Penny closing the shutters at the front of the house. Poor dear, Esther was thinking glumly to herself, she really doesn't have any idea.

Chapter 10

'Congratulations! It's your lucky day!' David grinned, closing Penny's office door behind him and coming to sit down.

'Well, as it so happens, I could do with one of those,' Penny answered, selecting the printer's ID on her computer, ready to transmit an editorial for the third edition of *Nuance*. Then, deciding to abandon it for the moment, she turned to David and to her dismay felt her heart churn. Why was it, she asked herself irritably, that after managing to hold herself together perfectly well all day one look at him was making her want either to dissolve into tears of frustration or scream like a mad woman?

David frowned and looked at her closely. 'Is something bothering you?'

'No,' she lied. David was the last person she was about to tell that she was making a total idiot of herself over the fact that though Esther Delaney had sworn she'd passed her message on to Christian, he still hadn't called. That he was proving so elusive was simply making Penny more determined than ever to meet him, and being unable to do anything about it was driving her to such a pitch of frustration she could barely contain it.

'Pauline Fields was pretty impressed with you,' David told her, apparently trying to cheer her up.

'I liked her too,' Penny said, forcing a smile. 'She's coming to the party, by the way.'

'So she tells me.'

Penny's eyes dropped to the paperwork in front of her as once again her mind started to wander.

'Hey, remember me?' David said softly.

Penny looked up. 'I'm sorry,' she said. 'What were you saying?'

'I was asking if something was bothering you.'

'And I said no,' which was the answer she'd been giving Sammy these past two weeks. 'So, come on, then: why is it my lucky day?' she said, forcing another smile.

'I'll come on to that in a minute,' he said. 'First I want to get to the bottom of what's eating you.'

'I'm just tired,' Penny said, snappishly. Why wouldn't he leave it alone?

'OK, I can understand that. You've been burning the midnight oil for months, but I'd have expected you to be on a real high right now, ready for the launch.'

'I am,' she said tonelessly.

'Yeah, looks like it,' he said, using the same tone. 'Marielle still giving you a hard time over the Pauline Fields thing?'

'I can handle Marielle.'

'Yeah, I guess you can. But she's on your case, Pen,' he warned. 'She's after getting you out of here and I can't ignore what she's been telling me. So let's talk about it, shall we?'

Penny's face paled with fury. 'There's nothing to talk about,' she seethed. 'OK, I made a mistake in one of the editorials, but it's cleared up now. There was no danger of it going to press, so what's the problem?'

'That's what I'm trying to find out. I'm gone ten days and I come back to find you falling to pieces. It's not what I expected of you, Penny.'

'Well, I'm sorry about that,' she said sarcastically. 'But, quite frankly, I couldn't give a flying fuck what you expected of me.'

Compressing his lips, he nodded slowly. 'OK, let's

take this another way. How are your plans coming along for LA?'

'Fine,' she answered.

'Who have you been in touch with out there?'

'A few people.'

'Like who?'

'What is this!' she exploded. 'You come in here telling me this is my lucky day, then you start giving me the third degree. Well, I don't need it right now. Do you hear me? So get off my case, you and Marielle both. And while you're at it get those thugs, whoever they are, to back off too. I've had just about a guts full of it.'

David's face darkened. 'Who's hassling you?' he said.

'Some fat guy in a Mercedes. Keeps crawling along the kerb after me, telling me he wants to talk to me. He's called here I don't know how many times and he's calling me at home too.'

'Shit,' David seethed, dropping his head in his hands. Then, looking up again, 'What did you tell him?' he asked.

'To fuck off,' Penny answered, really not interested right now in what it was all about.

The ghost of a smile passed over David's lips, but his eyes remained serious. 'I don't want you talking to him, Pen, have you got that? Don't, whatever you do, get in that car . . .'

'I have no intention of getting in his car. But I would appreciate it if you didn't keep doing this disappearing act of yours and handled the situation yourself.'

Again he nodded. 'You got it,' he said. 'So is that what's been getting you down?'

'Yes,' she said, seizing the excuse.

'Then I'll see what I can do. Meantime, I'd say it's a good thing you're off to LA for a couple of weeks. You can do with the break and with any luck it'll all be sorted by the time you get back.'

'You don't sound too confident about that,' Penny

203

retorted.

'No, but it's my problem, not yours, so I'll handle it. Do you want to talk now about LA?'

Penny shook her head. The very thought of leaving France, even if only for a couple of weeks, was anathema right now, when for all she knew Christian Mureau was on the point of handing himself in and she might end up missing a golden opportunity for an interview. Oh, how you do fool yourself, she told herself scathingly. But if she didn't buck her ideas up a bit then it was on the cards that David would send her back to London anyway. 'I need to finish putting through this editorial,' she said. 'Can we talk about it later?'

'Sure.' The humour that was never far from his eyes was making a reappearance. 'Well, I've got to tell you,' he said, 'I'm crushed. I thought maybe it was because you'd been missing me that you were messing up here.'

Despite herself, Penny started to smile. It was true, actually, she *had* missed him; in fact, she'd missed him a lot more than she was prepared to admit, especially to him. 'What's the lucky day about?' she pressed.

'You're going to just love it,' he teased.

'David, get on with it, will you!'

'I'm coming to stay at the villa with you,' he grinned.

Penny's jaw dropped. 'You're *what*?' she cried.

'I'm coming to live with you. Well, for a couple of weeks. I'll be out again by the time you get back from LA.'

'I don't remember inviting you,' she said indignantly.

'You don't? Funny that, I don't remember it either. Still, I'll move my things in this afternoon if it's all right with you.'

'No, it most certainly is not all right with me,' she cried, thumping the desk. 'What's the matter with your own place?'

'I've been burgled,' he answered, not seeming in the least bit put out about it.

'When?'

'While I was away. They made a bit of a mess of the place. The decorators are starting tomorrow.'

'What did they take?'

'Usual stuff. TV, video, hi-fi and a couple of other bits and pieces. Nothing that's not replaceable.'

'I see,' she said. 'Well, why can't you go and stay in a hotel?'

"Cos I thought it would be nice if you and I got to know each other better. And now I know about Fatso in the Merc, well, all the more reason for me to come and stay, wouldn't you agree?'

'No, I wouldn't. I can look after myself, thank you very much.' Oh dear God, she was thinking, he was the last person she wanted around when there was still a chance Christian Mureau might call. If David were to answer the phone he'd probably end up blowing everything, and even if he didn't she wasn't at all proud of the way she was becoming so obsessed with Mureau, which, knowing David, he would have no problem detecting. On the other hand, though, she'd been working so hard lately and was feeling so worn down that right at that moment she felt so disgustingly feeble that all she wanted was for David to put his arms around her and tell her everything was going to turn out all right.

'Well,' David said, 'I reckon you need some looking after and, since I'm available, I'm going to see what I can do about cheering you up and convincing you that you're doing a terrific job and things wouldn't have worked without you.'

'Do you know what?' Penny said, looking up at him. 'For a total bastard, you can be a pretty nice guy sometimes. But I want you out of there by the time I get back from LA.'

David's eyebrows lifted, a gentle reminder that he was the one calling the shots around here. 'I think maybe now's the time to tell you,' he said, 'that I won't be coming alone.'

Penny's eyes dilated. 'Oh no!' she cried. 'No! No! No! No! I am not having Marielle set one foot across my threshold, so you can just—'

'Hold up, hold up,' he said, laughing. 'I'm not talking about Marielle. I'm talking about a friend who's coming over from the States. She'll be here the day after tomorrow, in time for the launch.'

'Who is she?' Penny asked stiffly.

'Like I said, just a friend.'

'What sort of friend?'

He grinned. 'That sort of friend.'

'Do you have any other kind?' Penny remarked sourly. She wasn't one bit happy about playing host to David's girlfriend but didn't see how she could object without him accusing her of being jealous or something equally as infuriating and inaccurate. Still, Pen, she told herself, look at it another way. It was going to get right up Marielle's nose, David having another woman in tow, especially for the launch, and anyone who did that was OK by Penny.

'What's her name?' Penny asked.

'Cassandra.'

Penny nodded. 'Is she the one you mentioned before, the one you're serious about?' she asked.

David's grin widened. 'Now, that would be telling,' he said, and giving her a wink he walked out of the door.

Left alone with her thoughts and her calls on hold, Penny turned back to her computer and stared at the screen. She was, she realized, almost as annoyed as Marielle was going to be that David was taking someone to the launch, though for totally different reasons. In her own case, it was simply that David was at liberty to parade his love affairs as publicly as he liked, whereas she couldn't even get to meet the man she was tying herself up in knots over, never mind be seen with him in public. Suddenly her fists clenched and she slammed

206

them down on the keyboard. Why was she doing this? What the hell was the matter with her? She knew that the chances he'd call were practically nil, so why didn't she just let up on herself? David would be there, theirs was the triumph, and if she hadn't been so damned stupid as to have had the idea of inviting Christian Mureau to the launch she might not be dreading it so much or putting herself through this ridiculous misery.

After transmitting the editorial over to the printer she turned in her chair to gaze out at the serenity of the sky. Her mind wandered back to David and the fact that she was sensing a closeness to him lately that she was finding hard to define. And this obsession she had with Christian, the bizarre influence that he, a perfect stranger, was having on her life, was so out of character for her that it felt as if it was happening to some irrational and manipulative *alter ego*. Overtiredness was of course in the most part to blame for the way she feeling, but there was something about this dazzling sunlight and torpid heat that seemed to haze the edges of reality in a way that took the sense, the responsibility even, out of everything she did.

She started as her telephone rang and, leaning across her desk to push the button on her intercom, she said to Brigitte, 'I thought my calls were on hold.'

'It's the Baron von Bergenhausen,' Brigitte answered. 'He's insisting he speak to you personally.'

'OK,' Penny sighed, 'put him on.' She flicked the switch and picked up the receiver. 'Hello. Penny Moon.'

'Hello,' said the voice at the other end. 'It's Christian Mureau.'

Penny's heart flipped as her mind suddenly spun into chaos. 'Oh, uh, yes, hello,' she said, feeling the blood rushing to her cheeks. 'How are you?'

'Pretty good,' he answered. 'How are you?'

'Oh, fine. Yes, I'm fine. Um . . .' Oh God, she couldn't think straight.

'Esther Delaney gave me your message,' he said.

'Ah, yes, I hoped she would,' Penny responded, hardly knowing what she was saying. 'It was just, well, you left a message on my answerphone saying you thought we should meet and, well, I was hoping you still felt . . . Uh, that we could do that.'

'I would like that very much,' he said. 'But I think I should warn you that I don't give interviews.'

'That's OK,' Penny answered, feeling herself start to smile. 'I'm sure we can find something else to talk about.'

He laughed. 'I'm sure we can,' he said. 'I should be back in the South of France some time in the next couple of weeks. I'll call you when I get there.'

'We're having a launch party for our magazine on the thirtieth,' Penny said hastily. 'I was wondering if you would like to come.'

There was a short silence before he answered, during which Penny's heart felt like a stone falling through a bottomless cavern. 'If I can, I will,' he said. 'Thank you.'

Chapter 11

On meeting Cassandra Mulholland, David's American girlfriend, Penny couldn't have been more shocked. The woman was, without question, absolutely stunning – blonde, brown-eyed, long-legged, big-busted; you name it, she had it – but if there were more than two brain cells struggling for life behind those enormous, vacuous eyes that seemed never to stop blinking she clearly had yet to connect with them. Never in a million years would Penny have imagined David going for a woman who unabashedly boasted the title Miss Texas nineteen eighty-something-or-other and who flashed a set of teeth so big and white and fascinatingly plentiful Penny could only wonder how she got them all in her mouth. And as for those boobs! Well, words quite simply failed Penny. She'd always thought her own were on the large side, but Cassandra Mulholland's were positively frightening.

Still, she was easy enough to have around. She spent a third of her time by the pool, another third hanging on to David's every word and, no doubt, the remaining third with her legs wrapped round his back. That was something Penny didn't dwell on, though, since her own need for sexual fulfilment was now bothering her quite seriously.

However, these last couple of weeks, since Christian had called, she had been feeling much calmer. Wasn't it one of the real perversities of human nature that once something was within your grasp you didn't want it quite so much any more? Well, perhaps that was pushing it a bit, for she still very much wanted to meet him, but thankfully she seemed to have things in a much better perspective now. And with the first edition of *Nuance* rolling off the presses she had little time to think about anything more than the launch – and of course the possibility that he might come.

It was a beautiful, late August morning when she pushed open her bedroom shutters and wandered out on to the balcony. The rain during the night had left everything looking fresh and washed and gloriously rejuvenated after the enervating humidity and blistering scorch of the sun over the past few weeks. As she gazed out at the clear, sparkling blue sea, feeling a cooling breeze whisper around her, she was thinking of the day ahead. In just over an hour the caterers would arrive, along with the people from the ad agency who had handled pretty well everything to date, and then the preparations for the party would begin. Penny had no plans to go to the office – urgent calls would be relayed to her here – and later in the day she was driving to the airport to collect Sylvia. A suite had been booked for Sylvia at the Majestic Hotel despite Penny's insistence that there was more than enough room at the villa. As it turned out, Sylvia had brought a friend with her and wanted the privacy.

'Seems like everyone's getting it except me,' Penny remarked to Sammy, as she strolled into the kitchen after depositing Sylvia at the hotel. 'Thanks,' she added as Sammy passed her an iced lemonade.

'Well, those two are certainly doing their fair share of bonking,' Sammy told her, nodding towards where David and Cassandra were sitting beside the pool, seemingly oblivious to the chaos going on around them as billboards were erected, tables were laid out and boxes of wineglasses and crockery were unpacked. 'They've only just surfaced and it's,' she glanced at her watch, 'past midday.'

'I wonder what they find to talk about,' Penny said putting her head ponderously to one side. 'I can never think of a single thing to say to the woman.'

'Perhaps that's why they're always screwing,' Sammy suggested, 'because he can't think of anything to say either.'

'He doesn't seem to be having much trouble at the moment,' Penny commented as Cassandra burst out laughing. For some absurd reason Cassandra's laughter was annoying her. 'But then, when have you ever known David lost for words?' she added, taking a sip of her drink.

They both turned as a sudden explosion erupted just outside in the summer kitchen.

'*Oh là là,*' the chef roared. '*Tu me dis que nous n'avons pas de coriandre? Tu es un imbécile! Tout le temps je dois travailler avec des imbéciles. Je t'ai dit que j'ai besoin de coriandre. Il faut que j'aie de la coriandre.*'

Reaching up to unhook a bunch of dried coriander from the overhanging herb rack, Penny wandered outside and handed it over.

'Does it bother you, her being here?' Sammy asked as Penny came back.

Penny looked at her in surprise. 'Who?'

'You know who,' Sammy said. 'Cassandra.'

'No. Why on earth should it?' Penny responded, feeling herself start to tense.

Sammy shrugged. 'Well, actually,' she said, 'what I thought was that maybe he'd brought her here on purpose, to make you jealous. And I was wondering if it was working.'

Penny was half laughing, half annoyed, as she said, 'Sammy, I thought we dealt with that before. David doesn't give a damn what I think, or what anyone else thinks, for that matter. And as far as I'm concerned he can screw whoever he likes – it's nothing to me.'

Sammy's eyes narrowed. 'So you keep saying,' she said. 'But frankly, Pen, I'm not convinced.'

'Well, I'm sorry about that,' Penny replied smoothly, 'but I'm not about to start delving into the way I feel about David for your benefit – or anyone else's come to that. But I will tell you this: as far as David is concerned' – to her surprise she could hear a note of anger creeping into her voice and seemed unable to control it – 'I am nothing more than the editor of *Nuance* and the person he can poke fun at whenever the mood takes him. Because that's all I am to David, a joke. Now, go and answer that phone.'

Before Sammy could object, Penny had walked out to the summer kitchen. It was bedlam. Cooks were whizzing about all over the place, waiters and waitresses were zooming back and forth between the neat, round tables set out on the lawns, and the organizers were racing about with clipboards under their arms yelling for everything from an electrician to a musician. She was on the point of asking if there was anything she could do, when Sammy called out that Esther Delaney was on the line.

Penny's heart skipped a beat as she turned back into the house. She hoped to God that this wasn't going to be a message from Christian to say he couldn't make it; that would put a damper on the whole day as far as she was concerned. 'Hi,' she said into the receiver. 'How are you, Esther?'

'Oh, I'm very well, thank you,' Esther answered, in her familiar clipped tones. 'Just calling to say that I'll be a teensy bit late this evening. Wally will be there early, though.'

'That's OK. Thanks for letting me know,' Penny replied.

There was a pause, then Esther said, 'Christian told me you invited him.'

'Do you know if he's coming?' Penny asked, her heart pausing for the answer.

'He might. Yes. Yes, he might,' Esther replied.

Penny's spirits soared. 'Good. And if you see him before then, please tell him I'm looking forward to meeting him.'

'Righto,' Esther trilled. 'Toodle-oo for now, then. *A ce soir*, as they say around here.'

When Esther rang off, Penny stood holding the receiver for a moment, feeling faintly odd. It was nerves, of course, but she mustn't get her hopes too high. Esther had only said *might . . .*

'Pen? Are you all right?'

Penny swung round, to see David standing in the doorway. 'Yes, yes, I'm fine,' she said, putting the phone back on the hook. 'Just deep in thought.'

'Problems?' he asked.

'No, no, not at all. Quite the reverse, in fact.' She smiled. 'Things seem to be going pretty well out there, don't they?' Why was he looking at her like that? Anyone would think she'd just grown another head. 'Can I get you something?' she offered.

'No,' he answered. 'I've just come in to get changed. I'm popping down to Cannes for a couple of hours.'

'OK,' she said. 'Are you taking Cassandra?'

His eyes started to dance. 'To be honest, I could do with a bit of a break,' he said. 'You don't mind if I leave her here, do you?'

Penny shrugged. 'It's all the same to me.' She started to walk away, then turned back. 'Incidentally, if you're seeing Sylvia while you're in Cannes will you tell her the limousine's booked to pick her up at seven. If you're not seeing her, I'll call the hotel myself.'

'I'll get the message to her,' he said. 'By the way, did anyone think to turn off the sprinkler system for tonight?'

'Oh hell, no!' Penny cried, starting for the door.

'Before you go, Pen . . .' David said. 'About tonight. I'd like us to present a united front. No bitching, no sarcasm, no anything that might give Sylvia – or anyone else, come to that – the idea we don't get along. Does that give you a problem?'

'No,' Penny answered. 'I'm all for it, in fact. And who says we don't get along?'

He laughed. 'You know what I mean. Anyway, got to run. Enjoy Cassandra.'

'Probably not as much as you do,' she responded airily and swept out into the garden.

By eight o'clock almost everyone had arrived. Mercedes, Jaguars, BMWs, Porsches, a couple of limousines and umpteen lesser cars were crammed on to the tarmac in front of and behind the house and spilling on to the far lawns, while car jockeys raced up and down the drive, organizing the chaos. The waiters and waitresses were now all decked out in their neat black uniforms, the five-piece band were playing gentle jazz sounds on their platform by the pool and giant billboards of the *Nuance* front cover glistened in the soft, pastel lights.

The turnout was stupendous. Everyone had come, from the part-time odd-job boy at the office to Princess Stephanie herself. David was looking after the princess, while Sylvia chatted away with the mayor of Nice as though she'd known him for years. Probably she had, Penny reflected, hardly able to contain the pleasure that was swelling inside her. Though only a third of the magazine was going to be in French at any one time, at a conservative estimate she'd guess that at least fifty per cent of those present were French. And they all looked so chic! That wasn't to criticize the Scandinavians, the Dutch, the Germans, the English, the Italians or any other of the many nationalities there, it was simply that the French really had it. Though not even they could out-shine the gentle beauty that smiled down at them from the posters.

'It's you,' Penny said softly to Pauline Fields, who was standing beside her on the steps of the terrace surveying the gathering. 'You, who's made this what it is tonight.'

Pauline smiled. 'It was my pleasure,' she said. 'But don't do yourself out of the credit. You've worked hard to get to this point – damned hard, from what I hear – and you deserve the recognition that this,' she started to laugh, '*exalted* company has bestowed upon you.'

'We've had hundreds of requests from all over the world to run your interview,' Penny told her.

'So David tells me.'

They stood quietly for a moment watching the milling crowd and listening to the soporific hum of conversation and clink of glasses. A pale haze was already beginning to gather overhead as thin coils of smoke from mosquito spirals, candles and cigars wafted gently upwards.

'Tell me,' Pauline said, leaning in a little closer to Penny as the band struck up a livelier beat, 'who is that over there – the woman who keeps glaring in your direction?'

Penny followed the direction of Pauline's eyes and started to laugh. 'That,' she said, 'is my deputy, Marielle Descourts. She wanted to do the interview with you and hasn't quite forgiven me yet for not allowing it. Well, actually, it was David who made the decision, which is very likely the other reason she's looking so rattled, because he's got his girlfriend here from the States.'

'Oh, I see,' Pauline said. 'And which one is David's girlfriend?'

Penny scanned the crowd. 'I don't know where she is at the moment, but just look out for a mountainous bust. You won't be able to miss it.'

Pauline laughed. 'Does he ever see anything of his wife these days?' she asked.

Penny shook her head. 'I don't know. I don't think so,

215

but he's never discussed her with me. Why? Do you know her?'

'Not really. I just met her a couple of times.'

'What's she like?'

'Very beautiful and, from what I could tell, totally besotted with David. I've often wondered what went wrong there. But hey, come on, here I am hogging you all to myself and you're the hostess. Go mingle some more and have yourself a good time. I'm going to go rescue Sylvia from the old boy over there; she looks like she needs it. But before you go, tell me, is it true she brought a paramour with her?'

Penny grinned.

'So where is he?' Pauline laughed.

'Back at the hotel, I imagine. He's young enough to be her grandson, but you didn't hear it from me.'

'My lips are sealed,' Pauline promised and, patting Penny on the arm, she floated off in a cloud of perfumed chiffon to join Sylvia.

As the evening wore on, so Marielle's sour mood was evaporating. She'd had plenty to drink before coming and now, as she flitted from guest to guest, revelling in the admiring glances her bare midriff and long legs were attracting, she could feel the delicious tingle of lust she always felt when shedding what few inhibitions she had.

However, before she decided on her particular prey for the evening there was someone she was keen to meet, whom she'd just spotted over by the pergola. She'd never met him before, but unless she was greatly mistaken the bellicose-looking throwback to the days of the British Empire with the cigar and ginger moustache was Wally Delaney, who was, amongst other things, Penny's next-door neighbour. Marielle wasn't sure if he'd noticed her yet; probably not, since he'd been pretty intent on chatting up the waitresses or rattling on to other businessmen about whatever business he was in. But he was standing alone now and as Marielle moved

216

towards him she watched his eyes bulge at the blatant carnality gleaming in hers. She'd tease him along a while, brush up against him a couple of times, watch his face twitch and let him imagine all the things she might be prepared to do for him in return for the one little favour he could do for her . . .

As Penny moved through the crowd, picking up on snatches of conversation here, stopping to join in others there, she could feel the joy and excitement of the evening going straight to her head. So far she'd had very little to drink, but she was high on hope, high on the promise of what the evening might bring, and, she had to confess, was almost totally overwhelmed by the fact that as from tomorrow *Nuance* would be on the newsstands. And not even the knowledge that David's money and influence had played the biggest part in getting it there detracted from the pleasure of knowing that she too had played a key role.

'Am I allowed to tell you you're looking pretty terrific this evening?' David smiled down at her as she joined him and Sylvia. The evening was already half over and this was the first time they'd run into each other.

'You are,' Penny replied, her bright blue eyes sparkling. She guessed the compliment was probably more for Sylvia's benefit than hers – united front and all that – but she didn't mind hearing it anyway. Besides, she was really quite pleased with the way she looked – ecstatic, more like, since she'd never have believed she could squeeze herself into this dress, never mind move in it. As it turned out, it had been more of a push than a squeeze, and since blue was such a good colour on her she thought David was probably right, she did look terrific.

'You're looking pretty dapper yourself, as a matter of fact,' she said, winking at Sylvia. 'Men always look so good in tuxedos. You made quite an impression on the princess, from what I could see.'

'It's my natural charm and good looks,' David shrugged. 'They get 'em every time.'

Penny's eyes moved back to Sylvia. 'Don't you just love him?' she said sweetly.

'I adore him,' Sylvia laughed. 'I adore you both. You've done a fantastic job here, better than I'd ever imagined.'

'Mainly thanks to David,' Penny said.

'Not true,' he objected.

Penny glared a warning at him, knowing he was about to give her some honey-coated compliment that would make her want to throw up.

'It's been a team effort,' he grinned, evidently receiving the message.

'Do you mind if Penny and I have a little chat on our own?' Sylvia said.

'Carry on,' David answered. 'But beware, anything she tells you about me is only going to be half the truth. The other half is she's as crazy about me as I am about her.'

'Get lost, will you,' Penny muttered; then, turning a smile back to Sylvia, she suggested they stroll over to the other end of the pool, where it was relatively quiet.

'It seems to be turning out well for you down here,' Sylvia remarked, raising her voice as they passed in front of the band, who were becoming decidedly more lively as the evening wore on. 'Better than you'd hoped, I think?'

'Yes, I think you could say that,' Penny confirmed, smiling at a group of guests.

Sylvia waited until there was no longer any need to shout. 'So you're glad you came?' she said.

'Very.'

'And you want to stay?'

'Yes, I want to stay.'

'Good,' Sylvia said, smiling. 'That was what I hoped you'd say. Have you made many friends?'

'There hasn't been a lot of time,' Penny grimaced as

218

they parted a moment to walk either side of a palm. 'But yes, I've made a few.'

Sylvia nodded and treated Penny to one of her famous silences, which Penny knew she was supposed to fill but didn't.

'Is there anything you would like to discuss with me?' Sylvia offered.

Penny thought for a moment. 'No,' she said. 'No, I don't think so. Everything's running pretty smoothly. Hectically, actually, but it's all under control.'

'And your relationship with David is good?' Sylvia said, stopping and turning to face her.

'Very good. We get along like a cat and dog on fire.' She plastered an instant smile to her face. 'What I mean, of course, is we get along just fine.'

'He's very complimentary about you. In fact, so much so that I was wondering if maybe something wasn't developing between you. Something of a ... more personal nature?'

What was going on here? Penny was thinking to herself. Why was everyone so intent on telling her that she and David were becoming an item? In fact, it was beginning to feel like there was some kind of conspiracy to push them together. 'No,' she said, 'there is nothing of any nature at all between David and me, other than professional.'

Sylvia's face lost its intensity. 'Well, that's a relief,' she smiled.

Penny blinked, not sure whether she liked that response. 'A relief?' she repeated.

Sylvia thought for a moment. 'Well, maybe relief's not quite the right word,' she confessed.

Penny was tempted to invite her to try another, but refrained. She'd just seen Esther Delaney beetling up the drive in a flurry of fringes and feathers and wanted to get away as quickly as she could.

'What I suppose I was trying to say,' Sylvia went on,

'is that I don't want you to end up being hurt, and I'm afraid my godson has something of a reputation as a heartbreaker.'

'Don't worry, his secret's safe with me,' Penny whispered.

Sylvia gave a splutter of laughter.

'So has that got everything cleared up for you?' Penny said cheerfully. 'I'm not in love with David and neither am I ever likely to be in love with David.'

'I'm glad to hear it,' Sylvia smiled, 'because I would hate you to come back to London for the wrong reasons. It suits you down here, you're looking radiant, and one issue does not a magazine make. Now, I can see that you're dying to go and talk to someone, so off you go. I'll catch up with you again before I leave.'

Penny was about to depart, when curiosity got the better of her and she turned back. 'Will you answer me something, Sylvia?' she said. 'Why am I getting the impression that everyone, David included, seems to think I'm falling for him, when as far as I'm aware I've never done a single thing to make anyone think that?'

Sylvia chuckled. 'My dear, you told me yourself on the way in from the airport that you've been suffering from sleepless nights, bad moods, an inability to concentrate, loss of appetite . . . Which, to me, all sound like symptoms of unrequited love. And David, well, I'd say he was the obvious choice, wouldn't you?'

'No, actually, I wouldn't,' Penny responded. 'And what they are symptoms of is overwork. However, just to set your mind completely at rest, I will tell you that there is someone, but it certainly isn't David.'

Sylvia's eyes remained on hers, glimmering with affection. 'I wonder,' she said.

'Then don't, because it's not.' Penny smiled. 'And since Monsieur Villers appears to be on his way to join us, I'll leave you to grill him on how he feels about me.'

Sylvia was still laughing softly to herself as David

handed her a fresh glass of champagne. 'I am really very fond of that girl,' she told him. 'Very fond indeed.'

'You and me both,' he said, turning to watch Penny disappear into the crowd.

Sylvia's eyebrows lifted as she cast him a sidelong glance.

He laughed. 'Don't worry, she's safe.'

'Were you anyone else, David, I'd believe you.'

'Were I anyone else,' he replied, smiling, 'there wouldn't be a problem.'

'How true that is,' she sighed. 'Does she have any idea yet of the real reason for this magazine?'

'She doesn't seem to have. Sure, she's asked a few questions here and there when things haven't seemed quite right, but on the whole she seems satisfied with the answers I give.'

'Which are?'

'Vague. But, like I told you, she's been preoccupied with something lately. Did you manage to get to the bottom of it?'

'Not really. She says there is someone, but she didn't say who. However, she was quite insistent it wasn't you.'

'That must have pleased you,' he remarked.

'I won't deny it,' she responded. 'Did you seriously think it might be you, or were you just teasing her?'

'A bit of both,' he confessed. 'So, now we've got that cleared up, how about we go have ourselves a good time?' he grinned, taking her by the arm.

'We still have a lot to discuss, David,' she said, gently removing her arm.

'But not here,' he said firmly.

'Maybe not here. But I'm leaving tomorrow afternoon. I'd like you to come to my hotel in the morning.'

'I'll be there,' he told her. 'But no more about Penny, OK?'

'Maybe not about her, but definitely about the silly creature with the dreadful bosoms you've got staying

221

here. Who on earth is she and what is she doing here?'

'Cassandra?' he laughed. 'Cassandra is here for several reasons, not least of which was to bring me a message from my darling wife.'

'And what does Gabriella have to say?'

'Why don't we save that for the morning?' he suggested. 'I'm in the mood for a-moving and a-grooving right now,' and, clasping her much more firmly by the arm, he steered her towards the patio area that had been cleared for dancing.

As Sylvia followed him through the group of youngsters who were throwing themselves about wildly to the beat she caught a glimpse of Penny, who was talking to a rather awful-looking man who bore the most unfortunate resemblance to a slimline hippopotamus. Probably one of the local traders, Sylvia decided, unable to imagine why Penny had seemed in such a hurry to go and talk to him. It didn't occur to her that it might be the man Penny was getting involved with until she caught David glowering in their direction. Well, there was no accounting for taste, Sylvia thought, though some people really did push the limits. However, Penny's new beau was Penny's business and Sylvia was the last person to interfere. What she was unsure of, though, was whether she could say the same for David. It was Sylvia's guess that he hadn't been in the least bit prepared to discover that Penny was involved with someone and, now that he had, he wasn't liking it one bit. Yet surely David wouldn't see that great oaf as real competition? However, whether he did or he didn't was irrelevant, for romantic entanglements of any substance at this time in his life were very definitely a taboo for David and well he knew it. He might not like it, but he would just have to live with it, because if he didn't that wife of his was going to make him a whole lot sorrier than any man deserved to be.

Around eleven o'clock the older people and those who

had long journeys home started to say their goodbyes. Everyone had had a wonderful time, wouldn't have missed it for the world, and each, to a man and woman, wished Penny great success. Penny smiled politely, made all the right noises and waved them off. She wished they would *all* go, that they would just get out of here and leave her alone. She couldn't stand this seesaw of emotions, couldn't bear this waiting game any longer. Esther had dropped in, told Wally that she'd be back in an hour and had now been gone for over two. And now the only thing keeping Penny from screaming with frustration or doing the unthinkable and going in search of the old woman, was the faint hope that Esther would reappear when most had gone, when it would be safer for Christian to come.

Marielle, Penny could see, was in her element over there, sucking up to the stars, while Sammy and her friends were getting louder and drunker by the minute. David, who was not a bad dancer, had hardly left the floor this past hour and he, too, appeared to have had more than his fair share of champagne. How easy he always seemed to find it to enjoy himself, to let himself go and pull everyone else into that heady aura of recklessness that surrounded him. And if Marielle had been put out about Cassandra, she certainly didn't appear to be any longer, for she'd just shimmied her way on to the dance floor and was shaking herself at David so exaggeratedly he was in danger of having his brains bashed in by her boobs. What was it about him that made women throw their tits at him? Couldn't they see what idiots they were making of themselves? Oh God, she seethed inwardly as David, Cassandra, Marielle, Smithy and heaven only knew who else started stripping off ready to jump in the pool.

What's the matter with you, Penny Moon? she asked herself sharply. They're just having a good time. In fact, everyone was except her and she only had herself to blame.

But the instant she saw Esther coming up the drive her stony face was transformed into one of welcome. She all but ran across the lawn to greet the old lady, who, to Penny's dismay as she drew closer, looked more agitated than she had ever seen her.

'What's the matter?' Penny asked, fighting to control her irritation.

'No, no! Everything's under control,' Esther assured her, standing on tiptoe to peer past her. 'Oh, gosh, here comes Wally.'

Penny turned to watch him barrelling in their direction, willing him to drop dead on the spot.

'I really must talk to him in private a minute, dear,' Esther said. 'Do you mind?'

'Of course not,' Penny assured her, minding terribly. She desperately wanted to know what was going on, for it was evident something was, but she could hardly come right out and ask, especially when Wally looked as though he'd just swallowed a porcupine. Boy, was he angry! So angry, in fact, that Penny was somewhat reluctant to leave Esther alone with him.

'It's all right, dear,' Esther whispered, seeming to sense her dilemma. 'I'll come and find you as soon as I've spoken to him.'

It was some ten minutes later that Esther found Penny chatting with Sammy and Pauline Fields by the summer kitchen. Tapping Penny's elbow, she asked if she could have a quiet word.

'Of course,' Penny said and, moving a few paces away, she added, 'What on earth is going on?'

'I'm afraid Christian's not coming,' Esther told her. 'Says he's frightfully sorry, but something came up at the last minute, you see. Such a busy man, you understand.'

Despite the crushing disappointment Penny could sense there was more to it. 'I want the truth, Esther,' she said, more sharply than she'd intended. 'Whatever it is, I want to hear it.'

'Oh dear,' Esther replied, looking troubled. Then, glancing around to make sure no one was in earshot she said, 'Wally found out, I'm afraid . . . I'm in awfully hot water. Everyone's angry with me and I really didn't mean any harm. But you see . . .' She stopped as David went past them into the house, Cassandra and the others in noisy pursuit. Esther's eyes followed him; then, turning back to Penny, she said, 'He's your boss, isn't he? Very good-looking young man . . .'

'Yes, yes, I know,' Penny said impatiently. 'But go on. You were saying that everyone's angry with you . . .'

Esther frowned, obviously having lost her thread. 'Oh, yes, yes,' she said. 'Oh my, what a day it's been. He was going to come, right up until five o'clock he was going to come, but then he told Wally and Wally said not to trust you, which I think is frightfully unjust of him, but then the other one turned up and the next thing I knew Christian had booked himself on the next plane to Paris.'

'Which other one?' Penny asked, frowning.

'Our other employer,' Esther answered. 'Wally had told him that Christian was intending to come here and they had an awful fight about it. It's because you're a journalist, you see, dear. And Christian couldn't go against him—'

'Who is he? This other employer of yours?' Penny interrupted. 'You've never mentioned him before.'

'He . . . Oh dear . . . I'm afraid I don't know his name. We don't see him very often. But listen, dear, I have a message for you from Christian. He said to tell you that this evening wouldn't have worked out, but that he will call you again soon and . . .'

An explosion of laughter from the door drowned her voice and David came out holding up some sort of nobbly object, challenging Penny to tell him what it was.

Penny looked at it, looked at David, looked at all the stupid, sniggering faces around him, and suddenly she

225

couldn't take any more. 'Why are you doing this?' she yelled at him. 'Why can't you just leave me alone! I'm sick to death of you poking fun at me, making me look small, giving everyone else a laugh at my expense. I've got feelings, David! I know that might come as a surprise to you, but I have. And I just can't take any more.'

David's face had paled. 'Hey, hey,' he said. 'What is all this? It was just a joke, Pen . . .'

'That's it, a joke. That's what I am to you, isn't it, one great, big, fat joke? Hah, hah, everyone, Penny the Joke. Let's all go have a laugh at Penny, why not? Well, I'm not putting up with it any more. Let's present a united front, you said, let's pretend we can stand the sight of each other. I did my bit, David . . .'

'Penny, for God's sake,' he cried, 'I don't even know what the damned thing is. Someone tell me, for Christ's sake! What the hell is this thing?'

'It's Penny's anti-cellulite glove,' Marielle gladly informed everyone. Not *an* anti-cellulite glove, but *Penny's* anti-cellulite glove.

'Oh Christ,' David groaned. 'Look, Pen, I'm sorry. I didn't realize. I swear I wouldn't have done it . . . I just picked it up in the bathroom . . .'

'What the hell were you doing in my bathroom?' she yelled. 'You had no right to be in there.'

'There was someone in mine,' he shouted back.

'Oh God, I can't stand this,' Penny cried. 'I hate you, David Villers. I can't stand you. No, don't,' she said, shrugging Sammy and Pauline off as they attempted to put their arms around her. 'He's had it coming and now he's going to get it. You've made a fool out of me once too often, David, but this is the last time.' Dimly she was aware of him staring oddly at Esther Delaney, as if trying to locate the real reason for the outburst, but she was too blinded by rage now to register anything beyond the way he was still standing there holding that glove. 'If you don't move out tomorrow,' she seethed, 'then I will.

I don't want to be under the same roof as you, I don't want you anywhere near me. I've had you up to here, David.'

'Penny,' he said helplessly. 'I've never seen one of these things before. If I had . . .'

'No, well, you wouldn't have, would you, because you don't go out with fat women, do you? Wrestling with sex-starved Sumos isn't your scene.'

'Penny, just calm down,' he said. 'You're getting this way out of proportion.'

'But everything to do with me is out of proportion, David,' she screamed. 'Or hadn't you noticed?'

'No, as a matter of fact—'

'Like hell you hadn't,' she raged, cutting him off. 'Well, I might be a great big fat waste of time to you, but—'

'OK, time out!' he barked, his eyes flashing with temper. 'I want to talk to you now, in private.'

'Well, I don't want to talk to you,' she yelled. 'I just want you to get out of my life and go somewhere where I'll never have to see you again,' and unable to disguise the fact that she had started to cry, she pushed past him, ran through the house and up the stairs to her bedroom.

A few minutes later there was a tap on the door.

'Go away!' she shouted.

'It's me,' Sammy said, putting her head in.

Penny looked at her in the mirror; then, swivelling round on the dressing-table stool, she dabbed at her eyes with a tissue and held out a hand. 'I'm sorry,' she said, as Sammy came to kneel in front of her. 'I made a right fool of myself, didn't I?'

'Not really,' Sammy comforted her.

'You're just trying to be nice,' Penny smiled through her tears. 'Where's David?'

'Seeing everyone off.'

'Is he mad?'

'Hard to tell. What made you go at him like that? It left

us all speechless.'

For a moment Penny was tempted to tell her about Christian Mureau, but in truth she was so ashamed of the effect he was having on her she didn't want anyone, not even Sammy, to know. 'I don't know,' she sighed, wiping the back of her hand over her cheeks. 'Maybe I've just had too much to drink.' Groaning, she put her head in her hands. 'Of all the things for him to have picked up ...'

'But it wasn't so bad. Most women have got one.'

'Obviously not the women he knows.'

Sammy looked away for a moment, wanting to say a lot of things but understanding that perhaps the moment wasn't right. 'He wants to talk to you,' she said, bringing her eyes back.

Penny shook her head. 'No. I know I owe him an apology, but I can't face doing it tonight. I'm still too mad at him and—' She broke off with a humourless laugh. 'What am I talking about, he probably wants to tell me it's all over for me down here. Well, I can't face that either right now. Tomorrow will be soon enough.'

'It's all right, old thing,' Wally was saying, 'you can come out now. I'm not angry any more.'

'I didn't volunteer anything, honestly I didn't,' Esther wailed, her face pressed up against the bathroom door. 'Only her phone number. But he made me tell him, Wally.'

'I know he did,' Wally replied. 'But listen to me old thing. The girl who works with Penny, she was asking me about Christian tonight. So do you understand now, dear, that Penny is just after a story? They all are. And we can't let that happen now, can we?'

'No. Oh no,' Esther agreed.

'So what we're going to do in the morning, old thing, is start looking for a new house, the way we've been told to. And you must stop seeing Penny Moon now, do you understand? I know you're fond of her, but we have to think about ourselves, Esther. We need this job, remember? And we only have the job as long as Christian is around.'

'But if he's prepared to take the risk to meet her ...' Esther pointed out.

'Then it is up to us to save him from himself.'

Esther was about to say more, but she stopped herself, knowing that it would only make Wally angry again. But Christian would meet Penny Moon, she knew that, and when he did they were going to fall very deeply in love. Esther knew because Billy had told her.

It had been a long, stiflingly hot day, throughout which Penny had suffered in silence as Marielle strutted triumphantly around the office, clearly as certain as Penny was that last night Penny had gone too far.

David had already left the house when Penny had got up that morning. She'd known he was going to see Sylvia and that was what had turned the morning, the entire day, in fact, into such agony. Was he telling Sylvia that he didn't want her here any more? Was he saying that he couldn't, *wouldn't*, put up with her hysteria any longer? Sylvia must have heard the outburst, so had she reached the same conclusions: Penny Moon was good at her job, but she couldn't control her emotions? It was true, she couldn't, for throughout the unendurable wait to find out what her fate was to be, still all Penny could think about was Christian. She was at the point now where she'd do anything, anything at all, just to stay in France. It was irrational, it was insane, but as each obstacle presented itself all Penny could feel was an even deeper desperation and determination to meet him – before it was too late.

By the time she got home from the office she was convinced the only thing to do was to start packing. She hadn't heard from David all day, but his silence was enough to confirm her worst fears. She'd been surprised to find him there when she'd pulled up in her car. Surprised *and* embarrassed. Sammy had disappeared, so too had Cassandra, and the caterers who had come back to clear up had long since gone. There was only Penny and David and the two chairs beside the pool on which they now sat, half facing each other, half facing the black expanse of night beyond the circle of light surrounding them.

They'd been sitting there for a long time now, watching the sun go down and the moon rise, listening to the distant sound of yachts signalling to each other, the sibilance of night insects and the telephone ringing inside the house that went unanswered.

They'd talked about so many things that Penny could hardly remember them all. But some she could. He'd told her about his childhood, about his time in America and the death of his father, six years ago, that had been so devastating it had changed his life completely. He'd talked a little about his marriage, but mainly about his sons and how much he missed them. And somehow he'd made her laugh, had laughed himself, when she didn't think either of them were capable. Not a word had been mentioned about what had happened the night before.

'Are you cold?' he asked, looking over at her as she shivered.

'No,' she answered.

It was the first time either of them had spoken for a while and knowing that they couldn't put it off for ever Penny decided that now was as good a time as any to try bringing things to a head. 'I suppose,' she said, 'that I'm afraid.'

'Afraid? What of?'

'You and what you're going to say about the way I spoke to you in front of all those people last night.'

He bowed his head, looking down at his near-empty glass. 'Last night was my fault,' he said. 'I'd had too much to drink. I wasn't thinking about what I was doing.' He turned to look at her. 'I didn't mean to hurt you like that, Pen,' he said softly. 'In fact, it was the last thing I wanted.'

'I overreacted,' she said, feeling herself respond to the tone of his voice. 'Things have been getting on top of me a bit lately and I suspect I'd probably drunk too much too.'

'Sure,' he said.

It was a long time before he spoke again, so long that Penny turned to look at him. In the moonlight he looked ... But, no, she didn't want to think about the way he looked, and knowing that he was aware she was watching him she turned away.

'So where do we go from here?' he said, gazing out at the stars.

'I don't know,' she answered. 'All I know is that I want to stay, that I want to see things through, but ...'

'But what?' he said.

She shrugged. 'I don't know.'

Their whole conversation had been fractured by pauses, gentle silences in which they had absorbed the lazy intimacy of the night, easy in each other's company yet somehow moved by it too.

At last he stood up, walked to the edge of the pool, then turned back to look at her. 'Last night was a mistake on my part in a lot of ways,' he said. 'More ways than you know.'

'Then why don't you tell me?'

'Well,' he said, dropping his head, 'to begin with I thought ...' He rolled his eyes and looked off across the garden. 'Well, I guess I thought something was happening between us.'

As his eyes came back to hers Penny felt as though her insides were being crushed. Everything about him seemed suddenly so powerful. 'You could have fooled me,' she said in a half-hearted attempt to lighten things.

He continued to look at her; then, lowering his eyes to his glass, he said, 'Yeah, OK, I was wrong. I know that now, but last night it got to me. I drank too much, I went too far . . .'

'Why don't we just put it behind us?' she said.

His eyes came back to hers then slowly he started to nod. 'Yeah, why don't we do that?' and raising his glass he drained the rest of his wine. 'Do you want to talk about Los Angeles?' he said. 'You're leaving in a few days.'

Penny felt her heart sink. What she wouldn't give to be able to cancel this trip. 'OK,' she said. 'Let's talk about Los Angeles.'

'I'm going to get more wine,' he said. 'Do you want some?'

She nodded. They'd already drunk a bottle between them, but what did it matter?

When he was gone she found herself going back over all the things he'd told her that night, which was why, when he sat down again, she said, 'Why don't you come to the States with me?'

He laughed, but there wasn't much humour. 'I don't think so,' he said.

'But why? You want to see your children and you never know, maybe you can get things back together with your wife.'

He was shaking his head. 'It's too late for that,' he said. 'Besides, they're not in LA.'

'Then where are they?'

'Florida. Staying with my mother.'

'*Your* mother?'

'Yep, my mother,' he said flatly. 'It's a story you don't want to hear, so let's just leave it at that.'

Not sure what she wanted to say next, Penny pulled herself up from the chair and went to sit at the edge of the pool, dangling her feet in the water. When at last she turned round, drawing her knees up in her arms, she found him watching her.

He smiled. 'You've got the wrong idea about yourself, do you know that?' he said.

She could only just see him in the darkness, yet somehow it was as though she could feel him. 'What do you mean?' she whispered.

'You've got no confidence in yourself which is crazy when there's more to you than most women I've met.'

Penny laughed self-consciously. 'You didn't say that the first time we met,' she told him. 'Or maybe, in a roundabout way, you did.'

He frowned. 'Why, what did I say?'

Penny was on the point of reminding him, then thought better of it. What did it matter now? Why rake it up when she hadn't even really known him then? 'It's not important,' she said. 'I've just got a hang-up about my weight and—'

'What did I say?' he repeated.

'I told you, it's not important. Let's talk about my trip to LA, shall we? You obviously know hundreds of people there, so who are you going to put me in touch with?'

'Why have you got a hang-up about your weight?'

'Oh, for heaven's sake, David,' she laughed. 'Let's not fool ourselves here, eh?'

His face was deadly serious and as he leaned forward, resting his elbows on his knees and looking deep into her eyes Penny felt an incredible warmth moving through her as her heart started to quicken.

'Why don't you get undressed and let me look at you?' he said softly.

The flare of lust was so intense it took her breath away and the image of his naked body that had never quite left her was suddenly so razor-sharp in her mind it was as though the very hardness of him was even now beneath her fingertips. And, were it not for Sammy driving in through the gates at that moment, she knew that she would have done as he asked, for her need to be held, to feel a man in her arms and the power of a body like his pressing against her, was wholly overwhelming.

But as the headlights of Sammy's car bounced over the potholes in the drive she said, 'You're tempting, David, but I don't think either of us need another notch on the bedpost, do we?'

Chapter 13

Robert Stirling was in his usual position on the sun deck of the motor yacht, a pair of binoculars pressed to his eyes. The twilight bathers on the Cannes beaches were drawn so close by the lenses he could almost see the blackheads in teenage boys' ears.

As he tilted his head back, the creamy-white hotels and striped awnings of the apartment blocks along the Croisette rushed past in a blur until he came to focus on the wide, glassed-in balcony of David Villers's apartment.

'Fuck!' he spat as Villers, with his own set of binoculars, gave him a wave. 'Bastard,' he grunted, dropping the binoculars into his lap.

He was on the point of getting up and going into the cabin, when a messenger pulled up on his scooter, calling out that he had a package for Monsieur Stirling.

Stirling, whose corpulent frame was no hindrance unless he wanted it to be, swung himself out of the chair and on to the *passerelle*. Taking the package, he signed the messenger's docket and went back on board and into the cabin.

'D'you tell Villers where to find this boat?' he growled at Marielle, who was preparing supper.

'Of course not,' she answered, glancing over at him. 'What's that?'

'Mind your own business,' he told her, stopping a

moment to look at her, bare-assed in a bib-apron. Then, sliding the documents out of their wrapping, he went to sit at the table, where he began leafing hungrily through the reams of typewritten pages. At first glance there was no sign of what he was looking for, but they'd talked to Villers's wife, so it had to be there somewhere. He'd go through it later with a fine-tooth comb, looking for just one word, one nuance, one fucking anything, that would give him what he needed. But he'd do it tomorrow, when Marielle was out of the way and a couple of the boys were on board to lend a hand. He didn't mind waiting, especially not when he was in the mood for a few games right now. Shit, were things going well for him! Yeah, things sure were looking up.

'Get yourself over here,' he barked at Marielle.

Marielle looked back over her shoulder, then putting down the whisk she wiped her fingers on her apron and padded across the cabin.

'I need some help with this,' he said, putting his left hand on the documents while brandishing the index finger of his right hand. *Let's see how long it takes her to work this one out*, he was grinning to himself.

Marielle's tongue pushed out the side of her cheek as, frowning, she looked at the finger. To give her a clue he waggled it back and forth a couple of times, crooking it as though beckoning to her.

As enlightenment dawned, Marielle's eyes clouded and a small, catlike smile curled her sumptuous lips. Then, hooking up her apron, she parted the lips of her vagina and bared herself to him.

Stirling was impressed, she caught on quick, and wetting his finger in her sex he began to employ a laborious method of leafing through the document. Each time his finger dried he went back for more, digging it in slowly, sliding it back and forth a couple of times, then peeled away a few more pages. This was a good game, he was thinking, he kind of liked it. Being treated like a whore was obviously what Marielle got off on and he had no problem with that. 'Course she probably thought she was gonna get what she wanted out of him at the end of it, but she'd learn soon enough that she'd got the wrong guy here 'cos his head sure as hell didn't take no orders from his dick. He chuckled inwardly. Life felt real good tonight. Villers was in his sights, was gonna get what he had coming – and Stirling was pretty damn certain it wasn't gonna be long in the coming now.

'How long's Penny the Moon gonna be away?' he asked, not bothering to raise his eyes from the page to look at Marielle as he prodded around a bit.

'Another week,' she answered huskily. 'Why?'

'Just wondered. Must be a good time for you, having her out the way a while.'

'She's going to be gone a lot longer than she thinks,' Marielle answered, with a slight catch in her voice as he tapped his fingers against hers, indicating she should open herself wider.

This time he looked at her. 'What's that mean?' he said. 'You told me she was gonna be gone two weeks, three at the outside.'

'She is,' Marielle confirmed, wishing he'd stop looking at her and put his finger back where it belonged.

'Three weeks is up Friday,' he said. 'You telling me she's not coming?'

'She's coming,' Marielle said. 'But she won't be staying long.'

'Why? Where's she going?'

'I don't know,' Marielle answered, twitching her hips to signal she wanted more.

Stirling's top lip curled. 'You pull off whatever little stunts you want over there, Marielle,' he told her, poking her clitoris with his finger, 'but I don't want you getting in my way, do you hear? I want Penny the Moon back here in France and I want her staying as long as *I* say, not as long as *you* say. You got that?'

Marielle nodded. Just tell him what he wants to hear, she was saying to herself. 'I've got it,' she said. 'You're the boss. I do what you say.'

Stirling smirked. 'You're a fast learner, Marielle,' he said. 'I like that in you.' He put his finger in his mouth, sucked it, then withdrew it with a loud kissing noise. 'Tell you what,' he said, 'just to show how appreciative I am of how smart you are, I reckon I'm gonna fuck you.'

Marielle tried to look meek, but couldn't quite mask the triumphant gleam that shot to her eyes. He'd done plenty to her these last few weeks, got her to do even more to him, but what he hadn't done yet was screw her.

'Yeah,' he said, reaching under his belly to unzip himself, 'I reckon I'm gonna put this here dick in you, Marielle, and get you screaming out for your Maker. Now, what do you say to that?'

'Whatever you want,' she said humbly.

'Good girl,' he said approvingly. 'Now get yourself over this table and spread those pretty legs of yours nice and wide.'

Obediently Marielle bent over the desk, gripping the sides with her hands and resting her face on the documents.

'Oh no you don't,' he said, pulling the documents out from under her and patting her bottom. 'We're gonna find somewhere else to put these, so you just stay right where you are. I'll be back.'

Marielle did as she was told, her long slender legs widely parted, her smooth, tight buttocks tilted upwards, ready to take him. She felt so sluttish she could come just thinking about it.

'Well now, I do believe I recognize that smile,' a voice drawled from the doorway.

Marielle spun round to find David Villers grinning down at her, one shoulder resting on the door frame, his arms casually folded.

'Hello, Marielle,' he said. 'Having fun?'

'What the hell are you doing here?' she hissed, pulling herself up quickly and unsuccessfully trying to cover herself with the apron.

'I could ask you the same question,' he said, 'but I'm a big boy, I reckon I can work it out.'

Marielle was about to answer, when a door behind her opened and Stirling came in. 'Right, where were—?' He stopped dead as he saw Villers standing at the threshold.

'My, Bobby, I sure didn't expect you to be this pleased to see me,' David grinned, looking straight at Stirling's erection.

Stirling's face was beetroot-red as he fumbled his dick back in his shorts. 'What the hell do you want?' he growled. 'I don't remember inviting you here.'

'I just came over to say hi,' David answered. 'But I can see it's not convenient right now. I'll call back another time.' And with a quick glance at Marielle he left.

'That's the last time that bastard pulls one on me,' Stirling snarled, staring at the empty doorway. 'You tell him from me, Marielle, you tell that son of a bitch, I'm gonna blast his ass so fucking hard they'll still be looking for the pieces come Doomsday.' His eyes swivelled to Marielle. 'For Chrissake, cover yourself up,' he barked. 'Then get the fuck out of here and don't come back.'

The sound of laughter from behind the closed door of Sylvia Starke's office was becoming infectious. The production concourse was fairly full at that moment and as they all turned to look at each other a grin was spreading on every face. David Villers, Sylvia's cherished godson, had gone in a few minutes ago when just the sight of him striding through the office had caused more than a few female hearts to flutter.

In the comfort of Sylvia's plush seating area David had just finished recounting the story of how he had discovered Marielle with Stirling. Sylvia was dabbing her eyes and trying to catch her breath, she had laughed so hard.

'What I wouldn't give to have seen his face,' she gasped. 'But you must be careful, David. Stirling is nobody's fool: he's clever and he's dangerous. He isn't going to take this sitting down and you know it.'

'He's never taken anything sitting down,' David said calmly, 'but it's never got him anywhere yet.'

She eyed him for a moment, her expression alone warning him not to become cocky. 'What made you go over there?' she asked.

David shrugged. 'Seemed crazy not to when I'd just caught him spying on me with his binoculars.'

'But how did you know he was there? On that particular boat?'

'Easy. I got Pierre to follow Marielle.'

'Ah, yes, Marielle. So what happens to her now?'

David grimaced. 'I haven't made up my mind yet. Nothing, probably – at least, not for a while. My guess is, when Penny finds her feet a bit more she'll fire her, but she needs Marielle right now whether she likes it or not. And Marielle's harmless enough. A bit of a schemer, but she's playing out of her league here which she'll find out soon enough.'

'Well, just make sure she can't do you any damage before she does,' Sylvia warned.

'You got it.' David winked. 'You know,' he said, stretching an arm along the back of the sofa and resting a foot on his knee, 'I find I'm getting quite fond of old Stirling. I reckon I'm going to miss him when all this is over.'

Sylvia's mouth tightened as she looked at him from under her lashes. 'And when will that be, David?' she asked in a serious voice.

'Good question,' he sighed.

Sylvia watched him for a moment, then said, 'Have you heard anything more from Gabriella?'

He shook his head. 'Not for a couple of weeks.'

'Do you trust her?'

He laughed bitterly. 'With a woman like Gabriella, trust doesn't come into the equation.'

'Has she agreed to let you see the boys?' Sylvia asked after a pause.

'No way is she going to let me anywhere near them while she's staying with my old lady,' he answered, an edge of bitterness in his voice. The bitterness turned to anger as he got abruptly to his feet. 'It hurts, Sylvia,' he muttered. 'It hurts like fucking hell. They're my boys and I'm not even getting to see them grow up.'

Sylvia, watching him walk to the window, said nothing. There was no point reminding him that if he hadn't played around the way he had Gabriella might not be doing this to him for as true as it was, it sadly was now a very long way from being as simple as that.

'Stirling's after everything. You know that don't you?' he said. 'And he's not going to stop until he's got it.'

'He feels you owe him,' Sylvia pointed out.

David laughed and turned to face her. 'Now, there's an understatement,' he said.

Sylvia's answering smile was small. 'How's Penny?' she asked, changing the subject.

'Still in LA. Back the day after tomorrow.'

'Have things worked out for her over there? She hasn't called me at all.'

'I spoke to her last week some time. She sounded pretty pleased with herself, so yeah, I guess it must be going OK.'

'Good. Didn't you tell me you got the impression she didn't want to go?'

David nodded.

'The new man?'

'I imagine so.'

Sylvia frowned thoughtfully. 'How are things on the personal front between the two of you now? You've obviously made things up since your atrocious display of insensitivity the night of the party.'

241

'It was an honest mistake,' he defended himself. 'And yeah, we've made it up.'

Sylvia eyed him suspiciously. 'Not between the sheets, I trust?'

David's grin was sheepish. 'She turned me down,' he said.

'Wise girl,' Sylvia remarked. 'You know full well she's not someone for you to have a fling with.'

'It wasn't a fling I had in mind,' he said soberly.

'Well, whatever you did have in mind, I hope you've got rid of it now. I've told you before, I don't want her mixed up in any of this – and, if you do care about her, then neither will you. Gabriella is a dangerous adversary . . .'

'Thanks for reminding me,' he said tightly. A quick stab of temper suddenly flared in him and he slammed his fist into the wall. 'Jesus Christ, I'm beginning to feel like a criminal here,' he seethed.

Sylvia laughed. 'Why don't you tell Stirling that? I think he'd enjoy the joke.'

It was David's turn to laugh. 'Now, he could give lessons on what it feels like to be a criminal,' he said. 'God knows, he's not short on qualifications.'

'Robert Stirling's not short on a lot of things, David, and well you know it,' she said.

David turned back to look out of the window.

'We've got to get something sorted out soon, David,' she went on, starting to get up. 'If we don't, that man is going to drag us all—'

Wondering why she had stopped, David turned to look at her and his blood turned instantly to ice as he saw her slumped over the table. He was across the room in a second. 'Sylvia! Sylvia!' he cried, lifting her and cradling her head against his chest. 'Jesus Christ! Sylvia, what is it?'

'It's nothing,' she gasped. 'Nothing. Just a dizzy spell. It'll pass. I'm not as young as I used to be, remember,' she tried to joke.

'Bullshit!' he said savagely, a horrible, terrifying panic welling in him. Next to his sons there wasn't another person in the world who came even close to meaning as much to him as this woman. 'Oh Christ, Sylvia,' he cried as she clutched his hand. 'Shall I get the doctor? What do you want me to do?'

'Just hold me,' she smiled. 'It feels good, you holding me.'

'Let me get the doctor,' he said, pulling her closer 'You just stay where you are. I'll go get—'

'David, no – there's no need. I'm fine, really. Look, it's passing already,' she said, forcing herself to sit a little straighter.

'This is my fault,' he said, kneeling in front of her and holding her hands tightly in his. 'I didn't want you to get involved in this—'

'Shh, shh!' She smiled.

'I should never have let you. I should have just—'

'David,' she interrupted, 'I would never have forgiven myself if I'd let you go through this alone. Now, please, stop fussing. I told you, it was just a dizzy spell – nothing to get excited about.'

His eyes were still wide with alarm. 'Have you had them before?' he asked, knowing he wouldn't believe her if she said no.

'Yes, I have,' she told him. 'And I've already seen a doctor, which is how I know there's nothing to get excited about. Now, off you go and leave me . . .'

'No way am I out of here now,' he cried.

'I would like to lie down for a while,' she said, laughing.

'Then I'll wait outside.'

Shaking her head in exasperation, she said, 'I will never be able to sleep knowing you're pacing up and down out there and getting in everyone's hair.'

'Sylvia,' he said, 'since when have you started taking

naps in the afternoon?'

'Since this started,' she said. 'A few months, I suppose.'

'I want to see your doctor,' he declared. 'I want to speak to him myself.'

'David, I promise you, I'm not going anywhere yet. So off you go back to France . . .'

'Forget it,' he said.

'But Penny's back tomorrow. She'll be wanting to talk to you about LA.'

'Then she'll have to wait, because there's no way in this world I'm leaving London until I've spoken to your doctor and found out for myself just how serious this is.'

Chapter 13

Penny came awake with a start and looked up to find the stewardess standing over her, asking if she would like breakfast.

'Um, no, um, just tea, thank you,' Penny said, straightening herself up and trying to shake away the cobwebs. 'What time is it?'

'Seven-thirty,' the stewardess answered. 'We'll be arriving at Nice in just over an hour. Are you sure there's nothing else I can get you, besides tea?'

'No, just tea, thanks,' Penny smiled.

The stewardess turned back up the aisle and Penny fumbled around in the stack of newspapers and magazines on the seat beside her for the complimentary flight bag. She badly needed to clean her teeth and stretch her legs after this seemingly endless journey back to France. It felt as though she'd left Los Angeles a week ago rather than – she looked at her watch – well, however many hours it was . . . she was hopeless at working out time differences. Anyway, she'd had a long wait for her connection to Nice at New York and just at this moment she couldn't remember if it was Friday or Saturday.

By the time she returned to her seat she was feeling a little less groggy, though desperately in need of a shower. It wouldn't be long now, though, she reminded herself, and smiled at the wonderful shiver of excitement that penetrated her heart.

It had been a successful trip, one that she was now glad she'd made, since it had done her good to get away for a while. She'd met up with all the people David had put her in touch with, most of whom had passed her on to those she really needed to speak to. But David had opened the doors with his endless contacts and Pauline Fields had swept her out of the Four Seasons Hotel within days of her arrival and installed her in one of the guest rooms of her Bel Air mansion.

She'd had a great time, socially as well as professionally, and was now much more enamoured of Los Angeles than she'd been after previous visits. Actually, she'd never really been able to get the hang of the States and she couldn't quite work out why. It wasn't as if she didn't like the people, because on the whole she did, as long as she remembered that British irony didn't always travel too well. Still, she wasn't going to fall into the American trap of analysing every little thing she did or felt: the fact was that until this trip she'd always felt cut off, lonely and completely out of her depth in the States, despite the fact they all spoke the same language. What was important now was that she had made arrangements for several freelance film reviewers to furnish her with their critiques as and when the movies were released, which meant they would be available to *Nuance* way in advance of the cinema presentations in France. She'd also struck deals with gossip writers, who'd agreed to let her edit their columns for *Nuance* – with the proviso she make it known they were edited. She couldn't take the columns in their entirety, since her readers probably wouldn't have heard of most of the Americans featured. But still, there would be plenty of material there she could use and it was a column she was looking forward to taking charge of.

As the captain's voice came over the PA system Penny took out a compact and touched up her lipstick. David would be waiting at the airport. Those moments beside the pool before Sammy had made her timely arrival had played themselves through Penny's mind several times while she was away and she could only congratulate herself for not succumbing when the last thing she wanted was to add her name to David Villers's endless list of conquests. Lust was a pretty powerful thing, especially when someone had gone without for as long as she had – what was it, six months now? She shuddered: an unthinkable amount of time.

It wasn't until she was leaving the plane and making her way to the arrivals hall that the dreaded lethargy began dragging through her limbs. Flying always had played havoc with her system and it seemed that this time was going to prove no exception. Sometimes it could be days, even weeks, before she was back on an even keel. Not sleeping, wanting to throw up, getting paranoid about nothing: you name it, she did it, all on account of jet lag. With any luck, though, she was going to be too busy to let it get the better of her.

'Hi,' she said, finding Pierre waiting for her outside the baggage claim. 'I thought David was coming to get me. Not,' she added with a laugh as she kissed him on both cheeks, 'that I'm not pleased to see you. How are things at the office?'

Pierre looked troubled, but then if he ever displayed an emotion that was it, so Penny didn't take much notice.

'Marielle been behaving herself, has she?' she said, allowing him to take charge of her trolley and lead the way to the car.

'There are a few things we need to discuss,' Pierre said sombrely, 'which is why I've come to get you.'

'Oh dear, that sounds ominous,' Penny remarked, trying to make light of it when her heart was already thudding with apprehension. 'What's happened? What has she done? I thought I'd left everything in order for the next couple of issues. Don't tell me she's gone and

247

screwed it all up.'

'Not exactly,' Pierre answered, unlocking the boot of his car and throwing in Penny's suitcase. 'Do you want to go home or shall I take you to the office?' he asked, opening the passenger door.

'Maybe you'd better tell me,' Penny said, getting in. 'What's going on, Pierre? Where's David?'

She didn't get an answer until Pierre had slipped in behind the wheel and started the engine. 'David's over in London,' he told her gravely. 'He won't be back for a while.'

'Why? Oh God, Pierre, you're making me nervous. What's been happening? Why isn't David coming back?'

'He's staying with Sylvia. She had a bit of a turn a couple of days ago and he doesn't want to leave her.'

'What sort of a turn?' Penny demanded, her eyes wide with concern.

'Nothing serious, apparently, but he's going to stay a while.'

'But she's all right? Nothing's—'

'She's all right,' Pierre assured her. 'But you know how fond David is of her, she's like a mother to him, and he wants to spend some time with her. Which is why I'm here to pick you up and why I have to discuss with you what's happened while you were away, since I don't want to bother David with it right now.'

'Pierre!' Penny cried when he stopped. 'For heaven's sake come to the point, will you?'

'The point,' he said, as they joined the autoroute heading for Cannes, 'is that we're in danger of having a fairly serious lawsuit slapped on us.'

'Lawsuit?' Penny echoed incredulously. 'What for, for God's sake? Oh my God, I knew I shouldn't have left Marielle in charge. What's she done?'

'It wasn't Marielle,' Pierre said. 'It was your sister, I'm afraid.'

'*Sammy*? But Sammy's not in a position to—'

248

'It was her column,' Pierre said. 'She advised some woman to take a blunt instrument to her unfaithful husband and I'm afraid the woman's done just that.'

Penny looked at him, dumbfounded. 'Jesus Christ Almighty,' she mumbled, wanting to strangle Sammy even though she was already beginning to get a picture of what had happened. 'But how on earth did it go to press?'

'I don't know the ins and outs of it yet,' Pierre answered. 'It just blew up yesterday. But what I do know is that Sammy's disappeared and Marielle is demanding your resignation.'

'*What*?' Penny cried furiously. 'Take me to the office, Pierre. I want to see that woman *now*!'

Half an hour later Marielle was standing in front of Penny's desk not even attempting to disguise the disdain in her smile.

'I always knew,' Penny said in a dangerously low voice, 'that if I gave you enough rope you'd hang yourself, but what I want to know is what made you think you could possibly get away with this.'

'How *I* could get away with it?' Marielle laughed incredulously. 'It was *your* sister who wrote it. And it was *you*, Penny, who insisted she have the job.' She looked at her nails. 'I was never in agreement, as you know, and now look what she's done.'

'Marielle,' Penny said, pronouncing her name with great deliberation, 'you seem to be missing the point here. Both issues published while I was away were checked and cleared by me before I left, so I know what was in Sammy's columns and neither of them contained the advice that has gone to press. So that can only lead me to conclude that you, Marielle, made a last-minute change.'

Marielle's lip curled in disgust. 'For someone who's screwed up on her own editorials . . .'

Penny's eyes flashed with anger. 'My mistake did not

go to press—'

'Because *I* spotted it before it got that far,' Marielle cut in triumphantly. 'And *it* leads *me* to conclude that you aren't doing your job properly and that you didn't double-check the problem page.'

Penny looked at her long and hard. 'Where did you find the column?' she asked. 'Was it here, in my desk? Yes, I thought as much,' she said when Marielle coloured. 'And you know full well that it was a column Sammy gave me months ago as a joke.'

Marielle pounced on it. 'Then don't you think you should have thrown it away?' she challenged. 'Having stuff like that hanging around is dangerous and . . .' She smirked. 'Well, I think my point is proven, don't you? It found its way into the magazine and that poor woman who was looking for guidance is now up on assault charges. And, if you ask me, it was you, Penny, who was responsible, because it was *you* who didn't get rid of it.'

Penny was shaking her head in amazement. 'It's hard to believe that someone could be so stupid,' she said, a wave of tiredness sweeping over her. 'You're not even listening to what you're saying, are you? You don't even realize that with every word that comes out of your mouth you're incriminating yourself further. Now, go and clear your desk. Take whatever belongs to you and get out.'

Marielle was shaking her head. 'David's the boss here, Penny, not you. I'm not fired unless he says so.'

'You're fired, Marielle,' Penny said, starting to unpack her briefcase. 'Please remove yourself from these premises. You'll be hearing from our lawyers in due course.'

'Didn't you hear me?' Marielle hissed. 'I'm not going anywhere until David tells me. This is *my* magazine; I was the one who set it up, who found all the contributors, who—'

'Are you completely stupid?' Penny cried, rounding

on her. 'Do you seriously think David isn't going to back me on this? Do you really believe he'll—'

'Why don't we let David speak for himself?' Marielle challenged.

'David has other things to deal with right now,' Penny snapped, 'and your ridiculous attempt at sabotage is the last thing he needs. So if I were you I'd get myself out of here before he comes back.'

To Penny's amazement Marielle didn't appear in the least bit fazed. 'I can assure you that David will see things my way,' she said. 'Because, you see, Penny, there are things I know about David that David wouldn't want the rest of the world to know.'

Penny just stared at her. 'Excuse me,' she said, shaking her head. 'Was that a blackmail threat I just heard?'

Marielle shrugged. 'Call it what you like, but I'm telling you, Penny, it'll be your head that rolls over this not mine,' and with a contemptuous toss of her hair she swept out of the office.

Seconds later the door opened again and Pierre came in. 'She's impossible,' Penny said, sinking into her chair. 'She's threatening to blackmail David over something or other if we fire her and right now I feel too damned tired to deal with it.'

'Would you like me to take you home?' he offered.

'In a little while. I'd better check on things here first, make sure she doesn't have any more nasty little surprises in store. Anyway, I honestly don't see how we can avoid telling David.'

'No, I don't think we can,' Pierre agreed. 'I've just spoken to our lawyers. It seems the woman and her husband might accept some form of compensation— Penny, are you all right?'

'Yes.' Penny smiled, knowing full well she'd turned green. 'I'm always like this after a long flight. Go on, you were saying . . . about compensation . . .'

'Well, whatever the amount, David will have to

251

sanction it,' Pierre said. 'Do you want to tell him what's happened or do you want me to?'

'Let me think about that,' Penny answered. 'I want to talk to Sammy . . .'

'Do you know where she is?' Pierre frowned.

'Not at this precise moment, no. But I'll find her. Meanwhile, what do you propose we do about Marielle? Is there anything serious she can threaten David with?'

Pierre was shaking his head. 'No, not really. He has a few things going on that he wouldn't be too happy to have made public at this precise time, but it'll all come out sooner or later, so Marielle won't be able to do him much damage.'

Penny found she was smiling. 'So are you going to tell me what it is?' she asked, knowing already he wouldn't.

'I expect David will tell you himself,' he answered.

Penny's head went to one side. 'How does Marielle know about it?' she said, stung that David might have told Marielle and not her.

'It is very likely that Marielle has found out through a man by the name of Robert Stirling.'

'And who is Robert Stirling?' Penny enquired.

'Someone who will stop at nothing to ruin David. He's here on the Coast at the moment and Marielle's been seeing him.'

'Has she indeed?' Penny said. 'I take it David knows that.'

Pierre nodded.

'So, what has David done to this Robert Stirling to have earned himself such an enemy? No, I know,' she said, holding up a hand as Pierre started to answer, 'David will tell me himself.'

Pierre's smile was weak.

'Well, just so long as he isn't getting us involved in anything dangerous or underhand,' she said, stifling a yawn.

'All David's business dealings are straight down the

line,' Pierre retorted, obviously offended that Penny could think otherwise. 'And that's what's getting to Stirling. He wants to hang something on David and he can't find a single thing out of line. But he's going to keep on looking until he does find something – which he won't, but nothing will convince him of that – and Gabriella, David's wife, is in a position to make things extremely difficult for David if she chooses.'

'Then that suggests he does have something to hide,' Penny pointed out.

Pierre flushed. 'Look,' he said, 'you don't make the kind of money David's made without doing the odd shady deal here and there. But whatever he's done, he's done with his eyes wide open and the law, only just in some cases it's true, on his side. However, Gabriella could make things look a whole lot different if she wanted to.'

'Sounds like a happy marriage,' Penny commented.

'It was once. As it stands now, she won't see him and neither will she allow him to see his children.'

'Why?'

'Because she won't believe that David is capable of keeping his hands off other women,' Pierre answered with uncharacteristic bluntness.

'Well, i think i can understand that,' Penny remarked drily, wondering if, in fact, Pierre's answer was complete. 'Anyway, are you telling me that she would seriously stitch up her own husband, the father of her children, for the sake of . . . For the sake of what?' she asked him.

'You're a woman,' Pierre countered. 'Perhaps you're in a better position to answer that.'

Penny was shaking her head. 'I'm too tired to get into that,' she said, 'so let's change the subject. Remind me, what did we decide about Marielle?'

'We didn't. But my advice is we leave her where she is for the time being. David'll probably want to deal with

253

her himself.'

Penny mulled that over for a moment. 'OK,' she said, wanting to slump over her desk and sleep for a week, 'unless David says otherwise and providing we can sort out this mess before the press get hold of it, she stays.' She looked up. 'I take it that no one's got wind of why this woman is up on assault charges yet?' she said.

'Not that I'm aware of.'

'Then let's hope it stays that way. Now, give me a couple of hours, will you, then I'll take you up on that offer of a lift home.'

Later in the day, after taking a much needed siesta, Penny padded into Sammy's bedroom in the hope of finding a clue to Sammy's current whereabouts. To her dismay she saw a note waiting for her on the bed and, as she picked it up, more or less knowing what it contained, she could already feel the disappointment flooding her heart. 'Dear darling, beautiful, wonderful, talented, best sister in the whole world,' she read. 'Sorry not to be here to welcome you home, but Stefan got this fantastic offer of a job skippering a boat in the Caribbean, so I've gone too. I'll be in touch as soon as I know where exactly we'll be. Meanwhile, keep smiling. Love Sammy. PS Sorry about all the shit over the column, but I expect you've already guessed what happened. The Bitch found the joke one I wrote a while back and put it through. Anyway, bury her, then spit on her grave for me. I'm enclosing a couple more columns to see you through till you find someone else. Love you hundreds and thousands, Sammy.'

Stuffing the note in the pocket of her dressing gown, Penny wandered downstairs to the kitchen. The house felt horribly empty with both David and Sammy gone, and with the rain pattering against the windows and night approaching she was starting to feel quite lonely. Of course she had plenty of work to do, but right now, feeling so despondent about Sammy's abrupt departure even though she'd been half-expecting it, she didn't really have the heart to get down to it.

Filling the kettle, she put it on to boil, then, having switched the phone off earlier, she went to check if there were any messages. There was just one, from David, welcoming her home, telling her how much she had been missed and asking her to call when she had a minute. The sound of his voice warmed her and made her smile. It would be nice to think she'd been missed as much as he was insisting, but she knew David too well: it was merely the sort of thing he'd say. Still, she wouldn't mind talking to him right now; so, picking up the phone, she dialled Sylvia's number, presuming that was where she would find him.

A couple of minutes later she rang off, feeling slightly relieved that no one was in, for she'd momentarily forgotten about the problem with Marielle.

Looking down at the answerphone again, she grimaced ruefully. It had been full of messages earlier, but none were from Christian. However, telephone calls were like buses, they never came when you were waiting for one – and she wished to God she could stop herself waiting for this one. Her heart tightened as she wondered if he had been arrested, or maybe got the deal he was seeking from the DA and handed himself in.

To her surprise, when she called the Delaneys' number she got a France Telecom recorded message telling her that the line had been discontinued.

Frowning, she walked to the front door and peered through the darkness towards the Delaneys' villa. She could see no lights through the trees, but maybe they had already shuttered up for the night.

Dressing quickly she pulled on her coat and boots and went to investigate. She found the gates locked and in the fading light she could see that there were no cars in the drive. Nor was there any sign of Tilly, the dog, and no light was coming through the chinks in the shutters. The entire place was deserted and looked, she thought, as though it had been that way for a while.

Chapter 14

As soon as David heard what had happened over the agony column he was on the next plane back to France. From the moment he arrived Penny sensed the change in him, but though he was snappish and aloof with her there was no question it was Marielle he was gunning for. Penny never did find out what passed between them; all she knew was that Marielle continued to strut about the place like Miss Fleet Street herself, giving orders, crushing egos and generally getting up everyone's nose. She didn't appear in the least bit bothered by the severe pressure they were under from the press to explain the advice that had been printed in their agony column. It was as though she had played no part in it at all.

Fortunately no one seemed to have got wind of the fact that some unhappy, unstable woman had acted upon the advice and the handling of the woman and her husband was left to David to sort out. This he did, by parting with an unspecified sum of money on the condition that no mention of it ever reached the papers. To Penny's surprise she received no reproach from David herself, when she'd expected him at the very least to have told her not to be so careless as to leave that sort of thing lying around in the future.

In fact, over the next couple of weeks she didn't have much contact with him at all. Thanks to her crazy schedule, with meetings and functions to attend all along the coast, they were rarely in the office at the same time and, when they were, there was enough to occupy them to keep them out of each other's way. Not that she was actively striving to keep out of his way, but she had an uncanny feeling that he was deliberately avoiding her.

It was strange, she was thinking to herself one evening while sitting at home working, the way David didn't seem himself lately. Obviously Sylvia's ill health was worrying him, but from her short conversation with Pierre Penny guessed that David's other main preoccupation right now was saving his empire from this Stirling character. She'd meant to ask David about that, but since he hadn't been particularly approachable lately and with so much else on her mind she'd decided to leave well alone. But it wasn't the same around the office without David baiting her over something or other or strolling into her office and helping himself to a cup of coffee and sitting down for a chat. Was he mad at her for the way she'd turned him down that night, she wondered. But no, she couldn't see David getting strung out over something like that. So what was it? Why was he so agitated and why was he deliberately avoiding her?

For heaven's sake, pull yourself together, she told herself sharply. She was on the verge of becoming paranoid about his aloofness lately and it had to stop. His problems were his own, had nothing at all to do with her and it was as much conceit as it was paranoia that she considered herself important enough for him to be worrying about when there was no doubt, from the little she had managed to glean, that it was his wife who was uppermost in his mind right now. Funny, she thought, how she could almost feel jealous of his wife, a woman she didn't even know and probably never would. But knowing that Gabriella could affect David the way she was, that she could have such a hold over his life and cause him the pain she did by denying him the right to see his sons, made Penny want to reach out to him in a way that suprised her.

She hadn't seen it before, maybe because she hadn't allowed herself to, but now she was sitting here thinking about it she realized that a real friendship – unacknowledged, maybe, but none the less a friendship – had developed between them; and friends, at least in Penny's book, should talk to each other about things that were troubling them. Or maybe the friendship was just in her imagination, for there was no denying that lately David had quite definitely been shutting her out of his life.

And here comes the paranoia again, she admonished herself wearily. And wasn't she only concentrating on that particular fear because she didn't even want to think about what else was bothering her? There was still no sign of the Delaneys, the shop had been closed down and she'd just found out that day that the house next door was now for let. No one seemed to know where the Delaneys had gone or even if they were still in France.

The mystery of it was troubling her for reasons she wasn't in the least bit proud of, for vanishing into thin air the way they had had left her feeling strangely spurned, as though maybe she had done or said something, without even realizing it, that had driven them away. If she was right about that, then it could only mean that Christian had decided she wasn't to be trusted . . . As the thought pushed a horrible sinking feeling into her heart she could only thank God that no one knew how she was fixating on a man she had barely even met, and when, just to think of it, turned her hot with embarrassment.

The next few issues of *Nuance* hit the stands, one of them bearing a glorious colour photograph of Princess Caroline on the cover and, inside, the exclusive interview she had given Penny. Sales were on the up and the chance of an interview with Luke Pleasance, the ageing rock star who was making something of a comeback, had arisen – no doubt another of David's contacts, Penny thought – which meant she'd have to go over to New York. Well, that didn't matter, there were plenty of other things she could find to do in New York. Besides, it wasn't until the beginning of December and it was now still only the end of October.

David, like the rest of the world, it seemed, had done another of his disappearing acts, but although, on the whole, things were running pretty smoothly, Penny had to admit, as she strolled into the production office to find out what Marielle and Mario, the advertising director, were screaming about, that she much preferred it when David was around.

As usual Marielle and Mario were fighting over a right-hand page and Penny was in the midst of refereeing, when Brigitte told her she was putting a call through to her office.

'He said it was personal,' she explained as Penny looked at her curiously.

Penny's heart flipped. 'Is it David?' she asked, surprised by how much she wanted to hear his voice.

Brigitte shook her head. 'He didn't give his name.'

It was all Penny could do to stop herself running back to her desk. Of course by now she was thinking, *hoping*, it would be Christian Mureau, but, to her surprise, it was Wally Delaney.

'I'm fine,' she said in answer to his enquiry. 'How are you? Or maybe I should ask *where* are you?'

'Living over in Vallauris now,' he barked. 'Settled in nicely. Bigger house. More room for Tilly to run around.'

'Oh, that's good,' Penny said, a dozen questions gathering on the tip of her tongue which dignity made her bite back. 'And how's Esther?'

'Yes, yes, on splendid form,' he answered. 'Got to ask if you like the ballet.'

Penny blinked as she frowned. 'The ballet?' she said.

'Yes, as it so happens, I love it. Why?'

'Got to ask if you want to go tomorrow night,' he replied. 'American ballet company. In Cannes. My employer wants to know if you want to go with him.'

Penny sat down hard in her chair, her mind reeling with the shock of it. 'Well, yes,' she said, stunned by the fact that it was Wally who was calling her, when he'd always been so dead set against her and Christian meeting. 'I'd love to go. Uh . . .'

'Righto, then.'

'Wally, before you go,' she said, 'why didn't he call me himself?'

'On his way down from Paris. Call you later or tomorrow, he said. Don't want you to think I approve, because I don't,' he told her sharply. 'Remember that,' and the line went dead.

Penny looked at the receiver and suddenly started to laugh. To hell with him and his approval! She and Christian were going to meet at last and as far as she was concerned that was all that mattered.

'Marielle!' she shouted, putting the phone down. 'Marielle, I've got to talk to you.'

'Something wrong?' Marielle asked, all sweetness and light, as she appeared in the doorway.

'No, the reverse. I want you to tell me what people wear down here for the ballet. Better still, I want you to come shopping with me tomorrow to pick something out.'

Marielle couldn't have looked more shocked if she'd tried. 'You want *me* to go shopping with *you*?' she said.

'That's what I said. You'll know all the best places and I want something . . . well, something that's sexy but tasteful and you have the best dress sense of anyone I know.'

Marielle preened at the compliment. 'Then we'll see what we can do,' she said, giving Penny the once-over. 'What time do we start?'

'How long will we need?'

As Marielle's eyebrows went up, her eyes narrowed. 'A few months ago I'd have said all day and even then we'd be pushing it, but I guess a morning will suffice the way you are now.' And with a sugary little smile she left.

After raiding virtually every boutique and designer shop on the rue d'Antibes for the perfect dress, shoes and matching jewellery, at Marielle's insistence Penny agreed to go home.

'I don't know who he is,' Marielle said, as they walked back to the Noga Hilton car park, 'and I won't ask, but obviously this is a special date and you're not going to be able to concentrate on a thing. So off you go – and take a tip from me: whether or not you're intending to sleep with him on the first night, wear special underwear. At worst it will make *you* feel good; at best it will make *him* feel good. Is he French?'

'Yes, I guess you could say he is,' Penny told her.

Marielle smiled. 'Be warned,' she said: 'not all Frenchmen are as good in bed as reputation has it; take it from one who knows. But whatever you do, don't let your disappointment show.'

'Such negativity!' Penny laughed. 'It takes two, Marielle, which I'm sure is something else you know.'

'Or more,' Marielle said smoothly.

'I'll take your word for that,' Penny told her and since she was in such a jubilant mood she kissed Marielle on both cheeks before going off to find her car.

Watching her disappear through the sliding plate-glass doors of the hotel's shopping arcade, Marielle glanced at her watch and wondered who she should tell about this – Robert Stirling or David Villers? She almost laughed out loud. Why not let Stirling tell David? Now, wouldn't that be a neat little sting in the tale? Were Penny the Moon Canadian or American she'd know exactly who Christian Mureau was. But maybe Penny did know. Maybe that buffoon Wally Delaney had told her too, just as he had bragged about it to Marielle on the few occasions she'd curled herself round all that flaccid, pale flesh in the back seat of his car. Of course Marielle had already known exactly who Christian Mureau was, but after getting to work on Wally she'd not only managed to slot into place a few more pieces of the puzzle, she'd actually got to meet Mureau himself, at one of the Delaneys' tedious little soirées over in Vallauris. What a night that had turned out to be! She could almost feel sorry for Penny the Moon, since, were she not immune to such things herself, she might very easily have fallen hard for that man. Still, there was no doubt at all that Stirling would pee himself with excitement when he got to hear about Penny the Moon's date. What a shame she wouldn't be there to witness the scenes when Stirling told David and David turned on Penny. But, what the hell, as long as she, Marielle, got what she wanted out of this . . . And there didn't seem much doubt about that now that Penny the Moon, her new friend, was about to hand it all to her on a plate.

It was the middle of the afternoon when the telephone rang, snapping Penny from her doubtful scrutiny of that morning's purchases.

'Hi. Is that you, Penny?'

'Yes,' she smiled, her heart tightening at the sound of his partly French, partly American, accent.

'It's Christian Mureau,' he told her, a smile in his voice too. 'Are you still able to make the ballet this evening?'

'Yes,' she answered, a hand moving to her chest as though to deaden the beat of her heart.

'I'm sorry I didn't call myself yesterday,' he said. 'I was *en route* from Paris.'

'Mmm, Wally said. What time did you get here?' *Jesus, Penny, such a gift for the banal!*

'Late last night,' he answered. 'Are you concerned

about what you should wear tonight?'

Penny wanted to laugh, for only a Frenchman would ask such a question. 'A little,' she confessed.

'Smart, but casual,' he told her, his voice once again brimming with humour. 'I'll have Wally drive you to Cannes,' he went on. 'We should meet around seven. I'll be in the lobby of the Gray d'Albion Hotel. Do you know it?'

'Yes, I know it,' she said.

'There's a party after the ballet,' he told her. 'The choreographer's a friend of mine. Do you have to be up early in the morning?'

'Not especially,' she answered, wondering how, if Wally was going to drive her there, she was going to get home and not really caring.

'Voilà!,' he laughed. 'A ce soir.'

'A ce soir,' she echoed, and waited for the line to go dead.

Laughing to herself, though not quite knowing why, she went back to look at the dress Marielle had helped her choose. It was perfect. Smart, but casual. Marielle hadn't let her down. Holding it against her, she turned to the mirror. The dress was navy, almost black, with a straight velvet bodice buttoned through to the hip and shiny silk pleats to the knee. The neck was scooped, but not too low; the elbow-length sleeves were the same silk as the skirt. With her free hand Penny bunched her hair, wondering if she should wear it up. No, she thought not, and allowed it to fall back around her shoulders.

Now for the inspection of everything else.

Her heart sank. It was true, her thighs were better than they'd been in a long time, a whole lot better, in fact, but try as she might she just hadn't been able to shift all the cellulite. Her eyes travelled upwards to the distressing mound of her belly. The skin was creamy-white and pleasingly soft to the touch, but no amount of exercise had been able to force it flat. On the other hand, at least her waist had returned and those dreadful 'love handles' had all but disappeared. Raising her eyes still further, she examined her breasts with their full, rosy nipples and the faint blue veins beneath the translucent skin. Turning to one side she checked their pertness, though she wasn't sure that breasts as large as hers could actually be pert. But yes, she reckoned they could, for her nipples were still on the northern slopes and anyway she'd always considered her breasts one of her best features – providing, of course, the man in question liked big-breasted women. Would Christian? she wondered, as a shiver of pent-up desire coasted through her. Again she laughed. Would he even get to see them?

She looked at her watch. Just after four. She had plenty of time before Wally came to collect her. Glancing out of the window she saw that the sun was shining, that the clouds blown in earlier had been swept out to sea by the wind. It was strange how she was feeling, she thought: kind of floaty and unattached and surprisingly calm. And, she thought wryly, not in the least bit professional.

She started as the telephone rang.

'Hello?' she said huskily, wondering if it would be him again.

'Pen?'

'David!' she said. 'Where are you?'

'At the apartment. I just got back. I called the office, they said you weren't in today. Is everything all right?'

'Yes, everything's fine,' she laughed. 'Just fine. How are you?'

'Yeah, pretty good, I guess. Do you want to have some dinner tonight?'

'Oh, David, I'm—'

'I could use the company,' he said.

Penny's heart fell. It was so unlike him to admit to a vulnerability that under any other circumstances she'd have cancelled everything to see him. But in this instance she couldn't. 'David, I'm really sorry,' she said. 'I've got

265

other plans this evening. Maybe we could do it to-morrow?'

'Sure. OK,' he answered. 'Going somewhere special?'

'To the ballet, actually.'

'Sounds good. Well, you have yourself a great time. I'll speak to you tomorrow.'

'David!' she called.

'I'm still here.'

'Are you all right? You sound a bit down.'

'No, like I said, I'm pretty good,' he told her. 'Did Luke Pleasance come up with some dates yet for New York?'

'Yes. The beginning of December.'

'Great. He's a good guy, you'll like him. Anyway, I guess I'd better be getting on with things. Enjoy the ballet,' he said, and rang off.

What bloody awful timing, Penny groaned to herself as she went to run the bath. Other than Christian Mureau there was no one in the world she'd rather see than David, especially when she wanted to close this distance that seemed to have crept between them lately.

Still, there would be other times, she told herself as a tremor of excitement swept through her. Tonight was a night she'd waited a long time for. She wasn't going to think about what David would say if he, or anyone else she knew for that matter, were to find out who she was meeting, because they would all undoubtedly tell her she was insane – which she probably was, but when had that ever stopped her before?

'Oh my, don't you look simply splendid!' Esther declared when Penny pulled open the front door at six-thirty.

'Esther!' Penny laughed, feeling ridiculously pleased and surprised to see her even though the old lady had called to say that she, not Wally, would be chauffering her into Cannes.

'Would you like a drink before we go?' Penny offered,

embracing her.

'No, no. No time for that. He'll be waiting. Do you
have a coat? I think you should take a coat. There's a
definite nip in the air tonight. Don't want you catching
a chill now, do we?'

Smiling, Penny turned back inside to collect her coat
and make one final check on her hair and make-up. She
now knew, from the brief conversation she'd had with
Esther earlier, that she had been right about the reason
behind the Delaneys hasty departure from the house
next door: Christian had got cold feet about trusting her
and, suspecting that Esther was more influenced by
Penny than was good for any of them, he had ordered
the Delaneys out of harm's way. The reason for his
change of heart now was something Penny had yet to
find out, but she had decided to ask Christian himself,
rather than hear it second-hand from Esther.

It wasn't until some fifteen minutes later, as they were
crossing the *voie rapide* to head down towards the *Palais
des Festivals* in Cannes, that Penny realized how un-
usually quiet the old lady had become. Being in such a
turmoil herself she'd been quite happy to spend the journey in silence, but now, glancing over at Esther, she
couldn't help wondering what was going through her
mind.

'Just a teensy bit worried,' Esther answered when
Penny asked.

'About what?'

'No, no. Nothing really.'

Penny smiled as realization dawned. 'You're still
afraid that my only motive for meeting him is to get a
story, aren't you?' she said.

Esther's eyes remained fixed on the road ahead.

'And if I don't get it,' Penny went on, 'you're thinking
that I will go to print with what I know anyway. Such as
where he can be found these days and who's working for
him to keep him out of the hands of the law.'

Esther blinked rapidly.

'It's all right,' Penny assured her, 'as far as I'm concerned, this is a date. I've left my journalist's hat at home.'

Esther threw her a nervous smile. 'He's a good man,' she said. 'I think you'll enjoy your date.'

A few minutes later they were parking the car beneath the Gray d'Albion Hotel.

'Wow!' Penny exclaimed as Esther slipped off her coat. 'That's a great suit.' And for once it was, since its subtle colour and tailoring was much more becoming to a woman of Esther's age than her usual attire. 'Are you going somewhere when you leave here?' Penny asked.

'Just out for dinner with Wally and a couple of friends. How are you feeling?' She smiled, seeming to sense Penny's nerves.

'Don't ask,' Penny shivered.

Esther walked ahead into the lobby of the hotel, Penny close behind her. To the right was the bar with its luxurious carpets, brass rails and mirrors, an extension of the lobby. But Penny's eyes were sightless. For some peculiar reason she was trying to remember something she had read just a few days before, by Henry Miller. For a moment it felt as though it was the most important thing in the world to remember, but the words eluded her and then she wasn't thinking about it any more . . .

Esther was walking into the embrace of the man Penny had pictured so many times in her mind's eye since the night of the *vernissage* that she couldn't help smiling to herself now as, seeing him in the flesh, she realized how deficient her memory had been. His pleasure at seeing the old lady was clear and as Penny watched them she began to feel faintly light-headed. Esther was chattering and laughing, but Penny couldn't hear what she was saying. There was a buzz of conversation coming from elsewhere in the bar, but Penny didn't hear that either. Then she realized that Christian was looking at her, holding out a hand to greet her. Penny took it and to her surprise he leaned forward and kissed her on both cheeks.

For one insane moment, as her heart seemed to stop beating, Penny wanted to run. Nothing, just nothing, should be as powerful as this. Having never seen him up close before, it was almost terrifying to find that his eyes were so arresting that she couldn't drag her own away. They were a dark, muddy brown with a light of humour in them that almost, but not quite, disguised an intense sensuality that sent a thrill of excitement chasing through her. His nose was long and straight, his smile was easy, his teeth white and even. His skin was swarthy, his hair, slightly receding at the temples, though dark, was a few shades lighter than she remembered. It was dishevelled, cut short at the sides and curled over his collar at the back. He was tall, though maybe not quite so tall as she'd thought.

'It's good to meet you at last,' he said, and the way he was looking so directly into her eyes seemed to be telling her that she had been on his mind every bit as much as he had been on hers these past few months.

'It's good to meet *you* at last,' she echoed, feeling, to her dismay, a blush creeping over her cheeks.

'Can I take your coat?' he offered.

Penny slipped it off and as he took it her eyes started to dance at the appreciation he showed of the way she was dressed.

'We're meeting the others in half an hour,' he said, 'just over the road. I thought we'd have a drink here first.'

He turned back to the table where he'd been sitting and Penny saw there was champagne and three glasses.

When they were seated Penny watched the way he turned his attention to Esther, listening patiently and fondly as she wittered on, seemingly oblivious to the fact that her chaperonage was no longer required. Once or twice he caught Penny's eye, narrowing his own as though letting her know that he was far from forgetting she was there. But as Esther chattered on about things and places and people that meant little to Penny, Penny was glad of the opportunity to study him further.

Though he wasn't a conventionally handsome man he had the most compelling presence and unbelievably magnetic eyes she had ever come across. When she realized what else she was thinking, that there was nothing about him that in any way suggested he was a wanted man, she almost laughed. What did she expect? That he would go around with a sign on his head, or dress totally in black and carry a little jolly swag bag? He was wearing a brown polo-neck sweater, the most awful fawn checked trousers that appeared to be at least one size too big, tan cowboy boots, and an expensive-looking brown leather jacket was slung over the arm of his chair. The sweater fitted tightly over his chest and arms, showing the powerful muscles beneath. His movements, his whole demeanour, exuded a confidence that held not a trace of arrogance or conceit.

At some point, she wasn't sure when or how, he drew her into the conversation and it was a while before she realized that, whenever she spoke, his deceptively lazy eyes were holding her, seeming to reach far into the private realms of her thoughts. She could feel herself responding, as though moving into him, becoming a part of his mind, merging with his concentration. Esther Delaney seemed to recede from the scene, as though they were closing off their surroundings, isolating themselves in the silent discovery of each other.

It was ten minutes or more before Penny realized she had sunk into some kind of stupor and couldn't remember a thing they had said. Politeness had made him return his attention to Esther and Penny could only hope that her mouth hadn't fallen open as she'd watched him. Shaking off the stupor was a startling experience, as though she had just brought her head above water. The sounds around her suddenly sharpened and the faint feeling of suffocation was gone. *Jesus Christ*, she thought, what is he doing to me?

'Hey,' he laughed as she downed her champagne, 'not so fast. We've got a long night ahead of us.'

Penny's bottom jaw went to one side as she sheepishly grinned. Thank God he couldn't read her mind right now. If he could, he'd probably blush.

'Have you ever visited the Far East, Penny?' he asked.

Penny raised her eyebrows, puzzled. Then, belatedly realizing that was what he and Esther had been discussing, she said, 'No. Never.'

'Christian's speciality is oriental art,' Esther informed her proudly. 'He's written a book about it and made a TV documentary.'

Christian laughed at Penny's look of surprise. 'I did have a life before all this, you know,' he told her. 'Quite a full life, in fact. One I hope to return to one day.'

'Which particular aspect of it?' Penny asked.

He smiled and once again Penny felt herself blushing. 'That's easy,' he said. 'The sea. Do you know the sea, Penny?'

She frowned and smiled. 'I don't think I can say I do,' she answered.

'Then you must get him to introduce you,' Esther laughed. 'It's his passion.'

Penny's eyes moved back to his. His face was serious now as he looked at her. 'Will you forgive me?' he said. 'There is a call I must make.'

When he had gone, Penny turned to Esther.

'How are you feeling?' Esther smiled.

Penny took a moment to think about her answer, wanting to find the right words. 'To tell you the truth,' she said finally, 'I can't seem to get a handle on what's going on inside me at all. It all seems, well, so unreal.'

Esther chuckled. 'Well, you make a very handsome

pair,' she said, swallowing the last of her champagne.

Penny smiled. 'Who's he calling?' she asked.

Esther shrugged. 'No idea. He's always on the phone to someone. Business here, business there. He's got to keep things running as best he can so he'll have something to come out to – that is, if they don't confiscate it all.' She stooped to pick up her bag. 'Well, I don't think you need me any more. Say *au revoir* to him for me and I hope you have a splendid evening.'

It was a while before he came back by which time Penny was into her third glass of champagne. As he sat down she couldn't help sizing up his body and wondering when was the last time he'd made love.

'Esther asked me to say *au revoir* for her,' she told him.

He nodded, picking up his glass. Then, after staring down at the floor for a moment, he lifted his eyes back to hers and said, 'How do you feel about giving the ballet a miss?'

Penny swallowed hard as her heartbeat faltered. 'That's fine by me,' she said softly.

Suddenly he screwed up his eyes and pressed his fingers into the sockets. Penny watched him, wishing she could think of something to say. In the end he looked at her again, searching her face with his eyes. 'You understand everything about me?' he said. 'What has happened? The position I am in?'

She nodded. 'Yes, I understand it.'

'You realize that at any moment someone could come through that door and I will have to leave with them?'

'Yes,' she said.

He paused, his eyes still on hers. 'It would give you quite a story, wouldn't it?'

'That's not why I'm here,' she said, holding his gaze.

Several seconds ticked by as he continued to look at her, the infinite depths of his eyes seeming to convey the thoughts that were in her own mind. 'Did you know this was going to happen between us?' he asked finally.

272

Penny's heart felt as if it was turning inside out. 'Yes, I think so,' she whispered. 'Did you?'

He shook his head. 'I don't know. I guess so, but I try not to think too much about these things.'

There was a craziness to this that must have reached him too, for they both started to laugh.

'This is a hell of a time for you to come into my life,' he said.

Penny's lips compressed in a smile. 'I was beginning to think I never would,' she said, watching him closely.

Laughter sprang to his eyes and emptying his glass he put it back on the table. 'I confess,' he said, 'to questioning your motives for wanting to meet me.'

'Do you still?'

Again he laughed and rolling her eyes, Penny said, 'OK, if you did, I wouldn't be here. So what happened to convince you?'

He shrugged. 'Call it instinct,' he said. Then, with a wry smile, he added, 'I guess we both know that something happened between us the night of the *vernissage*, which was why I called you afterwards. I hadn't met you, but I'd seen you and, well, I guess I wanted to know more about you. Esther told me you were a journalist, but,' he shrugged, 'I wouldn't be in the position I'm in now if I didn't take risks. But things have changed a lot this last year or so, I have to be more careful, so I did a bit of research and everything I found out indicated I could probably trust you.'

'So,' Penny said, her eyes sparkling with mischief, 'what took you so long?'

Grinning, he said, 'Don't take this badly, but I'm afraid, affected as I was by you, you weren't at the top of my list of priorities.'

Feeling herself flush, Penny looked down at her glass. 'Of course not,' she said.

He waited for her eyes to come back to his, then said, 'Do you want to go somewhere to eat?'

She nodded, though whether she'd be able to swallow a morsel was another question altogether.

After settling the bill they left the hotel and strolled towards the Croisette. The November night was crisp and clear and as they drew closer to the sea they could hear the gentle sough of the waves and the rustle of wind in the palms. She told him about *Nuance* and he told her more about the world of oriental art. His English was so perfect she could almost believe he was American, but then a trace of an accent would break through and she would find herself responding to the warm, gutteral sound.

They chose a sparsely populated seafood restaurant between the Carlton and Martinez Hotels, where they were shown to a window seat and waited no more than a minute before champagne was brought to the table.

'Did you order this?' Penny laughed.

He nodded.

'I didn't hear you.'

'Would you prefer something else?'

'No, champagne is just fine.'

As the waiter poured, she watched her fingers idly playing with a fork. She desperately wanted to ask him more about the crimes he had committed, but knew that if she did he'd be sure to think she was trying for a story after all.

When they were left alone he picked up his glass and tilted it slightly towards her. 'Go on,' he said, 'ask away.'

Pursing her lips in a smile at having been so easily read, she touched her glass to his. Then, after taking a sip, she said, 'This is genuine interest, you understand? I mean, I've never met anyone who's . . . How shall I put it? . . . *in your position* before and I have to tell you that you're nothing like how I imagined a drug baron would be.' She grinned self-consciously as he laughed at her description of him. 'Is it true,' she said, 'what I read about you? How you organized the whole thing, all those container ships and the decoys and the enormous quantities of marijuana that were taken into the States?'

He nodded. 'Yes, it's true.'

She looked at him, feeling, not for the first time, slightly in awe of his ... was it genius? Certainly it required a brilliant mind to succeed as he had, when you considered the sheer scale of the operations he masterminded. As for the money he had made ...

'A hundred million dollars?' she said.

He laughed. 'An inflated figure by my estimation. But sure, it was a lot.'

She was tempted to ask where the money was now, but thought that perhaps that would be pushing too far. 'How did you get into it all?' she asked.

He took a breath and let it out slowly. 'Well, I guess I'd been looking around for some time for something that presented a real challenge since that was lacking elsewhere in my life. I'd been dealing in art for years, I had plenty of people working for me who could run things perfectly well without me and what I really wanted was to get back to the sea. I knew a few guys who were into the smuggling game – it's hard to avoid them in the East – but they were pretty small-time. So we got together and ... well, the rest is history.'

'Didn't it ever concern you that you were likely to end up in prison?'

He shrugged. 'Sure, but I guess that was half the fun, outsmarting the DEA and the straight Thai or Hong Kong cops, of which there aren't many, I'm here to tell you. It's a real battle of wits and when the adrenalin gets going, when you've got FBI choppers buzzing the ship, or you're flying a plane loaded with cash into the Caymans or wherever, and you don't know what the hell might be waiting for you when you get there ... well, it beats the hell out of a nine-to-five existence.'

Penny looked down at her glass, realizing that she felt horribly parochial in her role as the editor of a small-time magazine where the highs were so insignificant in comparison they couldn't even be measured against those he was talking about. Not that she wanted to go out and commit a crime, but she could easily imagine the excitement of his life, the fear and the glamour and the sheer exhilaration of pulling it all together. For a moment she almost wished that she didn't lack the nerve to get involved, for her cowardice made her feel so dull.

Bringing her eyes back to his, she said, 'The newspaper cuttings I read about you all date back to two years or more ago. Was that when you came to Europe? Two years ago?'

'Yeah, around that time.'

'To the South of France?'

'No, to Paris, actually. Paris and London. I don't spend much time here on the Riviera. It's a great place to visit, but it lacks energy. Most of the people are half asleep – they don't appear to have a clue what's going on in the world around them and I guess they don't much care either.' His eyes were dancing. 'Of course, there are exceptions.'

Penny smiled, but she was thinking that, not so long ago she had held the same view of the Riviera and now, listening to him, she realized she'd been too busy to notice that he was right. There wasn't much stimulation to be got down here and it felt suddenly as if the rest of the world was moving on without her.

'You know, there is something that intrigues me,' she said.

His eyebrows were raised as he waited for her to go on.

'Well, how on earth did you come to choose people like Esther and Wally Delaney to look after things for you when they seem the least likely people on earth to become involved in . . .' She started to smile as she belatedly realized how dense she was being. 'Which is, of course, precisely why you chose them,' she said, answering her own question.

His eyes were simmering with laughter. 'To tell you the truth,' he said, 'they don't do that much for me. Esther is just one of many who courier things back and forth to the States for me from time to time, or drive me between cities here in Europe. And the guys who organize false identities and passports for me occasionally deliver them to Wally. But don't tell him I told you that, because he likes to think he's running the show.'

Penny nodded, thinking that he was far more tolerant of Wally than she would ever be. 'He's very protective of you,' she remarked.

Christian grimaced. 'He's protective of an income he needs badly,' he responded.

Penny's eyes slanted towards the window for a moment as she thought about what she wanted to ask next and considered how to phrase it. In the end she said, 'The night of the launch party, the party to which you *almost* came,' she added, looking at him teasingly, 'Esther mentioned that there was another boss, someone whose name she didn't know . . .'

He nodded and his smile was wry as he said, 'Most of the guys are in jail now, but there are still a few of us this side of Gomorrah. The others are mainly in South America or the Far East. We meet up occasionally, either there or here and Esther wouldn't know the name of the guy who was here at the time of your launch, because it's safer for her not to know. And the reason she'd think of him as a boss is that Wally told him about you and he came on pretty heavy with me about how crazy I was to be even considering putting myself at risk by meeting you. I didn't argue, because he had a point. You see, it's only a matter of time for all of us now.'

Penny looked at him, wondering what it must be like to have something like that hanging over your head and feeling slightly dazed by how casually he seemed to accept it. 'Are you really considering giving yourself up?' she asked, feeling her heart trip on the dread of his answer.

'Considering, yes,' he said. 'But there are things I still need to straighten out before I go.'

'You mean the deal with the DA?'

He nodded. 'That, yes. Other things too.' His smile was self-mocking. 'You see, when the boss gives himself up, the pressure will be off the rest.'

'Meaning they might keep their freedom if you give up yours?'

'They might.'

'Which is why the pressure is so great for you?'

As he looked at her she could see that he was wondering if she really understood. 'It's hard,' he said in the end, 'but it's life. It was all just an adventure when it began. I don't think any of us ever dreamt we'd make so much money or get the kind of thrill we did doing it. It got so we couldn't stop.'

'But you've stopped now?'

He laughed. 'Yes, we've stopped.'

'Do you have any regrets?'

His eyes seemed to cloud as he looked searchingly into hers. 'Sure, I have regrets,' he said softly. 'More now I've met you, which is another reason I resisted you for so long. I was kind of afraid this might happen.'

Penny swallowed hard and, taking a breath, she said, 'Earlier, when I arrived at the hotel, I was trying to think of something I read the other day and now I know what it was.'

His eyes were dancing as he waited for her to go on.

'It was by Henry Miller,' she said. 'He wrote: "Nobody can feel better than the man who is completely taken in. To be intelligent may be a boon, but to be completely trusting, gullible to the point of idiocy, to surrender without reservation, is one of the supreme joys of life." '

Christian gave a shout of laughter. 'And do you consider yourself to be so gullible?' he said.

'I think I could be,' she said, her eyes dancing.

'And do you think that I'm trying to take you in?'

'No. But if you are, then I surrender without reservation.'

Instead of laughing, as she'd expected him to, he simply looked at her as though trying to fathom her. 'Tell me about you,' he said softly. 'Have you ever been married?'

'No,' she answered. 'But I know that you have.'

He was quiet for some time; then, looking down at his glass, he said, 'It's in the past. Let's leave it there, shall we?'

He's still hurting, Penny was thinking as she looked at the shadows on his face.

At last he brought his eyes back to hers and as she gazed into them he reached across the table and took her hand in his. The touch was very gentle, yet Penny's eyes and heart fluttered as she felt the incredible force of him flowing into her. Then, as his fingers curled around hers and he willed her to look at him again, she experienced such a heightening of emotion that the panic she had felt earlier at the power of what was happening between them swept through her again.

'Can we go?' she whispered.

'Yes,' he nodded. 'I think we should.'

They made love all that night and into the next morning. For Penny there were moments when it was hard to make herself believe it wasn't all a dream. But harder still was making herself accept that it wasn't going to last. Her hunger for his embraces, his passion, his extraordinary gift for knowing what she needed and then showing her more was something she couldn't bear to think of coming to an end. He was blinding her. All she could see was him, all she could feel was the incredible force of the sensations racing through her body. Once he accused her of being alone, of taking her pleasure and shutting him out. But when he discovered how long it had been since she'd made love he made her lie back on the pillows and allow him to bring her back to life.

What he did to her was indescribable as he took her from one spectacular release to another, and another. He made love to her in every possible position, throwing her across the bed and driving himself into her until she could take no more. And then he was tender, stroking her, caressing her, kissing her and telling her to look into his eyes.

'You're not with me,' he whispered. 'I can see you're not with me.'

'How can you say that,' she groaned, 'when I've never been more with anyone in my life?'

He smiled and kissed her softly on the mouth. 'Maybe,' he said, 'the fear of losing you has already become too great.'

'Don't let's talk about that,' she said, tightening her arms around him. 'Don't let's even think about it, not now.'

Rolling on to his back, he took her with him and looked up at her in the dawn light. 'Make love to me now,' he whispered. 'Make love to me and tell me you love me.'

'I love you, Christian,' she whispered, tears starting in her eyes. 'I don't understand it, but I do.'

'Shh,' he said softly, wiping away her tears. 'I love you too.'

Pulling himself up he put his mouth to her breast and sucked gently on the tender nipple. She looked down at him, running her fingers through his hair then pulling his face up she held it between her hands.

'Look at me,' she pleaded. 'Look at me and tell me what's happening between us. I don't understand it, I don't know how to deal with it. I . . . I feel so afraid.'

'I know,' he said. 'I can sense it. But don't be afraid — we'll deal with this together, take our days as they come,

280

be grateful for what we have while we have it.'

'But I don't want to lose you. I just can't bear to think about it.'

'Shh,' he soothed. 'I thought we weren't going to talk about it now.'

'You're right,' she sighed.

'Why don't we sleep for a while?' he said, easing her down and drawing her head to his shoulder.

'I would if I wasn't so afraid that when I wake up you'll be gone.'

But he wasn't. He was still there, holding her as he breathed slowly and rhythmically in his own sleep.

Gazing at him, the dark line of his brows, the tiny scar beneath his eye that she hadn't noticed before, the sharp bones of his cheeks, the inky-black stubble around his jaw, the pale redness of his mouth, she thought how terribly vulnerable he looked. It made her think of David and the moment of vulnerability he had shown the day before. She found herself wondering what it would be like to lie there looking at him this way, feeling the firmness of his body against hers, the gentle whisper of his breath on her cheek. Then all thoughts of David were gone as Christian's eyes opened and he started to smile.

Smiling too, Penny turned away and reached for her robe.

'Hey, where are you going?' he laughed, pulling her back.

'To the bathroom.' Romance like this was bliss, was what fantasies were made of, but in reality she had to clean her teeth.

A few minutes later he came up behind her and stood watching her in the mirror as she moved the toothbrush back and forth. It was a while before the intensity of his eyes penetrated her, when it did she stopped brushing and turned to face him. Taking the toothbrush from her mouth, he lowered his lips to hers and pushed his tongue deep inside. Penny's arms went round him, her fingers digging hard into his buttocks as he pressed himself to her. Her head fell back as he moved his lips down over her neck, his hands pushing aside her robe, sliding over her shoulders and covering her breasts.

In a moment they were on the floor and he was inside her. She was still tender and raw, but the feel of him pushing into her was so much stronger than the pain. She lifted her knees, and turned to the mirror, watching the powerful thrust of his body as he rode her.

'Where are you?' he whispered, turning her face back to his.

'I was there,' she smiled, 'in the mirror with you, watching you make love to me.'

He turned to look and laughed softly. 'Come back to me,' he murmured to her reflection. 'Be with me here.'

As she looked up into his eyes she pushed her fingers into his hair and traced a thumb over his lips. For a moment his eyes fluttered closed as he reached total penetration. Then, raising his hips, he started to pump gently in and out of her, all the time holding her eyes.

'Oh God,' she groaned as he started to move faster. 'What are you doing to me? I never knew I . . . Oh, God!' she cried as he pushed a hand between them and touched her. 'Christian!' she sobbed, clinging to him as he stroked his fingers back and forth.

Then, pulling himself gently out of her, he eased her on to her side and entered her from behind, moving his fingers faster and faster over the front of her until she felt the incapacitating shudders of orgasm begin. And he was there with her, opening her legs wider as he rolled on to his back and pulled her on to him. Then he was sitting with his chest pressed against her back, pushing her forward until she fell on to her knees. Her orgasm was exploding in exquisite, torturous bursts, seeming to go on for ever.

'Ah, *mon Dieu*,' he gasped as he rammed himself hard into her and held himself there. He was so big inside her that she could feel the pulsating beat of his climax. 'Oh, Penny, Penny,' he groaned. 'My love, what are we doing to each other?'

As she collasped beneath him he fell over her, moving the bulk of his weight to the floor.

It was a long time before either of them had the strength to move. When they did, it was only because he complained he was getting cold.

Laughing, Penny turned over and cupped his face in her hands. 'I want to do it again,' she teased.

Closing his eyes, he started to laugh. 'Ah, saved by the bell,' he said as the telephone rang.

As Penny went to take the call she heard him turn on the shower. A few minutes later she was back, standing under the water with him and soaping him.

'Who was it?' he asked, holding his face under the spray.

'Just a colleague,' she answered, not about to tell him that it had been Marielle calling to find out how her date had gone.

'Do you have to go into the office today?' he asked.

'No. What about you? Do you have to go anywhere?'

'No.'

They spent the entire weekend together, only parting for the few, but lengthy, calls he had to make. She didn't ask about them: they were a part of another life, a life that was going to intrude upon them all too soon, so why invite it? They walked in the garden in the rain, drove up to Mougins and drank coffee behind the steamy windows of a café. On Saturday evening he took over her car and drove them to an out-of-the-way restaurant, deep in the forests of the Var. On Sunday morning, after another night of untold passion and broken sleep, he drove down to Cannes, collected the papers and took them back to her in bed. At lunchtime he raided the fridge; then, throwing everything back in disgust, announced he was taking her to lunch in Eze. They talked about so many things, exploring each other's pasts, sorely feeling the need for each other's futures. It was like, Penny thought, teetering on the edge of a precipice knowing that to go over was inevitable, it was just a matter of time. The first jolt of a near fall came on Sunday evening as they were driving back to the villa and he told her he would have to leave in the morning.

Penny's eyes dropped to her hands. 'Where will you be going?' she asked.

'Not far, just up to Paris. Will you miss me?'

'Do you need to ask?' she replied, smiling. 'How long will you be gone?'

'A few days. No more.' He glanced over at her, then returned his eyes to the road. 'Why don't you come with me?' he said.

Penny's heart somersaulted. Should she? Could she? She knew she didn't want to be parted from him, but . . . 'I'll have to call the office,' she said. 'I think they can manage without me for a few days, but I'd better square it with my deputy.'

When they got home Penny played back the messages on the answerphone, while Christian stood behind her, his arms wrapped round her. The first two were from friends in London. The third was from David.

Instantly Penny felt a flare of guilt. She'd totally forgotten to call him.

'Hi, Pen,' he said. 'I guess you got busy last night. Not to worry, I'll catch up with you tomorrow.'

'Who was that?' Christian said.

'My boss,' she answered, turning in his arms.

He looked down at her, studying her face and seeming as bemused as he did angry. 'Are you in love with him?' he asked.

Penny stared at him, stunned.

'Are you?' he repeated.

'No, of course not,' she answered, shaking her head in disbelief. 'How can you even ask it when we've just spent the weekend we have?'

His eyes were still boring into hers. 'The way he spoke sounded intimate,' he said.

'That's David,' Penny told him. 'He always sounds like that – with everyone. Hey, come on, there's nothing to be jealous of. I told you, he's just my boss.'

Christian tightened his hold on her. 'I guess the strain is too great sometimes,' he said. 'Meeting you, falling in love with you, everything happening so quickly.' He laughed. 'You're not the only one who's afraid. I don't want to lose you, but I know I'm going to.'

'No,' she said vehemently. 'You're not. You don't understand. I don't care how long it takes, I'll wait for you, Christian. I don't want anyone else, I never will, I already know that. What we have together only comes once in a lifetime – do you think I'd let it go that easily?'

'Brave words,' he smiled. 'But will you still be saying them three years, maybe ten years, from now? No,' he said, putting a finger over her lips, 'don't answer that. Just tell me you love me now.'

'I love you now,' she whispered, and as she gazed up at him she very nearly told him what else was in her mind. But in the end she couldn't say it. Things had gone fast enough already; they had to spend more time together, be even more sure of each other than they were now, before they started thinking about dispensing with the condoms. So far they hadn't made love once without one, not even yesterday morning in the bathroom, and in truth she could hardly believe she was considering such a move.

Could she really be wishing that upon herself? she was wondering as they walked into the kitchen. A life of single parenthood as she waited for him to come out of jail? What on earth had got into her to make her think of such things? Did she really love him that much or was she just losing sight of reality?

It was around midnight when Penny woke to find the

bed empty beside her. Trying to swallow the fear that he had slipped away quietly, she started to reach out for the lamp, then stopped as she saw him, silhouetted in the moonlit window, staring out at the garden.

'Christian?' she said hoarsely, turning on the lamp.

Immediately he turned. 'Shh!' he said. 'Put out the light and come over here.'

Obediently Penny killed the light and padded across the room to stand in the circle of his arm.

'Did you know you were being watched?' he asked in a whisper.

Penny's sleepy eyes flew open as an icy tremor coasted through her. 'What do you mean?' she asked. 'Who would want to watch me?'

'I don't know,' he answered, 'but someone is. Look, down there in the trees. Do you see him?'

Penny craned her neck to see, but everything looked perfectly still and as it should be. 'I don't understand,' she said. 'Surely if someone was watching here, they'd . . . well, they'd be looking for you.'

He laughed softly. 'Do you think if they wanted me they'd still be out there?' he said. 'And this isn't the first time I've noticed someone. We were followed over to Eze today.'

'But how do you know?'

He smiled. 'After two years of living the way I have I don't have too much trouble spotting these things. Have you any idea why someone would be having you watched?'

'No,' she answered, feeling faintly light-headed at the prospect. 'None.'

Sensing her fear, he drew her closer to him. 'Maybe I've got it wrong,' he said. 'Maybe it's just a prowler out there. Is the place alarmed?'

'Fully,' she answered. 'I've even got a portable panic button I can carry around with me.'

'Is it connected to the police?'

'No, a security company. They're pretty good,' she went on, as though to reassure herself. 'They can be here within a few minutes. Oh God, this is so scary,' she groaned.

'Shh,' he said, touching her forehead with his lips. 'I shouldn't have said anything, and nothing's going to happen to you while I'm here.'

As he started to lead her back to the bed Penny cast one last, lingering glance out of the window. Still there was no movement other than the gentle sway of the trees and within minutes of lying in his arms all her fears were forgotten.

Chapter 15

Getting away to Paris proved no problem. Marielle was only too ready to cover – in fact she was insistent that Penny should stay away as long as she liked. Both Penny and Christian laughed about that since she'd already told him how keen Marielle was to usurp her position. They caught a mid-morning flight from Nice airport, where Penny noticed that the name on his passport was Jacques Marchand. She teased him about it during the flight, making him recite his many aliases.

When they arrived in Paris just over an hour later it was to find the Delaneys' counterparts waiting to drive them into the city. They stayed in a quaint, cosy little hotel not far from the Pompidou Centre and fought like crazy over who was going to pay for it.

'I don't care if you're a multimillionaire,' she shouted at him. 'You paid for everything all weekend, you even paid for the flights up here, so it's my turn now.'

'But you don't get a turn,' he said, laughing. 'No! Penny, put your purse away, you're—'

'Take it!' she cried, thrusting a handful of 200-franc notes at him. 'Please!'

'No! Keep it. You never know when you might need it.'

There was nothing Penny could do to persuade him, so in the end she gave up trying. Instead, while he was seeing the people he'd come here to see, she shopped and bought him some decent clothes.

'What is all this?' he cried, holding up the shirts and trousers and jackets from Giorgio Armani.

'It's called style – something you're not big on,' she told him bluntly.

He gave a her a pained look, saying, 'But I live on the sea. I don't know about clothes for life ashore. Did I really look so terrible?'

'Yes,' she answered, smiling at him. 'You looked like you'd been thrown together by a bankrupt charity. But now you're going to look devastating.'

Which he did. The clothes fitted him well, since she'd taken some of his old ones along with her to match them for size. The only trouble was, now that she had spent so much money on him he was insisting he do the same for her.

'You know what,' she told him as they wandered, laden with parcels and carrier bags, into the Galeries Lafayettes. 'I feel a bit like Bonnie and Clyde doing this.'

'Is that supposed to be funny?' he remarked.

'Yes, it was actually,' she answered. 'I mean, don't you think so too? Us out here spending all your ill-gotten gains!'

'Shh,' he said sharply.

No, that wasn't very tactful, Penny, she told herself, wishing she could bite out her tongue, until she saw him watching her from the corner of his eye and trying not to laugh.

'We've been invited to dinner with some friends of mine this evening,' he told her on the way back to the hotel. 'Would you like to go? Or would you prefer it was just the two of us?'

Penny put her head thoughtfully to one side. 'I don't know,' she said in the end. 'I'd like to meet your friends . . .'

'But they aren't very interesting,' he finished for her, 'and personally I would prefer to have you all to myself.'

'Then you shall,' she told him.

They went to *Le Tour d'Argent* that evening, not because he particularly liked it, but because Penny had never been. It was while they were there, gazing down at Notre-Dame in the wintry moonlight, that he told her he wanted her to return to the South since things were getting a little complicated here.

Immediately Penny panicked. 'What are you saying?' she asked. 'Are you about to be—'

'No,' he said, holding up a hand for her to stop. 'It's nothing like that. It's just that I'm not going to be able to spend much time with you over the next few days and I don't like to think of you wandering Paris alone.'

'I wouldn't mind,' she objected.

He grinned. 'Don't you have a business to run?'

'Yes, I suppose I do,' she said wryly. 'I'd almost forgotten. And you're right: I should be getting back. But when will I see you again? How can I get in touch with you?'

'Don't worry about that,' he said. '*I'll* be in touch with *you*. And I'll be in Italy at the weekend, over at Lake Garda. Do you think you can get away?'

'Yes,' she answered blithely. In truth she wasn't particularly proud of the way she was shirking her responsibilities, though she'd called the office several times to make sure there was no crisis going on in her absence. Of course there wasn't, Marielle was perfectly in control, though what David was making of her sudden disappearance she hadn't stopped to find out. Besides, what did *Nuance* matter when weighed against what little time she and Christian might have left together?

'Are you sure you want to come?' Christian asked.

'Yes. Yes, of course I do,' Penny answered brightly.

'Then why do I get the impression you're not sure?'

'I don't know,' she said, not wanting to tell him how guilty she felt about David and the way she was letting him down after all he'd done for her. Actually, the more she thought about David, the worse she felt, and though it pained her to admit it she was almost afraid to face him.

Christian drove her out to Orly himself the next morning, assuring her all the way that he was crazy about her, that he was going to miss her more than he could bear and couldn't wait for the weekend when they'd meet up in Italy. He'd already given her the name and address of the hotel, telling her that one of the Delaneys would drive her there and he would take her back himself.

When she arrived at Nice she took a taxi straight to the office, to find Marielle and Mario engaged in battle.

Situation normal, Penny remarked to herself as, virtually unnoticed, she sailed past them into her office, where she discovered Brigitte sitting at the computer – because, she explained, hers had gone down.

'So what's new?' Penny asked, taking off her coat. 'Where's David?'

'I don't know. He hasn't been in today.'

'Pierre?'

'No, he isn't here either, but he called to say he'd be in this afternoon. There's a message there for you to call back the owner of that restaurant in Valbonne we gave a bad review to. He's been calling since Monday, but Marielle said to leave it to you. She thought you'd prefer to handle it yourself, since you approved the write-up.'

Penny picked up the message. There was nothing more than a name and telephone number. 'OK, I'll call him,' she said as the evening she had spent there with Céline, the restaurant critic, came back to her. 'But I hope he doesn't think he's getting a retraction after the bloody awful service we got. Did I tell you what he said when I asked where the food was after we'd been waiting over forty minutes for the starter?' She knew she was gabbling, trying to hide her embarrassment at taking off the way she had. Had Marielle told them it was because of a man? 'He said,' she went on, ' "If you don't like it you can always go somewhere else." Which of course we did. And which, of course,' she laughed, 'Céline reported in the piece! Anyway, it might keep him on his toes a bit and make him realize that not every English-speaker down here is a tourist and even if they were that's no way to run a restaurant.'

'I'd love to have seen his face when he picked up your card from the table,' Brigitte giggled.

'So would I,' Penny commented, 'but, alas, we'd already left by then. Anyway, what else has been happening? Any news about the fashion shoot Babette's organizing?'

'It's all going ahead. We've got the lobby of the Hermitage in Monte Carlo and François Ruault is doing the photographs.'

'Great!' Penny cried. 'I thought he was in Paris.'

'He was, but apparently he's managed to squeeze us in.'

'Well, Marielle really is surpassing herself these days.'

'Not Marielle: Pierre. He called François and asked him to do it.'

'For Pierre, read David,' Penny smiled. 'So, you don't know where he is?'

'No. I can try his apartment if you like?'

'Not to worry, we'll run into each other soon enough,' Penny responded, showing nothing of the nervousness she felt at the prospect. 'Now, I need to get down to some work. No interruptions unless vital. Oh, except if there's a call from—' She stopped. What name would he give? 'It doesn't matter,' she said, 'you can put the calls through. Tell Marielle I'd like to speak to her when she's finished tearing into Mario.'

To her surprise Penny found it easier to concentrate on her workload than she'd expected and by the end of the day she'd managed the beginning of a short story, as well as a couple of editorials, and had successfully fought her way through a barrage of telephone calls. By the time she left at seven o'clock there was still no sign of David and Pierre had come and gone so quickly she hadn't even seen him.

'Well, there's no point putting it off,' she told herself wearily as she walked into the villa and turned on the lights, she had to face the music some time. She stood for a moment listening to the silence of the house, glancing up over the stairs as though she could hear the dying echoes of her and Christian's laughter. Then, dropping her bags in the hall, she went through to the sitting room and picked up the phone to call David's apartment. She let it ring for some time, but there was no reply and it appeared he'd forgotten to put on his answerphone.

'Well, at least he can't say I didn't try,' she said aloud as she replaced the receiver. Which, she added glumly to herself, was more than she could say for Christian, since he hadn't called all day.

Penny wasn't sure when, or even how, it started, all she knew was that by the time eleven o'clock came round she had worked herself to such a pitch of anxiety that she couldn't sit still even for a minute. She'd tried calling the Delaneys, but there was no reply; she'd tried the hotel she and Christian had stayed at in Paris, but he had checked out. She'd even considered driving over to the Delaneys to make sure no one was there, that they weren't trying to avoid her again, but she'd stopped herself at the last moment, refusing to give in to her paranoia. Christian had said he would call and anything, just anything, could have happened to prevent it.

She kept thinking about the prowler he had spotted outside whom she'd forgotten until now. All the shutters were closed, the doors were locked, there was no way anyone could get in, but in this house of creaking antique furniture every sound was tearing her nerves to shreds. And then there was David. Where was he? Where had everyone gone? Why did she feel so alone, so inexplicably threatened by the silence, by this horrible feeling of desertion?

Her heart was beating too fast. She paced up and down, her mind racing. He had said he loved her, he wanted her with him at the weekend, so why was she worrying like this? Because she was going to lose him. Because sooner or later they would take him away and she just couldn't bear it. They should be together now; she should have insisted she stay in Paris. Why had he sent her back? Why wouldn't he share what was going on in his life, allow her to support him? Because he was trying to protect her. Because he loved her.

Oh dear God, she prayed silently, *don't let them have taken him away yet. Please, please, God, let me see him again.*

She started, almost screamed, as the telephone suddenly shrilled through the house. Running to it, she grabbed it and in her haste, dropped it.

'Hello? Penny?' a voice was saying.

'Yes? Esther, is that you?'

'Yes, dear, it's me. How are you?'

'Oh, I'm fine,' Penny answered, taking a steadying breath. 'I was just . . . Oh God, I'm behaving like such an idiot here, Esther. Do you know where Christian is? Have you spoken to him? He said he'd call, but—'

'He's right here,' Esther interrupted.

'Where? Where are you? I tried your house . . .'

'I'm in Paris,' Esther said. 'And Christian's right here. He wants to talk to you.'

Penny waited, listening to the muted voices at the other end, then Christian's voice, low and intimate and sounding almost as anguished as she felt, came down the line. 'Hi,' he said. 'How are you? I'm sorry I didn't call

294

earlier. Things have been hectic here.'

'That's OK,' Penny answered.

'Are you missing me?'

'Do you need to ask? Are you missing me?'

'I can hardly think about anything else. But listen, I'm not sure any more about the weekend. Things have changed a bit and maybe I won't be in Italy after all. But I'll call you, OK?'

'Yes,' Penny whispered. Then, unable to stop herself: 'Can I come wherever you'll be?'

'Of course. I'll let you know where as soon as I know myself.' He paused, giving Penny the impression there was something he wanted to say, but obviously he decided not to for all he added was, 'I have to go now. I love you, *chérie*,' and the line went dead.

After she'd hung up Penny put her hands to her face and took a deep, shuddering breath. At first she thought it was relief she was feeling, but then she realized that it was something more akin to fear; as if she was beginning to drift in a sea of hopeless and tormented emotion.

'You've got to pull yourself together,' she told herself sharply. 'This is only the beginning – and if you can't cope now, when *will* you be able to?'

For some reason the sound of her own voice seemed to calm her, seemed to pass through the maelstrom inside her and quell it. She felt suddenly exhausted, as though she hadn't slept in so long she no longer knew what it was to sink into the oblivion of dreamless escape.

Dragging herself up the stairs, she turned out the lights behind her, trying not to see the towering shadows that loomed from each corner. She'd never been afraid in this house before, but tonight her nerves were so raw they jarred at every noise; her senses were wired and razor-sharp, yet all she wanted now was to sleep and sleep and sleep.

As she got into bed she pulled the panic button from the drawer and slipped it under her pillow. She didn't want to be here alone any more: she wanted Christian to be here, to reassure her that there was nothing to be afraid of. Was he right, was there someone watching her? She hadn't seen anyone, but why would he have said it if it weren't true? Why would anyone be watching her? She was nobody, a nobody who knew nothing . . .

It was in the early hours of the morning that a noise somewhere in the house roused her. Drugged by sleep, she turned over, telling herself it was just Sammy coming home, and started to drift back into oblivion. Then suddenly, as the thought of Sammy penetrated needle-sharp in her brain, the veil of sleep tore open and her heart hammered with fear. Sammy didn't live here any more. Sammy had gone.

A white-hot burn of terror slid through her heart. There was someone in the room with her, she could hear someone breathing. Not a trace of moonlight was coming through the shutters, there was nothing to see . . .

Suddenly one corner of the room was flooded with a sluggish light. Penny's eyes were still closed, feigning sleep, as panic pulsed through her. Slowly, very slowly, she was inching her hand towards the emergency button under her pillow.

'I know you're awake, Penny.' It was a stranger's voice, but he knew her name! Terror thundered through her brain.

'Open your eyes, Penny,' he said. 'There's nothing to be afraid of. I'm not going to hurt you.'

It was a nightmare. She would wake up in a minute. Somehow she would manage to drag herself from this mind-numbing terror.

As though they had a will of their own, Penny's eyes opened. There was a man, sitting in the corner, watching her.

'Hello, Penny.' He smiled. 'Please forgive the un-orthodox—'

He got no further, for suddenly every siren in the house started to wail and alarm bells shrilled as Penny leapt from the bed and made a frantic dash to the bathroom. Once inside, she bolted the door, pressed herself against it and feverishly pleaded for help. She could hear nothing above the pounding in her ears and the scream of the sirens. No one was forcing the door the other side, but she wouldn't, couldn't, let go. Her whole body was seized by shuddering spasms of shock, her mind was a screaming vortex of terror.

It seemed an eternity before she heard the piercing squeal of brakes, and the barking of dogs, carry through the din of the alarms. Her heart was still racing; she was too afraid to move.

A minute later everything went silent. The sirens had stopped. Then she heard the dogs tearing through the house and, almost immediately, someone calling her name.

'I'm up here,' she shouted. *Oh thank God, thank God, thank God.* 'I'm in the bathroom, in the master suite.'

Even before the security guard found her the Alsatians were there, scratching the door, growling, barking, frantic to get in. Two sharp words from the guard and they backed off.

'It's OK,' he called out to her. 'You can come out.'

Tentatively Penny unlocked the door and pulled it open. She could hear more dogs outside, racing through the grounds in search of an intruder.

'Are you all right?' the guard asked. 'What happened?'

Penny swallowed and took a breath. 'I'm sorry,' she said shakily, 'it was just so . . .' She took another breath. 'There was someone in here. Someone,' she said, point-ing at the chair, 'sitting right there.'

The guard turned to look at the chair.

'He woke me up,' she said. 'He said my name. He was

... Oh God, I'm sorry, I'll have myself together in a minute.'

'It's all right,' the guard said comfortingly. 'Just take your time. Would you like to go downstairs?'

'Yes,' she breathed. 'Yes, I think so. Is he gone?'

The guard nodded. 'The dogs would have found him if he hadn't. Was it anyone you know?' he asked.

Penny nodded. 'Yes. I mean ... I'm not sure. It all happened so fast.'

As the guard led her gently down the stairs his colleague came in through the front door. 'No one out there,' he told them.

The first guard nodded, then told him to round up the dogs.

'What I want to know,' Penny said, as the guard poured her a brandy, 'is how he got in.'

'Good question,' the guard responded. 'We'll check the place over, but if he got past the alarms that suggests he was already in here before you went to bed.'

'Oh God,' Penny groaned, feeling the fear slide through her again.

'Is there someone you can call?' the guard asked a few minutes later. 'Someone who can come and stay with you?'

Penny shook her head. 'No, I don't—' She stopped, swallowed another mouthful of brandy and said, 'Yes. Yes, there is someone. What time is it?'

The guard looked at his watch. 'Ten past two.'

Twenty minutes later Penny was standing in the hall with the guards when David's car skidded to a halt outside and he came racing up the steps and in through the front door.

The moment she saw his pale, anxious face, Penny started to shake all over again.

'It's OK, it's OK,' he said, pulling her into his arms. 'What the hell happened?' He was looking at the security guards.

'There was an intruder,' one of them told him. 'The door to the laundry room has been forced. It would seem he got in before the alarms were set, but we're checking the system to make sure there isn't a fault.' Then, in a lower voice. 'She's had a nasty shock . . . Would you like us to call the police?'

'Do you want the police, Pen?' David asked, his voice muffled by her hair.

She shook her head and pulled herself away. 'No. No, it's all right. I'm all right now.'

'Would you like us to leave one of the dogs outside?' the guard offered. David nodded. 'Right, no problem. We'll come back for him in the morning. If you need him any longer, we'll run through his commands with you. His name's Brutus, by the way.'

As soon as the front door closed behind the guards, David locked and bolted it, then went back to Penny in the sitting room. Her face was buried in her hands, and her shoulders were shaking she was sobbing so hard.

'Hey, hey,' he said, going to her. 'It's all right. Come on, nothing's going to happen.'

'Oh David!' she wailed, turning into his arms. 'I'm sorry. I'm so sorry. I'm making such a fool of myself. I just . . . Oh God, I can't even speak. I was so afraid you weren't going to be there. But I was afraid to see you. I thought you were angry with me. I don't blame you if you are. I shouldn't have gone just like that. I wanted to be there for you, but I let you down. I'm sorry, David. I'm so sorry. I'm making such a mess of things and I just don't know what to do.'

'For someone who can't speak, you're not doing so bad,' he laughed. 'Now, what's all this about? Why am I going to be mad at you?' he asked, squeezing her.

'For going off the way I did,' she said, turning away from him and moving towards the piano. 'I know I shouldn't have done it. I know I should have cleared it with you . . .'

'Why should you have cleared it with me? And did the world fall apart because you weren't there? Now, come on . . .'

'But that's not the point,' she cried, wringing her hands. 'You've done so much for me and I let you down. I didn't call you back at the weekend . . .'

'OK, time out,' he said softly. 'This isn't about apologizing to me for something you don't have to apologize for. This is about an intruder in the house . . .'

Suddenly coming to her senses, Penny spun round. 'It was the man from the Mercedes!' she said shrilly. 'The one I told you about. The fat one. I swear it was him. He was sitting there in my bedroom, watching me.'

David's face drained. 'Are you sure?' he said.

'Yes.' Then, shaking her head: 'I don't know. I think it was him. But if it was, then what was he doing here, David? Why did he break into my house?'

'I don't know,' David answered, almost to himself. 'But I'll find out. Did he say anything to you?'

'No, not really. Just that he wasn't going to harm me.' Her eyes came up to his. 'David, do you think he might be having me watched?' she said. David's eyes bored into hers, but even through her agitation she could see that his mind wasn't really with her. 'Do you?' she implored.

'I don't know,' he answered. 'He could be.'

'Oh God,' she groaned. 'I can't stand this. It's like a nightmare. Nothing makes sense any more. Why would he be having me watched?'

'That's something else I'll have to find out,' David said and, putting an arm around her, he led her to the sofa. 'Come on, sit down,' he said. 'I'll go get some blankets. Where are they?'

'In the cupboard on the first landing. Who is he, David?'

'I guess you could call him my nemesis,' he answered, staring sightlessly at the empty brandy glass beside her.

300

'Do you want some more of that?' he said.

Penny shook her head. 'No. I just want this night to be over.'

He found the blankets and brought them back to the sitting room. Penny was hunched into one corner of the sofa, her eyelashes still wet with tears, her face even more strained than it had been when he'd left.

He said nothing as he wrapped a blanket around her as though she were a child. Penny started to look up, found she couldn't meet his eyes, and turned away. She knew he was still watching her as he went to sit on the opposite sofa and sensed something in him she couldn't quite define.

'Was it a man?' he asked softly. 'Was that the reason you took off the way you did?'

Penny nodded. Despite the gentleness of his voice it sounded strangely hollow, as though it was causing him more effort to speak than it was her.

'Where did you go?' he said.

'Paris,' she answered, her voice faltering on the word as tears threatened to overwhelm her again.

'Didn't it work out?'

Screwing up her eyes Penny swallowed hard. 'Yes, it worked out,' she said. 'It's just . . . It's just a bit complicated, that's all.'

His laugh held no humour. 'Aren't these things always?' He waited a moment, then said, perhaps too casually, 'Anyone I know?'

She shook her head. 'I'm sorry, but if you don't mind I'd rather not talk about him.'

At last her eyes came up to his. In the dim light she couldn't make out his expression, but there was a tension about him that disturbed her, brought back the guilt she had felt when she hadn't called him. 'Is there anything I can do?' she said, hoarsely.

At first he seemed surprised by the question; then, understanding what she meant, he said, 'No. I'll handle it. Just you get some sleep. I'll be right here. Do you want me to hold—' He stopped, pulled a hand over his tired face and forced himself to smile. 'Try to sleep,' he said.

A few hours later, as the first rays of dawn were seeping through the shutters, David got up and went to the phone. It didn't take Pierre long to get there, by which time David was waiting on the front steps, his face drawn with exhaustion as he held Brutus on a chain.

'She's still asleep,' he said as Pierre, unshaven and warmly wrapped in a fur-lined coat, got out of his car. 'Stay with her until she wakes up. I don't know what she'll want to do today – it's probably best if she goes to the office. Then we'll have to arrange things so someone stays here with her.'

'Not you,' Pierre said. It wasn't a question, nor was it an order: it was a simple statement of fact.

'No, not me,' David said wearily. Then, releasing the dog from the chain, he said, 'I'll be in touch when I've seen Stirling. Have you got your mobile?'

Pierre patted his pocket.

David nodded, then, getting into his car, he turned it around and drove off towards the gates.

The yacht moored at the far end of the Canto Port in Cannes rocked gently in the water as David strode across the deck, his taut, handsome face showing nothing of what he was feeling inside.

As he banged open the cabin door Stirling looked up from his breakfast, feigning surprise with pleasantly arched brows, but when he took breath to speak David's voice cut across him, a whiplash of fury.

'You've gone too far this time, Stirling,' he growled. 'I could have you up on charges of harassment . . .'

'So you've told me many times before,' Stirling answered mildly, leaning back with his coffee. 'So you go right ahead and—'

302

'I'm not talking about me!' David seethed. 'I'm talking about Penny Moon and what you're doing to her. She's an innocent party in this, Stirling. You'll get nothing from her.'

'No?' Stirling said, the smugness in his voice inciting David's temper further.

'There's *nothing* to be got, Stirling! You're wasting your time and you know it.'

Stirling was shaking his head. 'No, David, what I know, what we both know, is that I'm pretty close now to getting what I'm after. And from what I've been hearing, Penny the Moon could bring me a whole lot closer.'

'Are you crazy!' David yelled. 'What the hell do you think she knows that no one else does?'

'That's what I was trying to find out last night,' Stirling answered. 'And I might have done if she hadn't tried raising the dead with that fucking alarm of hers. Still, I got outta there before having to face the embarrassment of a break-and-entry charge. That would have given you a moment's light relief, wouldn't it, David? Sorry to have disappointed you. So what did she tell the cops?'

'Wouldn't you like to know!' David said savagely.

'Not really. 'Cos, you see, I already know she didn't call them.' He cocked his head thoughtfully to one side. 'Funny that, wouldn't you say, that she called you and not the cops? But you know what that tells me, David? It tells me that our friend Ms Moon is trying to protect someone.'

'And you don't think waking up and finding the fucking bogeyman in her bedroom that someone might just be herself?' David snarled.

As Stirling shook his head he was grinning at the description of himself. 'Nah,' he said, 'what I reckon is she was protecting you.' His eyebrows came up as his smirk widened and he looked at David through

303

narrowed eyes. 'Or someone else.'

'You're in fantasy land, Stirling,' David snapped. 'I told you, she's an innocent party. She knows nothing, because there's nothing *to* know. Christ Almighty, you've turned my life upside down trying to find something, anything, and you can't do it. So why don't you just back off . . .'

'But Gabriella knows something, doesn't she, David? Isn't that why she won't let you see your kids? Isn't that why your mother won't have anything to do with you?'

'What goes on between me and my wife is none of your god-damned business,' David raged.

'But I reckon it *is* my business, and my guess is when Gabriella gets to hear about Penny the Moon she'll make it my business.'

David's face was ashen. 'To hear *what* about Penny Moon?' he said quietly. 'There's nothing to tell, nothing . . .'

Stirling chuckled. 'Does Penny the Moon know?' he said.

David knew exactly what Stirling meant, knew too that he was on very dangerous ground now. 'I told you already,' he answered tightly: 'she knows nothing.'

Stirling sat forward, helped himself to more coffee, then turned his gaze back to David. 'It's a cosy little set-up you got yourself over there with that magazine,' he said, dropping three lumps of sugar into his cup. 'But it don't fool me, David. Not for one minute is it fooling old Robert here. And I wonder what Penny the Moon will have to say if she finds out how you've been using her?'

David's jaw was like rock. 'No one's using anyone here, Stirling. No one except you.'

Stirling seemed to find that amusing and laughed for some time. 'My, oh my, how we do fool ourselves,' he said. 'But this wasn't something you expected, was it, David? You didn't count on falling for that woman, now did you?'

'I don't know what you're talking about,' David responded icily. 'But what I will tell you is this: if you don't lay off her now ...'

Stirling's chubby, ringed hand came up. 'Spare me the threats,' he said calmly. 'I'm gonna bust your ass, Villers, and you know it.'

'So you keep telling me,' David snapped, 'but you're never going to find what you're looking for, Stirling, because it isn't there to be found.'

Stirling licked his lips, as though relishing what he was about to say. 'I guess you know that Penny the Moon's got herself involved with Christian Mureau?' he said, apparently studying his nails but all the time watching David from the corner of his eyes.

David was very still. 'Christian who?' he asked.

At that, Stirling started to laugh again. In fact, he seemed to find it so funny that he went right on laughing until eventually he started to choke. 'Nice try,' he wheezed, wiping his mouth with a napkin. 'Yeah, that sure was a good try, Villers. Pull the other one next time, we'll get to hear a host of heavenly angels. Better still, we might get to see a few laurels sprouting their way through those boyish curls of yours.'

David's eyes were fixed on him; not even by so much as a flicker of a muscle did he betray what he was really thinking. 'You're going to have to make yourself clearer, Stirling,' he said smoothly.

'Is that so?' Stirling said, rocking his bulk back and forth. 'Then let me do just that. Penny the Moon is seeing Christian Mureau. And you, Villers, just like me, know exactly who Mureau is. And by my reckoning that's gonna do your little set-up over there no end of good. What do you say?'

'What I say is Penny's life is her own affair. It's got nothing to do with me and even less to do with you. So butt out, Stirling, and leave her the fuck alone or you're

305

going to have some serious explaining to do to people you won't want to explain to.'

Stirling's grin was so wide it was almost painful. 'Did Gabriella ever tell you,' he said, 'you're kind of cute when you're mad?' Then suddenly his expression changed completely, and as he leaned forward the darkness of hatred and vengeance clouded his eyes. 'Start counting the days, Villers,' he warned, and, tightening the belt on his dressing gown, he got up and walked out of the cabin.

'So Italy is still on,' Penny smiled, nestling the phone with her shoulder as she annotated a document in front of her. 'When will you be there?'

'Saturday morning,' Christian answered. 'The Delaneys won't be able to take you, I'm afraid. Can you get a train?'

'Of course. How long will you be staying?'

'A few days, maybe a week. Do you think you'll be able to get away for that long?'

Penny hesitated as an unbidden thought of David suddenly flashed in her mind. 'Yes. Yes, I think I can stay that long,' she answered, pushing the guilt aside and rotating her chair to look out of the window.

'Good.' Then after a pause he said, 'Penny, I wish it didn't have to be this way . . .'

'It's all right,' she assured him, the intimacy in his voice warming her right down to her toes. 'It doesn't matter which way it is as long as we're together.'

'I love you,' he said softly.

The words hit Penny's heart in soft ripples of joy and she was about to answer, when her door flew open and David stormed in.

'I have to go,' she said, colouring. 'Call me again soon.' She hung up, then turned to David and almost cowered from the rage in his eyes.

'What the hell do you think you're doing?' he hissed,

306

slamming the door behind him.

'What am *I* doing?' she cried, guilt instantly inflaming her temper. 'What I want to know is what *you're* doing, barging in here—'

'You know what I'm talking about,' he cut in viciously. 'I'm talking about Mureau. *Christian* Mureau. How long have you been seeing him?'

'How dare you speak to me like that! What I do and who I see in my own time is none of your damned business.'

'It is when you're associating with the Mureaus of this world,' he told her savagely. 'Don't you care what he is? Shit! Do you *know* what he is?'

'Yes, I know,' she said defiantly. 'So there's nothing you can tell me—'

'You know!' he seethed. 'Then, Jesus Christ, how can you be such a god-damned fool? Don't you realize the position he's putting you in? You're harbouring a criminal, Penny! He's wanted by the United States Government for drug offences the like of which you can't even begin to imagine.'

'Well that's just where you're wrong, David Villers. I know what he's done. I know everything there is to know about Christian Mureau. And you, just because you've heard a few stories here and there, jump to conclusions that—'

'I don't believe I'm hearing this,' he seethed. 'Are you blind, or are you just plain fucking stupid? We're talking about drugs, Penny. *Drugs*. You've heard of them, I suppose? You know what they are? They *kill* people, Penny.'

'You can leave out the sarcasm,' she spat. 'Of course I know what they are. But it was only marijuana and that doesn't harm anyone.'

David's eyes closed as he slapped a hand to his forehead. 'You can't seriously believe that,' he said, struggling to get his temper back in control. 'You're not

307

seriously sitting there telling me that you believe a man who's made the kind of money Mureau's made has done it through a few dumb suckers spacing out on pot?'

'Yes, I do believe it,' she cried. 'He's not what you think he is. He's never dealt in other drugs and he's only ever sold to people who want it and know how to use it.' The words sounded naïve even to her, but why not say them when she knew them to be true?

'Christ, Penny,' he raged. 'Don't you know anything? Don't you read the papers? He's not some kind of hero and neither is he a dealer only in marijuana. The man's a *gangster*, Penny. A gangster who ran an operation that netted him more than a hundred million dollars and I for one don't even want to think about how many lives he put in danger, or how many might even have lost their lives because of him. No! No!' he shouted as she tried to speak. 'I don't care what he's told you. All I care about is that you get out of this *now*!'

Penny's nostrils flared her indignance but it was a while before she spoke. When she did, her hands were pressed tightly together and her eyes were a steely morass of resentment. 'You can believe whatever you want to believe about Christian Mureau,' she told him, 'it makes no difference to me. But let me tell you this, David: I've met him, I know what kind of man he is and I, just like anyone else, am perfectly aware of how the press can distort things when they want to. So I don't blame you for what you think. I'm just surprised that you of all people could be so easily taken in.'

David was shaking his head and looking at her as though the extent of his incredulity was exceeded only by his bitter disappointment. But there was more – she could sense it so acutely that it might have been she who was feeling the pain that was clouding his eyes. 'It's not me who's being taken in,' he said, 'it's you.' He gave a mirthless laugh. 'Brainwashed, more like. Shit, how can *you*, of all people, be so gullible?'

Penny looked away as the uncomfortable memory of Henry Miller's words flashed through her mind.

'Look, Pen,' he said, putting his hands on her desk and leaning over her, 'if it were any other man I'd tell you to get on with it. I might not like it, but I'd be the last one to stand in your way. But, take it from me, Mureau isn't the man you think he is. You're a decent woman, Penny, with morals, scruples, all those things that decent people have. So why are you doing this to yourself? You know it can't go anywhere. They'll catch up with him in the end, and where's that going to leave you?'

Penny's face was stony as she kept her eyes fixed on the wall beside her. 'I love him,' she said, almost wincing at what even to her sounded trite. Then, clearing her throat, she added: 'And I don't care what you say, David, he's not the man *you* think he is. If you'd met him, you'd know.'

David's head fell forward as the nightmare of the past few years of his life swamped him. If only she knew, if only he could tell her. Maybe he should, but he knew what he was up against with Mureau and he was afraid that even if he did tell her it wouldn't make any difference.

'Anyway,' she went on in a small voice, 'what is it to you what I do?'

Lifting his head he looked down at the confusion in her eyes and felt his throat constrict. 'You just don't get this, do you?' he said hoarsely. 'You don't get it at all. I care about you, Penny. I care what happens to you. I care what that man might do to you, to your future.'

As Penny inhaled, her breath was shaken by an involuntary sob. 'I'm not going to stop seeing him,' she said defiantly. Then her eyes opened wide as the pain that seemed to cross his face pressed a quiet shock into her heart. 'But thank you for caring,' she whispered.

'It's not your thanks I want,' he answered gruffly. 'It's

your promise that you'll call this to a halt.'

Penny was shaking her head. 'I can't give it,' she said. 'I don't know how much time we have left together . . .'

'And when they do pick him up, assuming they don't pick you up too, what are you going to do then?'

Penny lowered her eyes.

'Oh Christ, Penny,' he laughed harshly, 'please don't tell me you're intending to wait. You've got your whole life ahead of you, you can't waste it that way. And did it ever occur to you that if he really loved you he wouldn't want you to?'

'He hasn't asked me to,' she countered, as embarrassed now as she was desperate for this conversation to end.

'I never dreamt you were this capable of romanticizing a situation,' he said, a note of anger creeping back into his voice. 'It's like you've taken time out from the real world. Christian Mureau is a wanted man. He's a criminal, Penny. For God's sake, don't let him turn you into one too.'

'I have no intention of ever dealing in drugs,' she responded hotly.

'You know what I mean. Penny, look at me. Look at me and tell me that in your heart you believe he loves you.'

As Penny's wide eyes came up to his the echo of Christian's parting words on the telephone was ringing in her ears. 'I know he loves me,' she said. 'And I know it's hurting him as much as it's hurting me. So, David, please don't spoil what we have left together. I'll take the consequences, whatever they might be . . .'

Banging a hand on the desk, David turned and walked to the window. There was so much more he wanted to say as he stood there gazing out at the passing traffic, things that made him want to get hold of her and shake her with all the frustration he had locked inside. But he knew already that he'd handled this badly, that he

310

hadn't given himself enough time to think it through before storming in here and telling her how to run her life. But Jesus Christ, Christian Mureau! How the hell could this be happening again?

Seeing him standing there looking so tired and so heartbreakingly defeated was having an unsettling effect on Penny. She wasn't used to seeing him this way; he was always so in control of himself and any situation he was in. She thought of last night and wondered what it had all been about. Now didn't seem the time to ask, for she was sure it was that, as much as her relationship with Mureau, that was causing him to appear so agitated and . . . well, yes, powerless. Once again she felt that puzzling desire to reach out to him, to help him through whatever was going on in his life. But how could she when it meant making a choice between him and Christian?

'Would you prefer it if I handed in my notice?' she asked quietly.

He gave no response and after a while Penny got to her feet and walked over to him. 'I'm sorry,' she whispered. 'I don't know what else to say, except I'm sorry.'

He turned to look at her, his dark, blue eyes filled with a heavy emotion. Then silently he reached out for her, drawing her into his arms and holding her close.

'This is hard for me, Penny,' he said after a while. 'I just wish you knew how hard.'

Pulling back to look into his eyes, she said, 'Don't let it come between us, David.'

His answering smile was one of resignation and incomprehension. His mouth was so close to hers it seemed the most natural thing in the world to touch it with her own.

'I know you don't understand,' she said softly after she'd kissed him, 'and I only wish I could explain it. But it's like something inside me belongs to him and for better, for worse, and because there is no doubt in my mind

311

that we love each other I'm going to go on seeing him.'

After a while David started to nod slowly and as she laid her head back on his shoulder he tightened his arms around her, saying, 'I just wish you knew what you were really doing.'

Chapter 16

Even as Penny boarded the train she knew that it was going to take much longer than the journey time to Lake Garda to free herself from the terrible confusion and even foreboding that had taken a hold on her since that morning with David in her office. Of course she understood why he thought she was crazy: hadn't she always known that anyone she told would think that way? Except she hadn't told David, someone else had. But what did it matter who? The fact was he knew and it hurt so much to be doing this to him. She wondered why it hurt like it did, or why it should matter to him so much, but she had no answers. She hadn't told him where she was going now, but of course he'd have guessed that it was to see Christian. Just as he'd have guessed that the reason she didn't want anyone staying with her in the house was in case Christian turned up.

Finding an empty seat beside the window, she dropped her holdall between her feet and, slipping off her coat, she sat down with a heavy sigh. Prepared as she was to let her relationship with Christian turn her life upside down, to know that it was doing the same to David's disturbed her as much as it baffled her. She was sure there was something he wasn't telling her, that there was more to his aversion to Christian than the fact that Christian was a wanted man. She'd even wondered if David actually knew Christian, if maybe their paths had crossed before. But if they had, why hadn't David said so? And the night Christian had listened to David's voice on the answerphone he hadn't seemed to know who David was. Then she remembered, with a sudden stab of unease, that he had been absurdly jealous at the way David had spoken to her. So maybe they did know each other; maybe there was a history between them that neither man wanted to admit to. It made her head spin just to think of it, for though the connection could be as simple as David purchasing marijuana from Christian there was always the chance that it went much deeper and was much more sinister.

Her eyes suddenly widened and her blood turned slowly to ice as she remembered Esther Delaney talking about another boss. Could it be David? But no, that was crazy, she could never imagine David doing anything to put himself in the kind of position Christian was in. And if he had, then why was he free to come and go in a way that Christian wasn't? But what about his unexplained disappearances, those times when she had no idea where he was or how to reach him?

Closing her eyes, she covered her face with her hands and tried to recall everything David had said that morning in the office. But through the monontous chant of the train the only words that seemed to stand out with any clarity now were those he had used when he'd told her he cared about her. She cared for him too, but was there more to his feelings than he was telling her? Was that why he didn't want her to go on seeing Christian? There was a time when the very suggestion would have made her laugh for the absurdity of it, but now it simply made her feel unbearably sad and disloyal.

What was going on? she sighed anxiously. Why wouldn't anyone tell her what she needed to know? She would ask Christian when she saw him, but for the moment uppermost in her mind was the fact that she didn't want this to come between her and David. But wasn't it already too late for that? It *had* come between them and, if she were honest with herself, the thought of losing David was frightening her. She didn't know why it should frighten her, except lately almost everything did.

The night before, Esther Delaney, in one of her motherly moods, had helped her try to rationalize her fear, explaining that living life on the edge was bound to take its toll. Christian had had plenty of practice and when Penny was with him she would find herself much more able to cope than when she wasn't. Which was another reason, Esther had gone on, why she should spend as much time with him as she could. David had been in love before, she'd said: he would know what it was like, wanting someone so much you couldn't think about anything else, feeling terrified the whole time that something was going to go wrong. And for Penny and Christian those feelings were doubly felt because of the situation Christian was in. Which was something else David would understand, even though he might not like.

'He's really very much in love with you, dear,' Esther had told her, 'and it's as difficult for him as it is for you.'

'I thought we were talking about David,' Penny said.

The old lady smiled fondly. 'No, Christian,' she said.

Turning to look out at the passing scenery, Penny pulled a cigarette from the packet she'd bought at the station. She lit it, but within seconds she'd stubbed it out. Nothing felt right any more. In truth it all felt horribly wrong, and for a moment she couldn't understand why she was sitting here on this train. But then the thought of Christian and the intensity of what they had shared, of what they already meant to each other, seemed to break through her fears like a comforting light flaring in a world of darkness and doubt. She was going to him because in her heart she knew that they belonged together and because he needed her perhaps even more

315

than she needed him.

And the instant she stepped off the train and saw his face, his eyes anxiously searching the platform, any lingering fears she might have had simply vanished. It was hard to believe that someone with eyes so gentle and unsure could have committed the crimes she had read about. In fact, as he spotted her and came running towards her and swept her into his arms, it was hard to believe he had committed any crime at all, he looked so happy and carefree and relieved to see her.

'Chérie,' he murmured, hugging her tightly. 'I've missed you.'

'I've missed you too,' she said, gazing up at him and inhaling the warm, masculine scent of him.

Cupping her face in his hands, he kissed her softly on the mouth. 'I want to make love to you,' he whispered. 'I want to lose myself in you and feel only the love I have for you.'

'How far is the hotel?' she asked, making him laugh with the mischief in her eyes.

'Not far. But much as I want to hold you, we have to talk, chérie. Esther told me about your conversation with her last night . . . I understand why you are afraid, chérie, but I don't want you to be – not of me, not of anything I have done. I will let you go, I will give you up and never see you again if that is what you want, because the reality of my life will not go away. It is hard for us both having to live this way, but you have a choice, Penny, you don't have to do this . . .'

'But I do,' she told him earnestly. 'And I've made my choice. I love you, Christian, and it doesn't matter how hard it's going to be for us or what other people might think. All that matters is how we feel about each other.'

His dark eyes were suffused with love as he gazed searchingly into hers, still holding her face in his hands and letting their feelings flow between them. Then suddenly a roguish smile danced across his lips. 'I think we are becoming something of a spectacle,' he whispered, as passers-by turned to look at them. 'Let me take you to the hotel. I think you're going to like it.'

He was right, she did, and not only for the enchanting winter-misted views over the lake, but for the way he could make her heart throb with their beauty just by being with her and sharing it with her.

It was dusk as they stood, unselfconscious in their nudity, at the window of their room, gazing out at the muted greys and purples and vermilion of the sky where the sun had set. Christian's arms were around her waist, his chest pressing gently against her back as she rested her head on his shoulder.

'I'm glad we talked,' she smiled.

He laughed. 'I promise you it was my intention before we made love.'

She lifted his hand to her mouth and kissed it. 'I only have doubts when I'm not with you.'

'I don't want you ever to doubt me, Penny,' he said, stroking her lips with his thumb, 'but I understand why you do. And I doubt you too when I'm not with you. I doubt that you could really have fallen in love with someone like me. I doubt that you will come when I ask . . . There are so many things I fear and losing you is one of them.'

Several minutes slipped by before Penny braced herself to ask the question she dreaded the answer to. 'Have you heard from your lawyers?'

'Yes,' he said, in a voice that was barely audible.

Penny's heart turned over. 'Does that mean,' she said gazing sightlessly out at the still waters of the lake, 'that you have the deal you asked for?'

'More or less,' he answered.

Penny's eyes closed as the pain of losing him so soon engulfed her. 'So you'll be going?'

He turned away from her and went to sit on the edge of the bed. 'I don't know,' he said, his head in his hands.

Then, as though feeling her watching him, he looked up. 'It's hard, Penny,' he said. 'So hard. I know what I did was wrong, that I should pay for it, but that you should pay for it too . . .'

Moving swiftly to his side Penny put her arms around him. 'There's nothing I can say to make this any better,' she whispered brokenly, 'except—'

When she stopped he lifted his head to look into her eyes. 'Except what?' he said.

'Nothing,' she answered, shaking her head.

Smiling, he brushed the hair from her face. 'Don't worry,' he said, 'I have thought of the same thing myself.'

Penny's eyes opened wide in surprise.

He laughed. 'I can think of nothing I would rather do than take you somewhere a long, long way from here where we can live out our lives together, free from the pressures of now . . .'

'Then why don't you?' she cried recklessly.

'Ah, Penny,' he sighed, 'would that I could. But it wouldn't work. They'd find me one day and to live looking over our shoulders all the time is no life for either of us. It would make us unhappy, it would make you start to resent me . . .' His voice trailed off as he leant towards her and kissed her gently on the mouth. 'But you see,' he said, 'I have my dreams too and they are the same as yours. But that is all it is, Penny, a dream. Reality is much harsher, much more difficult to face.'

Looking down at the floor, Penny listened to the few distant sounds that trespassed the silence. Finally she said, 'What is the deal? How long will you get?'

'They are saying ten years, of which I will serve between five and six.'

It felt like an eternity, yet at the same time it felt as though it were being swallowed into some kind of timeless vacuum that had no meaning at all. 'Is that longer than you were expecting?' she said.

'No, it was about the best I could hope for.' He pushed her back on the bed and gazed down into her eyes as his hand travelled lightly, exploringly, over her body. 'I haven't made a decision when to go yet,' he said, 'so why don't we forget about it until I do?'

Penny's smile was weak. She doubted very much if he could stop himself thinking about it and knew that for her it would be impossible.

Lifting a hand to his face she trailed her fingers gently over his jaw, running them to his shoulders, to his chest, then down over the hard muscles of his abdomen to take him in her hand. As she squeezed him his eyes fluttered; then, easing her legs apart, he lay between them and pushed himself slowly inside her.

Over the next three days they behaved and were treated like a honeymoon couple. They walked and talked, roaming the meandering paths in the hills, stopping in remote little villages to drink hot spicy wine and explore their surroundings. It was so cold they could see their breath in front of them, could feel the dry, frosted bracken cracking beneath their feet. It was a time apart from the rest of the world, a time that was as filled with happiness and laughter as it was by the spectre of what was to come. But despite how much they talked, never once did either of them touch upon the subject that was uppermost in their minds, and again Penny could only marvel at the way he seemed to slip so easily away from it, refusing to allow it to intrude upon this special time together.

She watched him with other people around the hotel and found herself loving him more for the way he was able to laugh with them and absorb himself in the tales of their daily excursions. It was as though he was trying to soak it all in, store it away and use it to sustain himself during the unthinkable time when there would be nothing, a time that no matter how hard she tried Penny just

319

couldn't imagine.

Occasionally he disappeared for a few hours, sometimes to be alone and sometimes to meet with people she never got to see. Whether it was with them that he was discussing a date for his surrender she didn't know; all she knew was that he wouldn't discuss it with her. While he was gone she would take out her computer and attempt to write the editorials she had assured Marielle she would fax over. Plenty of faxes had arrived for her, meaning that by now David would know where she was, but he hadn't called and neither had she expected him to. There were moments, though, when she badly wanted to talk to him, but what was there to say? She'd asked Christian if he and David knew each other and Christian's surprise at the question had been answer enough. Their association lived only in her imagination, along with David's feelings for her. So maybe the need to talk to David was rooted in the need to touch reality again, for as the time passed and she and Christian became closer than ever the more distanced she seemed to feel from her emotions. Sometimes when she looked at Christian she felt almost dazzled, as though she was seeing the afterburn of a light before it eventually disappeared completely. She knew she loved him, that she wanted only to be with him, to touch him and feel him and see him, so where had the moments of uncertainty smuggled themselves in from? Was it because of the way he seemed to be shutting her out, not allowing her to take part in a decision that was going to affect her so drastically?

'No, Penny,' he told her when she put that to him, 'I'm not shutting you out, I'm just trying to spare you more pain. And besides,' he added with a smile, 'if the decision were left to you I would never go.'

'That's true,' she admitted with a grudging smile of her own as she went to stand behind him at the mirror and slid her arms about his waist. 'I suppose it's just that

I want all of you and that is something I simply can't have.'

'But you can and you do,' he said, looking at her reflection. 'I just wish that I had all of you.'

Penny was clearly perplexed.

'When you came,' he explained, 'you brought your work with you. I suppose I thought, hoped, that when we were together you could let go for a while. But it is no matter because I know that you have a life which I can be no part of. I am jealous of that life, I detest it, because I know I must never touch it, must never allow it to be tainted by the things I have done.'

'Christian!' she cried, shocked. 'For God's sake, don't ever think of yourself that way. You *are* a part of that life, you're a part of everything to do with me. And the reason I brought it here was because, like you, I have responsibilities to others, loyalties that no matter how much I might want to ignore I just can't.'

'Are you speaking of your boss, David Villers?' he asked solemnly.

Penny frowned. 'Yes,' she said, 'amongst others.'

'You speak of him a great deal, you know.' He smiled. 'More than anyone else. More than yourself.' He turned from the mirror and looked down at her. 'Do you think of him when we are making love?' he challenged quietly.

'God, no!' Penny cried. 'How can you *say* that! Do you really think I'd be here with you if I were thinking about another man, especially in that way?'

He nodded. 'Yes, I do. Because you are.'

'Oh God, Christian, what do I have to do to prove how much I love you?'

'Maybe it isn't me you need to prove it to,' he said. 'Maybe it is yourself.'

Penny was shaking her head. 'Please,' she said, 'don't let's fight. I love you, Christian. I'd do anything, *any-thing*, to stop you going away, but I know you're going

321

to and . . . I know it's selfish, but I have to think about what I'm going to do when you're gone. And yes, I do have loyalties to David, I owe him a great deal, but you're the one who matters, Christian. You're the one I love and want to be with.'

'But?'

'You know all the buts,' she cried helplessly.

To her amazement he turned to her computer and flicked it on. Then, after tapping in the relevant commands, he stood back and pointed to the screen. 'Can you explain this?' he said.

As she moved hesitantly towards the screen, Penny knew already what she was going to see. 'That's my diary, Christian,' she said. 'You had no right to read it.'

His eyes were hard. 'Your diary?' he said. 'Or my life story ready to go to print?'

'Oh God,' she cried, pushing her hands into her hair. 'Please don't do this.'

'Answer me, Penny,' he said.

'It's my diary,' she cried. '*My* diary, *my* life. And you're a part of my life, the most important part of my life, so of course yours is there too.'

As she finished speaking he turned away, putting a hand to his eyes.

'Christian, please,' she begged. 'Talk to me, tell me what's really going on here. You've made a decision, haven't you? You know when you're going and you're afraid to tell me.'

Turning back to her he took her hands in his and stood looking at her, allowing a long time to tick by. 'You're right,' he said in the end: 'I shouldn't have read the diary. But I did it because I have to be sure of you, Penny. I have to know that I can really trust you. I know it probably hurts you to hear me say that, but being in the position I am it isn't easy and often isn't wise to trust. And you are a journalist, Penny. I need to

322

be sure that you aren't here just to . . .' He stopped and raised his hand to her face. 'I love you,' he said, his voice shaking with emotion, 'I didn't want to believe that of you, but, please understand, I had to be sure.'

'I understand,' she whispered.

Pulling her into the circle of his arm, he led her to the sofa. 'I want you to listen to what I have to say now,' he told her softly. 'It will explain even further why I had to be sure of you before I could tell you this. I want you to hear me out, and when I have finished I want you to think about what I have said before you give me your answer. It is a big decision I am asking you to make, Penny, probably one of the biggest of your life . . .'

Her eyes were darting between his even as the fear slid into her heart.

'I'm not going in,' he said. 'Not yet, anyway. But my time here in Europe has run out. They're too close to me now, too many people have seen me . . . So tomorrow I am leaving for the Far East.' He took a breath, then, looking deep into her eyes, he said, 'I want you to come with me, Penny.'

Penny's heart was thumping; her mind was in such chaos she hardly knew what she was thinking.

'I am going to leave you alone now,' he said. 'While I'm gone I want you to think about the implications it will have on your life if you come with me. And if you decide not to come I want you to know that it will change nothing for me: I will still love you. And I will understand.'

Penny remained where she was for a long time after the door had closed behind him. Her mind was unable to function. Any thought she had seemed to be snapped short by the next. Were all the strange feelings she'd been having lately a prelude to this? Was there some innate warning system inside her that had been challenging her to face what she really felt for him should this moment arrive? She had no answers, neither for herself nor for him. All she knew was that she wanted him to come back, that she didn't want to think about what he must be putting himself through now wondering what she was going to say.

She got up, walked over to the window and stared out at the night. It was so dark she couldn't even see the lake. For some reason it troubled her. Had she expected to find the answer there? Did she really think that the Lady of the Lake would rise up from the depths and show her the way? No, of course she didn't; yet there was something soothing about looking at the waters. But right now there was nothing to see, nowhere to turn, except to herself and the unanswerable question: did she really love him enough to do what he was asking?

A tiny *frisson* of excitement suddenly grazed her heart and she started to smile. It would be the craziest thing she had ever done, to run away with the man she loved, but did she really have it in her to leave everything behind and never look back? It made her light-headed just to think of the danger they would be in, but if he was prepared to face it, then why shouldn't she? Yes, she had questioned how much she loved him, but wasn't that only because she had been trying to protect herself? Trying to deny how unbearable her life would be without him?

'Oh God, this is insane,' she groaned, turning away from the window. She'd truly believed that this was what she wanted, but now it was here she felt so torn, so frustratingly unsure of her own mind. She pictured his face and felt her heart melt with love even as it contracted with fear. He hadn't said it in so many words, but she knew that he was doing this for her, that had she never come into his life he would have surrendered himself now and returned to the States. The responsibility weighed heavily on her; it was as though she had become his judge and jury, was holding his fate in her hands. She wondered what would become of them, where they would end up. Did it really matter as long as they were together? She pictured her life in France and felt suddenly breathless and panicked by the thought of losing it.

She stood by the phone for some time, staring down at it, a bewildering emptiness spreading throughout her body. In the end she picked it up and dialled quickly, not knowing what she was going to say, not even thinking about why she should need to speak to David now.

'Oh hi, Penny,' Marielle's voice drawled from the sitting room of David's apartment. 'We weren't expecting to hear from you for a while yet. How's it going?'

'Fine,' Penny answered dully. She couldn't speak to David now, not while Marielle was there. Then suddenly she wanted to scream. What was Marielle doing in David's apartment? Why was she there *now*, when she, Penny, needed to talk to him! Then, as though she'd asked the questions, Marielle told her.

'David's not here at the moment,' she said. 'He's gone to the airport to pick up his wife and children.'

'His wife and children?' Penny repeated, dimly aware of how alien the words sounded.

'That's right. Apparently they had a long talk on the phone and have decided to give it another go.'

'Oh, I see,' Penny said.

Marielle laughed. 'He got me out buying flowers to welcome her with – that's what I'm doing here now,' she said. 'You just caught me, in fact – I was about to leave.'

She gabbled on then about some faxes she had sent through that day, asking Penny if she'd read them and what she thought. Somehow, through the debilitating numbness, Penny managed to answer.

'Is there any message I can leave for David?' Marielle asked in the end.

Penny let the question hang for a moment, thinking, quite suddenly, that there were a thousand and one things she wanted to tell him, but knowing now that even if she could he wouldn't want to hear them. Then, as the door opened and Christian walked in, she looked up into his eyes and felt her heart turn over. He gazed down at her in the semidarkness, his face pale and strained, and she could sense his fear as deeply as she could sense her own. 'No, no message,' she said softly and, replacing the receiver, she turned into Christian's arms.

Pierre was trying very hard not to notice how ill Sylvia looked. It had been several months since he'd last seen her and in that time she had lost so much weight it had aged her ten years.

Did David have any idea she was this bad? he was asking himself, as Sylvia turned from the drinks cabinet in her Regency sitting room and carried two glasses to the table. Should he tell David, he wondered.

'Your face,' Sylvia smiled, 'is not normally something that gives you away, Pierre, but I'm afraid on this occasion it is letting you down. However, I am not going to die – at least, not this evening – so you can relax.'

Pierre was unsure whether or not to smile, but since her own called for a response he forced one.

'It's cancer,' she said bluntly. 'David doesn't know that, of course, and neither will he until I judge the time to be right.'

'Is it treatable?' Pierre asked, hoping it was the right thing to say.

'They think so,' she said, sitting in a chair opposite him. 'But you're not here to discuss my health, are you?'

Pierre stiffened with discomfort. No, he wasn't, but

how could they dismiss such a delicate and vital subject as though it were the weather?

'I take it there's still no news of Penny?' Sylvia said, coming straight to the point.

Pierre shook his head. 'All we know is that they left Italy three days ago.'

'And what does David say about it?'

'He refuses to discuss it.'

Sylvia nodded, tapping her fingers on her glass as she stared thoughtfully into space. 'But no doubt, like the rest of us, he is assuming the worst?' she said, turning her eyes back to Pierre.

'Yes, I think so.'

'And you're afraid,' she said, 'that he might do something to try and get her back.'

Pierre looked at her.

'You're right to be afraid,' Sylvia told him. 'I suspect David is too. Does Penny know how he feels about her? Did he ever tell her?'

'I don't know.'

Sylvia laughed mirthlessly. 'If he didn't, then he's shown uncharacteristic restraint. I take it Gabriella knows about Penny?'

'Stirling knows,' Pierre answered, 'so I think we must assume that Gabriella does too by now.'

'Which would explain why she wasn't on that flight,' Sylvia sighed. Then, shaking her head, she added, 'It would never have worked. There's too much bitterness between them now.' She took a sip of her drink. 'So, what do you want me to do?'

Having seen for himself how sick she was, Pierre was sorely wishing he hadn't come. But if he backtracked now those shrewd, still beautiful eyes would see right through him. 'I want you to help me find Penny,' he said.

Sylvia nodded. 'I thought that's what you might say. And if we do find her, what then?'

Pierre flushed. 'I was hoping you might persuade her to come back before ... well, before David does something he'll regret.'

Sylvia leaned forward to put her drink on the table. Then, after several more moments of deliberation, she said, 'This wise old bird isn't as immune to mistakes as she might like to consider herself, Pierre, and I have to confess that Penny Moon was a mistake. Not for the magazine, but for David. I chose her to go to France for two reasons, the only two that mattered. The first was because I knew that in her own unique way she would do a good job and I am fond enough of her to want to see her succeed. The second was because I didn't see her as a woman who would cause David any problems.' She shook her head sadly. 'What a misguided fool I was. But then I had never seen David with a woman who wasn't so beautiful it almost hurt your eyes to look at her. However, Penny's qualities go much deeper than the skin – we've all seen that and we've seen, too, the effect it has had on David. But Penny Moon is a headstrong girl with a mind of her own. It's true she doesn't always know that mind, but what's important is she thinks she does. And if she believes herself enough in love with Mureau as she must to have taken off with him the way she has, then I'm not sure there's anything I can say to influence her.'

'But will you try?'

Sylvia took her time before replying, but it didn't take long for Pierre to know that he wasn't going to get the answer he wanted. 'To be frank with you, Pierre,' she said eventually, 'unless you can persuade me otherwise, my belief is that the damage has already been done, meaning that Penny's return will serve no purpose now. That isn't to say that I approve of what she's doing or wouldn't like to see her back in France; what I am saying is that I can't see any way of it helping David now – any way at all.' Her brilliant eyes were holding firmly to his.

'We all know who Mureau is and there's no point fooling ourselves, Pierre, that as far as Stirling is concerned Penny's association with Mureau is the final nail in David's coffin. Or it will be if any of us try to get her back.'

Chapter 17

Penny was standing at the foot of the towering grey obelisk of the Hong Kong and Shanghai Bank. The sun was glancing off its myriad windows and thickening the air with a syrupy heat. In front of her the traffic roared past, a perpetual flow of tourist-toting rickshaws, red-and-white taxis and densely packed double-decker trams emblazoned with garish colour. The noise was cacophonous; the crowds moved in an amorphous mass of humanity, gathering at crossings like flies settling on treacle. The rank, humid air was an odorous cocktail of drains, incense and diesel. Looking down on it all, as she had many times these past few days from the terrace of their suite, was like watching the furiously changing pattern of a kaleidoscope at the base of a long, grey tunnel of skyscrapers.

As she waited for the rhythmic click of the pedestrian-crossing to change to an urgent pulse she forced her arm up through the tightly packed bodies around her to look at the diamond-studded Chopard watch on her wrist. It was almost five o'clock. Christian had been expecting her back by four.

The traffic slowed to a halt and, surging forward with the crowd, she made yet another futile attempt to shake off Lei Leen and Tse Dong, the couple Christian had assigned to escort her wherever she went and take care of her every need. At five feet four Tse Dong bulged with fiendishly rigid muscle, his squat face and thin, shifting eyes as inscrutable as the culture that had bred him. Lei Leen, his wife, was as readily obsequious as she was round-cheeked and plain, but after their first meeting Penny had detected a trace of humour in her blank, staring eyes that had both surprised and heartened her. But it hadn't taken long to discover that there was no getting close to Lei Leen. She was as much Christian's minion as she was Tse Dong's wife and, as such, she had no right to friendship with the *gweipo* her boss had fallen in love with and was paying her to serve and protect.

On reaching the other side of the street Penny turned towards Statue Square, where hot, sweaty tourists were pointing cameras at the colonnaded façade of the Legislative Building. As she looked at their pale, western features her throat tightened as a surging desire to run to them merged despairingly with her envy of their freedom. Feeling Tse Dong press in closer, she averted her eyes and hurried on through the crowds towards the Mandarin Hotel, almost choking on her frustration.

By the time they reached the hotel she had herself back in control and, as they entered the lift and rose swiftly up through twenty-four floors, she was successfully coaxing herself towards the excitement of showing Christian the outrageously chic and expensive designer clothes her afternoon shopping spree had produced.

This wasn't the first time he'd allowed her to go out without him; yesterday she'd ridden the tram on the precipitous route up to the Peak, where she'd stood with a straining mass of spectators watching a Hong Kong film crew staging a frenetic struggle between a martial-art expert and a revoltingly bloated python against the picturesque backdrop of a misted city and harbour. The day before she'd visited Aberdeen to take a boat trip out past the luxury yachts and the ornate floating Chinese restaurant in the harbour to where gnarled and timeworn old fishermen lived in putrefying squalor on board their rotting sampans. There had been other excursions too, to the decorously named and vibrantly oriental Thieves Market; the Fung Ping Shan Museum with its ancient Chinese pottery and Yuan Dynasty crosses; and a brief though tranquillizing stroll through the pergolas and statues of the Aw Boon Haw Gardens. She'd enjoyed them all, for her inherent fascination for anything new enabled her – with some effort, it was true – to suspend the despondency of her predicament and indulge herself in the comforting fantasy that she was simply a tourist. But those moments were preciously few for Tse Dong and Lei Leen were as omnipresent as the soggy air, silently stalking her every move, crushing her space and suffocating her mind like grim, Orwellian jailers. There was nothing she could do about it because Christian was adamant that unless she was with him Tse Dong and Lei Leen must never leave her side.

'But why?' she had cried the night before, her bright blue eyes flashing with anger and frustration. 'I feel like you're keeping me prisoner.'

Christian's face darkened with anguish.

'I'm never on my own,' she went on heatedly, 'not even for a minute, and I can't stand it. I need to breathe! I need to have time for myself. What is it? Are you afraid I'm going to run away?'

'Chérie,' he sighed, attempting to pull her into his arms and looking hopelessly dejected when she resisted. 'You have to understand the position we're in here,' he said. 'I know it's hard, but there are certain things I have to tie up and arrangements to be made for how we're going to live once we leave Hong Kong. If I could I'd come sightseeing with you myself, I'd like nothing more than to spend all my time with you, but right now it just isn't possible. So please, try to be patient. It won't be for much longer.'

'You're missing the point, Christian,' she cried in exasperation, her voice echoing around the pale marble walls of the opulent bathroom. 'The point is that I don't want Tse Dong breathing down my neck every minute of the day, treating me like I'm some kind of god-damned *prisoner!*'

'I'll have a word with him,' Christian responded, reaching up to adjust the towel that was tumbling from her hair. 'He is a little overzealous, I know, but he knows how much I care about you and I'd never forgive him if anything happened to you.'

Had the telephone not rung at that moment, as it constantly did day and night, she might have pursued it further; but, knowing she wouldn't win anyway, she'd sunk herself irritably into the vast, foaming jacuzzi bath and flicked mindlessly at the remote control, changing channels on the TV monitor in the gold-painted dome overhead.

With the jets of water pummelling her body, she felt the anger seep steadily away as the weight of despondency and shame began to erode the pretence she had enclosed herself in. At times it was as though she were standing aloof from herself, watching herself with the curious detachment of a stranger. But there were so many recriminations begging to be heard, so much regret and dread waiting to flood her mind with the enormity of what she had done, that as always she turned herself away from it, unable to face either the pain or the guilt.

Now, buoyed by the fleeting intoxication of having spent something in the region of thirty thousand dollars at the designer emporiums of Landmark and Prince's Building, she let herself in through the door of their suite eager, despite all her misgivings, to see Christian. He took such pleasure in giving her things and though she'd been unaware of possessing such a wanton materialistic streak before she seemed, to Christian's delight, to be having no problem at all in giving it free rein.

333

Leaving Tse Dong and Lei Leen to struggle into the hall with her parcels she pushed open the door of the sitting room, to be met by a fog of cigar smoke mingling with the bitter smell of alcohol and the gutteral murmurings of Cantonese. The light in her eyes instantly died as the voices fell into silence and her face tightened with resentment.

'Ah, *chérie*,' Christian said, extricating himself from the group of fat, hostile little men who were turning on the sofas in the raised seating area to look down at her. Behind the contorting lenses of pebble glasses their eyes were implacable, but their malice, along with the murky corruptness of their dealings, stained the air.

'I was beginning to worry,' Christian said, walking around the statue of the Tang Dynasty horse and coming down the carpeted steps to greet her. Though his eyes were shining with indulgent laughter, his face was strained and he seemed uncharacteristically on edge.

Putting an arm around her, he turned back to the men, who were getting reluctantly to their feet. Penny recognized some of them, for they had become regular visitors these past few days and they did no more to disguise their resentment than she did. She knew that as a woman she was so far beneath their contempt that it was only Christian's presence that forced them to acknowledge her at all. Even so, only one or two muttered a greeting, calling her by the name on her new passport, Madame Sevier.

'So, have you bankrupted me?' Christian asked, smiling and bringing her further into the room.

Penny was about to respond, when a telephone rang and numerous hands made ridiculous lunges towards briefcases and pockets. The door opened behind her as Tse Dong and Lei Leen came in, followed by the oval-faced butler with his soft Confucian eyes and long-toothed smile. He was carrying a tray of steaming *dim sum*. Christian waved him towards the dining table, while raising his voice to the man who was shouting into the phone. Since both were speaking in Cantonese Penny had no idea what was going on as a couple of the others rapidly punched out numbers on their mobile phones while the fax pumped through messages in an untidy, illegible calligraphy.

The door opened again and Penny felt Christian tense. She turned to follow the direction of his eyes and instantly felt her own tension mount as she watched a scrawny, wide-faced man, who had obviously been in the cloakroom across the hall, swagger into the room, thumbs hooked in his belt loops, the customary mobile phone poking out of his Versace leather jacket. His eyes were masked by wraparound Porsche glasses and heavy chunks of gold dripped from his neck and wrists, while his thin mouth worked frantically at a thick wodge of gum. He was at least half the age of the other Chinese in the room, but managed to ooze twice the arrogance and apparently revelled in his thuggish, gangland image.

As his hidden eyes alighted on Penny he stopped and she felt her skin crawl at the way his lips curved in a grin. 'So, this is Penny Moon,' he drawled in a heavily accented English.

Penny's face tightened. It was the first time since she'd been there that anyone had used her real name and that it should be this insolent, noxious little specimen of lowlife was as ominous as it was offensive.

'*Chérie*, this is Benny Lao,' Christian said.

'How do you do?' Penny said coldly as his gaze travelled the length of her body, turning her blood hot with revulsion.

His grin widened as, reverting to his native tongue, he began speaking to Christian in insulting, mocking tones. Almost instantly Christian cut across him and Penny's eyes shot to Christian's face. His fingers were digging into her shoulder, pulling her closer as his eyes darkened with rage and the others started to laugh. Until now Penny had never seen Christian anything other than in control, but it was clear, as Benny Lao's tauntings increased the laughter in the room, that whoever Benny Lao was he neither respected nor feared Christian Mureau.

'What's he saying?' Penny demanded, knowing that, whatever it was, it was about her.

'Nothing,' Christian snapped, not looking at her as Lao continued his unintelligible gibes, obviously as spurred on by Christian's impotence as he was by his audience.

Penny's eyes, blazing with fury, moved back to Lao. Her rage seemed to incite him further and, sensing Christian to be suddenly at a loss, she shouted again, '*What* is he saying?'

'Nothing,' Christian said, pulling her away. 'It doesn't matter.'

'Don't!' she cried, shrugging him off and turning fearlessly back to Lao. 'I want to know what you're saying,' she demanded.

'Penny, leave it!' Christian barked.

'No! I know you were talking about me, so I want to know—'

'Penny!'

'Tell her,' Lao said, idly grinding his chewing gum while relishing the scene he had created.

'No! You tell me!' Penny seethed. 'Or don't you have the courage?'

Lao laughed and, to Penny's horror, as he removed his glasses to reveal the scarred and callous slits of his eyes he rubbed a hand suggestively over his groin.

Her lips curled in disgust as she turned to Christian. For the moment she was too enraged to feel the fear that was burgeoning inside her. 'Get him out of here!' she spat. 'Get him out now!'

'*Chérie*, please, just go into the other room,' Christian responded, his face pinched with unease as his eyes bored into Lao's.

Lao's telephone suddenly rang, stealing the tension from the moment. He snatched it from his pocket and put it to his ear. His eyes remained on Christian's as he listened to the voice at the other end. The smirk never left his lips as he worked his gum and clicked his fingers for someone to present himself at his side. As someone hurried forward, Christian drew Penny away and steered her towards the door of the master bedroom.

Penny was about to speak, when she saw Tse Dong, who'd been standing to one side throughout, slide a hand out from under his jacket. Knowing that was where he carried his gun, she turned her panicked eyes to Christian. 'What's going on?' she demanded in a whisper. 'Who *is* that man?'

'A necessary evil,' Christian answered. 'Now, please, *chérie*, do as I say and go into the other room. Tse Dong will go with you, you'll be safe there.'

'Meaning I'm not here, with you?'

'Yes, of course you are,' he soothed, 'but he's using you to weaken my position and I don't want any blood shed over threats that are being made worse by your temper.'

'What kind of threats?' she said, flinching at the rebuke.

Before he could answer, Lao interrupted. 'Did you tell her?' he jeered, digging his phone back into his pocket.

Ignoring him, Christian turned back to Penny. 'I'm sorry,' he said softly.

Penny looked into his eyes, unsure what he was apologizing for. Then a sudden, icy fear slithered through her veins as she wondered just how powerless he was against Lao and if he was apologizing for something that he was about to let happen.

They both turned as Lao sauntered towards them, slaking Penny with his eyes. 'He tell you I going fuck you like a dog?' he hissed, poking his face towards her. 'He tell you I going make you suck every cock in the room?'

When Christian didn't speak, fear wrenched the blood from Penny's heart. She drew breath to speak herself, then froze as she saw the knife slide out of Lao's sleeve. A blinding rush of terror dizzied her. The lacquer chests and Chinese curios loomed in a grotesque parody of menace. The room was spinning, colours and faces were merging. A flicker of light glanced off the blade as he came closer. Obscenities dripped from his lips. Waning sunlight pooled in his eyes. Dear God, wasn't Christian going to stop him? She whirled round in panic, then was thrown against Christian as Tse Dong moved in front of her, his hand back inside his jacket, his muscles bulging with intent. She could no longer see Lao's face, but the violence in the air was palpable. Christian pushed her behind him and barked something in Cantonese. Lao shouted back and Christian turned to Tse Dong. Tse Dong didn't move. Christian spoke again and Tse Dong whipped his hand from his jacket. Christian's face hardened. The gun was pointing at Lao. It was a weapon that was powerful enough to blast Lao's head from his shoulders. Christian snatched it away. Instantly Lao thrust forward with the knife. The gun crashed down on his wrist, splintering the bones. Lao screamed and the knife fell. Tse Dong kicked it across the floor. Lei Leen pounced on it. Christian pushed the gun inside his jacket and held out his hand for the knife. Lei Leen passed it to him. He nodded and she quickly opened the bedroom door, pushing Penny inside and coming in after her.

'You OK, ma'am?' Lei Leen asked.

Penny stared at her, unable to speak.

'Take deep breath, ma'am,' Lei Leen said.

Penny did as she was told, hearing the breath shudder into her lungs as her heart pumped the numbing shock from her brain. It had all happened so quickly. A man had almost been blown apart in front of her eyes. If he'd touched her, he would have been. Another had come within inches of a blade plunging into his throat. The violence had been cut through with a madness that was barbaric. These men didn't fight, they killed! All that had stopped them then was Christian's swiftness of hand. What would have happened had he not been there?

She sank down on the edge of the *chaise-longue* and buried her face in her hands. Only then did she realize how badly she was shaking. How much power did Lao have? she was asking herself. What would the reprisals be for this abhorrent loss of face? Would she be the one to pay, or would it be Christian? She bunched a fist to her mouth to stifle the sob that was choking her. How did Lao know her name? Why had he made such a point of using it? Why was he using her to torment Christian?

She looked up as Lei Leen handed her a glass of water. Taking it, she tried to force a smile, then her head spun towards the door as she heard a burst of laughter in the next room. As it died she turned her eyes back to Lei Leen.

Lei Leen shrugged. 'They men, ma'am,' she said simply.

Penny looked at her, unable to believe that Christian could be laughing so soon after such a confrontation. But maybe he wasn't. Maybe it was the others who were laughing because he was already being forced to pay for the humiliation he had inflicted on Benny Lao. But it was unusual for the Chinese to move so swiftly. Except what did *she* know about the Chinese? It was impossible for her to fathom what was going on out there and as her mind shied away from the horrific images her imagination was so ready to conjure she found herself slipping towards the void of despair she had been fighting so hard to resist.

Her eyes closed as the anguish rose from her heart and rushed helplessly to her throat. Her breath stopped; her body shuddered with the futile power of her feelings. The torment was moving through her with more severity and desperation than she'd ever known. She couldn't bear it, it was too harsh, too real, too overwhelming and hopeless. She was more afraid than she had ever been in her life. She was adrift in a world that was as alien as it was terrifying and that she could ever have dreamt, even for a moment, that this was what she wanted was as shocking and unbearably painful as the reality of why, in the end, she had done it.

As her heart contracted with the tender bitterness of loss she turned her face to the window and gazed blindly out at the dying crimson of the sunset. She didn't want to think about why she was here, she didn't want to confront the terrible mistake she had made or why she had made it, but it was there and she knew that no amount of denial was ever going to make it go away. Her heart twisted as she wondered how she, who had always believed she knew her own mind, who had never knowingly hidden from a truth in her life, hadn't recognized the incredible power of her feelings when they had been governing her life for so many months? How could she ever have considered her life to be parochial or dull when nothing could ever be that way with David around? *Nuance* wouldn't be small-time much longer, not the way they had been building it, and with each day every frustration and every shared triumph had brought them closer and closer together, so that she had reached a point when the hours he wasn't with her had seemed empty and disjointed, mere bridges to be crossed until he returned. Dear God, why hadn't she realized how she felt when her own heart had been telling her all along – in the way it flipped with the pleasure of seeing him, the way it responded to the turmoil of his life, the way it warmed with the sound of his laughter and almost melted at the teasing intimacy of his voice. Where was he now? she wondered helplessly. What was he doing? Did he care that she had gone? Was he happy with his wife? Her eyes closed again as the pain folded around her heart. How could she have loved him this much without knowing? How had it managed to root itself in her so deeply when she hadn't even known it was happening? It was as though he had taken each part of her and painted it with his touch, his scent, his humour, filling her so full of himself and taking her in exchange that it was only now that he was no longer there that she could see what he had done. But even if she'd known, what difference would it have made? It wasn't her he wanted, so what was the point in tormenting herself this way?

'You OK, ma'am?' Lei Leen asked. 'You want I bring you something?'

Penny shook her head. 'No,' she said hoarsely. Then, reading Lei Leen's concern as genuine, she reached out for her hand and squeezed it. 'I'm fine, really,' she said, smiling.

'You want to open this now?' Lei Leen said, walking over to the bed and taking a small box from between the bronze and ivory silk cushions. 'Or you want wait for the boss?'

Penny was barely listening as she feasted her eyes sightlessly on the intricate beauty of the silk screens. In her heart she was still crying out for David. Then, with a humourless laugh, she said, 'Tell me, Lei Leen, why have your fellow countrymen taken such a dislike to me?'

'Oh no, they like you, ma'am,' Lei Leen protested, keeping her head lowered as she rearranged the cushions. 'Everyone like you, for everyone know that the boss, he not give himself up because of you. We not want him to go and now he stay because of you.'

Penny moved restlessly, as though to pull herself away from the encroaching heaviness inside her, and fixing her attention on what Lei Leen was doing she said, 'Well, they've got a funny way of showing it.'

'They just men, ma'am. They think women should not be where they discuss business.'

'And what do you think, Lei Leen?'

'Me? I no paid to think, ma'am.'

Penny watched her as Lei Leen turned to reveal the mockery in her eyes.

'What I think, ma'am,' she said, 'is that the boss, he love you very much. I see it in his eyes,' she put a hand to her chest, 'I feel it here in his heart. And you, ma'am, you are beautiful woman.' Her expression became suddenly serious. 'Not your face,' she said. 'No, no, not your face. But your soul, ma'am. You have beauty in your soul.'

Despite the way she was feeling, Penny laughed. 'I suppose I should thank you for that,' she said.

'No thank me, ma'am. You want open this now?' she said, holding out the box.

Penny looked at it, then swallowed hard to hold back the tears. She could guess what it was but, exquisitely beautiful though she knew it to be, she didn't want to take it. Except what choice did she have? He had bought it now and the very thought that he had paid almost four hundred thousand dollars for a necklace because she had foolishly stopped to admire it as they'd strolled through the hotel galleries that morning made her want to scream for the sheer insanity of it.

Instead she held out her hand and took the box. Lei Leen came to stand beside her, eager to see what it was.

Even though she knew what to expect, Penny's heart

almost stopped as she opened the leather case and gazed down at the sixty-two-carat, emerald-cut sapphire set in a bed of glittering fifteen-carat diamonds and the strands of sea pearls interwoven with smaller blue sapphires.

'Oh, ma'am,' Lei Leen gasped, clasping a hand to her mouth. 'You no tell the boss I give you this now,' she pleaded. 'I not know it was this. I think it is—'

'It's all right, Lei Leen,' Christian said. Penny turned to see him standing at the door. 'You can go now, Lei Leen,' he said.

He waited until she had passed him, then closing the door he came over to the *chaise-longue* and sat down beside Penny.

'Do you like it?' he murmured, looking down at the necklace.

'How can I not?' She smiled through her tears. 'It's the most beautiful necklace I've ever seen.'

Christian lifted a hand to her chin and turned her to look at him, sweeping her face with his eyes. 'Are you still upset about what happened out there?' he said, dismissing the necklace as though it were no more than a trinket.

She nodded. 'A bit.'

Sighing, he pulled her into his arms and laid her head on his shoulder. 'I'd never let anything happen to you, you know that, don't you?' he whispered.

Dumbly she nodded.

'If you weren't a woman,' he said with a quiet laugh, 'he'd apologize for his behaviour, but I'm afraid that not even I can make him stoop to that.'

'Who is he?' Penny asked.

'Like I said, a necessary evil. He works for someone I've been doing business with, someone to whom I owe a lot of money, which is what he believes gives him the right to push me around and try to humiliate me. He's learnt now that he can't.'

Penny lifted her head and looked searchingly into his

343

eyes. 'You're afraid of him, though, aren't you?' she said.

He nodded. 'I fear anyone who is without fear himself.'

'Would he have killed Tse Dong?'

'No. But only because Tse Dong would have killed him first.'

Penny shivered as the whole grisly scene played itself through in her mind again. Then, bringing her eyes back to his, she said, 'How did he know my name?'

He looked at her for a moment; then, lowering his gaze to the box on her lap, he lifted the necklace carefully from its bed of black velvet and draped it over his hand. 'Will you wear it tonight?' He smiled, looking back at her. 'We're entertaining in the Cartier room. Did you buy something today that will—'

'Christian. How did he know my name?'

'I don't know,' he sighed, shaking his head.

Penny waited, expecting him to say more, but he didn't. 'Who does he work for?' she asked.

His expression was pained as he answered. 'Penny, please don't ask these questions,' he said. 'You know that I have committed crimes, but that is all you need to know. I don't want you to be sullied by the types I have dealt with in the past . . .'

'But you're still dealing with them,' she reminded him.

'No,' he said. 'What I'm doing is winding things up once and for all. Benny Lao's boss will receive the money that is due to h—' He stopped as there was a discreet tap on the door and Lei Leen peeped in.

'There is call for you, boss,' she said.

'Who is it?' he said, obviously annoyed at being interrupted.

Lei Leen's eyes shot to Penny as her cheeks suffused with colour. 'No give name,' she said awkwardly.

'Then get the name,' he said shortly. He was on the point of turning back to Penny, when Benny Lao appeared, grinning, in the doorway.

344

'Why you not tell him is Gabriella?' he drawled. 'That get him running.'

Christian immediately stiffened and as Lei Leen blanched Penny felt the shock ripple through her.

David was sitting on the south-facing terrace of Penny's villa, rocking steadily back and forth in a wicker chair. The collar of his coat was pulled up to shield his neck from the wind, his hands were stuffed deep into his pockets. It was a cold, wet, early winter's day, the kind of day that made the whole world seem bleak. He wasn't sure why he'd come here, though he'd always found something soothing in the semi-remoteness of the place – not too far from the world, but far enough to pretend for a while that it didn't exist.

The shock of Penny going off the way she had coming right on top of the crushing disappointment of not seeing his children had hit him hard. The repercussions of what Penny had done were already making themselves felt, but he didn't blame her for that – she had no idea what her association with Mureau would do to his life. He couldn't help wondering if it would have altered her decision had she known. He'd often teased her that she was crazy about him and, in truth, there were times when he had almost come to believe it. But, whatever her feelings for him, they obviously weren't even in the same league as those she had for Mureau, considering she had given up her life for him.

He moved restlessly in the chair. Jesus Christ, what a mess, and there wasn't a single god-damned thing he could do about it. He knew where Penny was, but to call her would be a madness he'd have a very hard time explaining to himself in the months, maybe years, ahead. Stirling was watching him like a hawk now and, besides, what arrogance was it that made him think she'd even want to hear from him? Yet she'd called just before she'd left: she'd wanted to speak to him then, so why not now?

He sighed wearily. This was a pointless exercise and he knew it. He wasn't going to call and neither was he going to dwell on what might have been between them when he knew full well there could never have been anything. He had to look out for himself now and the two boys who meant everything in the world to him. His senses were blunted by the pain of not seeing them in so long. They were growing up, finding their places in the world, without him. He felt a moment's blinding hatred towards Gabriella who was making him suffer this way, who was depriving his sons of their father and threatening to wreck all their lives. But he had only himself to blame, for if he'd managed to stay faithful to Gabriella none of this would be happening. The ridiculous part of it was that he'd loved Gabriella, but even that hadn't stopped him wandering. He guessed he just hadn't loved her enough, or maybe he was just one of those pitiful jerks for whom infidelity was an incurable disease.

He turned his head to gaze out across the dismal garden to the murky grey smudge of the sea. The bleakness seemed to reflect what he'd been feeling inside since Penny had gone; it was as though the colour had bled from his life, the light had dimmed and the last echo of laughter had finally died. He'd never dreamt he'd feel the loss as deeply as this, had never, until she'd gone, realized just *how* much he loved her. Funny how everyone, except Penny, seemed to know how he felt about her.

A quick memory of the day she had flung a *tiramisu* in his face flashed through his mind and, despite the way he was feeling, a smile curved his lips. God, that seemed such a long time ago now. Was it really only eight months since they'd met? It felt so much longer. Yet in another way it felt like no time at all. So much had happened during that time, things about which she knew nothing. They hadn't been easy months, but knowing

346

Penny, having her there and sharing what he could of his life with her was what had made them bearable. How she'd laugh if she heard him say that – she probably wouldn't believe him, but it was true. She had come to mean more to him now than he had words to express and it was feeling this way that was going to make what came next so much harder to bear.

Hearing footsteps, he kept his eyes on the sea until they stopped, then he turned to see Esther Delaney standing at the corner of the house. Her slight, compact little frame was hidden in the sumptuous depths of a full-length mink, her normally immaculately set hair was being tossed about by the wind.

'They're still in Hong Kong,' she told him, her pale, solemn face pinched with unease.

'Where are they headed next?'

'We still don't know.'

David sucked in his bottom lip, sat a few moments longer, then got up from the chair. He walked past the old woman and around the front of the house, to his car.

'David, I'm sorry,' she cried after him, her face twisted with misery. 'David, please listen to me. He made us do it. We didn't have any choice . . .'

David turned and stared at her. 'You could have come to me,' he said.

Esther's gaze fell away as tears rolled down her cheeks. 'He loves her,' she said wretchedly. 'He won't harm her.'

David opened the car door.

'No! Please don't go like this,' she implored, starting towards him. 'He was so lonely, David . . . David, *please*,' she cried as he got into the car.

By the time he drove through the gates David had reached Pierre on the phone.

'Book yourself on a flight to Hong Kong,' he said shortly. 'I'll take care of things this end— I don't care,' he roared when Pierre interrupted. 'I've got to find out if this is what she wants. I need to know why she called before she left. That's all, Pierre. Just get to her and find out or I'll damned well go myself.'

Chapter 18

It was just after eight in the evening. Christian had left
the hotel an hour or so ago, saying he would be back by
ten to take Penny to the China Club for dinner. Penny
hadn't asked where he was going, though he'd muttered something about Gabriel Lamont, the man who
had called the other day. Though Penny remained convinced Benny Lao had said Gabriella, Christian was
adamant that she had misheard. He knew no one by the
name of Gabriella, he had insisted, and even if he did he
didn't understand why it would upset her so much. Not
wanting to explain, Penny had assured him she believed
him, but whether his call had come from a Gabriel or a
Gabriella there was no mistaking the effect it had had on
him. It had taken her a while to persuade him to tell her
what the call had been about and why it appeared to be
troubling him so deeply, and when he had finally told
her she sorely wished he hadn't. The call, whoever it
had been from, had been to inform him that all deals
were off now and that if he was caught he would be
facing twenty-five years in a federal prison.

The odd thing was that living as openly as they were,
though admittedly under false names, Penny had almost
lost sight of the threat hanging over him, but hearing
that, when she knew that he had given up the chance of
a lighter sentence just so he could be with her, had been
like hearing the deafening slam of her own prison door.

Earlier, when he had said he was going out, she had simply waited for him to leave, then had turned her eyes to Lei Leen. Lei Leen had looked away, but when Tse Dong had entered the room a few minutes later she had whispered into his ear. As she spoke, Tse Dong's impenetrable gaze had fallen on Penny; then he had turned back to his wife and dealt her a stinging blow, knocking her to the floor. Penny gasped and started forward, but Lei Leen's glance stopped her from doing anything to intervene. Lei Leen didn't fight back but neither did she give up, and in the end, Penny doubted she would ever know how, she had persuaded Tse Dong to do as she was asking. Which was how they now came to be driving through the dark, garbage-strewn back-streets of Kowloon, heading for Mongkok – one of the most densely populated areas on earth and one of the most dangerous.

Gloomy trails of light passed listlessly through the car, illuminating their faces as they crept deeper into the tangled maze of the slums. Tse Dong and Lei Leen were sitting either side of her in the back seat while a man Penny had never seen before drove the limousine through the festering mounds of debris and silent clutches of humanity. Everything outside was shaded in grey – the smoke, the dust, the ragged, meandering bodies drifting like shadows through the opium-drugged night. Penny was as tense as the other two, knowing what a risk they were taking bringing her here.

When they finally came to a halt in a narrow, dimly lit street, Tse Dong opened the car door and Penny instantly recoiled from the ammonia stench of urine wafting from the gutters to mingle with the pungent odour of incense. As she and Lei Leen stepped out into the street, blank, sickly faces turned in their direction and watched them with blurred, desensitized eyes.

Tse Dong's hand gripped the gun in his pocket as the

three of them watched the driver steer the limousine out of the street towards the glaring neon and seething, stall-crammed lanes of the night market. It was where they were headed next, but only as a cover lest Christian should find out they had been here.

As they walked past the blackened holes of alleyways and gaping doorways of squalid, rat-infested opium dens, soft moans of pain and euphoria seeped into the thick, humid air like a muted lament of death. Tse Dong led the way silently across the street towards the crystal gazers, palmists and geomancers whose decrepit felt-covered tables edged a park railing, behind which monotonous pleas for release rolled through the murky night as the stupefied bodies writhed in the needle-littered earth.

Penny had had no idea it would be like this; if she had, she would probably never have come, but now she was here she could only stare in appalled fascination. The sharp, glittering lights of Hong Kong, the soaring, gleaming façades of its skyscrapers, the vibrancy of the bustling, colour-splashed city streets, all seemed an entire world away from this hell.

'Remember, we not stay long,' Lei Leen whispered as Penny stopped in front of a fortune-teller's table and looked down at his long, bony fingers hovering over a cluster of indefinable objects. Did she really believe that this stranger with his sparse, rotting teeth and wart-blemished face could tell her what she had come to find out? As she looked at him she could feel the omnipresent power of ancient beliefs threading a hypnotic circle around her mind. The hallucinogenic substances in the air were casting chimerical fringes over her vision. She looked down as, in the gutter beside her, a foul, disorderly pile of rags shifted and slumped, to reveal the deadened face of a child, eyes rolling vacuously in their sockets, saliva drooling from pale, cracked lips. Penny knew she had stepped beyond the realms of her imagination and felt herself flood with pity and horror and disgust and fear.

The geomancer was speaking, his thin, drooping moustache quivering like weeds in a torpid breeze. His spidery fingers reached out for hers and as he turned her palm to the sluggish lamp at his elbow Penny's heart started a slow, expectant throb. She turned to Lei Leen, making sure she was there to translate. Lei Leen's head was bowed as she counted out the dollar bills to pay.

As the money was placed on the table the old man signalled for Penny to sit. The chair rocked as she lowered her weight on to it. The distant screech of sirens and a brief pulsating beat of music stole the sound from the soothsayer's words. The festering rankness of the street penetrated her throat, making her gag. She glanced up at Lei Leen's face. It was shrouded in shadow. The whole world seemed to have slipped into a penumbra of timelessness and delusion. Then everything in her began to turn slowly to ice as she felt the old man curl her fingers over her palm, closing her hand in a fist. She raised her head to look at him. His jaundiced eyes were staring past her, glazed and sightless; his trembling fingers were digging hard into hers.

'What? What is it?' she croaked, turning back to Lei Leen.

Lei Leen's eyes were fixed on the old man. She was stooping towards him, trying to fathom his mutterings. Then, looking at Tse Dong, she put a hand on Penny's shoulder.

'Come,' she said. 'We go now.'

Penny got to her feet. 'Lei Leen, what did he say?' she implored, fear shaking her voice.

'He say he is finished up for tonight,' Lei Leen answered, guiding Penny away from the table. 'Sometimes it happen that way. They do not always have the sight.'

Penny's mind was reeling at the old man's sudden loss of skill. Though she wasn't sure whether or not she believed in these unearthly powers she'd needed something to give her hope that this nightmare would end, that somehow she would find a way to disentangle herself from the terrible mistake she had made. And now all she knew was the paralysing fear that the old man had seen no future at all.

Her eyes were blinded by tears of loneliness and defeat. Lei Leen, Tse Dong, even Christian, all seemed like strangers, strangers who were controlling her life, strangers from whom she could find no escape. Coming here had been the foolish, desperate act of a woman who had lost her courage and no longer knew how to retrieve it.

As they rounded the corner, the sudden glare of neon burned into her eyes. Overturned refuse carts, with skeletal dogs rooting among them, lined the way into the bustling night market where cheap toys, lewdly sloganned T-shirts and fake designer watches vied for space with exotic fruits, squawking hens and squealing pigs. As they merged with the crowds the musky scent of sandalwood was obliterated by the stench of frying onions and pungent raw fish. Unwashed tables spilled on to the street, where hungry men crouched, tucking into jellyfish and octopus, swilling it down with San Miguel beer. A path in a crowd opened up and Penny watched in mute horror as a man holding a snake by its throat slit open its belly and sucked the innards into his mouth. As the blood and guts trickled down his chin Penny started to retch.

Lei Leen moved beside her and put a soothing hand on the back of her neck. As she continued to throw up, a space cleared around them. A man rushed forward and sloshed a pail of grey, greasy water over their feet. The sound of raucous laughter and vibrating sex aids rose above the general hue and cry. The rustle of paper bags, the squeaking of wheels, the wailing of sirens, the buzz of battered toys, the shrieks of humans, the barking of dogs, the blare of music, the honking of horns: the terrifying madness of noise pressed into her ears as though to crush her.

Then suddenly there was silence.

An eternal second of perfect stillness elapsed before an ear-piercing cacophony of screams tore through the night.

Penny barely knew what was happening as she hit the floor with Tse Dong on top of her. It was only when more gunshots rang out that she realized what had caused the panic. Stampeding feet raced before her eyes, knocking over stalls, kicking into them, trampling and falling over them. Tse Dong rolled over and, feeling someone dragging her from the mêlée, Penny turned to see Lei Leen frantically begging her to run. Scrambling to her feet, Penny clutched Lei Leen's hand, and together they plunged into the heaving, screeching mass of humanity struggling to escape. Tse Dong was right behind them, holding tightly to his gun and screaming instructions to Lei Leen. As they entered a side-street they broke from the crowd and dashed into a restaurant, knocking over tables as they went and skidding in the slithery remnants of abandoned meals. Penny yelped with pain as her hip struck something hard, but she was moving too fast to see what it was. The rapid bursts of machine-gun fire were once again audible over the din. She was thrown forward as something hit her in the back, but as she sank to her knees Lei Leen and Tse Dong wrenched her to her feet and dragged her on.

As they burst out of the back of the restaurant the limousine screeched to a halt in front of them. Tse Dong threw Penny inside, pushed Lei Leen in after her, then just managed to leap in himself as the limousine sped away. Lei Leen was crouched over Penny, holding

Penny's head down, while Tse Dong shouted at the driver.

It was only when they had left Mongkok and were speeding through the Eastern tunnel towards Central that Lei Leen finally took her weight off Penny and allowed her to sit up. By then Penny was limp with fear and exhaustion. Her eyes were wide and dry, her heart, her very soul, felt wrung out and drained of all emotion. She was living a Kafkaesque nightmare and didn't know how to make it stop. Whether those gunshots had been intended for her she didn't know; nor, right at that moment, did she care. The fact that she'd thought she'd been hit didn't matter either. Nothing did. It was as though her whole existence had been torn from its roots and transplanted into the empty air of some lawless, dehumanized other world. There was blood on her arm, but as Lei Leen lifted it to inspect it Penny turned her face to the window and gazed out at the passing landmarks.

'Just scratch,' Lei Leen pronounced, letting the arm go. 'I wash and dress it when we get back.'

Dully Penny wondered what had hit her hip and her back, but since there was neither pain nor blood and she could move she dismissed the thought. It was a while before she became aware of the heated argument going on between Lei Leen and Tse Dong and, guessing what it was about, she heard herself say in a cracked, toneless voice, 'Don't worry about what Christian will say. I'll be fine. There's no need for him to know. No harm was done.'

Lei Leen turned to look at her. Her face was drawn and frightened. 'Tse Dong say that the boss must know.'

Penny looked at Tse Dong, then turned away, not wanting him to see the tears stinging her eyes. 'Then I'll tell him,' she said.

A few minutes later they arrived at the Mandarin Hotel. There was no sign of Christian, but the butler

355

had been in to turn back the bed and draw the curtains. Penny walked through to the bathroom and went to stand in front of the mirror. The woman she saw looking back at her was a woman she no longer knew. Her face was ashen and smudged with dirt, her large, blue eyes appeared colourless and empty. She closed them as the tears threatened to overwhelm her again; then, hearing Lei Leen come in, she turned towards the shower.

'Can I get you something, ma'am?' Lei Leen offered. 'You like brandy or whisky?'

'No, thank you,' Penny answered.

Lei Leen hesitated, then said, 'Tse Dong send driver for boss. He be here soon.'

Penny nodded.

'You like I stay and keep you company?' Lei Leen said.

'Not unless you want to tell me what all that was about,' Penny challenged quietly, turning to face her.

Lei Leen was silent for a moment; then, shaking her head, she said, 'Ma'am I not know what it was about. Maybe they not shooting at us. Maybe they shooting at someone else. Mongkok is dangerous place. Lots of gangs.'

'But if they were shooting at us, *why* would they have been?'

Lei Leen bowed her head.

'Lei Leen, please,' Penny implored. 'Why would anyone want to shoot at us?'

'I not know, ma'am,' she answered. Then, shrugging, she added, 'The boss, he very rich man, maybe someone try kidnap you.'

'Oh God,' Penny groaned, covering her face with her hands. 'Where's Christian now?'

'He forget take phone. Tse Dong send driver for him.'

Penny felt the weariness creep through her limbs. She might just as well be speaking to the dour-faced, hand-carved statues of Chinese attendants standing either side of the jacuzzi.

'I'd like to be alone for a while, Lei Leen,' she said. 'I mean totally alone. I don't care if you wait outside the door, but please, just give me some space at least until Christian gets here.'

Lei Leen bowed her head meekly and left.

After she'd showered and washed her hair Penny wrapped herself in a voluminous bathrobe and wandered through to the dining room. The lights were low, casting a soft, dreamy glow over the eclectic splendour of Chinese antiques and plush, modern sofas and carpets. As she padded up the steps to the sitting room, trailing a hand over the Tang horse and highly polished teak banister on which it sat, she could smell the lingering traces of Christian's cologne in the air. She wondered how long it would take him to get there and prayed that it wouldn't be too soon. This was the first time she had been alone in over a week and she needed the time to decide what she was going to do.

A quick stab of unease pierced her heart as she recalled how the geomancer had closed her hand. Had he really lost the sight, or had he just not wanted to tell her what he had seen? Maybe there had been nothing there to see; maybe she was never going to get away from this place where each day brought a fresh madness and each night a demand for pretence she no longer knew if she could sustain.

What she did know, though, was that she could no longer close her eyes to what was going on around her. The snatches of English she had overheard these past few days were generally numbers, names or total *non sequiturs*, but it was the numbers that had first aroused her suspicions about those with whom Christian was doing business. They were always made up of three figures, usually in the four hundreds, and each number was divisible by three. She wasn't too sure how she knew, but how wasn't important; the fact was that someone had once told her, or maybe she had read it somewhere, that all Triad members were assigned a number divisible by three – and those in the four hundreds were the higher-ranking officials. Though she knew little else about the Chinese mafia she did know that their level of corruption and barbaric methods of killing, coupled with their infiltration of governments, banks and worldwide organizations, gave them the kind of power and omnipresence that made their Sicilian and Columbian counterparts seem as threatening as measles in comparison. And when she added to that where in the world they were, so close to the Golden Triangle, in a city that was littered with heroin refineries and which boasted a customs service that was as notoriously corrupt as it was overworked, she'd have to be a first-class fool to believe that Christian's seemingly inexhaustible fortune came only from the trafficking of marijuana.

A wave of misery swept through her as she recalled how David had tried to warn her. It was the same day that he had told her he cared for her. But caring for her wasn't loving her and she knew that, no matter how strong his affection might be, it wouldn't, couldn't, support the way she had walked out on him.

The thought of David had brought fresh tears to her eyes and a painful tightness to her heart. Her suspicions had taken such frightening twists and turns since the call from Gabriella, but still she couldn't make herself believe that David and his wife were involved in all this. Apart from that one phone call there was no evidence at all to link them to Christian – and even if the call had come from Gabriella and not Gabriel, what was there to say that it was Gabriella Villers?

Her head was spinning and feeling claustrophobic in her gilded prison she pulled back a curtain, and sliding open the glass door she stepped out on to the terrace to gaze down at the glittering, perpetually moving lights of

Victoria Harbour. It was a city as filled with secrets as her mind was filled with the fragments of doubt and suspicion. The roar of traffic rose up from the streets as the ferry-terminal clock chimed out the hour. Christian would be back soon and she was no closer now to deciding what she should do than she had been since she'd arrived. She swallowed hard and screwed up her eyes in an effort to hold herself together, for in her heart she knew that there was nothing she could do. Christian was never going to let her go and as long as they stayed here she knew she would never get away. If she were being honest with herself she didn't even know if she wanted to leave, for she could hardly bear to contemplate how much it would hurt Christian if she left without a word, and she knew she didn't have the courage to face the pain and betrayal in his eyes if she told him she wanted to go. The perversity of that didn't escape her, but it wasn't easy to imagine him as a gangster when he never treated her with anything but love and kindness and such overwhelming generosity it could almost split her heart in two to think of it. She wondered if she should be afraid of him, but when she considered to what lengths he was going to protect her the very idea seemed absurd.

Sighing, she turned back inside and closed the terrace door. She was thinking of Sammy now and when, if ever, she would see her again. Christian had assured her she would, but what if Sammy needed her now? Grief and longing swelled in her chest as she thought of how much she needed Sammy, how much she would give to see her now. Was she worried, afraid, did she even know that Penny was no longer in France?

As she walked past the desk her foot knocked against something and looking down, she saw her computer. She stooped to pick it up and was about to lay it on the desk, when her head fell forward as a great, choking sob tore itself from her heart. It seemed crazy that it should be this cold, inanimate object that had finally brought her to tears, but as all the pain and guilt, shame and desperation, engulfed her she hugged it to her chest and wept as though her heart would break. It was all she had now of her past. All her clothes, all her possessions were back at the villa, left for someone else to clear up, as was the mess she had left at the office. Dear God, how could she have treated people who had cared for her so much with such callous disregard? Between them, David and Sylvia had given her their trust, their support, their friendship and affection – and how had she repaid them? By throwing everything back in their faces. What kind of woman was she? What must they think of her now? How she longed to pick up the phone and call Sylvia, to tell her how sorry she was, how desperately she wanted to turn back the clock and pretend that none of this had happened; that the thousands upon thousands of dollar bills she had seen pass through this very room this past week were no more than a figment of her imagination; that Christian's connections with one of the world's most brutal organizations were nothing more than the far-fetched deductions of a panicked mind.

Stopping to catch her breath, she wiped a hand over her face and tried to calm herself. Should she trust her instincts now? she wondered, as she placed the computer on the desk and sank into the chair. Should she believe that Christian loved her and that were it not for her he'd have taken the DA's deal? She didn't want to believe it: if she didn't, it would make things so much easier. Maybe then she could go and never have to deal with the guilt the way she was having to deal with the other guilt that now tormented her – at having turned her back on David.

She gave a short, bitter laugh. What a pathetic fool she was! What had happened to her mettle and courage now when she needed it most? She surely wasn't just going to let this continue as though she had no say in her life? If

Christian really was dealing in heroin, then she owed him nothing, nothing at all. But how could she find out? It was madness to think he'd tell her himself and, even if he did, all it would prove was that he had lied to her. It still wouldn't gain her her freedom.

She started as the telephone rang. For a moment she was tempted to answer it; but then, guessing that it was Christian calling to tell her he was on his way, she just let it ring. When it stopped, she got up from the chair and wandered into the bedroom. She couldn't cave in now, she just couldn't. It was foolish to keep thinking of David this way, to wonder what he would tell her to do if she called him. It was all very well to imagine him sorting this out for her, for she'd never yet seen him fazed by anything, but the reality was that they had the barrier of the law between them now and she doubted that even he could overcome that. No, she had to forget about David and accept that she was on her own, that she had to face the consequences of her actions and somehow try to find out what she was really up against here. Then if, *when*, she did, she would have to decide how she was going to deal with it.

As the telephone rang again her head fell back and, biting hard on her lips to stop herself crying, she hugged herself tightly. She hated this weakness that was making her repeatedly turn to David, that was sweeping through her with such hopelessness and sapping her inner strength. But this was the last time, she swore to herself. After tonight she was never again going to indulge herself in the torment of loving him or believing she could depend on him. She had to accept that there was nothing he could do and, even if there was, why would he? She had got herself into this mess, it was for her to get herself out of it. But even as her resolve gathered it began to fracture and unable to stop herself, she fell to her knees beside the bed and sobbed his name.

*

As Christian sprinted up the steps into the crowded, black marble lobby of the Mandarin and moved swiftly towards the elevators, Lei Leen watched him pass Pierre, who was making his way back from the house phone. Neither man noticed the other; both were too intent on their own thoughts.

'What did she say?' Lei Leen asked as Pierre joined her.

'She didn't answer,' he said, his face strained with the frustration of being so near to Penny yet so powerless to get closer when Tse Dong was right outside her door.

Lei Leen lowered her eyes. 'What are you going to do now?' she asked.

'I don't know,' he answered. 'Call David, I suppose.'

Lei Leen nodded, then got up from her chair, walked off across the lobby and disappeared into the lift.

A few minutes later Pierre was dialling David's number in France. It rang only once before he picked up.

'I'm at the Mandarin,' Pierre said into the receiver.

'Did you see her?' David asked carefully. 'Did you speak to her?'

'No. I can't get near her.' Pierre paused, knowing how hard it was going to be for David to hear all this. But now wasn't the time to pull punches and David wouldn't thank him for it if he did. 'I went up to the suite,' he said, 'but Tse Dong is outside. There's no getting past him.'

'Did you speak to Lei Leen?' David asked.

'Yes.'

'And?'

Pierre took a breath. 'She says that Penny's where she wants to be.'

There was a long and painful silence, during which Pierre could only imagine David's anguish, and knowing he was about to add to it only made him feel worse.

362

'There was some kind of shooting in Mongkok tonight,' he said flatly. 'Penny was there with Tse Dong and Lei Leen. No one was hurt, but I talked to a character by the name of Benny Lao earlier and, to quote him, Mureau's been pissing a few people off. There's no way of knowing who was behind the shooting or if it had anything to do with the way Mureau's been upsetting people, but the coincidence of Penny being there is ominous. Lei Leen is convinced that if Mureau's enemies wanted to kill or kidnap Penny they'd do just that. Which means that if the shooting was in some way related, then it has to be read as a warning.'

It was some time before David answered. When he did, his voice was perfectly steady. 'Where's Penny now?' he said.

'In the suite. Mureau's just gone up there.'

Several seconds ticked by before David spoke again. 'So,' he said hoarsely, 'where do we go from here?'

Pierre didn't answer. The decision was David's and his alone.

David laughed harshly. 'Tell me, Pierre,' he said, 'how the hell do you rescue someone who doesn't want to be rescued, who probably doesn't even know that she needs to be?'

'You don't,' Pierre told him frankly.

'Not if you're in the position I'm in,' David added bitterly.

Pierre's silence was confirmation enough.

'Does he love her?' David asked.

'Lei Leen is certain of it.'

'And she's where she wants to be?'

'Yes.'

'Then there's no more we can do, is there?' he said, and the line went dead.

After slamming down the receiver David walked across the apartment, pushed open the french windows and stepped out into the raging wind. The storm was reaching its peak and as the waves crashed over the beach, flinging themselves menacingly against the sea wall, driving rods of rain ricocheted up from the street. It was the middle of the day, but behind him the main lights in the apartment were on and a desk lamp glowed in a meaningful circle over the stack of papers scattered on the table.

His face was pale with tiredness, his temper as foul as the weather, but if he was going to deal with this rationally he had to take charge of himself. Whichever direction he took now was likely to be as disastrous as the next and it was going to take every ounce of skill he had to get them all through it. He'd meant it when he'd told Pierre there was no more they could do for Penny, but it had been in the heat of the moment and deep down he knew that he was going to help her whether she wanted it or not. He'd already gone much further down that road than even Pierre knew, because despite what Pierre had told him he was convinced Penny did want his help. Whether she was too proud or even ashamed to ask, or was never alone long enough to make the call, he had no idea. But one thing he was sure of was that, damned hot-headed and impulsive as she could be, she certainly wasn't stupid. She'd have worked out for herself by now that Mureau was still dealing heroin and that was something David knew she would find as abhorrent as he did. Whether or not she'd discovered who was behind Mureau he had no way of knowing. A part of him hoped she hadn't, for, unless Mureau started behaving himself with those Chinese thugs he was involved with, Penny could very well, out of sheer ignorance, end up putting herself in even more danger than she was already in. But if she did know and she was as scared as she should be to discover that she was a weapon the Triads could point at Mureau's head, then he could only pray that Mureau really did care for her as much as he had managed to convince everyone he did. If he did he'd surely do everything in his power to protect her, which on the face of it he was, by having Tse Dong and Lei Leen go everywhere with her. Both were trained killers and both were as loyal to Christian as Pierre was to him.

Be that as it may, the sensible thing for Mureau to do now, after those warning shots across his bows, was to get Penny out of Hong Kong pretty damned quick. David didn't want to underestimate Penny, but faced with what she was now she couldn't be expected to think rationally enough to use what influence she had to persuade Mureau into leaving. He just hoped to God she didn't try to escape alone – if she did, she would very soon discover what it was to long for death. He dismissed the thought quickly, seeing no point in trying to deal with an eventuality that was a worst-case scenario, for with any luck Penny would stay put with Mureau until he, David, could get himself over there.

Walking back into the apartment he went to the table and stared down at the paperwork. Rain trickled from his hair and dripped on to his collar. He knew what he had to do now, but doing it was another thing altogether. This was a cruel and bitter hand fate had dealt him and he could but hope that Mureau hadn't managed to exert the same kind of influence over Penny as he had over Gabriella. If he had, then God only knew where all this would end. But for the moment he was going to ignore that possibility for the simple reason that, whatever else Penny thrived on, he knew it was certainly neither revenge nor greed.

He smiled grimly to himself as he picked up the phone and dialled Stirling's number. Throughout all this he'd never dreamt that he'd end up turning to Stirling for help. There was no guarantee he would get it, of course; in fact, there was every likelihood he wouldn't. But it was his last shot: he could go no further without

Stirling's influence to assist him and the only way he was going to get that was to give Stirling what he wanted.

Chapter 19

Ever since they had flown in over the flooded rice fields on the outskirts of Manila Penny had been trying to find the words to tell Christian she wanted to go home. There were moments when she wondered if he sensed what was in her mind, for the way he so often spoke over her as though afraid of what she was going to say or held her to him as though to crush her with his love seemed like the acts of a frightened, almost desperate man. And there was a hollowness to his laughter as he tried to engage her enthusiasm for their future, telling her of all the things they would see and do in even more remote and far-off places than they were now. He was trying so hard to make her smile, was almost beside himself in his attempts to convince her how happy they were going to be, that she simply couldn't find it in her to destroy his illusion.

Persuading him to leave Hong Kong had been much easier than she'd expected, for he'd seemed as keen to get away as she was, but getting him to admit he was still dealing in drugs hadn't proved so successful. He'd appeared genuinely astonished when she'd asked him about the three-figure numbers and if they meant what she suspected they did.

'The Chinese mafia?' he'd said incredulously.

Penny nodded. 'It's how they identify themselves and virtually every number I've heard mentioned since we got here has been a three-figure number divisible by three.'

He'd shaken his head, his eyes clouded by confusion as he thought back over the meetings that had taken place while she was there.

'Four two three,' she told him. 'Four five six. Four four one.'

He had put a hand to his head, still thinking, then finally he'd started to laugh. 'I don't know what those numbers have to do with the Hong Kong Triads,' he said. 'I've never even heard of this divisible-by-three thing. It could be that you're right, but in this instance, *chérie*, they're the tonnage of the marijuana shipments we sent over to the States.'

Of course it was possible, but the coincidence was too great and though she made a pretence of believing him, in her heart she remained convinced she was right. She hadn't pushed it, though, for a sixth sense told her that the less she knew the safer she would be. She couldn't quite qualify the feeling, but she was pretty certain that if the people he was dealing with ever got wind of the fact that she knew more than she should her life would be in serious jeopardy. And Christian's eagerness to get her out of Hong Kong after the shooting in Mongkok only heightened her fears that it already was.

They'd flown out on a private plane the morning after the shooting, travelling under false passports again, this time in the names of Paul and Gillian Anderson. Tse Dong and Lei Leen had stayed behind and for the time being she and Christian appeared to be alone in Manila. Not that the phone calls had stopped, if anything they were even more frequent than before – and always in Cantonese, so Penny still had no idea what they were about.

They were staying at the grand old turn-of-the-century Manila Hotel, not in a suite this time, but in a spacious double room with a clear view of the harbour. This attempt to blend less noticeably with the other guests, coupled with Christian's evident unhappiness and unease, was enough to tell Penny that the need for anonymity was growing. Whether this was because the DEA was closing in on him, or whether it had something to do with the Chinese, she didn't know, but what she did know was how deeply it was affecting her to see him looking so vulnerable and lonely.

They had left the hotel an hour ago, crossing the busy intersection of Bonifacio and Ayala Boulevards, where brightly coloured jeepnies crammed with solemn-faced passengers vied for space with beaten-up American cars and glossy white hotel taxis. They'd strolled around the *Intramuros*, watching Filipino schoolchildren in their smart, checkered uniforms explore the ruins of the old Spanish fort and romp excitedly around the Wall of Martyrs picnic ground, feigning executions and bloody, agonized deaths. With his smattering of Tagalog Christian had joined in the fun, allowing himself to be shot, but only after delighting them by falling to his knees and reciting a few badly memorized lines from José Rizal's *Noli me tangere*. As she watched him Penny smiled and laughed and fought back the tears of guilt at not loving him enough. How much less complicated things would be if she could despise him for the crimes he had committed, but life was rarely, if ever, that simple and she knew that despite everything he would always hold a very special place in her heart.

The children had caught up with them again as they'd roamed Rizal's shrine at the heart of the fort, but Penny had seen what an effort it was for Christian to resummon his earlier light-heartedness. It would have been easy to put his increasing depression down to the morbid exhibits in Rizal's house – the national hero's discarded pens, his sister's letters, the echoing emptiness of the room in which the great man had spent his final days before execution – but Penny knew there was much more to it.

As they left the fort and wandered through the pitted, dusty streets to Rizal Park it was left to her to turn down the bicycle and sidecar rides, to tip the beggars and smile at the sweet Filipino faces that watched them pass. She could sense him withdrawing deeper and deeper into himself, as though he was closing her out, preparing himself for the moment she left, when he would be forced to face the aimlessness and futility of his lonely existence. She ached with pity and wished she could find the words to comfort him, but what could she say? Besides, she wasn't such an egoist as to believe that it was she alone who was causing this despair, for something was happening, something that she was sure went far beyond his fear of her leaving.

'Christian, speak to me,' she said, sliding her hand into his as they strolled into the exotic tranquillity of the Chinese Gardens. 'Tell me what's troubling you.' She guessed she probably wouldn't want to hear the answers, but she just couldn't bear to see him suffering like this.

Squeezing her hand, he looked down at the clustered lily pads meandering languidly over the dark, rippling water. Then he turned to walk on, leading the way across the footbridge towards the ornate, colourful gazebos with their tall red pillars and curled roof edges. With the exception of an old man sleeping peacefully in the shade of a flowering magnolia they were alone in the garden.

'Christian?' she prompted.

Letting go of her hand, he walked on, wandering up the wide, terracotta steps into the welcoming coolness of a gazebo.

'Don't you find it beautiful here?' he said, as she came to join him. 'It's so peaceful and . . .' he turned to look at her, a hesitant tease lighting his eyes '. . . and romantic?'

he said.

'Very,' she smiled.

Drawing her into his arms, he kissed her forehead, then laid her head on his shoulder. 'I love you,' he whispered, holding her tightly.

She stood quietly in the embrace, listening to his heartbeat and trying to find her way through the impossible tangle of her emotions.

Eventually he let her go and turned to look around.

'Christian, what is it?' she said, putting a hand on his arm.

He was staring past her, his eyes unfocused and steeped in anguish. 'Will you marry me?' he said softly, still not looking at her.

Penny felt herself tense as her heart contracted and her eyes closed against the terrible realization that she was wrong, he wasn't preparing himself to let her go at all.

Hearing footsteps, they both turned and watched a young man with a camera approach. He took several shots of the gazebo; then, coming inside, he seemed surprised to find someone there even though he must surely have seen them when he was pointing his camera in their direction.

When he spoke, Penny wasn't too sure whether or not it was English, for his accent was too thick, but from his gestures it was evident he was asking if he could take their picture.

Smiling, Christian looked down at her. 'What do you say?' he said.

Penny shrugged. 'Why not?'

At the time it didn't seem odd to her that a shabbily dressed, badly nourished Filipino youth should possess such an expensive-looking camera; nor that Christian, who was a fugitive from the law, should so readily agree to his photograph being taken by a stranger. In truth she barely thought about it at all as she smiled into the lens, grateful for the timely interruption.

371

When the boy had finished, he thanked them, shook their hands and walked away. But once again Penny was saved from answering, this time by Christian's mobile phone.

As he spoke he walked out of the gazebo, though whether to prevent her from listening or to improve the connection was impossible to say. By the time he'd finished, Penny could see the change in him. Putting the phone back inside his shirt pocket, he bounded up the steps, grabbed her hand and ran with her to the gates.

'What is it?' she cried, having to shout to make herself heard above the roar of the traffic. 'Where are we going?'

'Back to the hotel,' he answered, plunging into the interminable stream of vehicles and weaving a path to the other side.

When they reached the hotel lobby he stopped, turned her to face him and spoke quickly, his words shortened by his breathlessness. 'That was the call I've been waiting for,' he said, his eyes shining with an emotion she found impossible to fathom. 'I have to go out now. I won't be long. I'll explain everything when I get back.'

'But where are you going?'

'Not far,' he answered. 'I want you to go up to the room and wait for me there. Lock yourself in and don't answer the door to anyone. Don't answer the phone either. And . . .' He stopped, swallowed hard and as his eyes flooded with pain, he said, 'Please, don't walk out on me now. I know you want to, but . . .' he lowered his head '. . . please, don't go,' he said hoarsely, and without waiting for an answer he left.

Penny watched him until he'd disappeared through the garden; then, looking around her, she started across the vast, pale marble lobby with its numerous red sofas and glittering chandeliers. There were at least a hundred people either sitting or standing around in groups and though she caught no one looking in her direction she had the distinct and uneasy feeling that someone was. When she reached the lift her heart began to thud as she waited for the doors to close, afraid that someone would get in with her. No one did.

When she got out on the fifteenth floor she was still alone. The floor attendant was at his desk, singing, and he treated her to a beaming smile as she passed.

'Good day, ma'am,' he said.

'Hello, Teddy,' she answered. 'How are you?'

His smile widened. 'I happy because my girlfriend call from Hong Kong last night,' he told her.

Penny smiled. 'Then I'm happy for you,' she said, thinking how wonderfully benign and ingenuous the Filipinos were.

'You enjoy your stay with us, ma'am?' he said, falling into step beside her.

'Very much, thank you,' she said.

'This your first time in Philippines?'

'Yes.'

'Where you from, ma'am?'

Penny was about to answer when she suddenly realized that she couldn't remember what it said on her new passport. But what was the harm in telling this boy the truth? 'England,' she said.

He seemed pleased by her answer. 'I know you not American,' he told her. 'I can tell by voice. You live in London, ma'am?'

She nodded. 'I used to, yes.'

'Where you work now?'

'France,' she said, wishing it were true.

'What you do there?' he asked.

'I'm a journalist.'

'That's nice, ma'am,' he said, taking her key card from her as they reached her room. 'You journalisting here in Manila?'

'No,' Penny smiled. 'Just visiting.'

373

'Then enjoy your stay,' he said, pushing the door open for her.

A few moments later Teddy was back at his desk. There was no one else around as he picked up the phone and dialled the number he had been given the day before.

'Hello?' a voice at the other end barked.

'Is Teddy,' he said. 'She here. She in room 1514.'

'How do you know it's her?'

'She say she English. She say she work in France journalisting.'

Penny had been standing at the window for some time, gazing down at the harbour. The sea was a metallic grey, the sky was translucent. There was none of the activity of Hong Kong harbour, just a few workmen meandering about the pier and a dozen or so tankers and container ships, resplendent in their ugliness, anchored randomly across the still waters of the bay.

Behind her the twin double beds, silent TV and empty bathroom seemed almost menacing in their obdurate stillness. After Teddy had closed the door she had left it unlocked until she'd checked that she was alone; then, after putting the chain across, she had taken an Evian water from the fridge and walked to the window, telling herself that she should be seizing this opportunity to leave. Her bags were there, already packed, except of course she wouldn't have taken anything with her. She tried to imagine how Christian would feel if he returned to find her gone, leaving behind everything he had given her. The hurt such an act would inflict on him wrenched at her heart and frowning, she closed her eyes.

She'd thought that leaving Hong Kong and freeing themselves from the omnipresence of the Chinese would give her the chance to think more clearly, to decide how she was going to break it to Christian that she didn't want to go on with him. But all it had done was bind her more tightly to him and bring a new edge to her fear that she was never going to find the courage to leave. Of course she would in the end, she'd have to, because she was even less capable of living a lie than she was of causing him pain. It seemed so pathetic, so ill-judged and absurd, to be giving such consideration to the feelings of a man who was wanted by the law for crimes she just knew were far more heinous than he'd told her. But trying to connect that man to the man who had asked her to marry him not an hour ago was impossible. He neither looked nor behaved like a criminal and were it not for the false passports and the residue of certainty that his Chinese contacts were Triad members she could almost believe that this was all some kind of elaborate trick. And in truth it was really only the shooting in Mongkok that persuaded her it wasn't. That and the unshakeable feeling of danger that, for no reason she could pinpoint, seemed to have increased since they'd left Hong Kong.

Leaning forward she rested her forehead against the window. She should get out of there now and she knew it. She should pick up her purse and take a taxi straight to the airport. So why didn't she? Why was she standing here, waiting for him and knowing that when he came back she would have to give him an answer she'd give almost anything not to have to face? She knew why, of course, she was afraid of who might be lurking in the hotel, who might be waiting even now for her to make her escape. If they were Christian's people, then she believed she had little more to fear than the awkwardness and pain of explaining to him why she had tried to leave. She might be a fool for thinking that way, but no matter what else he was capable of, nothing in the world would persuade her that Christian meant her any harm. But if they were Christian's enemies there was no knowing what they might do. Common sense alone told her that there had to be those who were afraid of how much she knew, those who would quite happily see her dead rather than run the risk of her telling what little she had learned. There might also be those who would see her as a means of exerting pressure on Christian, of increasing their power over him by employing methods of torture she didn't even want to think about. That was why she was still standing here, gazing out at the opaque waters of Manila harbour and the unsightly jungle of ships' cranes.

She had already turned away, when something she had seen suddenly registered in her mind and she turned back to look again at the group of four men standing at the far end of the pier. Though the distance was sufficient to deceive, she was certain that one of them was Christian. Going quickly to their bags she rummaged inside one of them until she found the binoculars, almost dropping them as the telephone startled her. Ignoring it, she returned to the window and trained the glasses on the men at the end of the pier. She was right, it was Christian, and when she saw who was with him her blood ran cold. It was Benny Lao. She moved the glasses around a little, trying to get a look at the other two, but, though they seemed familiar, for the moment she couldn't quite place them.

And then it hit her. Of course: they were the customs officers who had been on duty at the private airfield when they'd flown in the day before. She frowned, wondering what they could be doing out there with Christian and Benny Lao. The shorter of the two officers was pointing out to sea, or, she thought, following the direction of his arm, maybe he was pointing at one of the container vessels.

'Oh God,' she groaned aloud, lowering the glasses as the suspicion of what they were doing dawned on her. Of course, he was pointing at a ship: wasn't it just such vessels as these that were used to transport drugs? And wasn't the sprawling archipelago of the Philippines as renowned for its role as a transhipment centre as it was for its easy corruption?

Looking through the binoculars again, she watched as they continued to gesticulate and discuss whatever business they were about. If she was right in her suspicions, then she'd be a fool to wait a moment longer. It made no difference whether it was heroin or marijuana – both were illegal; and if they were caught, then she, by mere association with Christian, would be as guilty as they. But her fear of what she could become embroiled in did nothing to eliminate the fear of who might be waiting for her downstairs . . .

As the dilemma hung unresolved in her mind she watched the four men begin to walk back along the pier and tried to make herself think clearly. Her heart began to race with the sudden speed of her thoughts as she attempted to weigh up which risk was the greater, to stay or to run. But how could she run when God only knew who might be waiting for her downstairs? She could always call hotel security; but even if she could think of a rational explanation for requesting an escort out of the building, once they'd seen her safely into a taxi there was every chance the taxi would be followed. A surge of panic gripped her as she realized she couldn't think of anything else. It was as though her mind had ceased to function. She was trapped here and, short of calling the British Embassy, there was nothing she could do. So why didn't she call the Embassy? Because, she realized despairingly, it would be tantamount to handing Christian over. And, fool that she was, she just couldn't do it.

She was so preoccupied with her dilemma that she didn't hear the faint rustle of a note being pushed under the door; nor, when she turned to the phone, did she see it.

As she picked up the receiver her heart was beating

hard. She'd sworn to herself that she wouldn't give in to this again, that somehow she would make herself accept that even if he could there was no reason in the world why David would want to help her. But she didn't know who else to turn to.

As she pressed out the number her stomach churned with nerves. The very thought of hearing his voice was making her fingers shake and her eyes burn with tears. It would be seven in the morning in France. Please God let him be there and please, please God let it be him who answered, not his wife.

David was in the shower when the telephone rang. Hearing it, he banged open the screen, leapt over the edge of the bath and ran into the bedroom.

'Hello?' he snapped, grabbing a towel off the bed. 'Hello?'

His heart leapt as he heard the muffled echo of a satellite link. It was her. *It was her!*

'Hello?' he shouted, but after a faint buzzing the line went dead.

He turned as Stirling came to stand in the bedroom doorway, drawing on every ounce of self-control he had to stop himself smashing the receiver into the wall.

'It might have been Pierre,' Stirling said.

David nodded and put the receiver back on its base. Yeah, it might have been, but it was rare to get a satellite delay from Hong Kong. Not from Manila, though, so it might have been Penny. It might be that the floor attendant had done what David asked: had slipped a note under her door telling her to stay right where she was, not to try to get away until he got there – and to call him if she could. He'd tried to reach her only minutes ago, but there'd been no reply. She should have been there, though; the boy, Teddy, had told him she was alone in her room. So why hadn't she answered the phone?

Shaking his head, he turned and walked back to the bathroom. There could be any number of reasons why she hadn't answered then and even more why she hadn't spoken just now, but to torment himself with them would serve no purpose. Besides, there was every chance he was fooling himself here. The call might not have been from Penny and, even if it had been, what was there to say that she'd been calling for help? He still had no idea what her feelings were for Mureau, but since she had made no attempt to turn him in he could only conclude that she loved him so much she was prepared to overlook everything just to be with him. That was presuming, of course, that she knew the truth about Mureau. But no, that couldn't be the case. He was sure, he would stake his life on it, that Mureau had not divulged his connection with David. Maybe it would make no difference to Penny were she to know, but David just couldn't bring himself to accept that. OK, maybe he was fooling himself again; loving her the way he did and being so god-damned afraid for her, it would be easy to lose sight of his judgement. But he couldn't just stand by and watch her ruin her life. He had somehow to get her out of there, whether she wanted it or not, and the price he would have to pay for doing so was something he'd think about later.

Turning back, he looked across at Stirling.

'Do you want to make the call or shall I?' Stirling asked.

David stood still, tensing with the revulsion of what Stirling was referring to. He knew he had little choice but to go ahead with it now. 'Do it,' he said shortly; then, kicking the door closed behind him, he returned to the shower.

Penny looked across the room at Christian. He was standing at the door, reading a note he had just picked up from the floor. Her hand was still on the receiver; her heart was crying with the torment of having heard David's voice only to have been forced to cut the call short. She slid her hand carefully into her lap, before Christian noticed where it was.

When he'd finished reading the note he pushed it into his pocket and looked up. Penny's heart turned over as she saw how pale he was.

'What is it?' she whispered.

Briefly he shook his head, but as he tried to force himself to smile his mouth twisted and he averted his head.

'Christian!' she cried, moving swiftly across the room. 'What is it? What's happened? Oh my God,' she murmured as she took his hands from his face and saw the tears. 'Christian, please, tell me what's happened.'

'It's no good,' he said brokenly as he pulled her into his arms. 'I can't do this to you. I can't go on making you suffer like this, I love you too much.'

'What are you saying?' she said, gently pulling back to look into his face.

'You know what I'm saying,' he answered, trying again to smile. 'I know you don't love me, at least not the way you thought you did, and I . . . well, I guess I'm having a hard time coming to terms with it. But I will. I'll go on alone from here— and you . . . you must go back where you belong.'

Tears were starting in her own eyes now as she looked back at him and felt all the devastation in his heart. 'Oh God, I'm sorry,' she whispered. 'I don't know what else to say . . .'

'Hey,' he said, forcing a laugh as he pulled her against him again. 'Come on, don't you cry too. We've known for a little while now that this was going to happen, so let's both of us try to be brave.'

They walked quietly over to the bed together and sat down facing each other. Endless minutes ticked by as he looked at her, tracing her face with his eyes as though imprinting it on his memory. When at last he spoke, his voice was choked with emotion. 'There's a plane that will take you directly to London,' he told her. 'It leaves Manila four days from now. Will you stay until then?'

She reached up to wipe a tear from his cheek.

He caught her hand and squeezed it tightly. 'Don't say no,' he whispered. 'Please, don't say no.'

Right at that moment she wasn't sure she could leave him at all. 'Won't it make things harder if I stay?' she said, knowing it would for her.

'Yes,' he answered. 'But . . .' He looked down at their hands and linked her fingers through his. 'I can't lie to you, Penny,' he said, 'not any more. If I let you go now the people Benny Lao works for will catch up with you before you even get to the airport. The only reason they haven't taken you so far is because the threat of them doing it is enough to make me do as they're asking.'

'And what – what are they asking?' she said.

He laughed mirthlessly and turned his face to the window. 'One more shipment,' he answered.

When she didn't speak, he brought his eyes back to hers and lifted a hand to stroke her cheek.

'I lied to you,' he said, 'about everything. There have been other heroin shipments too. Not many, nothing like the marijuana, but they were there. And the Triads? You were right, Lao is. . . No, it's better you don't know who he is. His superiors know the risk they're running by using me this time when the DEA is closing in on me, but they're prepared to take it in exchange for getting me to a place where no one will ever find me, where I can never tell what I know.'

'Is that what you want?' Penny said, her heart aching with pity. 'I mean, isn't that just a prison of another sort?'

He shook his head. 'I don't know. Maybe. But in time, with a new identity, a new face, I can start a new life.

That's got to be better than twenty-five years in any prison, even a federal one.'

Penny looked away, moving her eyes over the delicate cane furniture and glass-topped tables. 'Is that what you were doing out on the pier?' she said. 'Organizing the next shipment?'

'Yes,' he answered, showing no surprise that she'd seen him. 'The crew are flying in from Stockholm in three days' time. We'll sail on the fourth.'

'To where?'

He smiled. 'It's better you don't know that either,' he told her. 'But I won't stay with it for long. Another ship will be waiting for me to take me . . .' Again he smiled, then closed his eyes to hide the pain.

'Oh God,' Penny groaned, pulling him into her arms. 'This is all my fault. I should never have led you—'

'No! Stop!' he said sharply. 'None of this is your fault, Penny! Remember that. The crimes were committed before I met you and the decision not to go in was mine and mine alone. So, please, don't ever blame yourself. Promise me you'll never do that.'

Swallowing hard, she stroked his hair and held him close. She couldn't make the promise, but to tell him that would only serve to make his guilt worse.

'I love you,' he said, tears fracturing his voice again. 'Letting you go will be the hardest thing I've ever had to face, but—' He stopped suddenly and wrenched himself away. 'Shit, what am I doing here? Don't listen to me, I'll have myself together . . .'

'It's all right,' she said softly. 'I understand. It's going to be hard for me too.'

He walked to the window and stood there, staring out at the vessel that even now was being prepared for its next voyage.

'If you stay,' he said quietly, 'there will be no question about your safety. I've done everything they've asked of me and will continue to right up to the end. Once I've gone, Benny Lao will return to Hong Kong and you will be free to board the plane to London.' He turned to face her; then, unable to meet her eyes, he looked to one side. 'There is just one thing I have to ask you to do,' he said. 'On Sunday evening, the night before your flight, I need you to take a telephone call for me. It will come here, to the hotel, and it will be followed by another. The first will be Benny Lao giving the go-ahead to sail. The second will be from the skipper of the—' He stopped, realizing he had almost given the name of the ship. 'Will be either from the skipper of the boat taking the shipment or from me,' he said. 'All you have to do is relay Lao's message, then as far as you are concerned it will all be over.'

'But why can't Lao call you direct?' she said, unable to disguise her reluctance to play any part at all.

He looked at her for some time; then, sliding his hands into his pockets, he turned back to gaze out at the bay. 'He could,' he said finally. 'But this is his way of getting you involved, to make sure that you're never tempted to go to anyone with what you know. I'm sorry,' he added. 'It was the best I could do. If Lao had had his way, then . . . Well, you don't need to know what he wanted you to do.'

'And if I say I want to go now?' she said.

'Then I'll do everything in my power to help you,' he answered, turning back to her. 'It would be a risk, one hell of a risk, and we'd both very likely end up losing our lives. But if that's what you want, to go now . . .'

He left the sentence unfinished and watched as Penny got up and walked into the bathroom.

She was gone for some time and when she came back she found him slumped in a chair, his head buried in his hands. As she came to stand beside him he looked up and her heart tightened with pity when she saw the utter hopelessness in his eyes.

'I'll stay,' she said, reaching for his hand.

His eyes closed and he circled her waist with his arms. 'Oh God, Penny,' he sobbed, 'how am I ever going to let you go?'

Chapter 20

More than forty-eight hours had gone by since Penny had cut short her call. A few well-placed pesos, dished out by Stirling's contacts at the American Embassy in Manila, had got David the confirmation he was seeking: that his number had been dialled from room 1514 early on Wednesday afternoon – seven in the morning French time.

During those interminable two days David and Stirling had taken little time out for sleep as they'd made endless calls around the world, striking one deal after another, sending millions of dollars in cash and assets back to the United States in their negotiations for David's downfall. David was resigned to it now and only wished it could be over. The bitter irony of it was that the only thing that would be left at the end of it was Penny's magazine. That was how he thought of it now, as her magazine. But would she ever come back for it? Would she even want it if she did?

He almost laughed. That he could be thinking that way in light of the disaster he was facing was incredible. Even more incredible was the fact that it was for her that he was doing it all. His fists clenched as a bolt of anger passed through him. Who was he kidding? He was doing it because she'd left him no choice. He loved her, damn it, but were he to see her right now he'd be more likely to wring her neck than wrap her in his arms.

Wearily he got up from the sofa and wandered over to the window. There was no point in venting his fury on Penny, for the only one to blame here was himself. He should have been straight with her from the beginning, should have told her who Stirling really was and why he was here in France. But he hadn't, so it was just a question now of striking the right deals in order to salvage something that would make his and his sons' lives worth living when it was all over.

He'd spoken to Gabriella the night before. It had been a difficult conversation, fraught with accusations and fear. He was sure the money meant more to her than he did, though she'd denied it. She'd sworn she still loved him, that she was prepared to start over if he'd give them the chance, but he hadn't committed. He was in no position to commit anyway, not until he had sorted out this mess with Penny. After that he would be in Stirling's hands.

He looked across to where Stirling had planted himself on a hardbacked chair. He looked the way David felt, just about all in. They'd been waiting for this one call for over four hours now and it could be that they had another four to go. It was a call that David wouldn't mind waiting the rest of his life for, even though it was one that, ultimately, might just bring Penny to her senses. He wondered what she was doing now. He knew she was still at the Manila Hotel and the idea that she might be making love with Mureau made his stomach churn with jealousy and frustration. In truth he'd never been more furious with anyone in his life, but it didn't stop him loving her. He doubted anything was going to do that even though he knew there was no future for them. But he wasn't going to let himself think that way, for who could say what the next few days would bring?

It was early the following morning when the telephone finally rang, rousing Stirling from an unsteady and noisy slumber. As his head came up from his chest his bleary eyes fixed themselves on David's. David held the look, then turned to the phone.

'David?' a scratchy male voice demanded.

'Yeah, it's me,' David answered, moving his eyes back to Stirling.

Stirling leaned forward and stabbed the button to turn on the speaker.

'We've found the sister,' the voice announced into the room. 'She's working charter boats out of Antigua.'

'How soon can you get there?' David asked flatly.

'Couple of hours.'

'OK, you know what you've got to do. I'm trusting you on this, so don't blow it.'

'When did I ever?' There was a smirk in the voice. 'I'll keep in touch,' and the line went dead.

David's face was white as he put down the phone.

'OK,' Stirling said, stretching. 'It's gonna be a while yet, so I'm gonna get something to eat. Care to join me?'

'No,' David responded. He wasn't proud of what he was doing; his appetite was dead.

When Stirling reached the door he turned back. 'Don't be too hard on yourself,' he said gruffly. 'It could work out.'

David's eyes were hard as he looked at him 'For whom?' he said.

The corner of Stirling's mouth pinched in a smile. 'I reckon maybe all of us,' he said.

The ambiguity of that remark sat with David for a long time after Stirling had gone. In the end, considering all that Stirling already had and given his current mood of compliance, David decided to allow himself a quiet optimism. It lasted only as long as it took the telephone to ring again, bringing him the very news he didn't want to hear.

'They checked out late last night,' the DEA agent in

Manila told him.

'What do you mean, checked out?' David cried. 'I thought you were watching them.'

'We were,' the agent confirmed, 'but they managed to give us the slip.'

David's head was spinning. 'So where did they go?' he said through his teeth.

'We're still working on that. I'll get back to you as soon as we know more.'

David banged down the phone. Then, out of sheer fury, he slammed it against the wall. Everything, just *everything*, had depended on them staying at the Manila Hotel and the fact that they hadn't could only mean that Mureau had got wind of the DEA's presence.

'Hey,' Christian said, pulling Penny into his arms, 'you've gone quiet on me. What are you thinking?'

'I'm thinking,' she said, smiling sadly as she gazed out at the sunlight dancing across the lake, 'that I'm going to miss you. But I guess I shouldn't be saying that.'

'No,' he sighed, 'I guess you shouldn't, but it makes me feel good to hear it.' Dropping his forehead against hers he rested it there a while, then he too turned to gaze out at the lake.

From where they were standing, at the end of a small, concrete jetty, they couldn't see where the *Laguna* joined the Pasig River. But neither of them had any trouble imagining the boat that would come for him that night to ferry him, under cover of darkness, along the winding stretch of the Pasig and out into the vast South China Sea, to rendezvous with the waiting ship.

'Are you sure it's going to be safe?' she said. 'I mean, if the DEA were watching us in Manila . . .'

'Shh,' he said softly. 'Let me worry about that.'

Penny turned to look at him, moving her eyes over the gentle contours of his face and feeling her heart fold around the anguish and uncertainty. 'What time will you leave?' she whispered.

Leaning forward he kissed her gently on the lips. 'Don't let's think about that now,' he said. 'We've only got this short time left to us, so why don't we at least try to enjoy it?'

Penny gave a wry laugh. 'That's a tall order,' she said, linking hands with him as they turned back down the jetty towards the remote, decrepit little fishing village it served.

The sun was beating down on them and the air was thick with flies buzzing around the rotting debris of dead fish and sewage that lapped the eroded edges of the pier. The stench of burning garbage carried on a listless breeze over the narrow, squalid streets, where thin, leathery-skinned fishermen and their families went about their business. They were no more than an hour or so's drive from the noisy, overcrowded metropolis of Manila, but it could have been another country, another world even.

'It's hard to imagine what it must be like to live like this,' she said, pausing to watch the unloading of an outrigger that had just come in from the fishing pens. A line quickly formed as the fish were dumped into baskets and carried to the waiting lorries. 'I wonder how often they see Westerners out here?'

'Rarely, I imagine,' Christian answered, batting away the flies and blowing on her neck to keep her cool.

Reaching up to her shoulder she put her hand over his and leaned into him. 'Shall we go and take a look at that church?' she said, pointing to the time-blackened dome of a small Spanish church at the end of the main street.

He shook his head. 'No. Let's get out of here for a while and go where the air's a bit fresher.'

The car was parked at the water's edge, between a mound of fraying bamboo baskets and a cluster of morose, scraggy mules. A fisherman moved his oars and tackle to allow them to get into the car, and obligingly waved down an approaching ox cart for it to wait while they reversed on to the road. Christian drove slowly, steering the rusty vehicle around rocks and potholes as they went back through the village, passing skinny, barefoot children playing in the dust in front of their makeshift houses. Skeletal, lethargic dogs slept in the shade of barren trees and car wrecks, or scavenged the mouldering piles of trash dumped carelessly on the roadside. At the other end of the village they passed a funeral procession, where mourners in faded T-shirts and ragged shorts followed the limping, flat-tyred car on foot, carrying torn umbrellas to shade them from the sun.

As she looked out of the window Penny's emotions were binding tightly inside her. The grimness of their lives was as heart-rending as it was incomprehensible. She turned to look at Christian. Feeling her eyes on him, he smiled and held out his hand for hers.

'Makes you realize how lucky we are, doesn't it?' he said, pressing harder on the accelerator as they left the village behind.

'Yes,' she said quietly, finding it hard to feel anything beyond the misery of such deprivation and the dread of the passing hours.

They were soon climbing the mountain roads, winding through dense, brittle hedgerows of bamboo and fern and soaring forests of coconut palms. When at last they reached a clearing on the brow of a hill, they got out of the car and walked over the coarse, sun-dried grass to look down over the lake and village. In the distance they could see the merging of the waters and the vague smudge of mountains through the haze.

Leading her over to a cluster of rocks Christian sat down in the shade and settling her between his legs rested her head back on his shoulder. Neither of them spoke for some time, but as they watched tiny green lizards scurry and dart over the slated rocks Penny could feel his melancholy as deeply as she could feel her own. In truth she felt so strangled by emotion she was unable to speak and almost wished that time would stand still so that neither of them would ever have to face what lay ahead.

Taking her hand he lifted it to his lips and kissed it softly. 'Did you know,' he said, 'that the British Airways plane is already here?'

For some reason she felt dizzied and strangely panicked. It seemed incredible to think that something as familiar as a BA plane with its supercilious stewardesses and confident pilots was here on this island.

'It takes off tomorrow night,' he told her. 'Your ticket's booked. The flight's at nine-thirty.'

Penny closed her eyes as they filled with tears. It was all coming too soon.

'What will you do when you get back to France?' he asked, breaking another long and difficult silence.

Her heart turned over. She'd been thinking about little else for days now, but not knowing how either David or Sylvia had viewed her disappearance was making it impossible for her to come to any decisions. 'I'm not sure,' she said. 'It may well be that I no longer have a job there, so I'll have to return to London.'

'You think David will have fired you?'

'Possibly. Probably.'

'You've only been gone a couple of weeks,' he pointed out. 'Not exactly a capital offence.'

'No, not exactly,' she said, her voice barely audible as she thought how much longer it seemed.

'My guess is he'll be glad to have you back,' he said, giving her a comforting squeeze. 'And if he's not, then he doesn't deserve you anyway.'

Penny smiled. 'Let's just hope he sees it that way.'

They sat quietly again, waiting and listening and watching the sun start to burn gold in the sky. Penny turned her head to look up at him and felt her heart spill over with sadness as his lips came gently, seekingly, down on hers.

They hadn't made love at all since the day he had told her he was letting her go and, though in some ways Penny had felt relieved, she had missed the closeness. But even as she felt his desire mounting now, she knew he was going to push her away. When he did, he got abruptly to his feet and walked back to the car.

After a while Penny followed him and found him slumped over the wheel, his head resting on his arms. As she looked down at him she found herself wondering how long it would be before he met someone else, how long he would have to wait before he could hold a woman in his arms again and make love to her. She could only guess why he was resisting it now, that the comfort of her body simply wasn't enough, not when what he really wanted was her love.

He turned to look up at her and as she gazed down into his dark, heavy eyes her heart started to falter. She knew beyond any doubt that David meant more to her, but, dear God, she loved Christian too. And what future was there for her and David when he already had a wife and two children he loved? What was she really going back for? What was waiting for her there, besides the loneliness of loving a man who didn't want her and the pain of worrying about a man who did. How was she going to feel in six months, maybe six years, from now if she read in the papers that Christian had been arrested? That his borrowed liberty was over and there was no one except him to care?

'Oh God,' she sobbed, turning away and burying her face in her hands.

He was out of the car in an instant. 'Hey, come on,' he said, pulling her to him. 'It's all right. It's going to be all right.'

'I don't know if I can do this,' she wept. 'I just can't bear the idea that I might never see you again.'

392

'You will,' he told her. 'I promise. One day.'

Tilting her face up to his he held it between his hands and looked tenderly into her eyes. 'And if, when you get back,' he said gruffly, 'you find that he doesn't want you . . .' He swallowed hard. 'Just get word to Lei Leen and I'll come back for you.'

Penny's eyes closed as she pulled her lips between her teeth and felt pain swamp her heart. 'You know?' she said.

'Sure I know.' He smiled sadly. 'I knew all along.'

'Then . . .'

'Shh,' he said, 'it doesn't matter now. All that matters is that you get tonight over with, then go back to your life and try to pick up the pieces.'

'But what about you?'

He smiled. 'Don't you worry about me. I'm going to be just fine. Now, what do you say we start back to the hotel?'

Nodding, she used her fingers to wipe the tears from her cheeks and leaning against each other they turned back towards the car.

'Do you remember the way?' he asked as they reached it.

Penny gave a splutter of laughter. 'Why? Don't tell me you've forgotten.'

'No, I know the way,' he answered. 'I just want to be sure that you do.'

'Why?'

'Because, *chérie*,' he said, turning her in his arms, 'this is where we say goodbye.'

Penny's heart jolted as her eyes widened with panic. 'Oh no,' she cried. 'No, please, don't let it be here.'

'Better here,' he smiled, 'than in the village. I don't want you remembering me along with the stench of fish and poverty.'

'But how will you get down there?'

'It'll only take an hour or so to walk it.'

'But you don't have anything with you. All your things—'

'Are right here in the car,' he interrupted, and kissing her briefly he went to haul his bag from the boot.

As he came back Penny was watching him, and though he was doing all he could not to show how hard this was for him she wasn't fooled.

'Christian,' she whispered.

'Shh,' he said, opening the car door for her to get in.

Obediently she slid into the driver's seat. Then, looking up at him again she so very nearly told him that she wanted to go with him, that, had he not leaned through the window at that moment to give her one last, farewell, kiss she knew the words would have tumbled from her lips.

'Look after yourself, Penny,' he said, his voice thick with unshed tears.

For a moment her throat was too tight to speak. 'Christian,' she sobbed. 'Christian, I'm sorry. I didn't mean to—'

Putting a finger over her lips, he stopped her. 'Just drive,' he said, 'and don't look back.' Then he pulled away from the window and waited as she started the engine. As she slipped the car into gear he said, 'The next twenty-four hours aren't going to be easy for you, I know, but be brave, *ma chérie*, and remember, I love you.'

As Penny pulled away, moving slowly along the narrow, stony track, she couldn't stop herself looking back. He was still standing there, his bag at his feet, his hair tousled by the breeze, his loneliness as stark and painful as the ache in her heart.

It took her almost two hours to find the hotel, hidden as it was in the thick, nerra forest of Antipolo. By the time she got there night had fallen and she was badly shaken by the fear that she had become so hopelessly lost she

394

would never find where she was going.

Leaving the car on the little patch of wasteland, she picked her way carefully through the darkness towards the feeble flicker of neon over the front door. She noticed, with unease, that there were no other cars around and the only sound was that of her footsteps treading the gravel. When they'd checked in the day before, after Christian had been warned that the DEA were watching him, there had been several other guests around. Now the entire place looked deserted.

A single candle lamp cast a shadowy glow over the dull wood panels of the lobby. It smelt of beeswax and mould. There was no one on duty and the dusty honeycomb of message boxes the other side of the desk held nothing but solid, old-fashioned keys. She looked around for a bell and, finding none, called tentatively into the silence. Her voice echoed eerily along a passageway as her heartbeat thumped in her ears.

'Hello . . . Is anyone there?' she called again.

A door creaked open and as a sliver of light fell over the desk a slender young girl emerged from the office.

'Can I take my key, please?' Penny said.

The girl looked at her blankly.

'Key,' Penny repeated, pointing and twisting her hand in a locking action.

The girl looked behind her, unhooked one of the keys and slid it across the counter.

'Thank you.' Penny smiled, her lips quivering slightly. She'd have liked to ask the girl if they were alone in the hotel, but since she clearly didn't speak English there was no point. But maybe it was better not to know, for if they were it would only unnerve her even more.

Her room, on the fourth floor, was a large, featureless square with a small balcony overlooking the woods. An attempt to liven it up a little had been made by placing a bowl of plastic fruit on the table between the beds.

Putting down her bag she went steadily from one lamp to another, flooding the room with light while trying to quash the mounting fear of how remote and vulnerable she was in this godforsaken place. If only they could have stayed on at the Manila Hotel, in the midst of civilization, where people spoke languages she knew and a constant flow of guests, floor attendants and maids populated the corridors and rooms. But they'd had no choice. The DEA had known Christian was there and were simply biding their time, waiting to catch him red-handed with the cache of heroin.

Not knowing what else to do, she wandered into the bathroom to shower off the dust of the day. By the time she came out again she had coaxed herself into an unsteady calm, reminding herself that she had only to wait for the phone calls, then she could get out of here. The temptation to go now was almost overwhelming, but the suspicion that Benny Lao was having her watched was even greater. Please God he wasn't planning to double-cross Christian and kill her anyway, thereby eliminating any lingering possibility that she might tell what little she knew.

Struggling to keep control of her fear, she slipped into a pair of blue leggings and a thin, loose sweater. Then, seeing the moon rising over the trees, she opened the balcony door and stepped outside. It was just after nine o'clock. Christian had told her to expect the first call some time around eleven. Gazing up at the moon, she wondered where he was now and how he was feeling. She had known that leaving him would be hard, but she had never dreamt that it would be quite so hard as this and even now she could feel herself weakening under the terrible sense of loss.

She sat down on a fraying bamboo chair and, leaning an elbow on the railing, stared out at the darkness. The night before, they had talked into the early hours, mainly about small, inconsequential things. Later, just before they had fallen asleep, he had taken her through the simple procedure she had to follow tonight. Then, unable to stop herself, she had tried to persuade him to hand himself in. It surely had to be better than this solitary life of exile he was planning for himself, a life that, no matter what he said, would continue to be at the mercy of the Chinese. But he had remained unmovable, determined to pursue the path he had chosen for himself.

'Of course,' he'd said, smiling, 'I'm in your hands. There's nothing to stop you turning me in. You know where I am, you know where I'll be tomorrow night—'

'No,' she'd interrupted, shaking her head. 'I'd never do it. It's not my life, it's yours, and I'd never be able to live with myself if I was responsible for taking your freedom away. I'm not a judge, nor am I a jury . . .'

'But you are a law-abiding citizen.'

She'd smiled weakly. 'I'm not even sure I'm that any more,' she said.

As she recalled the conversation now, Penny wondered if she would be made to face charges. The DEA obviously knew about her and, even if they didn't suspect her of drug trafficking, someone would surely want to question her about something. The idea of it brought the spectre of Benny Lao closer. Forcing it away, she tried to concentrate on what she was going to say if she was detained. She wondered if her disappearance had been made public. Not having seen an English or French newspaper since she'd left, she had no idea. What was it going to be like to go back? How much was she going to have to face?

She moved restlessly as her heart twisted with a terrible sense of foreboding. It wasn't the first time she'd had this presentiment of disaster, but tonight it seemed so much worse, so much stronger. It was as though some terrible, unthinkable repercussions were even now playing themselves out somewhere beyond her reach, and the dread of what she might find when she got back to

France was increasing all the time. For a moment she felt so panicked that it was all she could do to stop herself running out of there and getting on the next plane via anywhere to get back and stop whatever it was that was happening. But of course she was overreacting, giving herself an importance she just didn't warrant, for what possible consequences could anyone else face for a foolishness that was all her own?

She stiffened suddenly as something moved in the bushes below. Then, telling herself that it was nothing more than a night creature, she turned back into the room and started to put the few things she'd taken out back into her suitcase. It was incredible to think that this one designer trunk contained over half a million dollars' worth of clothing and jewellery. What would she do with it all now?

A door slammed down the hall, jarring her heart and causing her to drop the bottle she was holding. Then everything was so silent again, so still and unnerving. But even though she knew her fear was much more acute than she was admitting, she wasn't going to let it rule her. She just wished to God she could sleep or read or do something, anything, to make the time pass more quickly.

Seeing her computer sitting beside her case, she smiled bleakly. There was little chance she'd be able to concentrate, but why not indulge herself? *Nuance* might well be in the past for her now, but what was the harm in pretending, just for a short while, that her life could go back to the way it was? Her head fell forward as the stultifying dread that it might not engulfed her, but, raising it again, she took a deep breath and lifted the computer on to the table.

Thinking she could hear the distant sound of a car engine, she stood still, listening to the delicate hiss and sigh of the night, the persistent grating of night creatures. Something suddenly fell in the bathroom and she almost leapt from her skin. The burn of fear was still sore in her heart as she forced herself to go and see what it was. Just her hairbrush, which had tumbled into the wash basin.

Picking it up she walked back to the table, trying to persuade herself that she had nothing to fear. Then opening the computer she pulled out a chair. As she moved to sit down, the telephone rang, wrenching a startled scream from her throat.

Panicked, she looked at her watch. It was too early. Christian had said around eleven. It wasn't yet ten. Had something gone wrong? Was he calling to warn her to get out of there? Please God she could find her way back to Manila in the dark.

With her heart pounding in her chest, she gingerly picked up the phone and put it to her ear.

'Penny? Penny?' a faint, tremulous voice came down the line. 'Pen, is that you?'

'Sammy?' Penny whispered incredulously.

'Yes, it's me,' Sammy answered. 'Oh, Penny, I don't know what's happening, but you've got to help me!'

A bolt of alarm stiffened Penny's heart. 'Where are you, Sammy?' she said.

'I don't know where I am,' Sammy answered.

'Oh God, Sammy,' Penny muttered, 'please, don't do this to me now. I'm not in any position to bail you—'

'No, listen, Pen, you don't understand. I know where I was, but then these . . . these people came along and they're holding me here, Pen. I don't know who they are, but they've got a message for you. They told me to tell you if—' she stopped and sniffed – or maybe she sobbed; Penny couldn't be sure. 'They told me to tell you that if you don't do as they say, then— Oh God, Penny, they said to tell you you'll never see me again.'

Penny's eyes were wide with fear; her hands were shaking uncontrollably. 'Who are they, Sammy? Did they tell you—'

'I don't know,' Sammy wailed. 'They just want you to
... Hang on...' Penny could hear muffled voices at the
other end, then Sammy came back on the line. Her voice
sounded slightly stronger now, but there was no
mistaking her terror. 'They said that someone will be
coming to see you in the next hour and you're to tell
them where Christian is. If you don't, Pen, they said
they're going to take me out to sea and leave me there.'

'Oh my God,' Penny cried, closing her eyes as her
mind started to reel. 'Sammy, listen to me. Listen.' Her
chest was so tight she could barely breathe. 'Do you
think you can get away from them?'

'*No!*' Sammy shouted. 'There are four of them! They're
right here in the room with me! Oh, Pen, please, you've
got to tell them where Christian is.'

The vision of Christian standing alone on that rocky
road on the hillside was brutally sharp in Penny's mind,
splitting her conscience. 'Tell them,' she said, 'tell them
that I don't know where he is. He left here today, and he
didn't say where he was going.'

She waited with her heart in her throat as Sammy
relayed the message.

'They don't believe you, Pen. They say you know
where he is...' Her voice suddenly crescendoed into a
scream. 'Penny, please,' she begged. 'They've got guns!
They're going to kill me...'

'Sammy! Sammy!' Penny cried. 'Sammy, are you still
there? Oh my God,' she sobbed, banging the connectors.
'Sammy! Sammy!' But there was no reply.

Fumbling the receiver back on to the hook, she stared
sightlessly ahead, her heart thumping so hard it hurt.
What the hell was she going to do? It wasn't as simple as
choosing between Sammy's life or Christian's freedom,
for if she turned him in now she would be putting her
own life at risk. But what was she thinking? There was
no question it had to be Sammy. Sammy was her sister,
her own flesh and blood, who had committed no crime,

was an innocent pawn in this unholy mess that had somehow reached across the globe to the distant islands of the Caribbean. Pressing her hands to her face, she tried to stop the ragged sobs breaking in her throat. How was she going to bring herself to do this to Christian when she had sworn she would never turn him in; when he had trusted her to come back here alone, had given her her freedom at such heartbreaking cost to himself? What was she doing to his life? How had it ever come about that she was responsible for so much pain and bitter regret? But whatever happened she couldn't let Sammy pay the price. Surely Christian would understand that. Please God, he had to understand.

Her only hope now, as she waited for the arrival of the people Sammy had mentioned, was that they would come before the call from Benny Lao. If they didn't she had no idea what she would do. But what *could* she do other than pass on the message? Should she warn whoever called for Christian that he was in danger? But if she did that, what would happen to Sammy?

As another wave of panic swept through her she got to her feet and started to pace the room. Who, in God's name, could these people be who were holding Sammy? How had they even found out about her? How had they traced her to this hotel? Had Christian told them? But that was absurd when it was patently obvious that it was him they were after. Oh, Jesus Christ, what was going on? She couldn't make sense of anything any more. Perhaps it was the FBI or the DEA. But that was even more absurd, for they didn't go around holding innocent people hostage in order to get their man. Or did they? What the hell did she know about these things? But if it wasn't them, then that only left the Chinese. She felt suddenly sick with fear at the very idea that Sammy could be in their hands . . . 'Oh God!' she cried aloud, clutching her hands to her head. 'We're all going to end up dead!'

The time dragged slowly by, each minute inching her fear further and further into the realms of terror. She tried to fight it, tried to force herself to stay calm. To lose control now would help no one and only increase the danger. But her feeling of helplessness was total, for there was no one she could call, no one she could turn to for help. Everything would happen in less than an hour and even David would be powerless to stop it. She sat against the head of the bed, her feet curled under her, her eyes fixed on the door. Somehow she must convince herself that she and Sammy would pull through this; if she didn't, she would go to pieces. But what was going to happen to Christian? What in God's name had he done to the people holding Sammy to make them threaten her the way they had?

At last the heavy tread of footsteps sounded in the corridor outside. Terror sank into her bones. She couldn't move; she couldn't speak; she couldn't even breathe. When the knock came, her eyes remained rooted to the door, watching the twist of the handle. It opened slowly and two men stepped inside.

The moment she saw them Penny almost collapsed with relief. One was wearing the military-style uniform of the Manila police. The other was showing her his badge.

'Miss Moon?' the uniformed man enquired.

Penny nodded.

The uniformed officer turned to his superior, a stumpy man with a bulging forehead and receding chin, who, as his eyes travelled from her to something he was holding in his hand, introduced himself in perfect English as Chief Superintendent Jalmasco of the Philippine National Police, Narcotics Command.

Penny's eyes darted between them. Dread was suddenly stalking her again. She knew from Christian how easy it was to obtain false papers, so were these men really who they were claiming to be?

'We have reason to believe that you know the where-abouts of a man wanted by the United States Drug Enforcement Administration,' the superintendent continued.

Penny merely looked at him. Her heart was thudding so hard it was an effort to breathe. The uniformed man came towards her. Penny pressed herself back against the bed, but he moved past her and began picking things up, turning them over in his hand, then discarding them.

'Are you aware,' Jalmasco said, 'that it is a crime to protect a wanted man?'

Penny's eyes were wide. Again she turned to the uniformed man as he started pulling open drawers and checking inside. She took a breath and felt herself burn with guilt as the words came falteringly from her lips. 'He's – he's at the pier in Binangonan,' she said, flooding with shame at how easily she had caved in, but willing herself to think of Sammy.

The superintendent looked at her with raised eyebrows, then turned to watch the other man as he emptied the contents of her suitcase on to the bed.

'Are you holding my sister?' Penny said.

The superintendent seemed slightly taken aback by the question, but ignored it.

'Are you holding my sister?' she repeated.

'If I were you, Miss Moon,' he said, still watching his subordinate, 'I would be more concerned about myself right now. Is this yours?'

Penny turned and her eyes dilated in confusion and terror as the other man held up a transparent bag filled with a white substance.

'I repeat,' the superintendent said, turning back to her. 'Is this yours?'

Penny shook her head. 'No,' she cried. 'I've never seen it before.'

The superintendent nodded. The uniformed man laid the bag down on the bed and took a small white box covered in blue print from his pocket.

Penny watched in horrified disbelief as he opened the box and lifted out a plastic phial of clear liquid in which a single capsule bobbed at random. Then he pulled open the bag on the bed and tipped a small amount of the white substance into the phial.

Penny was numbed by terror. It was a nightmare. It couldn't be happening. But she knew, even before he pinched the capsule to break it, what colour the liquid would turn the instant the chemicals in the capsule contacted the substance.

As the colour seeped into the bag the superintendent looked back at her with a satisfied smile. 'Heroin,' he pronounced as Penny stared helplessly at the violet-blue liquid.

Then suddenly it was as if the whole world had gone crazy. More men burst in to the room. They moved so swiftly Penny had no chance to stop them. Someone was reading her her rights as her hands were wrenched behind her back, handcuffs were snapped on to her wrists and she was pushed towards the door. The room was wrecked as curtains were torn down, furniture was overturned, the beds were stripped and drawers were hauled out. The superintendent yanked open the door and shoved her through. Outside there were more police, crouching in the shadows along the corridor, inching forward with guns aimed straight at her head.

Her legs were so weak she could barely walk. Two men gripped her arms and dragged her downstairs to a waiting car. As they thrust her inside, Penny pleaded desperately with them to listen. No one would and as the car accelerated off into the night her head fell back against the seat as, with a sense of utter hopelessness and terror, she realized that they hadn't actually asked her

where Christian was, nor had they seemed to know anything about Sammy. So who, in God's name, were they
and where were they taking her?

Chapter 21

During the moments after Pierre told David that Penny had been arrested there was nothing but an excruciating silence.

'David? David, are you still there?' he said at last.

'Yeah, I'm here. What the hell happened?'

'I don't know. I don't have all the details.'

'Then give me what you have.'

'She was picked up by Narcotics Command at the hotel in Antipolo just over an hour ago. They found a kilo of heroin.'

'Jesus Holy Christ,' David muttered. 'I take it you know what that means?'

'Yes,' Pierre answered sombrely.

'Then let's hope to God she doesn't. Where is she now?'

'As far as I know, they've taken her to the local jail.'

David winced. 'Where's Mureau?'

'No idea. He's disappeared.'

David's face tightened. 'Where are you?'

'At the Shangri-La in Manila.'

'Then meet me off the plane when I get there. I'll call you from—'

'David, are you crazy?'

David's temper suddenly snapped. 'Don't you get it, Pierre?' he yelled. 'It's all over for me. I've got nothing left to loose. Not even the boys . . .'

'But—'

'Don't waste time,' David cut in. 'Just get out there and find her a lawyer before someone else does it for her.'

As a milky dawn light crept into the early-morning shadows of the cell Penny watched the old woman who lay crooked in an arthritic jumble on a wooden pallet beneath the wide, barred window. Her jaw was slack, saliva trickled from the corner of her mouth and her wrinkled, leathery face twitched in dream or pain. Outside in the dingy yard a set of pipes gurgled and clanged, then spewed a mass of thick grey liquid into the gutter. As it oozed a path towards the drains a scrawny, tailless cat leapt from the wall and darted across the yard, squealing as it knocked against a pile of tin cans. The noise caused the young girl who was asleep on the pallet beside Penny to stir and turn over. Penny, who was sitting hugging her knees to her chest on the end of the pallet, wondered how she could sleep on the bare, worm-eaten boards. As the girl's thumb found its way into her mouth she reached above her head with her other hand and twisted her fingers around the hem of Penny's sweater. She could be no more than fourteen years old. Another girl, probably around twenty, was curled up on the floor on a pile of rags beside the old woman's pallet, her thick black hair matted around her face.

It was a cell meant for eight women, though mercifully, considering it had only two beds, contained only four right now, including Penny. It was set in a corner of a high-walled yard littered with rusting oil drums and the corroded frames of bicycles and car parts. When she had been brought there during the night Penny had reeled in horror at the sight of what looked like an animal pen and tried desperately to struggle free. As she wept and pleaded with them to listen, her handcuffs were removed while someone unlocked the barred gate, and then she was pushed inside. The stench had hit her stomach like a physical blow and, seeing her about to throw up, the old woman had thrust a tin bowl at her.

It still sat there, at the foot of the pallet, adding its own nauseating smell to the stinking sewage seeping from the lavatory cubicle in the corner. This place wasn't fit for animals, never mind humans, and Penny knew that if she were made to suffer it for any length of time she'd never pull through. Her eyes closed as despair enveloped her heart and lodged in her throat. It was all she could do to overcome the urge to throw herself against the barred gate and scream hysterically for release.

Her throat was parched, but she was afraid to touch the water in the urn. She itched all over, her bladder was filled to bursting. Earlier she'd ventured into the lavatory, but the stinking foulness that had assaulted her had sent her reeling back into the cell. She'd tried again, with the neck of her sweater pulled up over her nose, but when she'd seen the hole in the ground and felt her feet slithering in faeces she'd only just managed to make it to the tin bowl in time.

Now, sensing someone watching her, she turned to look at the young girl beside her. She was staring up at her, her wide brown eyes steeped in awe that a Western woman should be sharing their cell. All three women had stared at her that way when she'd arrived, their soft, cowlike eyes unblinking and disbelieving, and uttered not a word.

Penny's eyes moved to the patch of pale sky she could see through the bars. It was no good trying to tell herself that this was a nightmare, that she'd wake up any minute and find herself back in France, for the horrific reality of rats combined with the unrelenting dread of what was going to happen to her had kept her awake all night. She still didn't know how the heroin had come to be in her bag, but could only presume that Benny Lao had planted it there while she was out with Christian, then tipped off the police. Whether or not they had arrested Christian too she had no idea, for she'd seen no one since they'd thrown her in here and doubted they would tell her even if they had. As for Sammy, she couldn't bear to think what might have happened to her and took shallow comfort from the hope that her captors, whoever they were, had heard of her arrest and had realized that she was now powerless to do as they'd asked.

More hours ticked by, monotonously and agonizingly slowly, as the distant clatter of street life carried into the yard. Now the other women in the cell were staring at her too. Never in her life had she been unable to get up and walk out of a room at any moment of her choosing; she'd never known what it was to be trapped like this. The dank, mouldy walls were closing in on her and the benign scrutiny of her cellmates was working her panic to such a pitch that her whole body shook with the effort of trying to suppress the hysteria. Her bladder was screaming the need for release and in the end, as the pipes outside splashed another viscous emission into the gutter, she lost control. As the urine seeped through her panties and leggings and trickled through the wooden slats on to the floor, tears of humiliation and hopelessness ran down her cheeks. She slumped over her knees, sobbing with shame and bitter despair. How long were they going to keep her here? Please God, they had to let her go soon or she would lose her mind. As it was, the terror and confusion and crazed speculation on what kind of sentence awaited her, coupled with what had really happened to put her there was pushing her closer and closer to the edge.

It took a long time for her bladder to empty. By the time it did, the old woman was sitting beside her holding out a rag for her to wipe away her tears. Penny took it, then the old woman lifted the water jug and emptied it on to the floor, sluicing the urine towards the gutter that ran beneath the iron bars of the door. Penny tried to thank her, but the act of kindness was making her cry all the harder. She could barely catch her breath as sobs of utter desolation and fear tore through her body.

'You American?' the old woman said.

Penny tensed, unsure she had heard right; then, lifting her head to look at the woman, she saw the hesitant light of friendliness in her eyes.

'No,' Penny sniffed, wiping her nose with the back of her hand. 'No, English. You speak English?'

'Leetle.' There was a moment or two's awkwardness, then the woman said, 'Why you here?'

Penny bit her lips as fresh tears threatened. 'I don't know,' she said brokenly. 'It's a mistake. They found heroin in my bag.'

The old woman nodded. Then, turning to the youngest of the two girls, she said, 'She here for drug.'

Penny looked at the girl, realizing from the blankness of her expression that she had no idea what was being said. 'How long has she been here?' she asked, dread of the answer squeezing her heart.

'She here five month,' the old woman answered.

Penny's head fell back against the wall as the sheer horror of it penetrated her. 'Five months?' she repeated. 'Hasn't she been tried?' Seeing the woman didn't understand the question, she said, 'Court? Has she been for trial at court?'

'She still wait.'

Oh dear God, Penny was moaning inside. Five months in this hell-hole just waiting for trial. 'And you?' she said. 'Why are you here?'

'I here for robbery. They let me go home, but I no have money for bail.'

Penny looked at her with a remote yet profound sympathy. She was probably so poor that she had been forced to commit the robbery that had put her here and now she had no way of raising the money to get out. 'Do you ever have any visitors?' she asked.

'My children, they come last week. But they not come often. They have no money for buses.'

Penny wished she could think of something to say, but couldn't. So instead she asked why the oldest of the two girls was there.

'Husband leave her with debt,' the old woman answered.

Penny's eyes closed at the pitiful injustice of it. 'How long has she been here?' she asked.

The old woman was about to answer, when they heard the heavy tread of boots coming across the yard.

'He bring food,' the old woman said in answer to Penny's look.

Penny didn't even want to imagine what kind of food it was. All she was interested in was getting someone to find her a lawyer.

'The court find you a lawyer,' the police officer answered, sliding a tray of inedible gunge under the door.

'But when?' she cried. 'You can't hold me here like this . . .'

'You eat,' he barked.

'I don't want your damned food,' she raged. 'I want to get out of here. Have you told the British Embassy you're holding me? You have to tell someone at the Embassy.'

'I don't have to do anything,' he told her haughtily.

Penny's eyes flashed with impotent fury. 'Not one single mouthful of that filth is passing my lips until you get me a lawyer,' she seethed.

The man grinned; then, sliding a key into the lock, he pushed the door open. 'You in luck,' he said. 'The lawyer, he here. Come this way, please.'

Feeling the shame of her stained, damp clothes, Penny got up from the bed and, keeping her head high as he snapped on the handcuffs, she followed him across the yard and round to the front of the police station.

Inside, it was heaving with people, all shouting and waving pieces of paper, or trying to get to the men in the crowded cell at the back. Penny was ushered through quickly and taken into a small, bare office where a portly, middle-aged Filipino with horn-rimmed glasses and a white embroidered shirt worn loose over his navy slacks was waiting for her.

'Ah, Miss Moon,' he said, getting to his feet and waving her to a chair as her hands were freed. 'My name is Atilano Sombillo. I have been appointed by the court to represent you. Please, sit down.'

Penny did as she was told, trying to control her badly shaking hands as she pushed a clump of matted, damp hair from her face. Already she was thinking that there was something not quite right about this, that something, or maybe it was someone, was missing from the normal order of things, but she was too nervous and exhausted to grasp the suspicion and pin it to a rational explanation.

The lawyer and policeman spoke for a few minutes and Penny looked around at the peeling paint, frosted-glass window and pin-dotted map of metropolitan Manila. It was still hard for her to believe she was there, so very far from home, so terrifyingly isolated from everyone she knew and all that was familiar. As another tremor of fear vibrated through her she reminded herself firmly that she had a lawyer now – someone who was going to help her to prove that it was all a mistake, that she had been set up – and that the living terror that she might never get out of there would soon be a thing of the past.

At last the policeman left and Sombillo sat down and opened the file in front of him. Penny waited only until the door had closed before saying, 'The heroin wasn't mine. I had no idea it was there. Someone planted it.'

Sombillo's head came up and a quick panic bit into Penny's heart as she saw the expression on his face. It was a burlesque of the long-suffering attorney who had heard it all before.

'It's true!' Penny cried. 'I'm telling you, someone planted it.'

Sombillo didn't answer as he continued to scan his notes.

'Have you contacted the British Embassy?' Penny demanded. 'Do they know I'm here?'

He nodded patiently. 'Yes, they know.'

'Then I want to see someone. Surely I have that right.'

'I'm sure they will send someone in due course,' he answered, looking down at the case notes again. 'Now, let me see. One point two kilograms of heroin.' He nodded again and raised his eyes back to hers. 'This is a very grave situation, Miss Moon.'

'I'm aware of that,' she snapped. 'But I'm telling you, it was planted on me.'

His solemn eyes gazed at her through the thick lenses of his spectacles. 'I should advise you,' he said earnestly, 'that to change your story at this stage is not going to look good when we go in front of a judge.'

'What do you mean, change my story?' Penny said, her head starting to spin. 'I haven't spoken to anyone until now to give a story.'

'I understand that you were informed of your rights at the time of your arrest,' Sombillo said.

Penny shook her head. 'I don't know,' she answered. 'I think so, but it all happened so fast . . .'

'It says here,' he told her, 'that you were informed of your rights, but that you waived them and confessed to being in possession of an illegal substance, namely heroin.'

The dizziness in her head increased to such an extent that her stomach churned with fear. 'I never confessed to a thing,' she told him. 'Why would I when the heroin wasn't mine?'

Sombillo sighed and folded his hands on the desk. 'I

413

should advise you that it would be in your own best interests if you were to make a clean breast of this now and provide me with the details of how you came by this heroin and for what purpose you intended it.'

Penny stared at him in abject horror. 'Didn't you hear a word I just said?' she demanded. 'The drugs were planted on me, so why don't you try asking me who might have planted them?'

Sombillo grimaced. 'OK. Tell me,' he said, as though humouring her.

'I think,' she said, forcing her rising temper under control, 'that it was a Chinese by the name of Benny Lao.'

'I see. And who is Benny Lao?'

'He's . . . he's a Hong Kong Triad member.'

Sombillo's eyebrows arched incredulously towards the ceiling. Then, continuing as though she'd never mentioned Lao, he said, 'Who sold you the heroin?'

'I don't believe this!' Penny cried, hitting her hand on the table. 'Why aren't you listening to me? It's your job, your duty as a lawyer, to hear what I have to say, so why are you presuming I'm guilty before you've even heard my side of the story?'

'Because, Miss Moon,' he said, 'you told the police you were guilty.'

'That's a lie!' she shouted.

'And in my opinion,' he went on, 'your association with a certain Christian Mureau is not helping the situation.'

'Then *fuck* your opinion,' she cried, infuriatingly close to tears.

'To become abusive with me isn't going to help your case at all,' he admonished.

'The only thing that is going to help my case is for you to listen,' she cried. 'I'm telling you that I have never smoked, snorted, injected, smuggled, bought, peddled or even touched a single milligram of an illegal substance in my life. You can check it out. Speak to the

414

people at the Embassy, they'll tell you. I don't have any kind of criminal record at all.'

He frowned curiously and looked back at his notes. 'Then how do you account for the fact that it says here that you are wanted in your own country for the falsification of passports, travelling under an assumed name and, er, let me see, ah yes, that you are also wanted in France for the harbouring of a known criminal.' He stopped and looked up at her with a benign little smile.

All Penny could do was stare at him as the numbing chaos in her mind splintered her anger into a thousand pieces and left her reeling with shock and terror. It was as though her last flicker of hope had just been extinguished by a raging wind of injustice.

'This information was delivered to me this morning by your Embassy,' he informed her. 'So it would appear that whilst you don't actually have a criminal record as such, you do have a number of charges outstanding against you.' He pressed down the top of his pen, annotated the document in front of him, then said, 'Now, perhaps we can return to the matter at hand. One point two kilograms of heroin were found in your possession last night—'

'Whatever charges might be outstanding against me,' Penny cut in, 'they bear no relevance to what I am charged with now.'

'Quite,' he said. 'I was merely pointing out that your claim that you have no criminal record, whilst true at this moment, is quite probably a temporary situation. To continue: a narcotics test was carried out at the premises of the Aurelio Hotel at approximately ten o'clock last night which showed the substance found in your bag to be of an illegal nature.' He looked up. 'China White, to be more precise,' he stated blandly.

Penny's fear was like acid burning into her thoughts, leaving them ragged and unformed and making it almost impossible for her to gauge what she was saying.

415

'Have you arrested Christian Mureau?' she demanded.

'I'm afraid that is priviliged information,' he responded.

'If you have,' she persisted, 'then he will tell you that the heroin was planted on me.'

'I'm sure,' he said, leaving her in no doubt that Christian's word would carry about as much weight as it would take to transport her to jail for the next twenty-five years.

'It was put in my suitcase by a man called Benny Lao,' she went on doggedly. 'I swear I had never seen it before the moment the police officer took it out of the case.'

Sombillo blinked, then turned towards the door as a lower-ranking officer knocked and put his head in. '*Telefono*,' he said.

'You will excuse me,' Sombillo said, getting up from his chair.

Penny watched him walk to the door, then sank her head into her hands as it closed behind him. She had never known such a terrible sense of foreboding as this. Discovering that she was wanted in England and France had added new and horrible dimensions to her already terrifying sense of abandonment. And Sammy, what the hell was happening to Sammy now?

Defeat was creeping into her bones, telling her that there was no way she was going to get out of here: she was going to have to face whatever judgment was passed on her and maybe spend the best part of her life in a Filipino prison for a crime she hadn't committed. The appalling injustice of it made her want to lash out at this preposterous little man who was refusing to listen to a word she said. What the hell kind of lawyer was he to presume his client to be guilty without even hearing what she had to say? There was something terribly wrong here, something that wasn't adding up at all, but in her weakened and agitated state she seemed unable to make her mind function.

Then quite suddenly her head jerked up as she finally realized who was missing here. Chief Superintendent Jalmasco. No arrest was ever made for a charge like this without an immediate interrogation and no one had asked her a single damned thing from the moment she'd been arrested until now. And yet there was a confession. Jesus Christ, how could she have been such a fool? Why hadn't she worked this out before? Jalmasco and Sombillo were both in Benny Lao's pay. They were all in Lao's pay.

Her heart was racing as she tried to make herself think clearly. Then her eyes fell on the file in front of her. She grabbed it and spun it round on the desk. Please God, she wasn't going to find a forged confession. But she did. It was there in black and white and signed by a hand that was so like her own that under any other circumstances she'd have sworn it was hers. Trembling with outrage and terror, she sifted frantically through the papers, scattering them over the desk in her hunt for the Embassy-headed notepaper that would tell her whether or not the charges in England and France were real. She found nothing bearing either the Royal crest or the Republican insignia of France, but what she did find turned her blood to ice.

Picking up the photograph, she sat back in her chair, too stunned for the moment to do anything but stare down at the clear, smiling image of her own face as her mind flashed back to the moment when Jalmasco had introduced himself the night before, looking first at her, then at something he was holding in his hand. Everything in her was recoiling from the sudden onslaught of all the ramifications this photograph presented. The background was fuzzy, but not too fuzzy for her to see where she was when the photograph had been taken. She remembered the moment clearly: she'd been in the gazebo in the Chinese Gardens with Christian when a Filipino boy had appeared out of nowhere and asked if he could take their picture. Yet there was no sign of Christian in the photograph she was holding. It was of her and her alone.

Her eyes moved sightlessly to the middle distance as the unthinkable question loomed horribly in her mind: had Christian known what the boy was doing when he'd set up his camera and, as the evidence here showed, focused his lens only on her? She could only conclude that Christian must have, for being in the position he was in he would surely never have allowed a stranger to take his photograph. And if he had known and that photograph had now turned up here in the hands of a lawyer who was so bent on establishing her guilt . . .

The photograph slipped from her fingers as shock drained the blood from her face. She couldn't be right about this. Surely to God she couldn't. He loved her, he'd do anything in the world for her, give her anything, take her anywhere; he'd even come back for her if David . . . Her eyes closed and, taking a breath, she forced herself past it. She'd believed everything he'd told her, she'd felt nothing but love and pity and heartbreaking empathy with his suffering. And all the time he had been . . .

Her hand flew to her head. She was unable to form the words, unable to make herself believe that he would do this to her. He'd bought the photographer, the police, the lawyer . . . Dear God in heaven, who else had he bought? But why? Why would he do it? To punish her for not going with him? It was the only explanation she could think of, yet—

Hearing Sombillo's voice outside, she hurriedly stuffed the photograph and papers back into the file, spun it round to face his side of the desk and waited for the door to open. She had no idea how she was going to play this now, whether she should let him know what she had discovered or whether, for the time being, she should keep it to herself.

'I apologize for the interruption,' he said, coming back

418

into the room. 'I took the opportunity to order you a coffee. I imagine you could use one.'

'I believe,' she said, looking him straight in the eye, 'that I have the right to change my lawyer at any time of my choosing. I wish to exercise that right as of this moment.'

'I see,' he said, scratching his face and showing no sign of either surprise or offence. 'May I ask why?'

'No.'

'Then may I remind you of the seriousness of the charges you are facing?'

'It is precisely because of their seriousness that I wish to change my lawyer,' she said, unable to keep the tightness from her voice.

'I should advise you,' he said, 'that I have tried a number of death penalty cases—' He stopped as the shock registered on her face. 'Do I take it,' he went on carefully, 'that you were unaware that the possession of more than forty grams of an opium-based drug is punishable by death in the Philippines?'

Weak with hunger and beaten half senseless by the repeated onslaughts of fear and shock, Penny started to sway in her chair. 'Death?' she repeated dully as the image of the geomancer closing her hand flashed in her mind.

'I'm afraid so, Miss Moon,' Sombillo answered. 'I thought a woman in your position would have known that.'

'No, I didn't,' she said, her voice barely more than a croak as a single, unbearable thought circled her mind. He had sentenced her to death. Christian, the man who had made love to her so tenderly, the man for whom she had so very nearly given up everything, had sentenced her to die in a Filipino jail.

'Would a glass of water help?' Sombillo offered.

Penny looked at him with unblinking eyes. 'I want to speak to someone at the British Embassy,' she said hoarsely.

'All in good time,' he said, smiling.

'Didn't you hear me!' she suddenly screamed. 'I want to speak to my Embassy!'

'Now, please, try to keep calm,' he said soothingly. 'I understand what—'

'I am demanding my rights as a British citizen to speak to my Embassy,' she yelled. 'You can't hold me here without notifying the British Government—'

'On the contrary, Miss Moon,' he interrupted. 'The police are empowered to hold you for up to thirty-six hours without informing anyone, which they frequently do. So perhaps you should consider yourself one of the lucky ones, since your Embassy are already aware of your arrest and you already have a lawyer.'

'You call yourself a lawyer!' she spat. 'What kind of lawyer is it that tries to persuade his client to sentence herself to death? What kind of lawyer takes money from a known criminal to make sure that death . . .'

Sombillo was clicking his tongue and shaking his head. 'These are very serious allegations you are making against me,' he scolded. 'Perhaps it would be in your own best interest if you returned to your cell and took some time to cool off and recognize the serious-ness—'

'*I do recognize the damned seriousness!*' she screamed. 'I more than recognize it, I'm fucking living it! Now get me a real lawyer. Get me someone who's not in Christian Mureau's pay!'

'Are you seriously suggesting that Mr Mureau has managed to bribe the head of Narcotics Command, not to mention all the other officers who took part in your arrest last night and myself—'

'I'm not suggesting it!' she seethed. 'I'm saying it right out. He's paid the whole god-damned lot of you to do this to me . . .'

'Miss Moon,' he said gravely, 'though it is totally

against the regulations for me to tell you this, under the circumstances, I think that you should know that Mr Mureau is at present also in the custody of the Philippine National Police and I can assure you it is most unlikely that he will manage to buy his way out.'

The breath left Penny's body as though she'd been punched. He was lying, he had to be. Unless Lao had set them both up ... But no, it was Christian who had allowed the photograph to be taken and it was Christian who had removed them from the Manila Hotel to the wilderness environs of the city, where the entire judicial system could no doubt be bought for a sum that wouldn't even dent his fortune. And it was Christian who had let her return to the hotel alone though there had been no reason for him not to return with her and remain there until it was time for him to go and meet the boat. No reason except he had known that she was going to be arrested, because he had set the whole thing up in order to ... To what? She still couldn't think why he would do it except to punish her for letting him down. Unless of course he was afraid that she would tell what she knew. But even that didn't make sense, since he was fully aware of how little she really knew, and, besides, she had no idea where he planned to go from here. So maybe he *was* in custody – maybe Sombillo wasn't lying about that the way he was about everything else.

As her eyes came back to rest on the lawyer she wondered who he really was. She'd seen no credentials. And Jalmasco, was he really a Chief Superintendent of police? She'd seen only a brief glimpse of his badge, but in a country as rife with corruption as this it wouldn't be hard to forge those things. There was no sign of Jalmasco today, yet there was no mistaking the fact that she was in a police station, so her arrest at least was genuine. What concerned, no, terrified, her now, though, was how many people had already been bought and how far

421

things would go before she managed to get word to
someone at the Embassy of where she was and what was
happening to her.

Chapter 22

Having managed to give Stirling the slip, David had flown first to Frankfurt; then, after an interminable five-hour wait, he had boarded the direct flight to Manila.

Whilst he was at Frankfurt airport he had spoken to Sylvia, then to Pierre, then last of all to Stirling. Sylvia had managed to contact the British Embassy in Manila, only to be told that they were aware of Penny's arrest but were powerless to help since Penny was currently refusing to see anyone. That alone had scared the hell out of David, but when Sylvia had gone on to tell him that Penny already had a lawyer with whom she was perfectly happy it had been all he could do to stop himself hijacking one of the jets on the tarmac and redirecting it to Manila. It was small comfort to learn that so far the press had been told nothing, for the last thing David wanted right now was a battery of cameras and loudly inquisitive journalists getting in the way. The whole story would come out soon enough and until then he could do without the publicity.

Pierre had confirmed what he'd already guessed: that the lawyer had not been provided by them. But time was still on their side, he'd reminded himself. Just as long as he got there before the thirty-six hours were up there was a chance he could buy off the cops who were holding her in the godforsaken backwater of Manila that Pierre had pulled no punches in describing.

Having been unable to get past the front desk of the police station, Pierre was now back at the Shangri-La, keeping in contact with the BPI bank who were to receive the funds Sylvia was wiring over. Now that he had all but bankrupted himself, David had no resources of his own to call upon – at least, nothing that could in any way match the sums Mureau would have paid out.

His final call, to Stirling, had gone better than he'd expected. Stirling had shown no surprise and little concern that he'd taken off the way he had.

'It's your funeral,' he'd told him bluntly.

'I know that,' David responded. 'But I just need these few days.'

'Seems like you got 'em,' Stirling said. 'But you ask me, you're crazy going out there, 'cos, if all you been telling me is true, then between them Mureau and that wife of yours are gonna bust your ass you go within ten miles of Penny the Moon.'

'It's a chance I'm going to have to take,' David said shortly.

'And what about Penny the Moon? You thought about what they might do to her if you go riding in like some half-cocked Gallahad?'

'I'm thinking about nothing else.'

'Then take my advice, boy: don't do it.'

'If I don't she'll go to jail and we both know it. They've set her up good and proper here—'

'Let the DEA boys handle it,' Stirling interrupted. 'They know what they're doing . . .'

'Like they knew what they were doing when Mureau skipped the Manila Hotel?'

Stirling grunted. 'Unfortunate that,' he said. 'How did you find her, by the way?'

'Another time,' David answered. 'The important thing is I found her and if the DEA had got off their fat butts a bit quicker than they did they'd have found her in the hotel alone. No hostage situation in that. She'd have

424

been clean away and Mureau would have been behind bars by now.'

'Uh, uh,' Stirling said. 'She might have been clean away, but so would Mureau.'

'Have you heard where he is yet?'

Stirling chuckled. 'No. But my guess is you'll find him. Or, more like, he'll find you. And do you want to know my next guess? He'll have her killed before you can get to her. Either that or he'll make sure you don't get to her before she's arraigned. She'll be facing the death penalty then – meaning there'll be no blood on his hands. But I'm going with the first. I reckon he'll have her killed the minute he hears you've set foot in Manila. And if by some miracle he doesn't manage to pull it off, then he's got that there death penalty as a back-up. Seems like he can't lose.'

'He's not a killer,' David said savagely.

Again Stirling laughed. 'He'd kill you, my son, make no mistake about that.'

'Then why hasn't he already done it? He's had plenty of opportunities.'

''Cos you've never had him in a corner so tight he can't feel his nuts before,' Stirling answered. 'If he's got any sense he'll cut his losses now and disappear for good. Maybe he'll do that, but I wouldn't put *my* money on it. He took Penny the Moon with him for a reason and that reason, by my reckoning, has got more to do with what's what going on out there than it has with getting under your skin.'

'I'm not convinced,' David said. 'He gains nothing if Penny dies.'

'Then maybe he's got something else planned for her. Something we haven't thought of. He's smart, David, and I'm beginning to wonder if he ain't a whole lot smarter even than you. So you take care of yourself out there, son, and come back to me soon, 'cos we got a ways to go yet and I'm kinda getting to like your company.'

'The feeling's not mutual,' David responded. 'But I'll be back – and Penny will be with me.'

'I wish I had your confidence, son,' Stirling said with a sigh. And with that, he rung off.

Now, sitting in the first-class seat that Sylvia must have arranged since he'd been unable to pay for it himself, David was jotting down names and numbers ready to hand to Pierre when he arrived. He'd give all he had twice over to know what was going on in Mureau's head right now, but could only pray to God, as he prepared Pierre's instructions, that he was covering all eventualities.

As the adrenalin continued to thump around his system he looked impatiently at his watch. Another five hours before he got to Manila. But that still gave them plenty of time before the arraignment. He guessed the DEA would be waiting for him when he got there, counting on him now to flush out Mureau. Having had him in their sights all this time, they sure must be kicking themselves to have let him slip through their fingers the way they had. But there had been nothing they could do while Penny was with him. They couldn't run the risk of what he might do to her had they gone in. He wondered if Penny realized that she had been a hostage all this time, but wondering what Penny did and didn't know, what she might be feeling now and whether she was as terrified as he imagined she was, wasn't something he was going to dwell on. He needed all his wits about him when he got there, so the best thing he could do now was try to get some sleep.

Miraculously he managed to drift off into some kind of semiconscious state for a while, but then he was suddenly jolted awake by the one terrifying eventuality that hadn't even occurred to him until now. He sat up straight and started to work it through carefully in his mind. Before Penny's arrest he had been prepared to believe that Mureau *was* in love with her – being in love

426

with her himself, it was easy for him to believe it of someone else, even Mureau. But the moment Pierre had told him Penny had been arrested David had discounted the possibility; it had been such an obvious frame-up that no one in his right mind would believe that a man would do that to a woman he loved. But what if he was wrong? What if Mureau did love her and ... Jesus Christ, he groaned, as the thoughts started tumbling in upon one another. What if he'd been right about Penny's feelings for *him*, David? What if she did feel the same way and somehow Mureau had found out? Of course he might be kidding himself here, telling himself something just because it was what he wanted to believe, but he'd be a god-damned fool if he dismissed it. For if he *was* right and Mureau did love Penny and was therefore planning what David was now very much afraid he was planning, then there was already every chance he was never going to see Penny again.

Penny was trying to prepare herself for another night in the damp, rat-infested hell-hole of a cell. Since the policeman had brought her back after her showdown with the lawyer she'd seen no one other than her cell mates. She hadn't eaten all day and though she doubted she'd manage to get even a mouthful past her throat without throwing it back up again she had promised herself that when the next meal came she would try. God only knew what the water was doing to her, but she would lose strength if she drank nothing. Though there were still all too many moments when panic and fear threatened to explode in a screaming, jibbering fit of hysteria, she had so far managed to keep that at bay. But for how much longer, she wondered, averting her eyes as the old woman scratched at the teeming lice in her hair and the younger girl stuffed old, balled-up newspapers inside her panties to absorb the flow of blood.

The falling darkness was acting like a blanket, holding

in the suffocating stench of human waste. The sluggish humidity in the air was dampening her hair and making it cling to her skull, while the persistent scratchings of rodent life caused shivers of revulsion to trample over her skin. Her urine-stained clothes were smeared with dirt, as were her hands and face.

Throughout the day the other women had been scrubbing police shirts in the old tin bowl in order to earn themselves a few pesos. The pesos, the old woman had told her, would be used to buy themselves larger helpings of the rancid, greasy slops they called food. Their situation was so desperate that even confronted with it the way she was, Penny found it hard to make herself accept it.

All that was keeping her sane now was the faint belief that she had found a way of letting someone know she was here. It was going to cost her her shoes, but that was all she had to bargain with now. Her diamond watch had been taken the moment she got here and no doubt the spoils in her suitcase had already been shared out between the arresting officers – with the lion's share almost inevitably finding its way into Jalmasco's pocket.

It was the old woman who, simply by staring at Penny's shoes, had first given her the idea of trading them. They were a pair of white leather Charles Jourdan pumps with small, gold-framed buckles on the toes which she had bought on one of her shopping sprees in Hong Kong and which had probably cost more than this woman would see in a month, maybe a year. Remembering what the old woman had said about not being able to raise the money to make bail, Penny had tentatively offered to give the shoes to her son or daughter the next time they came. In exchange she wanted the old woman to ask her son or daughter to go to the British Embassy and tell someone there where Penny was.

It was a long shot and Penny knew it, for if anyone got

wind of the fact that she was corrupting the other inmates it would probably be the worse for them all. Added to that was the likelihood that it could be days, even weeks, before the old woman's family came again, and Penny didn't even want to think about what kind of state she would be in by then. For now, she just had to force herself to go from one hour to the next – and if she thought about the future at all, then it must only be to a time when all this would be behind her and she and Sammy were together somewhere in France, or London, or some place anywhere in the world where they were safe.

She had no way of knowing then that she was wasting her time even thinking about bribing the old woman, that the time would never come when she'd be able to put her plan into motion; all she knew then was that the small comfort it gave her had calmed her enough for her to fall into an unsteady, dream-ridden sleep.

It was just after eleven at night when David landed at Ninoy Aquino airport. Pierre was waiting, ready to update him on what had been happening.

'Where's Penny?' David said, before Pierre could speak.

Pierre blinked. 'Still in the jail.'

David's tension seemed to relax for a moment. 'Thank God for that,' he said, starting to walk on. 'And the DEA?'

'They're waiting to talk to you. David, I don't think—'

'No, don't think,' David interrupted. 'I know what you're going to say, that I've got to be out of my mind coming here, but it's too late now, I'm here. Now, I've got to get out to that jail and fast. How long will it take?'

'An hour. Maybe more.'

'Where's the money? Did it arrive?'

'It's locked in the boot of the car. They won't arraign her for at least another twelve hours . . .'

'If I'm right about this,' David said, 'they won't arraign her at all. Where's the car?'

'Right outside. What do you mean they won't arraign her? They have to; there'll be hell to pay otherwise. The British Embassy knows she's there.'

'There's not the time to explain,' David said, pulling the notes he had made on the plane out of his pocket. 'Right now I want you to go back to the hotel and call these people. Get everything set up, including the plane, and make sure it's ready to fly out at a moment's notice.'

Pierre's face had turned white. 'David, you can't—'

'Just do it,' David snapped. 'Now, how the hell do I find this place?'

'You won't need to worry about that,' Pierre told him. 'You'll have company. There are two DEA agents in the car. The Manila section of Interpol have managed to get themselves involved too, and so have Narcotics Command.'

'Let's all go to the fucking circus,' David said scathingly.

A few minutes later he wrenched open the front passenger seat of the car and glared down at the DEA agent sitting there. 'Have you got someone watching that jail?' he barked.

'I guess you must be Villers,' the agent responded silkily. 'The name's Foreman. This here,' he added jerking his thumb towards the back seat, 'is Bertolucci, like in the movie director. We call him Lucci, or Looch.'

'Sure is a pleasure to meet you,' Lucci grinned.

'Are you in contact with whoever's watching the jail?' David snapped.

'Sure. You think Mureau's gonna get in there . . .'

'It's not Mureau I'm worried about,' David seethed. 'Now, get on that radio and find out if she's still in the jail.'

'She's still there,' Foreman answered. 'And I think

we'd better straighten out just who's giving the orders round here, 'cos it sure as hell ain't you, sonny boy.'

David was already walking round the car. 'You want to see an innocent woman lose her life, then you just carry on debating who's in charge here,' he said, getting in behind the wheel. 'Now, which way are we heading? What the fuck . . . ?' he cried as he started to pull away and a Disneyland of police lights started flashing in the rear-view mirror.

'Hit the brakes,' Foreman said. Then, turning to Lucci. 'Go tell them to cool it or we'll go out of our way to lose 'em and they'll miss out on all the fun.'

David threw him a filthy look, then said, 'Why aren't they out there already? The way I heard it, it's their own officers who took money from Mureau . . .'

'Which puts your girlfriend back in a hostage situation,' Foreman reminded him. 'One step out of place and good night, Penny Moon. Least, that's the way we see it. You want to tell me different?'

'No,' David answered shortly. 'What I want to tell you is why it's so god-damned vital they keep her in that jail till we get there, 'cos if Mureau's up to what I think he's up to, there's every chance in the world we'll never see either of them again.'

'Is that so?' Foreman drawled, his interest perking up. 'D'you hear that, Looch?' he said as Lucci got back into the car. 'Mr Villers here reckons there's a chance we might never see our friend Mureau again if we don't keep the girlfriend in jail. Now what do you reckon to that, Looch?'

'Reckon it calls for some sort of explaining, Jim, is what I reckon.'

'Yeah, s'about what I reckon too. So hit the gas, Mr Villers, and tell us what you know.'

'Before I do that, how about you telling me what kind of jurisdiction you have here?'

'*Carte blanche*,' Foreman answered. 'Mureau's our man

431

and the Filipinos aren't arguing the point. Turn right out of here. Head up to the next lights, then turn right again. So, what you got that we ought to know about?'

It didn't take David long to tell them what he thought Mureau was proposing to do, and even before he'd finished Foreman was on the radio to the agent watching the jail.

'She still there, Todd?' he shouted over the static.

'Sure, she's still here. Would've told you if they'd taken her anywhere, wouldn't I?'

'That's just it,' Foreman said. 'Don't let them take her anywhere. If they try to move her, shoot. D'you get that? Shoot!'

'What, are you crazy?' David yelled. 'If you shoot, everyone's going to end up dead, including Penny. If they try to take her anywhere, you just follow. How many men have you got out there?'

'Two,' Foreman answered. 'Enough for you?'

Before David could answer, the field agent's voice came back over the radio. 'Who the fuck is that, Jim?'

Foreman grinned. 'That's our friend Mr Villers, Todd.'

'Then tell him to keep his fucking voice down – it's making the natives nervous.'

'Where are you, for Christ's sake?' Foreman laughed.

'We're parked up in one of those crappy little bicycle-and-sidecar affairs right opposite the jail. No one comes or goes without us seeing.'

'What about the back? Who's watching the back?' David shouted.

'No back way in or out,' Todd answered.

'There's always a back way in or out,' David roared.

'Get him the fuck off the line, will you?' Todd grumbled.

'We got us a pretty serious situation here, Todd,' Foreman answered. 'More serious than I can go into right now. So just do as he says and double-check the back way.'

'OK, you got it. But you tell that bastard from me he ain't in no position to kick ass around here—'

'Over and out, Todd,' Foreman cut in and threw the radio back on the dash. 'We'll check in again five minutes before we get there,' he said to David, 'but if there's anything to report we'll know about it. You tooled up?'

'No,' David answered, swerving to avoid an oncoming truck.

'Sort it, Looch,' he said. 'We run into Mureau out there this guy's gonna need all the protection he can get.' Then, to David: 'The others keeping up?'

'They seem to be,' David answered, glancing in the rear-view mirror. His adrenalin was really pumping now and he was glad when the car fell into silence. He wanted to concentrate on this miserable excuse for a road, because the way they were going there was every chance they'd end up over a cliff. The bright lights and bottlenecks of Manila were behind them now and the lack of street lights and moonless sky were making the route as hazardous as any he'd ever driven.

They sped on through the night, passing derelict garages, convents and villages. The higher they climbed, the denser the forest became. The winding road narrowed to a single track. Overhead sharp tongues of static flashed across the sky. David's hands were tight on the wheel; his face was pale and his limbs rigid with tension. His mind was racked with thoughts of Penny. The crazy thing was that the closer they got to her the more jittery he felt at seeing her. He just prayed to God that she wasn't in on this with Mureau. But surely to God she'd never have agreed to being locked up in a festering hole just to humour Mureau? And it was even less likely that she'd put her sister's life at risk by not co-operating with the DEA. But they hadn't got there in time, had they? The outfit Mureau had bought himself had got there first, so there had been no opportunity to tell Penny who was really holding her sister and that there was no chance in

433

the world any harm was going to come to Sammy.

'Shit!' he swore, fighting to control the wheel as the car bounced up over a rock.

'Take it easy,' Foreman muttered. Then, glancing at his watch, he reached for the radio.

'You there, Todd?' he said.

'We're here,' Todd answered. 'Where are you?'

'Just coming up over the hill. We can see the lights of the town now. Be with you in about five. Any action your end?'

'Dead as a doornail.'

Foreman hung up the radio and looked at David. 'Could be you're wrong,' he said, 'and he's not planning on coming for her tonight.'

'That's your problem,' David answered. 'I'm here to buy her out of that jail, then we're out of here. You want to wait around to see if he shows, that's up to you.'

'She's the bait, Villers. She's gonna have to stay.'

'Could be he's long gone,' David said.

'Could be. But we need her in that jail a while longer yet.'

David didn't argue. He knew the only reason he was getting the DEA's co-operation here was because of their chances of capturing Mureau.

'This it?' he said a few minutes later as they bumped up over a mound in the road and turned into a rutted main street of the third world.

'This is it,' Foreman confirmed. 'Police station's down on the right. Look out for the Holy Trinity Dental Clinic – it's right next door.'

David had slowed the car now and as Foreman gazed warily around the shadowy shop fronts and deserted food stalls he reached for his gun. 'Where is everyone?' he murmured. 'It's a fucking ghost town.'

David's blood pulsed thickly through his veins as he glanced in the mirror to see the other vehicles turning into the street. 'What's it normally like out here?' he said.

'Heaving. But hell, it's nearly midnight; could be they've all gone off to grab some sack time.'

'Lights're on in the police station,' Lucci said. 'So someone's at home.'

'Like to know who,' Foreman commented, priming his gun.

'There're the boys,' Lucci said, pointing to a bicycle-and-sidecar, half hidden in shadow.

'The money's in the trunk,' David said, pulling the car to a halt on a dusty patch of land in front of the station. 'I'm going round the back to let her know we're here. Pay whatever it takes and follow up with the keys.'

Foreman turned to Lucci and rolled his eyes. 'Go tell the boys to stay put and cover our asses,' he said. 'All looks pretty quiet to me, but they're a bunch of bandits – no knowing what might happen in there.'

As the Interpol and NarCom vehicles pulled in around them Lucci got out and trotted towards the sidecar. David and Foreman moved to the front of the station.

'Any trouble afoot, we'd have been warned,' Foreman said softly. 'But no point taking chances. Get going. We'll follow up once we know what's what inside.'

David was about to break away, when a uniformed officer joined him. 'Oriel Maralit, Narcotics Command,' the officer told him. 'The cell's out the back.'

David nodded, then ran silently past the seething gutters and disappeared into the black hole of the side alley, Maralit close on his tail.

A dim light seeped into the darkness at the far end of the alley. David moved swiftly, fleetingly wondering if he should have picked up the gun Looch had prepared for him. When they reached the yard Maralit flicked on a torch and slid the beam over cracked, mouldering walls.

'Far corner,' Maralit whispered, pressing ahead.

In the torch beam David could see the barred window and ran towards it. The stench hit him, making him gag.

435

The beam slithered on to the gate and David's heart stopped. The gate was wide open; the cell was deserted.

He spun round as someone ran into the yard.

'She there?' Lucci shouted.

'The place is empty,' David shouted back, his voice strangled by fury.

'The boys have gone. No sign of 'em,' Lucci told him, coming to check the cell for himself. 'Must've gone in pursuit.'

David bolted back round to the front of the station. Foreman was coming out. Lucci dashed to the car and started shouting into the radio.

'Place is deserted,' Foreman told him.

'Jesus Holy Christ!' David seethed, banging his fist into the wall. 'How the fuck did this happen? You just called in five minutes ago.'

'I'm aware of that, son,' Foreman responded tightly. He turned to Lucci. 'Any luck?'

'Nothing,' Lucci answered.

NarCom and Interpol officers were swarming over the police station. Maralit had gone inside to join them.

'No sign of the girlfriend?' Foreman said to David.

'She's gone,' David confirmed through his teeth.

'What a fucking mess,' Foreman muttered, dashing a hand through his sparse, greying hair. 'You got any idea where they might have taken her?'

David glared at him, his dark eyes flashing with murderous rage.

They both turned as a NarCom officer came racing out of the door. 'They've just found the station commander, tied up in his office,' he said breathlessly. 'Seems the whole place has been under siege since they brought the girl here.'

'Does he know where they've taken her?' Foreman barked.

'He says it's a long shot, but he reckons they could—'

He broke off as Maralit crashed out of the door behind

him and sprinted for his car. 'I'll lead the way,' he
shouted. 'If Brillantes is right about this, then we got no
more than ten minutes.'

Penny's terror of the speed they were travelling was only
surpassed by the terror of where they might be taking
her. The night was so black and the speed so lethal she
could see almost nothing as they careered around bends
and shot up over humps in the road. Sombillo and
Jalmasco were either side of her, clinging to the
doorstraps as the driver swerved around potholes and
revved savagely out of ditches. The icy blast of the air-
con chilled her skin while inside she burned with
renewed fear.

They'd come for her ten minutes ago, throwing open
the barred gate and ordering her to move fast.
Jalmasco's gun was trained on her and as she stumbled
to her feet more men had poured into the yard. There
was a lot of shouting in words she didn't understand.
She was dragged forward and pushed into the alley-
way just as two shots rang out from the street.
Flinching, she'd shrunk back, but Jalmasco pushed her
on.

'We've got to get you out of here,' he'd hissed. 'Keep
moving.'

As they'd thrust her into the waiting car she'd seen
two bodies being hauled from a bicycle sidecar and
dragged off into the shadows.

'Oh my God,' she whimpered as someone sluiced
away the dark trail of blood that followed the bodies.
'Where are we going? What's happening?'

No one answered as they leapt into the car. The driver
pressed down on the accelerator, throwing up dirt and
stones behind them, then they were speeding down the
street.

'Please,' she begged now, almost screaming as they
swerved to avoid an abandoned jeep. 'Where are we

going?'

'We had to get you out before you were arraigned,' Sombillo told her, his eyes turned towards the night.

'But why? I don't understand,' she cried.

'You were facing the death penalty,' he reminded her. 'Is that what you wanted?'

'No. But . . . For God's sake!' she shrieked as they hit a bump and the car went on to two wheels. 'Why do we have to go so fast? *Can't you tell him to slow down?*' she cried as the car righted itself.

'We're almost there,' Jalmasco said, glancing at his watch in the passing glare of a single street light.

'Where?' she yelled. 'Where are we going?'

'I told you, we're getting you out of here.'

'*That doesn't answer my question,*' she screamed, her voice rising hysterically as the car ricocheted off a wall and skidded into a spin. The driver fought with the wheel, then swung left. Penny saw the rippling gleam of water in the headlights.

'Take it along the water's edge,' Sombillo said, leaning forward. 'The pier's right ahead.'

Penny's eyes darted frantically about her as the blinding throb of terror thumped through her head. She knew where they were now. She recognized the village, the jetty and the deserted outriggers bobbing on the fringes of the lake. But she had no time to order her thoughts before the car squealed to a stop and the back door was wrenched open.

She couldn't see his face in the darkness, but she knew, even before he spoke, who it was.

'Penny?' he cried as Jalmasco leapt out. 'Penny, thank God.'

Reaching into the car, he took her hand and pulled her out. But when he tried to take her in his arms Penny slapped them away.

'*Chérie,*' he gasped.

'I want to know what the hell's going on,' she seethed.

'You set me up, didn't you? It was *you* who planted that heroin. *You* who paid—'

'Penny, listen to me,' he cut in. 'Benny Lao planted the drugs. I should have realized he'd do something like that, but I didn't think he knew where we were. Then when I heard what had happened I skipped the boat and stayed to try to get you out of there. There is another boat coming for us tonight. We have to get away . . .'

'No!' Penny shouted. 'You're lying, Christian. It was you who set me up, you who paid *him*,' she spat, pointing at Sombillo, 'to scare the hell out of me . . .'

'He was trying to help you, *chérie*. He had to make you see what danger you were in . . .'

'What kind of fool do you take me for?' she yelled. 'I knew what danger I was in; I never doubted it for a moment. And I saw the photograph, Christian. I saw it. The one of me in the Chinese Gardens. The one you paid that boy to take so these bastards here would recognize me. So don't try telling me it was Benny Lao . . .'

Christian turned as Jalmasco spoke to him in Tagalog, then both looked out at the lake.

'The boat's here,' Christian said, turning back to Penny. 'You have to come, *chérie*. If you stay, the best you can hope for is twenty-five years.'

'No!' she screamed. 'I've committed no crime . . .'

'They've only got your word for that. Penny, don't be a fool. There's every chance they'll hang you for this.'

'Then I'll take that chance,' she responded, turning to walk away.

'Penny,' he cried, grabbing her arm. 'There's no time to argue about this now. I love you, *chérie*, and it's because I love you that I'm not just going to stand by and watch you throw your life away. You can't fight them, Penny. Do you hear me? They'll find you and make sure you never talk.'

Penny stood mutely staring out at the lake. In the flickering forks of lightning fracturing the humid air she could see the boat coming closer, weaving a path through the fishing pens and heading towards the feeble light at the end of the pier. What if she had got it wrong? What if it had been Lao who had set her up? God knew, she didn't want to believe it was Christian, but what about the photograph? He still hadn't explained that.

When she pressed him about it again, he turned to Sombillo. 'Where did you get it?' he asked.

Sombillo shrugged. 'It came with the case notes. I never knew its relevance.'

Christian turned back to Penny. '*Chérie*, I know how hard this is for you,' he said, 'but I swear I would never do anything to hurt you. Surely you must know how much I love you. I've put my own life and liberty at risk to stay here and help you. Do you honestly think I'd have done that if I'd set you up myself?'

Penny looked at him, then turned to gaze out at the lake again.

'And tell me this,' he said softly: 'what reason would I have to do that to you?'

'I don't know,' she mumbled. 'I don't know anything any more. I just want to go home.'

He pulled her against him and rested her head on his shoulder. 'Then we'll try to get things sorted out here so you can do that,' he told her. 'It'll take some time, but at least you haven't been arraigned, so nothing's official yet. But for now, Penny, you must come with me.'

Tears were gathering in her eyes as she realized that she had no choice. If she didn't go, then they would lock her up in that jail again – and, as he'd said, it was only her word that the heroin wasn't hers.

'We're not going to join the ship with the drugs . . .'

'Shh,' he soothed. 'That ship sailed the night it was supposed to. Now, come on, let's get you out of here before anything else goes wrong.'

As he led her down the jetty Penny watched the boat sliding towards them. Everything in her was screaming out to her not to do this, but as though her limbs belonged to someone else she just kept on walking, hearing and seeing nothing, moving beside him and letting him hold her.

When they reached the end of the jetty the boat was only a few yards away. She started to sob. She so desperately didn't want to do this, but she could see no alternative. Whichever way she turned now, her life was in ruins. And surely a life on the run with Christian had to be better than another night in that festering hell she had just left.

She felt him stiffen as a sudden commotion broke out behind them. Panic expanded her chest as she realized it was the police.

'It's OK,' he whispered, keeping his arm around her. 'Don't look back. Just be ready to jump the minute the boat is close enough.'

The engines chugged a laborious hum, drowning the kerfuffle on the water's edge. Someone aboard leapt on to the bow, preparing to throw the rope. Penny stared down at the water, watching the aimless drift of dead fish, splintered wood and rotting waste.

'It's all right,' Christian whispered, letting her go as the rope sailed through the air towards them. 'Are you ready?'

Penny nodded and tensed herself, ready to jump. At that very instant someone shouted her name.

Before Christian could stop her she had swung round, unable, unwilling, to believe her ears. Her heart was suddenly racing as her mind dissolved into a vortex of confusion and terror. The night was so black she couldn't see the end of the jetty, but when he shouted her name again she knew.

'Oh my God,' she cried, stumbling forward. It might just be a dream, maybe she had lost her senses altogether, but she didn't care, she had to get to him. She hardly felt it when Christian grabbed her arm, she

441

simply carried on trying to run.

'Penny! *Don't* get in that boat!' David cried.

Christian pulled her back. She staggered against him and felt the hard metal of a gun at her head. 'Don't listen to him,' he hissed. 'Just get in the boat.'

Penny's eyes widened with terror as Christian twisted her arm behind her back and yelled out to David. 'If you come any closer, I'll shoot!'

'Let her go, Mureau,' David shouted back. 'It's me you want, not her.' He was standing at the end of the jetty now, visible only in the jagged switches of static overhead.

Mureau laughed. 'You flatter yourself, *mon ami*,' he scoffed.

'Act like a man, Mureau. Stop hiding behind a woman's skirts.'

Christian swore under his breath and Penny felt the anger ripple through him.

'Christian, please,' she whimpered, 'just let me go.'

His face twisted with scorn. 'To him? Never,' he spat.

'But why? What's all this about? I don't understand.'

Christian laughed. 'She doesn't understand, David,' he shouted. 'Do you want to tell her, or shall I?'

'Don't be a fool, Christian,' David answered. 'It's all in the past. You've ruined my life; isn't that enough?'

'She comes with me,' Christian told him. 'Tell him,' he hissed at Penny. 'Tell him you want to come with me.'

'I can't do that, Christian,' she said, wincing at the pain shooting through her twisted arm. 'I don't want to come with you. I don't love you, not the way I love him.' She knew the instant the words had left her lips that it had been the wrong thing to say, but there was no way of taking them back now.

'She says she loves you, David!' Christian jeered. 'So what do *you* say? Do you love her?'

'I'm not playing that game,' David responded. 'She knows nothing about any of this, so for God's sake, man, let her go.'

'Gabriella know you're here?' Christian shouted.

'She will by now.'

Christian grinned. 'She's going to finish you for this, David.'

David was silent.

'Me and Gabriella together. We're going to finish you, David.'

Penny gasped as he tightened his grip on her arm.

'You do what you have to do,' David told him. 'Just let Penny go.'

'And how do you suppose I'm going to get out of here without her?'

'You won't get out of here, Christian,' David answered.

'Is that so? Well, you just watch me.'

As he turned Penny towards the boat she almost screamed as his grip tightened and a searing pain shot through her arm. 'Christian, please, don't do this,' she begged.

'What choice do I have?' he responded mildly. 'Now, just get into—' He swung round as a single gunshot exploded into the night. Penny seized her chance and started forward.

'Get down!' David yelled.

Another shot rang out and Penny hit the floor.

Christian lunged towards her and aimed the gun at her head. 'Get up,' he said.

Penny forced herself back to her feet, trembling with shock and blinded by tears of frustration.

'It's over, Christian,' David shouted. 'Haven't you realized that yet? Didn't Gabriella tell you?'

'It'll never be over,' Mureau responded. 'Not between you and me.'

'Then make it between you and me and let her go!'

'You want her back when you know I've screwed her?' Christian laughed. 'She's used goods, David. And I'll tell

443

you this, she's not like Gabriella. No way is she like your wife, David. Have you seen this body?' he sneered, making Penny shriek as he wrenched her arm further up her back. 'It was all I could do to get myself a hard-on.'

Even through the pain and the terror Penny could feel herself crumbling with shame at his words.

Everything had gone quiet at the other end of the pier and as endless minutes ticked by and no one moved, the dread that they had abandoned her overwhelmed her. 'Why are you doing this?' she sobbed. 'Please, tell me, Christian, what happened between you two.'

Before Christian could answer, another voice called out from the end of the pier. 'Mureau! We got two DEA officers out here and a whole army of Filipinos. You ain't going to get away with this, son, so come on in now before someone's blood gets spilled.'

'It'll be hers if any of you come a step closer,' Mureau warned. Then, to Penny: 'In the boat. Go! Now!'

Penny turned, then gave a startled gasp as a figure rose up from the water. Christian's response was like lightning. He shot the figure at point-blank range, then, grabbing Penny, he shoved her towards the boat. '*Jump!*' he hissed.

'Stay right where you are.'

Penny spun round. A wet-suited man, with lake water pooling at his feet, was holding a gun to Christian's head. Christian's foot lashed out. Penny fell back, hitting her head on a pulley. The man fired. At the same instant Christian elbowed him in the gut. Dazed, Penny tried to pull herself up. Blood was flooding her eyes. Christian's foot smashed into her chest. She jerked back, crashed to the floor, then rolled senselessly into the viscid depths of the lake.

David was racing along the pier. Seeing her go in, he dived right in after her. The scum and slime blinded him. He thrashed about in the darkness, trying to find her. Resurfacing, he took air, then went back down.

444

Gunshots exploded in his ears. He couldn't find her. Mureau was firing into the water. God-damnit, he couldn't find her! He twisted and turned, flailing out with his arms, kicking with his legs. His body jerked, once, twice, as more shots boomed into the water. Then everything went silent.

Foreman and Lucci stood staring down at the air bubbles in the lake. Any second now Villers would come up – with the girl. A minute went by, then another. Foreman was the first to tear off his jacket as the two DEA agents dived into the water after them.

Chapter 23

A host of faces swam before her eyes, melting, undulating in a liquid softness, fading into nothingness, then returning in a blurred, echoing infinity. There was a droning in her ears. She could hear her name, a distant reverberation, moving further and further away, then sharply beside her. Still the droning. She could see David. She wanted to touch him, but he'd gone. She tried to say his name but her tongue was too heavy, her lips wouldn't part. Sammy was there. Then a strange woman with dark, probing eyes that seemed to vibrate with the droning. David was there again. Then she saw her mother. Her eyes filled with tears. Her mother was smiling. Then everything was black.

A car was waiting on the runway as the light aircraft circled the island, then began its descent against the blazing orange hues of sunrise. Beneath them the South China Sea quivered like fire.

The passengers disembarked and were driven speedily, though carefully, through a forest of palms and multi-specied cacti. Everything was still as they passed – no ripple amongst the lily pads on the pond, no stirring of the slender reeds, no sound from the *casitas* buried in the tropical splendour of the island. The tang of salt mingled with the delicate essence of flowers to perfume the air.

On reaching the *casita*, the car stopped to let its

passengers out. No one spoke. The gentle sigh of the sea carried on the first whispering breeze of the day. As the door of the *casita* opened, David carried Penny through and laid her gently down on the bed. The nurse closed the door behind them.

More than two hours passed before the nurse came out again. Before getting into the car she turned to look at the *casita*. It was made up of two large triangular-shaped rooms with gently sloping red-tiled roofs placed together as though engaged in a cheek-to-cheek embrace and fondly observed by the caressing fronds of palm leaves and the lofty majesty of a glorious morning sky. Then opening the car door, she got inside and headed back to the airstrip.

For some time now Penny had felt herself rising through the misty, glutinous bands of sleep. It seemed like an endless journey, but as each one began finally to dissolve, receding soundlessly and effortlessly into obscurity, her eyes began to flicker. She turned her head, moaning softly as daylight penetrated the darkness. She blinked her eyes open, then closed them again, allowing her senses to gather from the deadening solace of sleep, waiting for the lucidity that would remind her of who and where she was.

For a long time nothing happened. She was fully awake, but her eyes remained closed as she recalled the visions of her sleep. David and Sammy. A stranger and her mother. And the terrible, monotonous droning. The droning had stopped; there was no sound at all now. A small frown appeared between her eyes as she remembered the jail. Then her eyes flew open as she recalled the scene on the pier. David and Christian. Something had happened between David and Christian.

As she looked around the room her eyes grew wide. There was a faint throbbing in her head, but otherwise she was sure she had the strength to move. She sat up, supported by vast, downy pillows at the head of a bed that was so big you could get lost in it. The room was triangular and luxurious. The two sloping walls were dominated by windows, through which she could see a smooth, wooden terrace, a small garden of tropical shrubs, then ... she shifted herself higher ... a pure white beach being lapped by a sun-spangled aquamarine sea.

She frowned as she thought that maybe she was dead and gone to heaven. Where was she? And how had she got here?

Peeling back the sheets she walked over to where the windows met in a point. In front of them were two dark wood day beds, both with mattresses the colour of the sand on the beach. She turned to look back at the room, gazing incredulously around her at the dark bamboo headboard of the bed, the highly polished wood of the floors, the ornate marble desk and the clay bowls filled with vivid flowers. Walking back across the room she slid open the double doors beside the bed and stepped into another triangular illusion that might have been designed for an Egyptian queen or a Moorish princess. The bath was set in a creamy marble block, facing the window, looking out on to the enticing blue of the sea. At the other end of the room the vanity units were set in the same delicate shades of marble, with an enormous mirror bordered in discreet, opaque lights. Pushing open a slatted wooden door beside it she found the toilet, and in a marble-tiled cubicle the other side was the shower. In the middle of the room was a neat round table, on which a white orchid preened in the dreamy glow of a single spot.

She turned back to the mirror and looked at herself. How, she wondered, had she come by what she was wearing? It was a white, man's shirt, crumpled because she'd slept in it, but meticulously clean. So too were her hair and her face. She peered a little closer and saw the bruise on her forehead. She touched it, winced, then gave a confused smile as her stomach growled with hunger.

She walked back across the bedroom and let herself out on to the wooden deck. The warm, scented air assailed her. Small details of the dreadful episode on the pier were beginning to come back to her. She wondered how long ago it had happened, or if, maybe, she had dreamt it. So desperate was her longing for David that maybe she had imagined it all. Then a sudden fear descended on her. Had Christian managed to get her into the boat? Was it he who had brought her here? Was this to be their retreat, hiding from justice, isolated from the world?

Her eyes alighted upon a hammock swinging gently in the breeze. She walked down the steps towards it, then continued along a short sandy path through the tangle of exotic shrubs and flowers to the beach. There she found two sun beds, sheltered by a parasol from the blazing sun. Their fabric was the same translucent white as the sand, the wooden frames were made from the same polished wood as the interior of the *casita*. Much further along the beach she saw two more sun beds and a parasol, more palms bowing towards the sea, and on the near horizon, across the dazzling sapphire waves, a small island rose gently out of the blue.

This truly was a paradise. But how had she come to be here? A tight band formed around her head as she tried to make herself think. It was as though fear had become a constant in her life now and fear, she knew, was born out of ignorance. But why was she here? Who had brought her? And why did she seem so alone?

Walking back, she looked down at her toes, watching them sink into the powdery crystals of sand. As she approached the steps to the veranda she lifted her head to look at the *casita*. The sun was glinting on the windows, dazzling her. She thought she could see someone standing there.

She stopped and put her head curiously to one side. Then her heart suddenly caught.

'Hi,' he said.

She started to speak, but her lips only trembled as her eyes watered and she wondered whether she should really trust what they were seeing. He looked so impossibly handsome with his tousled blond curls and deep, searching blue eyes laughing quietly, teasingly, down at her. Her heart was so full she could barely breathe. She felt shy, ridiculously tongue-tied and foolish.

'Out for a stroll?' he said, the laughter simmering wickedly in his voice.

Penny turned her head to one side, her lips pursed in a smile. 'David, I . . .' Her voice trembled and as she lifted her head to look at him her eyes were imbued with the power of her feelings.

He came down the steps; then, folding her in his arms, he said, 'I love you too.'

'Oh God,' she spluttered, laughing through the tears as her mind and her heart started to swim in the crazy flood of incredulity. The feel of him – the sheer strength of him and the intoxicating scent of his hair and skin – was flowing through her.

'That was what you were going to say, wasn't it?' he asked.

'No,' she laughed.

'It wasn't?' he said, sounding surprised and disappointed. 'Well, it sure looked like it was.'

There was nothing she could do to stop the tears. It wasn't that she had forgotten his humour, it was simply that she'd been so afraid she might never hear it again.

'So,' he said, tilting her face up to his and stroking his thumb along her jaw, 'what were you going to say?'

As she gazed up at him she could feel the force of her love stealing the words from her lips. 'I don't know,' she whispered. 'But you're right I – I do . . .'

'Love me?'

'Yes,' she nodded, swallowing hard.

'Well, that's a relief,' he murmured, dropping his forehead on to hers, "cos we're sure as hell in the wrong place if you don't.'

Laughing again, she raised her head to look at him. 'Where are we?' she asked.

'Well,' he said, looking skyward as though to think about it for a moment, 'we're at the Amanpulo, which, I guess you could say, is one of the world's most exclusive hotels.'

She turned to look out towards the first magical rays of the sunset. 'Are we still in the Philippines?' she asked.

'Yep.'

She shook her head disbelievingly. 'How did we get here?'

'By plane.'

She frowned. 'Then how come I don't remember it?'

'Well, I guess because you weren't conscious and because the nurse who flew out with us gave you something that kept you under a while longer than you might otherwise have been.' He brought her face back to his and gazed anxiously into her eyes. 'How do you feel?' he said. 'You were in that lake a pretty long time, you know.'

Penny frowned. 'I was in the lake?'

Rolling his eyes, he said, 'Just great. There am I risking my life to save her and she doesn't remember a single thing about it.' Lowering his head, he brushed his nose against hers. 'Do you remember anything that happened last night?' he said.

'Bits,' she answered. 'I think, well, I guess I still can't get over the shock of you being there. I mean, well, it all feels a bit unreal now, but— Oh my God!' she suddenly gasped. 'Sammy! What's happened . . .'

'It's OK. She's fine.'

She started to speak, then let her breath go in a laugh.

If David said Sammy was fine, then she was fine. 'I can't take all this in,' she told him. 'So much has happened and so far none of it makes any sense.'

'No, I don't suppose it does,' he said. 'But it will, once we've talked.'

'You and Christian,' she said, moving her eyes between his. 'What is it . . .?'

'Shh,' he said, putting a finger over her lips. 'How about we get you something to eat first? You must be ravenous by now.'

Yes, she was, but she wasn't sure she wanted to wait. 'Just tell me this,' she said. 'Is it all over? Is he in jail?'

'Yeah, he's in jail,' he answered. 'They're flying him back to the States tomorrow.' As for whether or not it was all over that was something David still couldn't be sure of; in fact, he was very much afraid it wasn't, but he didn't want to tell her that now. 'Come on,' he said, taking her hand and walking her back up the steps to the veranda.

Before going inside they stopped to gaze out at the spectacular beauty of the setting sun. As it turned the sky from azure to red and spread its burning splendour over the sea he lifted his hand to the nape of her neck and began gently to massage it. Penny's eyes closed as she leaned against him and desire began its slow burn deep inside her. His fingers moved into her hair, then down over her shoulder and around to her face. As his thumb touched her lips he felt a telling tremor pass through her and turning her in his arms he looked deep into her eyes.

Neither of them spoke as they gazed at each other in the fading light. His mouth came slowly to hers, touching it softly, pressing her lips open and caressing them gently with his own. Then his hands moved over her back and as he pulled her to him, allowing her to feel the swelling evidence of his need, he pushed his tongue into her mouth. She could feel herself merging with his

452

potency, felt his strength sweeping through her, filling her, spilling into her heart, plunging deep into her soul.

As he raised his head she looked up into his eyes and felt herself turn weak. 'This is still so hard to believe,' she whispered shakily.

'Then how about we make it real?' he said, bringing her mouth back to his. As his tongue found hers again his arms tightened around her, crushing her to him.

She could feel the masculine beauty of his body beneath her hands, the firmness of his muscles, the taut- ness of his skin, the coarse hair on his arms, the commanding pressure of his mouth. The incredible scent of him stole into her senses and the taste of him inflamed her; her whole being was alive with his touch.

He led her into the *casita*, then drawing her to him again he pressed himself so hard against her she moaned aloud at the exquisiteness of the urgency and pain.

It wasn't easy for her to tell him she loved him, but once she'd found the words she repeated them over and over, kissing him frantically, tearing at his shirt, ripping open his jeans and gasping at the consuming need that engulfed her as her fingers encircled him.

'Jesus, Penny,' he groaned, his head falling back as she tightened her grip. His hands were on her shoulders and she looked down at the solid, dark power of his erection straining in her hand. Every part of her ached with the need to feel him inside her, but as his fingers found her buttons she suddenly drew back, turning away from him.

'Penny?' he said, trying to pull her back. 'Penny, what is it? Did I hurt you? Penny, look at me.'

'I can't,' she choked. 'I just . . .' She couldn't go on. The shame of what Christian had said the night before had suddenly found her. She hated herself for letting it come between them now, was furious that she should even allow it to matter. But she was terrified that David too would compare her with Gabriella. And if he did, would he find her lacking too? She couldn't bear the humiliation and as her chest heaved with the misery she knew she couldn't tell him what was wrong. She didn't want him to remember too.

'I'm sorry,' she said, taking a breath as she wiped away the tears. 'I love you, David. I love you so much, but . . .'

'But what?' he prompted gently.

She tried to make herself smile, then dropped her head in her hands. 'Oh God, it's no good,' she cried. 'I can't do this. I can't bear you to see me . . . I don't want you to—'

'Hey, hey,' he interrupted, half laughing, half serious. 'If you're saying what I think you're saying then you're a bit late for such modesty.'

'Don't mock me, David, not now.'

'Who's mocking?' he said, his eyes softening as he stroked his fingers over her cheek. 'Who do you think bathed you? Who do you think washed your hair and dressed you in one of his shirts?'

She looked up at him, desperate to know, despite the gentle tease in his eyes, what he had really felt when he'd seen her naked.

His smile widened and, rolling her eyes, she started to laugh. 'How do you always manage to make me feel such a fool?' she said. 'Even at a time like this.'

'Beats the hell out of me,' he grinned, taking her hand and putting it back where it had been.

'Can we turn out the light?' she said, feeling as ridiculous as she knew she sounded.

'Uh-uh,' he said, shaking his head. 'I want to look at you. I want to see you when you—'

'No, David, please . . .'

'Yes,' he said.

His hands moved carefully, peeling away her shirt, lowering her panties, caressing her, then kissing her in all the places he had touched. When finally she was naked, he slipped out of his jeans, then led her to the bed and laid her down.

'I love you,' he whispered as he lay down next to her. She gazed at him, her heart too full to speak.

Then he propped himself on one elbow and, making certain she was watching him, he moved his eyes lingeringly to her breasts, to her navel, and down over her thighs, before returning slowly back to her face. 'I love all of you,' he told her, 'and one of these days I'm going to make you see how beautiful you are.'

As her throat tightened she turned her face away. The memory of Christian's words wouldn't leave her, the image of Gabriella's beauty was still diminishing her, and though she detested herself for it she seemed unable to banish it.

'Listen to me,' he said, turning her head back and kissing her gently on the lips. 'I love you, Penny Moon. I love you more than I know how to say and I want you right now like I've never wanted anyone in my life. But if you don't want to do this, then we don't have to. OK?'

She looked long into his eyes, half expecting him to laugh, but he didn't. It felt suddenly strange to be lying here like this with him. It was all happening so fast; the trauma of what she had been through was still stalking her. Yet she wanted him, she wanted him so badly.

His eyes remained on hers as he lifted a hand to stroke the hair from her face. 'How about we make love without having sex?' he whispered.

Despite herself, Penny laughed. 'That's not possible,' she said.

'Sure it's possible. Want me to show you?'

'Yes,' she whispered as his lips came back to hers.

He rolled her gently on to her back, exposing her to his touch. His fingers trailed a slow, tantalizing path from her neck to her breasts. He lifted them in turn, circled each hard, rosy nipple with his tongue, then pulled it tightly into his mouth.

'Watch me,' he whispered, slipping an arm under her shoulders to raise her. 'Watch my hands touching you.'

His words ignited such a fire of lust in her that any lingering inhibitions she had were instantly forgotten. All she wanted now was for him to do with her whatever he wanted, to go on and on until she could take no more. She watched his dark, masculine hand caressing the white, velvety softness of her flesh and moaned aloud at the exquisite sensation of her nipples between his fingers.

'Do you want me to make you come this way?' he murmured.

Weakly she shook her head. She didn't doubt that he could, but she wasn't ready for that yet.

Making sure she was still watching him, he lowered his hand to the gentle mound of her belly and circled it out over her hips, pressing his fingers into the abundant, creamy flesh, then trailing them down over her thighs. She was too far gone by now to care any more about their fullness: she just wanted him to go on touching her for ever.

His hand came back to her face and turned it to him. He sucked her lips between his own. 'Open your legs,' he whispered.

Obediently she parted her legs, then watched his fingers move into the dark thatch of her pubic hair. His eyes were on her face as she followed the path of his hand over the insides of her thighs, then back to her pubic hair. She gasped and turned her face into his neck as his finger found her clitoris and began to slide gently back and forth.

'Do you want my fingers inside you?' he asked, his voice thick with his own desire.

'Yes,' she whimpered. 'Oh God, yes.'

'Right up inside you?'

'As far as they can go,' she answered, her legs opening wider as he began pushing his fingers into her. 'Oh God,

456

David,' she cried as he entered her deeply.

She lay still, rigid with desire, feeling her body pulse to the point of explosion as he moved his fingers in and out of her while stroking her clitoris with his thumb.

'Feel good?' he murmured.

'Mmm,' she answered, unable to say more.

'Want my tongue there?'

'Oh David,' she groaned as lust eddied throughout her entire body.

'Is that a yes?'

'Yes. It's a yes.'

Removing his fingers, he knelt over her. She was so ready for him that even as his tongue found her she could feel the initial pull of orgasm beginning. He opened her wide with his thumbs and took her in his mouth, sucking her, teasing her, massaging her and penetrating her with his tongue. Her head rolled from side to side and her out-stretched hands clenched at the sheets, twisting them around her fingers as the impossible sensations throbbed through her lower body until she could take no more.

'David,' she murmured. Her eyes were glazed as she pulled herself up, moving to him, reaching for his hardness and finding it as his mouth found hers. Her fingers enclosed him; the excruciating hardness felt as though it might erupt at any second. He groaned into her open mouth and tried to push her back against the pillows, but she was already moving away. And then her mouth was where her fingers had been, closing around him, clenching him, sucking him and pulling him deeper and deeper into her throat. He was too big for her to take it all, but as her fingers massaged his balls, holding them, squeezing them, moving to his anus, pressing inside, she was driving him to the point of madness. He fell back against the bed, unable to feel or think beyond what she was doing to him.

It was only moments before his seed began its rapid, burning ascent that she let go and drew herself up to look at him.

His eyes were watching her, steeped in love and lust. He lifted a hand and stroked it lazily over her breasts. 'You're blowing my mind,' he told her softly.

'Is this making love without having sex?' she smiled shakily.

'This is making love,' he answered.

Her eyes moved to the straining bulk of his erection, then back to his face.

'I want to be inside you, Pen,' he said gruffly.

'Which way do you want me?' she asked.

'Oh, Jesus Christ,' he groaned. Then suddenly she was in his arms and he was rolling on to her, pushing his legs between hers. 'I want to see your face. I want to watch you come,' he said as she wrapped her legs around his waist.

Lifting himself up on one arm, he reached down and guided himself to her. As she felt the tip of him probing her she whispered his name.

Looking at her, he said, 'I love you, Penny. I love you so god-damned much.'

'I love you too,' she said, her eyes fluttering closed as she savoured every moment of the penetration. He pulled back, then pushed in again. The feel of her around him was exquisite. He waited for her eyes to open, moving himself gently in and out of her, but he could see that she was lost to the sensations of what he was doing. Then suddenly he slammed into her, penetrating her as far as he could. Her back arched as she cried out. Her hands gripped him; her legs tightened about his waist. His muscles were like steel as he hammered himself faster and faster into her. She was meeting each thrust, pulling him down to her, searching for his mouth.

'I love you,' he said again, bruising her lips with his own. His hands slipped under her buttocks, urging her up to him. Then, raising himself on his arms, he looked down to where their bodies were joined and together

458

they watched his penis plunging into her.

She looked up at his face, saw the hard clench of his jaw and ran her hands over the solid strength of his arms. Then suddenly he changed the rhythm and movement of his hips. He caught her scream in his mouth as he drove into her, harder and harder, faster and faster.

'David,' she moaned deliriously. 'Oh my God, I can't bear it.' Her shoulders pressed hard into the bed and her arms fell away. She was too weak to hold him, too overcome by the sheer power of what was happening to her. He reached for her hands and curled his fingers tightly around hers. The relentless assault on her senses was pushing her to the point of frenzy. Then the surging power of her orgasm erupted around him in a blinding mass of sensation.

'David,' she gasped. 'Oh my God, David!' She felt so full of him, so utterly a part of him, that the sudden flood of his own release and the seething might of the contractions that seized them both drew him deeper and deeper into her.

'David!' she cried. 'David, I can't.'

'Stay with it,' he gasped. 'You're there. Just stay with it.'

Her back arched and he grabbed her to him, holding her up and plunging into her as the final rush of his seed shuddered from his body.

'Don't stop,' she begged. 'David, please don't stop.'

Only then did he realize that she was about to come again, one orgasm right after the other. He spun her over, sat her astride him and continued to pump his hips while using his fingers to manipulate her back to the edge.

At last, as the fervour of the spasms began slowly to subside, she fell over him, her breath ragged with exhaustion, her heart racing with spent adrenalin. He held her close, stroking her and kissing her, as he waited for his own heartbeat to relax and his breathing to steady.

Their bodies were bathed in moonlight, their limbs entwined in an embrace of satiated love. They lay side by side, gazing into each other's eyes, silently marvelling at how long it had taken them to reach this when they should have known right from the start that it was where they would end up. It felt so right. Their bodies were so instinctively attuned to each other it was as though they had made love many times before. The initial coyness of lovers hadn't arisen, wasn't necessary for them. As she looked at his face she could only wonder at how she had ever imagined herself in love with anyone else, when just the depth of his blue eyes, the familiar scent of his skin, the dark shadow on his jaw, could turn her heart inside out. She had such an overwhelming sense of being where she belonged that her heart could barely contain it. He was the first man she had ever truly loved and it was only now that she realized how vulnerable a love as strong as this could make her. Her eyes closed as she thought of his wife, but she pushed the thought away. If he still loved Gabriella, then surely that was where he would be now.

'What are you thinking?' he said softly.

'I'm thinking,' she said, opening her eyes, 'that you're pretty inept when it comes to making love without having sex.'

Slowly he grinned.

Laughing, she said, 'You made me come twice, you know.'

Putting his lips over hers, he said, 'Want to try for a third?'

Her body instantly responded and as his tongue moved into her mouth she could already feel herself starting to melt in the growing heat of passion. But as he rolled on top of her her stomach gave a protracted growl of hunger, reducing them both to laughter.

'Come on,' he said, getting up from the bed and pulling her after him. 'Time to eat.'

'Is there a restaurant here? I don't have any clothes,'

she said, padding into the bathroom after him.

'There's a restaurant,' he answered, 'for which you will need clothes – and you'll find some hanging right there in the closet. I got them in the hotel shop; you can always change them if you don't like them.' He pulled her in front of him and turned her to face the mirror, then wrapped his arms around her waist and looked at her reflection. 'There's also room service – that is to say private dining,' he said, 'for which you won't need any clothes. God, I love you.'

Smiling, she leaned her head back on his shoulder and watched him smoothing his hands over her nudity. The light was so soft and flattering she almost felt beautiful as she basked in the warm shades of the room and the stirring sensation of his touch. After a while she raised her eyes back to his and, finding him watching her, she turned in his arms and pulled his mouth down to hers. Then, suddenly realizing that when he opened his eyes he would see her rear view, she began shuffling to one side.

Realizing what she was doing, he burst out laughing and gave her a playful slap on the buttocks. To her shame she felt the flesh ripple.

'You're going to have to get used to me looking at it,' he said, grinning, as he planted her firmly back in front of the mirror and ran his hands over the delicious fullness, 'because I intend to be doing it on a pretty regular basis.'

'Aren't I allowed any inhibitions?' she protested, her voice faltering slightly as she felt him hardening.

'Uh-uh,' he said, shaking his head. 'Not with me, you aren't. Want to take a bath before we eat?'

She nodded and letting her go he walked over to turn on the taps.

'OK,' he said, sitting on the edge of the bath and emptying the Floris bath gel into the water, 'come on over here.'

As she walked towards him he turned to watch her and she felt an incredible glow of pleasure burn through her as she saw the effect she was having on him. 'You know what I want,' she murmured, coming to stand in front of him and putting her hands on his shoulders, 'I want you to bath me and talk to me the way you did just now.'

As the steam rose up around them he got to his feet and lowered his mouth to hers. His erection was brushing against her, but when she tried to move closer he turned her away. Then, putting an arm around her waist, he placed a hand on the back of her head and bent her over the bath.

'Open your legs,' he said softly.

As she did as he told her she felt his hands on her buttocks, squeezing the ample flesh. 'I want to look at you like this,' he said, sliding his fingers inside her while with his other hand he scooped up her breasts. Then, letting her go, he stood back.

'David,' she protested weakly.

'You want me inside you?' he said, pushing his fingers hard into her. 'You want my cock where my fingers are?'

'Yes,' she gasped, dazed by the lust his coarseness had engendered.

'Then say it.'

'I want your cock inside me,' she said raggedly. 'Right up inside me. I want you to fuck me so hard— Oh God!' she cried as he suddenly rammed himself into her. Then her knees almost gave out as he reached in front of her to tease the most sensitive part of her.

'Tell me you love me,' he growled, banging into her and gripping her tightly around the waist.

'I love you.'

'Tell me again.'

'I love you, David. I love you.'

Reaching into the bath he scooped up the foaming water and began to soap her breasts. Then he pulled out of her, turned her to face him and buried his tongue deep in her mouth. Her hand found his penis, but as she stood on tiptoe to put it in her again he lifted her in his arms and stood her in the bath. Then he was in there beside her, his mouth on hers again as he sat on the wide marble slab the other side of the bath and pulled her on to his lap. As he penetrated her he leaned back to rest on his elbows and look up at her. Then they both started to laugh as they realized that neither of them could move.

His smile faded as she squeezed him with her inner muscles then, as he fell back, surrendering himself to her, she manoeuvred herself on to her knees and began to move up and down on top of him.

Looking up at her, he brushed his hands over her breasts. 'Don't ever hide anything of yourself from me, Penny,' he told her. 'I love you. I love every god-damned inch of you.' Then pushing his fingers between her legs, he began pumping his hips, watching her breasts bounce over her ribs as her head fell back at the building power of sensation.

'David, I'm going to come,' she cried as his fingers and hips started to move faster.

'I know. I can feel it.' Then suddenly the grip of her orgasm clenched him. 'Jesus Christ, Penny,' he seethed. 'What are you doing to me?'

'Just don't stop,' she begged, 'please don't stop.'

Within seconds he was on the point of shooting into her again. Raising himself up quickly, he folded her in his arms and held her close as the shuddering spasms of his own release ejected the seed from his body.

After a while he looked up at her and smiled tenderly into her eyes. 'You OK?' he said.

'I think so,' she said, smiling too.

'Do you reckon we should turn off the taps?' he said.

Laughing, she reached behind her and shut off the water. Then, carefully detaching herself from him, she sank back into the warm, silky suds.

'You know what I'm going to do now?' he said, resting his elbows on his knees as he looked down at her.

'Tell me,' she said.

'I'm going to order us some food, because if I don't do it now and we carry on like this we're never going to get to eat. And, speaking for myself, I'm pretty damned hungry.'

'Sounds like a good idea to me,' she said, sinking beneath the water.

He watched her as she came up, looking at the arch of her neck and the fullness of her breasts as she held her head back for her hair to fall behind her. Then, as her eyes met his, he smiled and stooped over her to kiss her. She looked so ridiculously happy and was so blissfully unaware of the terrible price he was going to pay for being there that he just couldn't bring himself to tell her. Not yet, anyway.

Chapter 24

When Penny finally awoke the following morning, after
a night of almost unbroken sleep, she found herself alone
in the bed. Pushing back the sheet, she picked up a discarded towel from the floor and wrapping herself in it,
wandered out on to the veranda. David was standing at
the edge of the sea, his hands thrust deeply into the
pockets of his shorts. Seeing him, a quiet intensity stirred
in her heart. The crystal waves lapped smoothly over his
ankles as he stared out towards the horizon. The sun was
already high in the sky, shedding its warmth over the
spectacular beauty of the island, deepening the
turquoise-blue of the sea, making the white sand sparkle
and the vivid green of the palms glisten. Even after all
the tender and passionate moments they had shared, it
still seemed incredible to her that they were there and
that they had had to go through what they had to find
each other.

She smiled sadly to herself. She still didn't know yet
what he had been through, but something had happened
since she'd left, that much was clear, and she had the distinct and uneasy feeling that, despite Christian's arrest,
they hadn't yet seen the last of him. She knew that David
had deliberately held back on this the night before, wanting to lose himself in the euphoria of their love-making
and, like her, pretend for a while that the rest of the
world was simply a place to which one day they might

return. She had no way of knowing what history he and Christian shared, but she knew he would tell her, was probably, even now, trying to find the right words. She wished there was something she could do to help him, but apart from letting him know that she loved him and that, no matter what, she would be there for him, there was nothing else she could do. Maybe, once he'd told her, there would be more, but she knew she must allow him to tell her in his own time and not push him.

She watched him as he lowered his head and walked a few feet along the shore. The fact that she could sense his turmoil so strongly, and that it was the role she had played that had brought them to where they were now, was causing a dreadful guilt to close around her heart. But now wasn't the time to indulge herself in her own emotions, for this was no longer about her, it was about David and Christian and Gabriella. Most of all, though, it was about David, and since it was too late to change whatever had happened, or what she herself had done, all they could do was go forward together, face whatever still had to be faced, and hope that one day soon they would be able to put it all behind them.

Turning back into the pleasing coolness of the *casita* she went into the bathroom and, dropping the towel, stepped into the shower. No amount of speculation was going to make her any the wiser, but there was nothing she could do to stop the thoughts chasing each other through her mind. A part of her wanted to resist ever knowing what had led up to the night on the pier, but an even stronger part was preparing to deal with it in the best way she could for David.

When, a few minutes later, she stepped out into the bathroom she found him standing in the doorway, watching her. Under the dark scrutiny of his eyes the heat of desire pulled through her.

'I love you,' he said hoarsely.

'I love you too,' she said, injecting such feeling into the

words that for an instant his eyes seemed to dull with pain.

Picking up a towel he walked over to her and using it to pull her to him he kissed her tenderly on the mouth. 'I just ordered some breakfast,' he told her, 'and then . . . Well, I guess we'd better talk. Do you feel up to it?' he added, looking searchingly into her eyes.

'Yes,' she nodded.

Smiling, he wrapped her tightly in his arms. 'How did I ever get to be this lucky?' he whispered. Then, with a dry, bitter laugh, he added, 'How did I ever manage to fuck up the way I have?'

'Did you?' she said, prising herself gently from the embrace and looking up at him.

'Yep, I sure did,' he answered flatly.

'Well, there's a relief.' She smiled. 'I was beginning to think you were invincible and I'm not sure I know how to handle invincible. Fuck-ups: now, those I can handle.'

'Then I hope to God you can handle this one,' he said as the fleeting humour in his eyes faded.

In that moment, when he looked at her that way, she truly believed that there was nothing she couldn't handle. It was only in the weeks and months ahead that she came to doubt her ability to be strong for him, but by then she was dealing with so much more than either of them could have foreseen.

Their breakfast of coffee, croissants, fresh papaya and mango was served on the veranda, by which time Penny was wearing the pale-lilac sarong dress he had chosen for her the day before, with her hair brushed back from her face and tied with a ribbon that matched the dress. As he looked at her he felt the tremendous power of his feelings tightening his heart. Not only was she a very special woman, she had a very special kind of beauty, one that shone through from the very depths of her soul, lighting her clear, blue eyes with honesty and courage and the kind of integrity that made him want to shield

467

her from all the sordid cruelties of the world. He smiled to himself as he thought of how she would laugh if he told her that.

They drank and ate in silence as butterflies flitted and glittered in the sunlight and the haunting song of a hoopoe bird carried on the breeze. Apart from the hotel staff they hadn't seen another living soul on the island.

'Well,' he said finally, 'I guess I've got to begin somewhere, but believe me when I tell you that no one comes out of this with a halo, least of all me.' He laughed mirthlessly and looked down at his coffee. 'That's an understatement if ever there was one,' he muttered, almost to himself. 'Anyway, in a nutshell, I had an affair with Christian's wife and one way or another I've been paying for it ever since.'

Penny waited, watching his eyes move out over the sea as he began to relive the past few years of his life. 'It wasn't the first time I was unfaithful to Gabriella,' he said, 'nor was it the last, but it was the only time it ever got to me the way it did, and, well, I guess it was the closest I ever came to leaving her. The only reason I didn't was because she was pregnant with Jack, our younger son. If she hadn't been, well, I'm pretty sure I'd have gone. I say pretty sure because I still don't really know. I loved Gabriella, I was crazy about her from the day we met, but it didn't stop me cheating on her, even while she was pregnant. She knew about most of my affairs. God only knows why she tolerated them, except I was rich and Gabriella worships at the altar of the Almighty Dollar. That's not to say she didn't love me, because I know she did. She also loved being married to a man who was British and when I had affairs I was, on the whole, pretty discreet. But with Jenny Mureau it was different and Gabriella knew it. Jenny was wild and crazy and so god-damned beautiful...' His jaw tightened for a moment; then, continuing, he said, 'She got me so screwed-up over her I didn't know what the hell I was doing. It was the same for her – it was like we just could-n't get enough of each other. We met at some party in LA and within half an hour of being introduced we were screwing our brains out in the spare room, while my wife and her husband were downstairs mingling with the other guests. I hadn't met Christian before, I hadn't even heard of him, but knowing him wouldn't have made a difference. I'd still have screwed his wife and I'd have done it right in front of him if that was what she'd wanted.

'Of course the minute we walked back in the room Gabriella knew what had been going on. She was stand-ing there, almost eight months pregnant, radiant and happy and flirting with some guy, like she was glad to have the attention when she was so heavy and close to giving birth. I don't think she'd ever dreamt that I would screw another woman while under the same roof as her, much less do it while she was pregnant.' The edge of bitterness that had crept into his voice was evidence enough of how digusted he felt at himself for what he had done. 'I'll never forget the look on her face when she saw me,' he said. 'The pain was raw. But it wasn't only pain, it was fear. It had frightened her to realize that I could hurt her that much; and it was like she knew already that this was the end, that there would never be any going back. I had committed the ultimate sin and no matter how much we loved each other she would never be able to forgive this single act of treachery that made all the others pale by comparison.

'We left the party soon after. I don't remember much of what we said on the way home. She was crying, I was yelling, trying to deny it, I guess, I don't really remember now. By the time we got home she was hysterical. She grabbed a knife and tried to stab me with it. I managed to get it away from her, but she damned near wrecked the place – throwing things at me and telling me to get the hell out of her life. I didn't want to leave her alone, but I knew I was only making things worse by being there, so I called a friend of hers and asked her to come over. When the friend got there I left and went to a hotel. And do you know what I did then? I called the party we'd just left and spoke to Jenny. She came right away and she was barely in the door before I was screwing her again.'

He was shaking his head in disbelief, as though he just couldn't connect with the man he was talking about. Sighing deeply, he forced himself to go on. 'We stayed holed up in that hotel for four, five, days, I don't remember now. No one knew where we were – Jesus, I don't think *we* even knew where we were except in some Orphic oblivion where nothing existed beyond the madness that had possessed us both. I tried to call Gabriella a couple of times, but she put the phone down on me and I just turned over and went on screwing Jenny like I couldn't give a damn. Of course, I did give a damn, I loved Gabriella, but I just didn't seem able to stop what was happening. It was like I had lost control. I could see everything slipping away from me, but none of it seemed to matter.' He pressed his fingers to his eyes. 'My father had died six months before and . . . Well, I'm not about to use that to make excuses for myself. All I'll say is that his death hit me hard. We'd always been close and when he went it was like nothing made sense any more. Nothing seemed to have a point to it. I had no idea just how fucked-up I was because of it, but, looking back, it was like I was on some kind of mission to self-destruct. But like I said, it's no excuse for what I did to Gabriella.

'At the end of the four, five, days I went back to her. She'd calmed down a bit by then, but, when she asked where I'd been, like a god-damned fool I told her. Don't ask me why, except I didn't want to lie to her, not when she knew I was lying. My mother had flown up from Miami by then with Tom, our eldest, who was two at the time. I don't even want to think about the scenes that went on over the next few weeks until Gabriella gave birth, but they were hell for us all, particularly for Tom. His mommy was constantly in tears, his granny hardly stopped shouting at his daddy and meanwhile all daddy could think about was Jenny Mureau. She was like an obsession with me. I couldn't get her out of my mind. I was on fire for her every minute of the day. She kept calling me at the office, begging me to see her. I held out for a while, but not for long. I couldn't. I can't explain it now, I don't even understand it now, but back then it was like it was eating me up, like I'd go crazy if I didn't see her. So I saw her.' He paused for a moment, frowning. 'You know, the strange thing is,' he said, 'I can't even say the sex was good. Maybe it was – I guess it *must* have been to have got me so worked up – but I can hardly remember it now. All I remember now was this compulsion to do something I knew right from the start was going to end up destroying my life. Which it has, but in ways I couldn't even begin to imagine then.'

Pausing again, he leaned forward and rested his elbows on his knees, linking his hands in front of him and staring down at the sunbaked deck. 'The turning point came when Jack was born,' he said tonelessly. 'I was there with Gabriella throughout the labour. She had a pretty rough time of it and the fact that my mother had located me in some hotel with Jenny to tell me the labour had started turned the whole thing into a bloody nightmare. It went on for hours . . . You don't need to know the details: just suffice it to say that Gabriella's pain, on all counts, was what finally started to bring me to my senses. And then, seeing our second son coming into the world, seeing Gabriella's love for him and the hesitancy in her eyes when she handed him to me . . .' He swallowed hard. 'She was afraid I wouldn't want him; she thought I was going to turn my back on them.' His breath caught on the words and he stopped.

Then, swallowing again, he said, 'My mother brought

Tom into the room then and as I looked at her face it was like I could see my father. It was like she or he was reminding me that I was a father too, a father who was fucking up his children's lives. And I guess it was then that I realized that nothing was as important as those two boys – no woman, no obsession, no amount of money or success, just *nothing*. They were all that mattered and I had to do something to get myself together before I ended up losing it all.

'In the weeks before Jack was born my mother had hardly been able to bring herself to speak to me. She was still dealing with her own grief over my father's death and seeing her son behaving the way he was, neglecting her grandchild, abusing his wife, bringing the kind of shame upon himself that would have broken my father's heart . . . Well, it was a lot tougher on her than I realized at the time and that's why I don't blame her for what she's done since. God knows, I've deserved it.'

Lifting his head, he gazed sightlessly out at the view.

'I saw Jenny one more time after Jack was born,' he said. 'We made love, but after, while we were going back in the car, I told her it was over. By then I knew who her husband was, mainly because she'd told me about him, but now that I knew his name I'd started to listen whenever it cropped up in conversation. On the face of it he was an art dealer, but it didn't take much scratching beneath the surface to know that the incredible sums of money he'd made had come from a more sinister source. At that stage of the game it was only marijuana – the heroin came later, much later . . .'

He stopped and turned his heavy eyes to Penny. She held his gaze, saying nothing as he smiled weakly then looked away. There were no words to ease his suffering, nothing to be said that could undo what he had done in those nightmare months between the death of his father and the birth of his son. He was paying for it now and she guessed that no one was going to be harder on him

472

than he already was on himself.

'Anyway,' he went on, 'like I said, I told Jenny we couldn't continue. Surprisingly, I didn't find it as hard as I thought I would. It was like the fever was coming to an end and, beautiful as she was, I couldn't work out what it was about her that had driven me to such a pitch. I knew it was Gabriella that I loved, that I had a long way to go before I got my marriage back together, but that was all I wanted then. Jenny was a madness I had miraculously and mercifully recovered from. The trouble was that those around us never recovered. Jenny did, but it took a lot longer for her than it did for me and by then it had destroyed her marriage. She didn't love Christian and wasn't sure she ever had, but he was as crazy about her as I had been. More so. He worshipped her. He lived for her. Everything he did was for her. So when she told him she was leaving it was like his entire world fell apart.

'I think the first he ever knew about me was when she told him she was leaving him because of me, even though we hadn't seen each other in months by then. She told him she couldn't go on living a lie, pretending she loved him when the only man she wanted was me. Whether it was true I don't know. As I said, I hadn't seen her in months and neither had I heard from her. I got to hear about it through Gabriella, who'd heard it from one of Jenny's friends. Of course, Gabriella presumed from that that Jenny and I were still seeing each other. Nothing I said could persuade her otherwise and who could blame her for not believing me when I'd never given her much reason to trust me even before all this.'

He stopped and rubbed a hand over his face, giving himself a moment to think. 'The months following Jack's birth hadn't been easy,' he continued. 'Gabriella had tried to forgive me, but we both knew she hadn't: in truth she wasn't even close. Then, when she heard that Jenny had left Mureau, she became convinced I was going to leave her and almost overnight she went crazy. I mean, she lost her mind. She did things . . .' He took a breath. 'She got a priest in to exorcise our house. She held a crucifix in my face every time I tried to go near her. She started talking to people who weren't there, or telling people who *were* there that I was trying to kill her. It was obvious she was heading for a serious breakdown; but when I finally got her to a doctor, it was like . . .' he shook his head incredulously '. . . it was like nothing was wrong. She was suddenly back to normal and I was the crazy one for saying she'd done all those things.

'Anyway, she might have had a better grip on her sanity by then, but the bitterness had reached an all-time high. Her sole purpose in life now was to make me suffer for what I had put her through. She started jeering at me and trying to humiliate me in public. She was spending to the point she might bankrupt us and threatened all the time to leave me and take me for every penny that was left or I'd ever make in the future. If it weren't for the boys I'd have got out then, but I couldn't leave them with a mother who was as unstable as that, and to take them away . . . Well, God only knows what that would have done to her.

'Then one day she just packed up and went. She did it without telling me: I just arrived home to find them all gone. I didn't know then what had happened to make her go. It was only later that I found out Mureau had called her and told her that I was seeing Jenny again. It was a lie, of course, but when I finally tracked Gabriella down at my mother's she wouldn't even speak to me and neither would she allow me to speak to Tom.

'Anyway, knowing that not seeing the boys would be what would hurt the most seemed to keep Gabriella happy for a while. But then, when I stopped calling, in the hope that my silence would provoke her into calling me, she went the other way and responded to the overtures Mureau had been making to her ever since Jenny had left him.

'I knew nothing about the approaches he'd made, of course. Not until Gabriella told me herself that she was divorcing me to marry Mureau did I know that he'd even been in touch with her. I flew straight to Miami and forced her to see me. I knew by then that we were never going to repair things. Oh, in our own miserable and pathetic ways we still loved each other, but too much damage had been done. She just couldn't find it in her to forgive me and I couldn't blame her for that when I couldn't forgive myself. Still, like I said, we saw each other. She broke down the minute she walked in the room, we both did, and for a while there it seemed like we might get it together. She broke off her affair with Mureau, I moved to Miami because that was where she wanted to be and though we lived separately we saw each other all the time. But she just couldn't let it go. Every time she saw me talking to another woman she accused me of sleeping with her. If I was as much as five minutes late to pick up her and the boys she'd put it down to me not being able to get out of another woman's bed in time. And every time I picked up Jack she'd remind me of what I had done while she was carrying him.

It got so that I couldn't take it any more. We were destroying each other and I could see what an effect it was having on Tom.' His voice had become unsteady now, strangled by unshed tears. 'Every time I looked at his little face and saw all that confusion and the way he was struggling so hard to make things better, like he was the one to blame . . . It damned nearly broke my heart. When his mother wasn't around he used to creep into my lap and hold on to me like he was . . . like he was trying to tell me he was sorry. He was three years old, for God's sake. Three years old and he was blaming himself. He didn't dare to show me any affection in front of

Gabriella because he knew if he did that she would shout at him and tell him what a bastard his father was. She didn't seem to care what she was doing to the child; all she cared about was making me suffer. So in the end I told her that the best thing she could do was file for a divorce and we would let the courts decide on custody of the boys. What a mistake that was. She thought I was threatening to take them away from her. I wanted to, it was true, but my mother had made it more than plain that if I tried she would fight in Gabriella's corner and I wasn't prepared to have the boys go through all that.

'Anyway, Gabriella didn't file for divorce, but she did take up with Mureau again. I still hadn't met the man at this stage. All I had was a brief recollection of seeing him at the party where Jenny and I had met. Well, if I thought Gabriella was bitter, I hadn't seen anything yet. Jenny had managed to get her divorce and was about to marry some Egyptian guy who was even more loaded than Mureau. But it wasn't the future husband that Mureau saw as the source of all his misery, it was me. So, believing I was going to try to take her sons away from her, Gabriella went along with Mureau's plan to break me.'

He turned to look at Penny and she saw the exhaustion and defeat lying heavily in his eyes though he tried to mask them with a smile. As she looked back at him she could feel his pain merging with all the other emotions in her heart.

'Gabriella knew about Mureau's involvement in the shipments of marijuana coming into the States,' he said. 'She went into it knowing what risks she was running, but to her they were worth it just to see what Mureau had told her it would do to me. And Mureau was right: her involvement would ruin me. I still don't really know what kind of role she was playing at that stage; all I know is that fantastic sums of money started turning up in my bank accounts. There was no way I could explain all the surplus funds that she and Mureau between them managed to deposit into my accounts. For sure, I was a wealthy man, but I sure as hell hadn't done anything to generate the kind of money I was making in the year or so after I told Gabriella to file for divorce. It didn't take us – by "us" I mean me, Pierre and the accountants – long to work out what was going on, and as soon as we did we started closing everything down and moving our assets around the world to countries and accounts Gabriella knew nothing about. I took the money because Mureau, deliberately, hadn't laundered it well enough for me to be able to explain it away and of course, if I had declared it, it would have been tantamount to sending Gabriella, or more likely both of us, to jail. Amazingly, no one asked any questions at the time. Maybe we'd got the money out before the IRS had a chance to build up any sort of case, I don't know, but they've sure as hell caught up with me now. Which of course is what Gabriella and Mureau always intended. But that's not all they intended, because when they planned my demise they made sure they looked into every possible way they could ruin me and booked their tickets.

'The first time the DEA pulled Gabriella in for questioning she turned to me for an alibi.' He laughed bitterly. 'Of course I gave it. How could I not when she asked for it the way she did? Did I want to see the mother of my children go to prison? Think what it would do to the boys' lives. Think of the stigma they would grow up with. Oh, she laid it all on and, sucker that I am, I bought it. Not because I couldn't see through what she was doing, but because I still felt I owed her for what I'd put her through. So the charges against her were dropped; Mureau was the one they were after, but since they still couldn't hang anything on him they were hoping that Gabriella might lead them to what they wanted.

'Anyway, the false alibi was just for starters. What they wanted now was for me to start masterminding ways of getting Mureau's shipments into the country. If

I didn't, Mureau and Gabriella were going to start singing about all those millions I'd managed to get out of the country. I was tempted to let them, but Gabriella really went to work on me, using my guilt in ways only she knows how until, like a fool, I went along with it. And, of course, once I was in, there was no way I could get out. I concocted ways you'd never even heard of to get those shipments into the States and I made fools out of the DEA into the bargain. On one occasion I even got them trying to arrest Customs officers who were trying to arrest them. The Keystone cops had nothing on them, they all looked such idiots, while Mureau's shipment sailed in at another port. Robert Stirling – you know, the guy over in France? – well, he was one of the DEA officers who spent the night in jail and had to explain the fuck-up to his superiors the next day. That was just the start of it between Stirling and me. I've run him around the block a few times since, until I earned him the suspension from duty he's now under. That's why he's there in France, freelancing. He knew I was behind it all and while the rest of them went after Mureau, Stirling came after yours truly. He's been acting without jurisdiction – his superiors have only just found out where he is and I don't imagine they know much about the Mafia boys in Nice who've been accommodating him all this time.

'Anyway, when the FBI added Mureau's name to the list of their most wanted, he left it to me to get him out of the country and set him up with people to look after him in Europe – your next-door neighbours being two of them. I paid them – and plenty of others – to do what they could to keep him out of jail because, if *he* went down, obviously he was going to take me with him, and probably Gabriella too. And where would that leave the boys? My mother's an old woman and, besides, Gabriella is right: what kind of lives would they have once it was found out that both their parents were in jail?'

He sighed heavily. 'I've made a complete mess of this and I've got no one to blame but myself. It's just up to me now to see that they don't suffer any more than they have to. I wish Gabriella had the same priority, but she doesn't. Her priority remains the same: repaying me for what I did to her when she was pregnant with Jack. It's a never-ending mission with her and one she never seems to tire of.

'Still, to condense the next two years into a nutshell: Sylvia came up with the idea of starting a business which she would finance, though I would pay her back through its own legitimate profits as well as those of other companies I have – or at least I did have, until recently. She wanted to do it so that if it ever did come about that I had to go to jail there would be something there for me to come out to. Something no one could touch because, whichever way anyone looked at it, it was only her money behind it. And of course a magazine was the obvious choice, since that was what she was already into. I was loath for her to get involved, but she wouldn't back down. She wasn't only thinking of me, she was thinking of the boys and the fact that if they did lose their parents to the judiciary system they had in some way to be financially supported. Of course there was no question that both my mother and she could manage that without even noticing it. But I'm their father and ... Well, without going into all the macho stuff, there we have *Nuance*. It's for them as much as it's for me and, although on paper it's as squeaky clean as any tax man could want, the back-handers I've paid out to get it up and running as fast as I did have come from Mureau's drug funds – the funds he laundered into my accounts.'

He turned again to look at Penny. He was aware that so far she hadn't uttered a word and wondered what was really going through her mind. He guessed she'd tell him when he'd finished; he just hoped to God she could forgive him. To think of the pain he was going to cause her only heightened his own, but there was nothing he could do to spare her. Things were already happening, thousands of miles from here, over which he had no control at all.

'Are you all right?' he said softly.

She nodded.

'Can I get you something? More coffee?'

'No. I'm just . . .' She shook her head. 'No, nothing.'

'Come on, tell me,' he coaxed gently.

'I'm just, well, almost afraid of what you're going to say next.'

He smiled in an attempt to reassure her, but the smile was empty, for she had good reason to be afraid. God knew, he was.

'Why did you choose the South of France for the magazine?' she asked.

He shrugged. 'Several reasons. It was time for me to get out of the States. Mureau wasn't there any more, but the drugs were still coming in and the DEA were making my life pretty damned difficult. I tried to persuade Gabriella to come with me, but she wouldn't. If I wanted her, she said, I had to stay. If I left, then she would never let me see the boys again.'

'But you went anyway.'

'I had to. Mureau had got involved with the Chinese by then – there wasn't just grass coming in now, there was heroin too. For the boys' sake as well as my own I had to get out. Their mommy and daddy going down for grass was one thing; going down for heroin was something else altogether. The strange thing was Gabriella never looked at it that way. Oh, she loves the boys, she's a good mother in every other way, but when it comes to me she's . . . Well, I don't know, it's like she gets a real kick out of seeing me hurt. I don't blame her for wanting to pay me back, but the bitterness has got like a cancer with her. She can't get rid of it. She'll do anything she can to twist the knife and you can see the pleasure she gets in doing it. When I first came to Europe she flew out to spend a few days with me and what do you know? she invites Mureau to come along too. She screwed him in the hotel room I'd booked for us and made sure they were both there, in the bed, when I came in. Mureau suggested I call up Jenny and make it a real party and Gabriella laughed till she cried. She paraded about naked in front of us both and Mureau loved it – he really got off on watching me humiliated like that. So did she. I let them do it in the blind hope that they'd get something out of their systems. But when they started to screw again, needless to say I walked out.

'Hell,' he said, running his fingers through his hair, 'there's no point going back over all this now: just suffice it to say that Mureau could play her like a puppet. He only ever had to mention there might be another woman in my life and, boy, did Gabriella dance to the tune. He was having such a good time doing it he didn't even see himself fall into his own trap until it was too late. Gabriella suddenly had us both by the balls and, wow, did she start squeezing. She doesn't get what she wants, she goes right to the DEA and tells them everything she knows. She's so crazy we'd have both been insane to try calling her bluff, so needless to say she's one wealthy woman now with two sons their father can't touch and the power to stop their father ever having another woman. "Oh, you can screw around all you like," she told me, "but the minute it starts looking serious..."' He sliced a finger across his throat. 'As for Mureau, he'd better just keep the money rolling on in. Well, he had no problem with that. He just kept right on doing what he'd always been doing, while I financed his protection in order to keep me and my wife out of jail.'

Penny was frowning thoughtfully. 'So as far as the Delaneys are concerned,' she said, 'you're both, you and

Christian, their employer?'

He pulled a face. 'I guess you could say that, yes. I never had much to do with them, at least not at first. I got to hear about them through some contacts I had in Singapore who told me they were living in the South of France now. Apparently they were in need of money and weren't too bothered about how they got it, so I put them together with Mureau who hired them – at my expense. Mureau was rarely in the South of France at that time so they had to travel to meet up with him. What more they did for him, other than keep him furnished with false papers and arrange decoys for him as he moved about the continent, I don't know. What I do know is that as soon as I moved into the South of France he started coming a lot more often.'

His eyes came up to Penny's and, smiling, he held out his hand. 'You sure you're OK?' he said. 'This isn't getting too much for you?'

'No, no, I'm OK,' she assured him, taking his hand and winding her fingers through his.

'So, where was I?' he said. 'Yeah, that's right: the South of France. I chose it mainly because Sylvia had acquired Fieldstone and *The Coast*, much more than the other magazines in that group, needed work. It would help her out if I did what I could to revive it and it would provide me with a company that was totally legitimate. So I chose France – and Sylvia,' he gave an ironic smile, 'chose you.'

Though she smiled in return, a tremor of nerves coasted across Penny's heart as his fingers tightened on hers. 'Let's go inside,' she said. 'It's getting too hot out here.'

He waited until she was sitting cross-legged on the bed; then, sitting down on the edge, he continued. 'So, I was getting things moving in France, Gabriella was still keeping my children from me, but, can you believe it, she was starting to make noises about some kind of reconciliation. Whether she meant it, I've no idea. She's played that tune so many times now, it's like you know all the words but you no longer hear them. Anyway, I'd have gone for it just so I could be with the boys, but my guess is that Mureau got wind of it and put a stop to it. He didn't have his wife, so I sure as hell wasn't going to have mine. Any sign of us patching things up, then he was going to take us all down. See, he could threaten her with the same things she threatened him. The ammunition we had on each other was like a ticking bomb that we kept tossing to each other, waiting to see whose face it would explode in first. The only thing they didn't have on me was the heroin, but Gabriella had already let me know that she'd perjure herself to make sure I went down for everything she went down for. That was, until the DEA made her an offer. If she delivered the goods on Mureau and me, she'd buy herself her freedom.'

'Oh God,' Penny murmured.

'Quite,' he said.

'How long ago was she made the offer?'

He thought a moment. 'Six, eight, months ago. I guess, around the time you came to France. You'll remember the way I was always disappearing, well, it was to see Gabriella. I never told anyone, other than Pierre, where I was going because I didn't want to risk Mureau finding out. Stirling had turned up in France by then and I knew that, with him sniffing around, things were likely to erupt at any minute. But now that Gabriella had her offer it at least meant that the boys wouldn't lose their mother to the prison system. Sure, she'd been more heavily involved than I had, but, if it came to it, I was prepared to take the rap, providing she didn't lie about the heroin. She agreed to that, but only on the condition I went back to live with her.'

'So why didn't you?' Penny asked.

'I thought about it, believe me. I thought about it long

and hard, but in the end I couldn't do it. Apart from owing Sylvia, I knew that if I went back the boys would suffer. She was no closer to forgiving me then than she'd ever been and during the meetings I had with her I could see it. She needs help, professional help, but it would take a braver man than I to suggest it. Because, of course, I am the root of her misery. If she'd got help, then I'd have been prepared to give it a shot, but I couldn't do it when I knew that the boys were better off not having to see the damage their parents were causing each other.'

'How did she take it when you told her you weren't coming back?'

'Oh, pretty well,' he said cuttingly. 'She had herself a new boyfriend by then, someone who was satisfying her quite adequately, she told me. But if I wanted any satisfaction in that area then I'd better just forget it.' Anger suddenly sparked in his eyes. 'There have been times, I can tell you, when I've come so close to putting my hands round that woman's throat and wringing the goddamned life out of her. *Anything* just to end this treadmill of misery she's got me on. There's no reasoning with her: she went beyond that a long time ago. She even told me that herself, the same time she told me to forget about other women. In fact, I hadn't had a relationship with a woman in I don't know how long by then. But her timing was perfect, because it was right after that, only days in fact, that you came into my life.'

He dropped his head and began slowly to shake it; then, to her surprise, she realized he was laughing. 'Right from the minute you flung that damned *tiramisu* in my face,' he said, 'I knew I was in trouble.' He turned to look at her and as his eyes softened with love she felt her heart reaching out to him. 'If you only knew what it was like to be around you at that time,' he said. 'You were like a breath of fresh air. No, you were more than that: you were like the sun coming out after the longest winter ever. You were so alive, so full of life and crazy paradoxes...' He looked incredulously into her eyes. 'You made me laugh when I'd almost forgotten what it was like to laugh. When I was with you I could be myself in a way I hadn't dared to be in so long. I used to pretend that everything was normal, that this was all there was in my life, just you and me and the magazine we were creating. I loved it when you got mad at me because I knew you couldn't stay that way. Watching you laugh when you were trying so hard not to, well, I can't explain what it did to me. I sometimes wonder if you've got any idea of the kind of effect you have on people. I was totally knocked out by you. And when I saw that your lack of confidence in your appearance was only making you more beautiful in my eyes... well, that was when I realized how hard I was falling. And once I knew it and started to look at you that way, I could see that to love you and share my life with you was all I wanted. Except, what life did I have to offer? Besides, I didn't know how you felt about me. And then, when I heard you were seeing Mureau...'

He was looking deep into her eyes as again he started to shake his head. 'I thought I would kill him,' he said quietly. 'The very idea of him even touching you... I knew what it was about, of course. I knew he'd done it to get back at me. That's not to say I don't think he had any feelings for you, because I think he did. But, take it from me, he's never got over Jenny leaving him, the same way Gabriella's never got over my affair with Jenny when she was pregnant. I think, if the truth were known, they keep it alive for each other.

'Anyway, you know yourself how you came to meet Mureau. The first time, at that *vernissage*, was just a co-incidence – at least, so Esther tells me. Mureau knew about you, of course, but he didn't know who you were until Esther told him.' He grimaced. 'Apparently, Mureau encouraged her to drop little nuggets of infor-mation about him that would whet your appetite as a journalist and get you wanting to meet him. She did it because she's got a real soft spot for Mureau, will do almost anything for him – for both of us, actually, because in that addled head of hers she's adopted us as her sons and sees it as her duty to indulge us. It was typical of her to overlook the real implications of you and Mureau meeting; all she thought about was the romantic element of it all, which was something Mureau played on. Though, in fairness, I have to admit that she didn't know the whole story about how Mureau and I had become involved with each other until I told her recently. Neither did Wally, but he was more prepared to be loyal to me: he knew who was paying him. But then Mureau managed to get to him too. He put the pressure on Wally to keep his mouth shut and, like a god-damned fool, Wally did. If he'd come to me when he should have I could have stopped all this happening, but Mureau had the old woman in the palm of his hand, and Wally – well, Wally's price is easily affordable to a man as rich as Mureau. And, of course, they're both in way over their heads; they don't really have the first idea how to handle something like this, which is hardly surprising, really, when most don't.

'Still,' he shrugged, 'you and Mureau met without me knowing anything about it. You know what, though? When I did get to find out, I could never make myself believe that you would run off with him. I don't know why. I guess I just thought that I and Sylvia and the magazine meant enough to you, that you wouldn't go for it when Mureau asked you – which, of course, I knew he would.'

'You're right.' Penny smiled sadly. 'You and Sylvia and the magazine did mean enough to me and I would-n't have gone were it not for the fact that when I called you, the night I went, Marielle told me that you had gone to collect Gabriella and the boys. I'm not proud of the way I ran away from that – in truth, I'm bitterly ashamed of it. But the thought of having to stay in France and watch you reconcile with your wife . . . Of course I didn't know then all that had gone on between you. I didn't even know how much I loved you till then. I just hadn't seen it. I suppose I wouldn't let myself because I just couldn't imagine what you would see in someone like me. Then, when I realized how I felt . . . Well, I never knew I was such a coward until I ran away like that.'

'Hey, come on,' he said, reaching for her hand. 'Don't be so hard on yourself. We've all made mistakes and you're looking at the guy who's made a lot more than most. It was just a shame you didn't call half an hour later. If you had, I'd have answered the phone myself and could have told you that Gabriella didn't show. She's always been fond of doing that – telling me she's coming, with the boys, then backing out at the last minute. That time she'd even called from the airport in Miami to tell me she was about to get on the plane. So I didn't know until the connecting flight came into Nice that she wasn't on it. Anyway,' he smiled, linking her fingers through his, 'what's important now is that I've managed to get you back.'

Penny's eyes dropped to their hands; then, bringing them back to his, she said, 'But at what cost to yourself?'

He grimaced. 'Well, I guess we'll know that in the next few days. I don't suppose I've left either Gabriella or Mureau in any doubt now how I feel about you and, of course, Mureau's already in custody. So I'm in their hands and it all hangs on how committed they are to seeing me go down.'

'How committed do you think they are?'

'I'd say about a hundred per cent, especially Mureau. I really don't think he counted on me doing what I did. I think he truly believed that he could take you from me, fit you up the way he did by planting the heroin, then spring you from jail so that you'd be on the run too, and in order to save my own skin I would do nothing about it. But the hell was I just going to stand by and watch you ruin your life. I knew he wouldn't have given you the whole picture and I knew you well enough to be certain you'd never go along with it if you did know. All that baffled me then was why you went at all, but of course we have rotten timing to thank for that. Well, rotten timing and Marielle, who's been doing her damnedest to get rid of you ever since you arrived and managed it in a way none of us could have foreseen, least of all her.'

He gave a wry smile. 'Beware of fools, eh? She was always playing out of her league, but she's arrogant enough and stupid enough to think otherwise. Stirling used her to try to get information on me that didn't exist – at least, not where the magazine was concerned, and that was all she had access to. But of course she was the one who told him you were seeing Mureau and in turn he told me. And I blew it! He knew instantly the way I felt about you then, and of course he told Gabriella in the hope she'd start composing her little eulogy of my sins. Which, I don't doubt, she is reciting right now.'

To Penny's amazement he suddenly started to grin, and for the first time that morning she saw the old, familiar humour dance in his eyes. 'What?' she said. 'What is it?'

He laughed. 'There's a twist to the tale that Gabriella knows nothing about, though whether it's going to do me any good has yet to be seen. But old Stirling, the guy I managed to get locked up by his own people, the guy who's vowed to see me rotting in jail – or, preferably, hell – for all eternity, has developed a bit of an attachment to me. I'm serious,' he said, when Penny's eyes widened with incredulity. 'We've spent the past week together, liquidating my assets, so to speak, and flying God only knows how many millions back to the US tax authorities, and during that time I told him the whole story. He's seeing things a bit differently now and, though there's no getting away from the fact that I have committed crimes, he's not going to push it. Of course, he's got no sway with Gabriella and Mureau, and he knows that between them they can stitch me up good and proper, but he's prepared to put in a word with the DA.'

'What does that mean? That you might not have to go to jail?'

'At best that's what it means, but I don't want to hold out too much hope on that score. Like I said, I am guilty of certain offences; it's just dependent on how far Gabriella will go – whether she perjures herself or makes a clean breast of how she got me involved. Not that it will excuse me, but there might be a case for extenuating circumstances. Anyway, it's her evidence that will count, more so than Mureau's.'

To Penny it seemed totally self-deluding to believe that Gabriella might suddenly find the compassion to see that she'd made him pay enough, but it was a delusion she was prepared to hang on to if only for the time being. 'So what happens next?' she asked, pulling him towards her.

'We wait for the phone call,' he said, propping his head on his hand in front of her and running his other hand over the 'V' of her crossed calves.

'From whom?' she said.

'Stirling. He knows where we are. I called him yesterday while you were still asleep to let him know. He's given me his word he won't send in the marines, not yet anyway. Seems he's a bit of a romantic at heart, but he does a pretty good job of hiding it. Anyway, he reckons he can trust me, which he can, and that I'll get myself back there just as soon as things start really hotting up.'

'That's quite a risk he's running, considering what a fool you've made of him in the past.'

'He said much the same thing himself, but in his own, uniquely eloquent way. And would you like to hear what else he said? He said he's counting on you to get me back there, because you he definitely trusts. Strange guy, huh, when you just ran off with a known criminal the way you did.'

Penny's eyes narrowed, making him grin, but as he began to massage her calf she lost her train of thought for a moment. 'So who'd have thought it?' she said. 'Wyatt Earp does an about-turn . . . By the way, did he ever tell you what he was doing in my bedroom? It was him, wasn't it?'

'Yeah, it was him. My guess is he was hoping to trap Mureau and when he found you were alone he decided to avail himself of the opportunity for a little chat about me, or Mureau – whichever one of us took your fancy that night.'

'Very droll,' she commented drily. 'Anyway, what about the Delaneys? What's going to happen to them now?'

He shrugged. 'If they're lucky, they'll get to stay right where they are. If not, they could find themselves up on charges of their own.'

Penny was frowning thoughtfully.

'What is it?' he said.

'Nothing particularly important,' she answered. 'I was just wondering about the night of the launch. Christian was planning on coming, so was it you who talked him out of it?'

He nodded. 'Wally told me earlier in the day and I know Mureau well enough to know what a kick he'd have got out of doing something like that. So, as you say, I talked him out of it.'

Penny was shaking her head. 'They're a pretty adept pair of liars, both Christian and Esther Delaney,' she remarked. 'Christian, well, that doesn't surprise me, but Esther . . . I must be losing my touch, because I'd have thought I'd have easily been able to see through someone like her. And to think that, all this time, she's managed to throw me off the track the way she has and keep it hidden from me that she knows you.'

490

'Oh, she's a shrewd little cookie when she wants to be,' he said. 'And if there was ever one explicit instruction I gave were she ever to meet you – I didn't know then that you were going to move in right next door to the woman – it was that she never let you know anything about my involvement with either of them or with Mureau. I guess she never did, but the shame of it now is that I didn't see her more often, which was what she wanted. The trouble was, I couldn't take the way she fussed around me, mothering me and driving me up the wall with her efforts to get "her boys", as she referred to Christian and me, to see eye to eye. Anyway, she's not someone I want to discuss right now. The person I want to discuss is you. You seem to have taken all this pretty calmly considering there's every chance that our time together's going to be somewhat limited. You do love me, don't you? I mean, you will miss me if I go?'

Knowing he was teasing her, Penny raised her eyebrows. 'Yes, I love you,' she said. 'But I'm not going to think about how much I'll miss you if you go until it happens. And the irony of having imagined myself in love with one man who was wanted by the law only to discover that the man I really love is also wanted by the law, has not escaped me. I don't know what I did to deserve this. Maybe my life was just running too smoothly before and the Divine Powers That Be decided it was time to bump me around a bit. But the fact that they gave me you at the same time is enough to make sure I can weather it. I love you, I'm going to be there for you no matter what, and to go to pieces now, which is in fact what I feel like doing, isn't going to get either of us anywhere. So what I shall do, as soon as we get back to France, is make damned sure that magazine continues to work for you, for your sons and . . .'

'For us?' he whispered.

'Yes, for us,' she smiled. 'But until we do go back I don't see any reason why we shouldn't at least try to

491

make the most of what we have here.'

His eyes were imbued with irony. 'I love you,' he said.

Looking down at him, she started to smile again, but her lips faltered as his hand moved in under the hem of her dress. Then, bringing his eyes back to hers, in a voice that wasn't quite steady he said, 'I want to make love to you.'

Desire instantly masked the laughter in her eyes and sliding down the bed to lie next to him she rolled into his embrace, pressing her body into his. They kissed for a long, sensuous time, allowing the needs of their bodies to flow unattended as they held each other tightly. Feeling his hardness straining between them, she lowered her arm, opened his shorts and took him in her hand. As he groaned into her open mouth she opened her eyes and watched his face tense, his long lashes fluttering as his desire mounted.

Then his eyes opened too and, gazing far into hers, he rolled on to her, pressing his hips hard into hers before moving down her body with his mouth, unbuttoning her dress as he went. When she was naked he silently took off his own clothes, then lay over her again, enclosing her body with his. It was a long time before he entered her as they lay there kissing and looking into each other's eyes and feeling the need of each other's bodies pulling them closer and closer together.

After they had made love he rolled on to his back beside her and lay quietly holding her hand until the quickening of their breath began to quiet and they could hear the soothing rhythm of the waves and the gentle swish of palm fronds. The honeyed scent of sea-grapes wafted in through the open windows, sweetening the air. His hand tightened on hers as at last he turned to look at her; then he pulled her tightly into his arms and held her as the tears ran from her eyes.

'It's OK,' he whispered, kissing her hair. 'Come on now, it's going to be all right.'

'I'm sorry,' she said in a strangled voice. 'It's just that I love you so much and it seems so . . . Oh God, I'm sorry. I promised myself I'd be strong for you, and look at me. I'll have myself together in a minute. It's just that . . .' Sniffing, she lifted her head to look at him. 'Oh God, David, I don't want you to go. I don't think I'll be able to bear it.'

'Yes, you will,' he told her. 'Besides, it might not come to that.'

Shaking her head and looking deep into his eyes, she said, 'I can feel it, David. There's no point trying to hide it from me, because I know what you're thinking.'

'You do?' He smiled.

'You think the worst is going to happen, don't you?' she said.

Sighing, he pulled her back into his arms. 'We're going to have to face it, my darling, that there's every chance it will.'

Chapter 25

The next three days were days that Penny would remember for the rest of her life. The island was an idyllic retreat from the world, its wild beauty, unspoilt by tourism and consisting of no more than the scattered *casitas*, which made up the one luxurious hotel, and a small airstrip. Though they occasionally saw the other guests now, no communication was forced upon them and they sought none. Exclusivity and privacy were paramount in this Utopian world that sat like a precious emerald in a shimmering bed of aquamarine. Once or twice they dined in the restaurant overlooking the moonlit pool while the gentle sounds of Filipino love songs drifted hauntingly over the terrace. But on the whole they took their meals in their *casita*, feeding each other and teasing each other in a way they would want no one to witness.

It took no more than an hour to stroll around the island, which they did once or twice, stopping to splash about in the waves and roll laughing in the sand. They swam and snorkelled, captivated by the spectacular beauty of the coral reefs as they watched the brightly coloured fish darting through the crystalline water. Penny made her first attempt at water-skiing, with a diver from the hotel driving the boat so that David could be in the water with her. She was hopeless and made him laugh so much with the way her legs kept splaying, or the way she was suddenly yanked forward and dragged like a piece of jetsam through the water, that she pretended to drown just to shut him up. By the end of the day, though, she was cutting a path through the waves, perhaps not as expertly as he, but certainly more exultantly.

They borrowed music from the hotel library and played it on the CD in their room while lying quietly in each other's arms on the hammock outside as they listened to Bach or Sinatra or Mendeiros, Penny's favourite. Sometimes they danced on the veranda, holding each other close as the sun melted like gold on the horizon and the shadows stole silently over them, as though to enclose them in their love.

On what turned out to be their last evening there they took a speedboat from the hotel and David drove them over to the neighbouring island of Manamoc, where Madeleine, the young girl who took care of their *casita*, lived with her family. She'd invited them because Penny, unlike most of the other guests she served, had shown an interest in her. All the locals turned out for the small feast of freshly caught *garoupa*, fried plantain and succulent mangoes. They sat beneath the stars, Penny between David's legs, watching the fishermen roast the fish while the women sang and passed around hand-thrown plates laden with food. They encouraged David and Penny to join in with the songs, but though they tried David was so woefully out of tune that even the locals couldn't stop themselves giggling when Penny finally lost the struggle to keep a straight face. In the end a young boy stood up and began to sing in a voice that was sweeter than the coconuts and as melodious as the waves lapping the shore. It was so moving that Penny wasn't the only one with tears on her cheeks when he had finished, even though she hadn't understood the words. With a tightness of emotion in his own throat David wrapped her in his arms and the islanders smiled at them while nodding knowingly and happily to each other.

'You know what Pamalican mean?' Madeleine asked them as they were leaving. 'Pamalican, the name of island where you stay?'

'No,' Penny said. 'What does it mean?'

'It mean the people keep returning to the island. So it mean you will come back.'

'I hope so,' Penny said, looking up at David.

'We will,' he said softly.

The call from Stirling came at eleven the next morning. Penny was out, at the other end of the island, fixing a surprise for David. As much as she dreaded it herself, she knew how badly he wanted to dive, but he wouldn't go without her. So she'd decided to pluck up the courage and was making the arrangements for that afternoon. But when she got back, one look at David's face was enough to tell her that they wouldn't be going.

Holding back the terrible onslaught of nerves she walked over to him and they held each other tightly, as though taking strength from each other.

'What did he say?' she whispered.

'Just that it's time to go home.'

'To France?'

He nodded and Penny felt herself turn weak with relief. At least it wasn't the States; not yet anyway.

'Did he give you any idea what to expect?'

'Not really. All he said was that my lawyers are flying over from the States in a couple of days.'

'So you don't know what kind of evidence she's given yet?'

'No, not yet.'

They arrived back in Nice in the middle of a chilly, wet, yet brilliantly sunny, morning to be met by Pierre and Ruth, an ex-*Starke* editor Sylvia had sent down to keep an eye on things until Penny returned.

To Pierre's surprise, as they came through to the arrivals hall, both dressed in dreadful pink, yellow and green anoraks they must have picked up before boarding the plane in Manila, they were arguing. It seemed that Penny, having spoken to Ruth on the telephone while they were waiting for their connecting flight from Paris, had decided she was going to New York in four days' time.

'But there's no need for you to go,' David was protesting. 'You can send someone else. You've been through a hell of an ordeal, for God's sake . . .'

'But I'm OK now,' she retorted, taking his hand as they followed Pierre and Ruth out through the revolving doors. 'And there are a lot of things I need to do in New York that are all important for the future of *Nuance*, as well as the interview with Luke Pleasance, which was set up before I went. So, I'm going.'

'Ruth, speak to her,' David pleaded in exasperation. 'Tell her, you've got everything in hand here, Marielle can do the interview and she should take some time to recuperate before she—'

'Don't get involved, Ruth,' Penny interrupted, winking at the older woman as they walked across the road to the car park. Then, stopping between two giant tubs of cacti, she slid her hands inside his coat and gazed plaintively up into his eyes. 'Humour me,' she whispered. 'Please.'

'But, sweetheart . . .'

'No, no buts. You're leaving again tomorrow and I—'

'Only for Marseille. I'll be back tomorrow night, Sunday morning at the latest.'

'Then you can come to New York with me,' she said.

Sighing, he dropped his forehead on to hers. He wasn't sure yet why his lawyers were flying into Marseille rather than Nice, though Stirling had said it was something to do with all the flights into Nice being booked up. 'OK,' he said. 'But we're going straight home now. I

497

want you to get some rest, because as lovely as you are with your tan you look just about all in.'

'Kiss me,' she said, holding her mouth up to his.

Pulling her closer, as though to shield her from the cold, he put his lips softly over hers.

'And you will come to New York?' she said.

He nodded, catching himself before saying, 'If I can.'

'I've sent someone over to the villa to put the heating on,' Ruth told them as they got into the back of Pierre's car. 'I'll courier over the flat plans and all the other things you asked for when I get back to the office. I didn't want to send them when there was no one there to receive them.'

As David turned to glare at her Penny grinned and glared back. 'It's OK, I won't do anything today,' she assured him. 'I'll do it tomorrow when you've gone.' In truth she knew she wouldn't be able to do it today, for apart from the terrible nerves she was already suffering about his meeting with the lawyers the next day, which would prevent any kind of concentration, she could already feel the debilitating effects of jet lag starting to claim her.

As they sped along the autoroute towards Cannes she laid her head on his shoulder and closed her eyes. It was hard to believe that little more than two weeks had passed since she'd gone. So much had happened in that time it felt more like a year. Christmas was now less than a month away and she prayed silently and desperately that they would be able to spend it together. Inside she was so pent up with fear that the effort of trying to keep herself together was exhausting her. But she had to go to New York, she had to make herself go on – for his sake as well as her own. Pressing herself in closer to him, she put an arm around his waist and turned her face into his neck. She felt his hand come up to stroke her hair, and as he and Pierre talked about *Nuance* the mellifluous sound of his voice lulled her into a state of semiconsciousness.

He woke her when they got to the villa and when she saw it her eyes shone with tears of relief and happiness. After Ruth and Pierre had gone, they strolled on to the terrace and gazed out at the wonderful blue of the Mediterranean and the glistening, snow-capped peaks of the Alps. Penny's heart swelled. There really was no more beautiful sight in the world. The air was crisp, spiked through with sunlight and frost, and as she looked up at the clustered red roofs of the village above them she felt her heart catch when she saw the sparkle of Christmas lights framing the church tower. Crossing her fingers, she said a silent prayer that they would be together; then, feeling his eyes on her, she turned back, to find him smiling.

'Welcome home,' he whispered; then, laughing, he pulled her into his arms.

'How about,' he said when they turned back into the kitchen, 'we take a nice long bath, then get ourselves into bed?'

'Sounds like a good idea to me,' she answered, looking around at the familiar pots and copper pans hanging on the nobbly stone walls. Smiling, she recalled the time they had eaten pizza at the table beneath the hanging herb rack, but when she turned to him to remind him her heart contracted at the look of devastation in his eyes.

'David?' she said. 'David, what is it? There's something you're not telling me, isn't there? Stirling said something when you called him from Paris . . . David, please, you've got to—'

'Hey,' he laughed, cupping her face in his hand. 'There's nothing. I told you what he told me – just that I have to go to Marseille tomorrow.'

'Then why were you looking like that?'

'Because,' he smiled, 'I'm so god-damned afraid of losing you.'

Still looking suspiciously into his eyes, she started slowly to shake her head. 'You won't ever do that,' she told him. 'I swear, no matter what happens, you'll never do that.'

When they woke up the following morning they made love sleepily, eyes closed, bodies entwined as the dreamy, unhurried magic of a shared orgasm floated between them. A while later he kissed her briefly on the nose, then got up from the bed. She looked up at him and they both smiled in an effort to disguise their nerves.

While he showered she lay where she was, staring out at the pale oppressiveness of the sky and feeling, irrationally, that if she didn't move then maybe the day wouldn't have to begin.

'Would you like some breakfast before you leave?' she said when he came back into the room, a towel draped around his waist as he rubbed his hair with another. It was the first time he had shown any modesty in front of her and just this small display of it twisted her heart with unease.

'That'd be nice,' he answered.

Finding her robe she went downstairs to the kitchen. It was cold and everything was so still, so encased in silence, that it was as though any sound at all might cause the very air to splinter like glass. She searched the cupboards but there was no milk, no bread, not even any coffee. Then, having found a packet of jasmine tea, she put the kettle on to boil. As she poured the water into the pot she heard him come in behind her. Taking a breath, she turned to face him, and when she saw him the breath was expelled on a current of laughter.

'You look terrible,' she told him. 'Don't you have any other clothes here?'

He shook his head forlornly.

'Then take them off and I'll press them for you,' she said.

'It's OK, I can do it,' he said with a laugh, unbuttoning the wrinkled shirt that Pierre had brought over from his

500

apartment the day before.

'I'll do it,' she said.

Grinning, he tossed it to her. 'You could be starting something for yourself here,' he warned.

'Don't count on it,' she responded archly, going into the laundry room to set up the iron.

She wanted to scream, to cry out in fury at the sheer madness of what they were facing. The not knowing was unbearable, but to know, to find out what was going to happen, maybe that would be even worse. She looked down at the stark whiteness of his shirt and as she smoothed the hot iron over the front it was as though she was spreading the heat of foreboding in her heart. Hearing him coming towards her, she looked up and, as he lifted a hand to sweep the hair from her face, she flinched.

'Hey,' he said, half frowning, half laughing. 'What is this? Did you think I was going to hit you?'

She smiled; then, handing him his shirt, she planted a kiss on his mouth.

'That's better,' he murmured, holding her chin in his hand and pulling her back to him.

As he kissed her again she could feel herself starting to shake, but, forcing a laugh, she said, 'I'm sorry there's no breakfast. Just tea.'

'Tea's fine,' he told her, laying his trousers on the ironing board and putting both arms around her. 'It's going to be all right,' he said gently. 'I promise you.'

Holding back what she really wanted to say, she forced another smile and nodded. 'I know,' she said. 'But I'll be glad when today's over.'

'That makes two of us,' he grimaced. Then, taking a deep breath, he turned back to the kitchen. 'So where's this tea?' he said in a poor attempt at enthusiasm.

The sound of the buzzer announcing Pierre's arrival at the gates came too soon for them both. They were sitting facing each other across the table and as he got up to go and get his coat Penny dropped her head in her hands, twisting her fingers brutally through her hair in a vain attempt to stop herself crying. Hearing him coming back down the stairs, she quickly wiped away the tears and lifted her head.

'Oh God, David!' she laughed and sobbed as he stood there in his pink, yellow and green anorak. 'You can't wear that.'

'I can't?' he said, looking down at it in surprise. Then, bringing his eyes back to hers, he gave her such a roguish grin that she just broke down and cried.

'That bad, huh?' he said, making her laugh. 'I guess I'd better take it off, then.'

She walked with him to the door, then, turning in his arms, looked up into his eyes.

'I'll call you later,' he said softly, touching his lips lightly to hers.

She nodded; then, letting him go, she stood back as he opened the door. Pierre was waiting in the Saab. David got into the driver's seat, circled the car round and drove off towards the gates. When he got there he hooted the horn and Penny, realizing he must have forgotten the remote control, leaned back inside the front door to push the release button.

As his car disappeared from view tears were spilling from her eyes. It was as though her whole body was straining to run after him. She didn't want to voice it, she didn't even want to think it, but she had a horrible, terrible premonition that this was the last time she would ever see him.

Closing the door she sat down on the bottom stair and burying her face in her knees she sobbed as though her heart would break. Panic was welling up inside her, as though to drown her in the terrible truth that he wouldn't be coming back. She tried to calm herself with reminders of how she was always plagued by morbid thoughts and paranoia after a long flight, but it didn't work. She just couldn't get it out of her mind that this was all they were going to have together, that the kiss he had just given her would be the last.

Dizziness and fatigue coasted sluggishly through her as she pulled herself to her feet. She knew she should go back to bed, but she just couldn't face it. So she stood where she was, her whole body racked with sobs as she stared down at the ridiculous anorak he had left on the stairs.

At last, in the faint hope of distracting herself, she walked into the kitchen. She saw the two empty cups on the table and the open door of the laundry room and, covering her face with her hands, she sank to her knees and wept uncontrollably. How was she ever going to keep things going without David when the mere thought of him not being there was making her fall apart like this?

Then suddenly she tensed and, lifting her head, she turned to look at the front door. Someone was calling her name.

'David?' she whispered hoarsely. She leapt to her feet, ran to the door and tore it open.

'David!' she cried.

'You weren't expecting anyone else, were you?' he said drolly. Then his eyes softened with concern as he saw her distress.

'I'm sorry,' she said, dashing a hand across her cheeks. 'I know I'm being foolish, but I suppose everything's just catching up with me.' She looked past him to the fore-court. 'Where's your car?'

'At the gates. I came back to bring you this,' he said, pulling a greasy paper bag from behind his back.

'Oh God, I think I'm going to cry again,' she choked when she saw the croissant. 'How did you get in?'

'I climbed the gates,' he told her, lifting her face up to his. 'Now, are you going to open them for me so I can get out again?'

She shook her head. 'I want to watch you climb.'

He laughed. 'Out of luck,' he said, reaching behind her to press the button. 'Now, you go get yourself some sleep and I'll call you later. OK?'

When he'd gone, Penny carried the croissant into the kitchen and sat down. What an idiot she had made of herself! To think she was never going to see him again and in a matter of minutes he had already come back.

At the other end of the drive, as he got back into his car, David looked at Pierre. 'She hadn't had any breakfast,' he said. 'I couldn't leave her without any breakfast.'

Pierre smiled weakly. 'She'll survive, David,' he said. 'It's time to start thinking about yourself now.'

'I know,' he said bleakly, staring down at the wheel. He sighed, then put the key back in the ignition and started up the engine.

Two and a half hours later they arrived at the Sophitel just outside Marseille airport. After giving their names at the front desk they took the lift to the second floor and walked down the long, featureless corridor to the conference room they had been allocated. The door was already ajar.

Pushing it open David walked in, Pierre right behind him. Sitting around the table were Stirling, three dark-suited lawyers, who had flown in the night before, and, as he'd known she would be, Gabriella.

Gabriella's obsidian black eyes were glittering with triumph as she watched her husband sit down on the edge of the bed. They were alone in her room, having just left the meeting that had gone on all day, the meeting that had so ruthlessly hammered home to David the impossibility of his situation. But it wasn't over yet, they still had a long way to go, and with all the trump cards in her hand Gabriella knew she couldn't fail to get what she wanted. She knew, too, precisely how she was going to play each card.

David's exhaustion showed in the paleness of his face and the deepening lines around his eyes. He sat with his head in his hands, staring down at the floor. He had never felt so impotent in his life.

'Would you like some food?' Gabriella offered, curling her long legs under her as she leaned back against the pillows. Her raven hair fell in an exquisite sweep over the side of her face; her full, red mouth shimmered in the glow of the bedside lamp.

David shook his head, then, getting up from the bed, he slid his hands into his pockets and went to gaze out at the night. He wondered what Penny was doing now and felt his heart sink. She'd be worrying about him, of course, and the fact that he hadn't called.

Gabriella waited, watching him, her eyes branded with malice and with a pain that had long ago been poisoned by the bitterness that now consumed her. 'Would you like me to spell it out for you?' she said sweetly.

'No,' he answered.

But she did anyway, using words and a tone that lacked any kind of finesse or sensitivity. 'Your pathetic little romance with Penny Moon is finished,' she said. 'There'll be no more jetting off across the world playing the big hero, no more shacking up in desert-island hotels or Riviera villas. She's history for you, David. You make a single attempt to contact her again, you've got my word on it: all deals are off. Do you hear what I'm saying? You want my help, then you do things my way. And that goes for Pierre too, so you can forget any ideas you might have of getting him to contact her for you, because, you'd better believe me when I tell you, I have ways of finding out that you haven't even dreamt of. And if I find out that either of you has as much as picked up a phone you can kiss goodbye to your freedom – and your children.' She smiled as he flinched; then she continued. 'Oh, Penny Moon can carry on with that pitiful little magazine you've got going over there in Cannes, we'll need someone to run it for us, but the minute I say she's out, she's out! Have you got that?'

When he didn't answer she went on, savouring every moment of the power she had over him. 'I've waited a long time for this, David,' she said, 'but it's been worth all the agony I've put myself through just to see you suffering the way you made me suffer, you bastard.' Her voice was now thick with hatred and spite; her dark eyes were flashing with the corroding fire of resentment she had raging inside her.

'You never were able to keep that dick of yours under control, were you?' she sneered. 'You had them all, didn't you, David? You screwed the whole god-damned lot of 'em – my friends, my enemies, anybody's wife, girlfriend, mother, daughter – you just didn't know when to stop. You never cared about me or the way you were humiliating me; all you ever cared about was yourself and which of the whores you could stick it into next. Well, you're paying for it now and, let me tell you, you'll be taking a vow of fucking celibacy by the time I've finished with you should you ever even speak to Penny Moon again. So, get it into your head now, David, your screwing days are over. You've had your fun. Now it's my turn. But just so you don't think I'm completely without feeling, let me tell you this: I intend to be there for you. I'm going to see you through this and if you keep your freedom I'll take you back into the bosom of your family. You see, I still want you, David. You've still got me panting for you even after all this time. I'd lie right here and let you screw me now if that was what you wanted, but you don't, do you? Well, maybe you'd like to reconsider that, because I'm getting horny just thinking about what all this is doing to you.'

At last David turned to look at her. 'Tell me about the boys,' he said quietly. 'How are they? Has Jack started his new school?'

'You want to know about the boys,' she said, sneeringly, 'you'd better ask nicely. So why don't you come over here and sit down?'

'Gabriella, you're demeaning us both doing this,' he said, staying where he was.

'Hah!' she cried, tossing her head back. 'You think I care about demeaning you after what you did to me?'

Frowning, he closed his eyes and pushed his fingers into the sockets. 'You've got to stop doing this, Gabriella,' he said wearily. 'Can't you see, it's hurting you every bit as much as it's hurting me.'

'All I can see,' she said, savouring the malice, 'is a man on his way to jail unless he gets himself over here right now.'

He waited, watching her, as she began slowly peeling off her clothes. She was still a stunningly beautiful woman with a body that could tempt a saint from chastity.

When she was naked she lay back on the bed and, spreading her legs, looked up at him. 'You want me, David, don't you?' she said thickly. Then, laughing, she cupped her breasts in her hands. 'You can pretend all you like,' she said, 'but I know you, David. You can't resist me. Even after all I've put you through, you still can't resist me. So why don't you just forget about Penny Moon? Come over here and remind yourself what it's like to make love with a real woman.'

Slowly he walked over to the bed, the urge in his groin pushing him on. Then, putting a hand either side of her, he lowered his face to hers until they were only inches apart. 'I'd rather go to jail,' he hissed; and, snatching up his jacket, he walked out of the room.

Early on Tuesday morning Ruth Elliot, one-time editor of *Starke* magazine and temporary editor of *Nuance*, arrived at the villa to take Penny to the airport. It was just getting light and a low-lying mist hung over the gardens as she pulled up in front of the house. The door was open and Penny's bags were already on the steps outside, so Ruth got out of the car and went to open the boot. She could hear voices coming from inside the house, then Penny came out and checked the luggage to make sure she had everything.

'Last-minute instructions for the cleaner,' she said as Ruth came to pick up her bags.

She lifted her head and smiled and Ruth felt a quiet shock pass through her. Though they had spoken frequently on the telephone these past few days, this was the first time she had seen Penny since she'd arrived back on Friday and she felt as though she were looking at another woman. Penny's tan had all but disappeared, leaving her skin pale and ravaged with exhaustion. Her sunny, blue eyes were dull and red-rimmed, though whether with tiredness or from crying it was impossible to say.

Ruth wasn't a woman given to prying, nor to handing out advice when it hadn't been sought, but in this instance the words were out of her mouth before she could stop them. 'Penny, are you sure you're up to this?' she said, her grey eyes looking worriedly into Penny's face. 'I'm sure we can find someone else to go . . .'

'No, I'm fine,' Penny assured her, looking at her watch. 'Do we have time to stop by the office to pick up a lap-top? I meant to ask you to bring—'

'It's in the car,' Ruth told her. 'But really, Penny . . .'

'I'm OK,' Penny said firmly and started towards the car.

As she got into the passenger seat Ruth put the bags in the boot, then slipped into the driver's seat and fastened her belt. She hadn't even turned the car round before Penny launched into a barrage of questions concerning *Nuance*. Ruth answered them all, never once mentioning the fact that they had discussed all this, at length, over the weekend.

By the time they reached the autoroute Penny had

fallen silent and was staring out of the window at the early-morning traffic. Every now and again Ruth glanced over at her, wondering if she should give in to the common sense that was telling her to come off at the next exit and take Penny back home whether she liked it or not. She was in no doubt that were David there he would tell her to do just that. But David wasn't there, which was of course what was causing the problem.

Ruth had no idea where he was, though she did know something of what had gone on, for Sylvia had filled her in before she'd come down here. She wished there was something she could say to Penny to help ease her suffering, but she sensed that even if she could find the words Penny wouldn't welcome the intrusion.

'So how are you getting along with Marielle?' Penny suddenly asked.

Ruth grimaced. 'She's a bit of a handful, isn't she?' she answered.

Penny laughed. 'Just a bit. How did she take it when you told her I was going to New York instead of her?' she asked.

'Actually, better than I expected. She seems to have mellowed a bit since you got back.'

'I wonder why!' Penny remarked drily, thinking that she would leave it until after Christmas to fire Marielle, since it wouldn't be a particularly charitable thing to do during the season of goodwill. The thought of Christmas caused her heart to contract and, retreating into silence again, she turned back to the window.

At last they arrived at Nice airport, but, when they pulled up outside the terminal building, though she turned off the engine Ruth made no attempt to get out.

Penny sat quietly gazing down at her lap. She was dreading this trip and would have given almost anything not to go, but, she kept reminding herself fiercely, life had to go on.

'David wouldn't want you to do this, you know?' Ruth

said gently.

'But it's not up to David, is it?' Penny answered, lifting her heavy eyes to look straight ahead.

Dropping her head for a moment, Ruth wondered if she should push it any further. In the end she said, 'I don't understand why you have this compulsion to go. It can wait, Penny. We can always find another interview to substitute—'

'It's all set up with Luke Pleasance now,' Penny cut in. 'And I've a lot of other people to see while I'm there.'

After a moment Ruth tentatively put out a hand and laid it over Penny's. 'I'm not going to ask what happened this weekend,' she said, 'but I do think you should speak to Sylvia before you go.'

Penny's heart twisted as she turned to look at her. 'Why? Has she spoken to David? Does she know where he is?' she asked desperately.

Ruth shook her head. 'No. At least, not as of last night.'

Penny's eyes moved blindly to their joined hands; then, attempting to smile, she said, 'He'll call when he can and in the meantime I have to keep things going here. I promised him I would . . .' Her voice failed her for a moment; then, forcing her smile wider, she said, 'He'll probably call the office when he finds I'm not at home. You've got my number in New York, haven't you?'

Ruth took a breath and, nodding, she said, 'Yes, I've got it.'

At last Penny brought her eyes to Ruth's and Ruth felt her heart falter as she saw the bewilderment and pain Penny was trying so hard to control. 'I know you think I'm crazy for going,' she said, 'but, believe me, I really will go insane if I sit around here waiting to find out what's happening.' She blinked rapidly as tears welled in her eyes. 'I don't even know if he's still in France,' she said, brokenly. 'For all I know he could—' She stopped; then, with a sudden flash of impatience, she made herself go on. 'I know I look as bad as I feel, but it's only lack of sleep. I'm fine really and I'll be a whole lot better once I get on that plane. I won't be able to stare at a telephone then or wake up terrified that I haven't heard it ring. And he'll call me when I'm in New York, I know he will.'

'But what if . . . What if he's calling to say he has to go back to Miami? Don't you want to be here to say . . . well, to see him before he goes?'

Penny shook her head. 'If he calls to say he's going back to Miami,' she said, 'he'll be going straight away. He won't come back here first. So I might just as well hear it in New York, where at least I'll be doing something positive for *Nuance*'s future. And if he's calling to say it's all OK, that the miracle has happened, then he'll fly out and join me.'

Ruth smiled, as though to inject some warmth into the brave yet distant hope in Penny's voice. 'Well, if you need to talk, I'm always at the end of the phone,' she said. 'And if I hear anything, anything at all, I'll call you straight away.'

'Thanks,' Penny smiled, 'I'd appreciate that.' But in her heart she knew that David would call her himself, that he wouldn't just go without saying a word, not when they meant as much to each other as they did.

Chapter 26

New York was ablaze with all its legendary Christmas magic. Santas of all descriptions and ethnic origins peppered the busy sidewalks, ringing their bells and booming out Christmas cheer, while sleet settled in tiny, glistening stars on their fluffy beards. Every store front, every office block and every hotel was a glittering mass of coloured lights and gaily wrapped parcels. Giant Christmas trees, laden with bright silvery balls and glossy fake snow, stood resplendent in their glory in every public place. The wintry night sky was speckled with icy raindrops which fell in the bitter wind over the teeming, noisy, steam-filled streets.

Penny had spent a long time in Bloomingdales, hovering around a strange, Red-Indian artefact that for no accountable reason she thought David might like. It was the third time she'd been back to look at it, each time certain she would buy it. But once again she had come away empty-handed, afraid that if she parted with her $300 before he called it would be tempting fate too far and she'd end up with it for ever.

She was nearing the end of her trip now. The interview with Luke Pleasance was on tape, the other meetings she'd arranged had all taken place and the new contacts she'd hoped to make had been made. The trip had been a success, but the toll it had taken on her was enormous.

Now, as she tried to flag a yellow cab to take her back

to the hotel, she felt so ill, so debilitatingly weary and weighted by fear, that the lively seasonal cheer seemed like a cruel mockery of her pain.

The wind was slicing into her skin, her cheeks were icy cold, her hands and feet were numb. She'd only been standing there a few minutes, but already she was chilled through to her bones. The winking neon lights blurred in front of her eyes, the roar of traffic crescendoed in her ears and as the distant roofs of the tower blocks started to circle and swoop she thought she was going to pass out. A cab came round the corner. She tried to lift her hand but her arm was too heavy to move. Rain, mingled with tears, dripped from her nose and chin, ran down her neck and slithered in icy tendrils under her collar.

Dimly she was aware of an inner voice struggling to make her obey, telling her to pull herself together, if only to get her back to the hotel. She tried to react, to push her way through the enervating layers of nausea and lethargy, but it was as though her movements, together with the hustle and bustle, the noise, the weather, were all happening in an unsteady whirl of slow motion.

'Are you all right, ma'am?'

Penny turned her head and watched two Santas' faces merge into one. 'Yes,' she heard herself say, but the sound of her voice was muffled by the fuzz in her head.

'Here,' he smiled, holding a car door open for her.

Penny looked at it and blinked.

'You did want a cab, didn't you?' he asked.

'Thank you,' Penny said hoarsely. Then, as she started to climb in, it was as though a thick veil briefly parted and everything slipped back into focus. 'Merry Christmas,' she said to Santa, smiling back over her shoulder.

'To you too, ma'am,' he responded cheerily. 'Where are you going?'

Penny gave him the name of her hotel, which he

promptly relayed to the taxi driver; then he waved her on her way.

A few minutes later she was in her room, sitting on the floor with her back against the wall and crying as though she would never stop. There were no messages again and she just didn't have the energy to deal with it any more. She was exhausted to the point of collapse, yet her mind just kept on and on going round and round in circles, swirling and spinning, swooping and swooning, churning her stomach and blackening her thoughts. Never, even in the gloomiest, ugliest and most painful moments of her life, had she ever felt like this before. It was as though someone, or something else entirely, had taken over her body and was trying to push her out.

That David's silence should be affecting her as badly as this was terrifying her, for there were times when she felt so crushed by the panic that her breath wouldn't come. She knew it wasn't normal to feel this way, that no matter how much she loved him, however desperately she wanted him to call, it shouldn't be affecting her physically like this. But it was and all she wanted now was to go home.

The car came late the following afternoon to take her to Kennedy airport. Mercifully there were no delays and once she was on the plane her anxiety subsided and she slept throughout the flight back to France. She had felt the beginnings of flu stealing in for the past couple of days, but as she stepped off the plane into the clear, crisp sunshine of the Riviera it was as though a cloak of darkness was being lifted from her mind and, with it, the lead weights from her limbs. She was home now, back where she belonged, and with only two weeks to go until Christmas she had a lot to get on with.

She took a taxi to the office and was treated to the kind of welcome normally reserved for returning heroes. Ruth popped some champagne, but though Penny tried hard to join in with the spirit of things the champagne made her feel nauseous and the clamour reverberated through her head as if it was trying to break out of her skull. She didn't ask anyone about David or Pierre: the closed door of their office told her all she needed to know. Neither of them had returned. It was almost two weeks now – two weeks in which she had been to hell and back, wondering what was happening to him and where on earth he might be. She couldn't bring herself to believe that he had gone without calling, but neither could she think of a reason why he hadn't.

As the day wore on, though an occasional dizzy spell unsteadied her she felt fine again a few minutes later and, since she'd just got off a flight from New York, she naturally put the shakiness down to jet lag. Marielle was out interviewing and didn't come back all day and Ruth had things so well under control that in truth there wasn't much for Penny to do. But she stayed at her desk the entire day, working on her interview with Luke Pleasance and collating all the information she had collected from editors and journalists in New York. At six o'clock she picked up the phone to call Sylvia. She was greeted by a voice she didn't know and which announced that Sylvia wasn't expected back until after the New Year. She tried Sylvia's home, but all she got was a recorded message telling her that no one was in right now.

Feeling herself in danger of becoming paranoid, that everyone had gone missing and they were all keeping their whereabouts secret from her, she quickly packed up her desk and asked Ruth to drive her home. On the way she asked Ruth if she knew where Sylvia was, but Ruth hadn't spoken to Sylvia in over a week and had no idea where she might be.

'Do you want me to stop at a pharmacy and get something for that cold?' Ruth offered as they made the slow crawl along the Carnot towards Le Cannet.

'No, I've got things at home,' Penny answered, gazing

out at the spectacular displays of Christmas lights and wondering why she felt so out of touch with the world, as though she were just passing through and might at any moment, like the snow in the air, fade into the nothing.

'Then what about getting you some food?'

'No, I'll just go straight to bed and try to sleep off the jet lag.'

It was clear when they got to the villa that Ruth was loath to leave her alone, but Penny insisted that all she needed was to sleep and asked Ruth to excuse her for not inviting her in.

The house was as cold and dark and empty as she'd expected it to be. For some peculiar reason it felt so much bigger than before and as she walked into the sitting room she found herself wishing desperately that she might find Sammy there. But Sammy was in the Caribbean with Stefan, fully recovered from her ordeal at the hands of David's people, if the last time they'd spoken was anything to go by. The messages on the answerphone were the same ones she had replayed over the phone earlier in the day, with the exception of the last one, which must have come in while she was on her way home, and Penny smiled as she listened to Sammy's voice, thinking that they must have some kind of sisterly telepathy. The message was simply telling her that Sammy had missed the last post so was calling to wish her a Happy Christmas and would call again on Boxing Day when she got back from her cruise.

Suddenly desperate for someone to talk to, Penny sat down next to the phone and dialled David's apartment in Cannes. It was a stupid thing to do, of course, because even though she hadn't expected a reply the fact that there was none made her feel lonelier and more afraid than ever. She wished she knew where the fear was coming from, but it had no coherence, no roots in logic or shape she could understand. All she knew was that it was there, billowing through her mind like a cloud of black smoke and pushing her deeper and deeper into a void of irrational dread. The desire to be strong for David, to prove to him and to herself that she could handle this and keep things going, was the single bright flame in the darkness of her mind, but even that was beginning to flicker in the chill air of portent.

She stayed where she was, huddled into her coat and staring at the empty hearth as she shivered and shook and wave after wave of exhaustion bore down on her as though to grind her into nothing. There was a hissing sound in her ears like the lasting echo of the sea in a shell and her skin was red-hot and tender. She felt so disgustingly sorry for herself, yet it seemed so unfair that she should be ill at a time when she needed her strength more than ever.

Sighing, she dragged herself up from the chair and went in search of some Lemsip or aspirin or a hot-water bottle. Finding all three, she put on the kettle and sat down to wait for it to boil. Before it did she was back at the phone, dialling the Delaneys' number in the hope that they might be able to tell her what was going on. But as soon as the phone rang at the other end she pressed the connectors, cutting the call. If there was anything to hear, she didn't want to hear it from them. Then, dialling again, she called Mally, her rock-star friend, whom she hadn't spoken to in months. She didn't hold out much hope of Mally being there, but her need to speak to someone kept her hanging on the line. At last Mally answered, having dragged herself from the bath, and to Penny's relief she was in for the evening so had plenty of time to chat.

For a while Penny wasn't at all sure what they were talking about as her eyes swam in and out of focus and the sound of their voices ebbed and flowed like a symphony playing behind closed doors. She wasn't sure how long they'd been on the phone when she heard

Mally calling down the line, 'Pen? Pen? Are you still there?'

'Yes, I'm here,' Penny answered, feeling Mally's voice penetrate the gelatinous mist in her head.

'So tell me what's been happening to you,' Mally said. 'You sound terrible, by the way. Have you got the flu or something?'

'Yes, 'fraid so,' Penny heard herself say.

'Too bad. Anyway, come on, out with it, what's been happening over there? Any men on the scene?'

Penny gave a splutter of laughter. 'Mal, I wouldn't know where to start,' she said, aware she was too tired even to try.

But Mally wasn't so easily put off and bit by bit she managed to coax the story out of Penny, until in the end she was silent and Penny was the only one talking. By the time she'd finished Penny felt more exhausted than ever, but her eyes had remained dry and for some reason the fire on her skin had lessened.

'So there you have it,' she said finally. 'Bit of a mess, eh?'

Mally didn't answer straight away, but when she did Penny felt her heart churn at the concern in her voice. 'You sound dreadful,' she said. 'I've never heard you like this before and frankly, Pen, I'm really worried. Why don't you come back to England for a while? You know you can always stay here.'

Penny's throat was tight. 'No,' she said. 'But thanks anyway.'

'OK, then I'll be blunt. Do they have any hospitals for tropical diseases nearby, because after what you said about being in that lake I think you should go and get yourself checked out.'

Penny's eyes closed. It was as though Mally had reached into the core of her fear and plucked out the very thorn she was afraid to confront. 'I don't know,' she said lamely. 'I'll have to ask someone.'

'Well, there's sure to be one somewhere and I want you to promise me that you'll go and see someone – and soon. Like *tomorrow*.'

'OK, I promise,' Penny replied.

But the following morning when she got out of bed she felt much better. Still a little fluey maybe, and slightly nauseous, but certainly not so ill that she couldn't work. Or go out to shop for a Christmas tree and turkey roasting dish in the vain hope that David might come back. On Sunday afternoon she fell asleep on the floor beside the half-decorated tree, then woke up and staggered to the bathroom, where she tried – and failed – to throw up.

On Monday morning she called in sick and went to see a local doctor, who sent her off to the labs to get her blood tested. They took so much blood she wondered what on earth he could be testing her for, but not wanting to dwell on it she rolled down her sleeve and, ignoring the doctor's advice to go back to bed, she went into the office. She had made David a promise to keep things going and nothing, but nothing, was going to stand in the way of that.

On Tuesday morning, despite a violent bout of sneezing and a dash to the loo to throw up when she smelt her own perfume, she felt strong enough to go into the office again and was on the point of leaving when the buzzer at the gates sounded.

Remembering that David didn't have a remote control, she ran to the entryphone.

'Penny? It's Esther Delaney,' the voice at the other end said.

It was as though a band of steel suddenly closed around Penny's heart. Why was Esther here? Did she have any news of David? A part of her wanted to die rather than hear anything from her, yet another part was almost ready to beg.

'Could I come in, dear?' Esther asked.

Penny braced herself. She didn't find it easy to be rude to people, but right now Esther felt like a deserving case. 'Why?' she said, shortly.

'I think it would be better if I came in,' Esther said.

As she waited for Esther to come up the drive Penny could feel the shallowness of her breath and a strange kind of fragility about the air that made her almost afraid to move. She pulled the door open and watched the car approach. The last thing on her mind was the way she looked, until she saw the shock on Esther's face.

However, Esther didn't comment. Nor did she attempt to greet her the way they always used to, with a kiss on either cheek. She simply walked up the steps to the house and followed Penny through to the kitchen, looking considerably less preposterous than normal in a sombre black dress and low-heeled shoes. Then, sitting down at the table, she opened up her handbag and lit a cigarette while Penny put on some coffee.

'So?' Penny said, sitting down opposite her and fixing her with anxious yet hostile eyes.

Esther flushed and looked down at her hands. Then, taking a quick draw on her cigarette, she said, 'He's gone.' Her hand snaked through the air. 'Gone, never coming back.'

As the words bit into Penny's heart she felt the room starting to spin. 'What do you mean?' she said angrily. 'Why can't you talk properly? Who are we talking about?'

'Stirling went back on their deal,' Esther answered. 'He's been arrested . . .'

The blood was draining from Penny's face. 'What are you talking about?' she cried. 'I know Christian's been arrested!'

'Not Christian. David,' Esther said.

Penny's insides turned to water; her throat was like chalk. She stared at Esther's pallid face, watched the cigarette go between her lips and the smoke rush out of her nose.

Esther's fingers were trembling as she took another long pull on her cigarette, then ground it out in the ashtray. 'He loved you, dear,' she said shakily. 'I didn't realize it until it was too late, but he really loved you.'

Suddenly Penny snapped. 'Stop it!' she yelled. 'Stop telling me things you know nothing about and tell me what's happened.'

Esther seemed cowed by the outburst and her voice was frail as she said, 'I'm not terribly sure yet. Wally will be able to tell you better than I can.'

'Then where is he?' Penny cried.

'I'm afraid I don't know,' Esther answered pathetically. 'All I know is that after David left you the other Saturday—'

'What do you mean?' Penny demanded. 'What do you know about that? For God's sake . . .' She stopped and squeezed her eyes tightly closed. She had to get a grip on herself, she had to make herself deal with this. 'I'm sorry,' she said, forcing herself to breathe slowly. 'Go on. When David left . . .'

Esther was about to continue when the telephone suddenly shrilled into the room. Penny went to answer it, momentarily tempted to hit the button for the answerphone, but guessing it was someone from the office calling to find out if she was coming in, she picked it up.

'Penny? Wally Delaney here. Just called home. The cleaner told me Esther was with you.'

Penny turned to Esther. 'I'll pass you over,' she said coldly.

As Esther took the phone Penny sat down again. She could only hear one side of the conversation, but it didn't take much working out what they were saying.

'Yes, I'm very well, dear,' Esther said. 'How are things your end? How is he?' Her eyes turned to Penny and she smiled. 'Yes, she's here – she's just answered the phone to you, old thing.' Then, to Penny: 'Have you been here all weekend, dear?' Penny nodded. 'Yes, she's been here all weekend,' Esther said into the phone. 'I don't know,' she went on. 'Maybe something was up with the telephone. I don't *know*,' she repeated. Then she listened for a while, said goodbye and put the receiver down.

'David's going to call you in a few minutes,' she said.

Penny's insides folded as she suddenly felt she must be losing her mind. 'I thought you said he'd *gone*?' she cried. 'Jesus Christ, Esther, what are you doing?'

'I'm sorry,' Esther said lamely. 'I absolutely thought he was gone. I haven't heard from Wally since Friday. I didn't know what was happening so I assumed the worst.'

Penny looked at her, dumbfounded. That she could sit there and lie at a time like this, that she could jump to her own stupid conclusions and tell her that David was gone and never coming back, that he had been arrested . . . then that he was going to call in a few minutes . . . What was the matter with the woman? Why was she doing this?

The telephone rang and Penny looked at it, half afraid it was about to play her a trick. Then, picking it up from the table, she said, 'Hello?'

'Pen? It's me.'

'David?' she whispered, an overwhelming tide of relief and love flooding her heart.

'Sure, it's me,' he said. His voice was croaky, but she could hear the smile.

'Where are you?' she said. 'What's going on?'

'It's kind of hard to explain right now,' he answered, 'but I'm in London. Sylvia's been rushed to hospital for emergency surgery and they've let me come to see her before I go.'

Penny felt the the panic, the nausea, the dizziness, everything start to swirl through her in a blinding choas. 'Go where?' she said breathlessly.

He gave a dry laugh and she could hear the tears in his

522

voice. 'I have to surrender myself,' he told her. 'Esther will be able to explain some of it and as soon as I can I'll write you a long letter telling you everything that's happened.'

'Oh God,' Penny murmured under her breath. This couldn't be happening, it just couldn't. 'Esther said Stirling reneged. Is that true?'

'His hands were tied,' he answered. 'There was nothing he could do in the end.'

She took a breath and closed her eyes tightly. 'Why didn't you call?' she said. 'I was so worried.'

'I know and I'm sorry. It's just been difficult and things . . . Well, nothing's gone the way I thought it would. I tried calling you all weekend. Where were you?'

'I was here,' she answered. 'Something must have been wrong with the phone.'

There was a pause as they both felt the sheer desperateness of the situation.

'How long will you be gone?' she asked, steeling herself for the answer.

'I don't know for sure. Five years, maybe less.'

Five years! This was a nightmare. She'd wake up in a minute and he would be there, grinning at her, teasing her and telling her it was all a joke. 'Oh God, David . . .'

'I'm sorry, Pen,' he said. 'I didn't think it was going to happen like this.' He paused. 'I love you. You know that, don't you? I love you very much.'

'I love you too,' she whispered.

'Keep that bed warm for me?' he said.

'Of course,' she said brokenly.

'I'm sorry,' he said again, and she could tell he was having as hard a time keeping it together as she was.

The need to touch him, to see him, was burning an unbearable frustration deep into her heart. 'When are you leaving?' she asked, the idea of flying over to London rushing into her mind.

'In about an hour. I'm at a hotel outside the airport. I'll have to go soon.'

Penny swallowed hard. There was so much she wanted to say, but nothing was coming. 'Where are you going?' she said.

'Miami.' Then, in a voice fractured with emotion he said, 'I wish you were here right now so I could hold you in my arms.'

'Oh David,' she choked. 'I wish I was there too. I love you. I'm never going to stop loving you.'

'No, me neither,' he said. Then, 'I've got to go now, got to get that plane. You'll be OK, Pen. *Nuance* is yours – they won't be able to take it away. Look after yourself, sweetheart,' he said. 'And remember . . .' His voice gave out for a moment. 'You know what I'm saying,' he whispered, and the line went dead.

'David!' she cried, tears streaming down her face. '*David!*' But there was no reply.

She looked helplessly at Esther.

'It's all right, dear,' Esther said soothingly, taking the receiver from her and replacing it. 'You'll be all right. We'll be here to take care of you.'

Penny's eyes closed as the nightmare of those words engulfed her. David was gone and she was left here with Esther and Wally Delaney. It was all so wrong, it shouldn't have happened this way. Why did life have to be so cruel as to prevent her seeing him one last time before he went? 'I'm sorry,' she said, unable to look at Esther. 'I need to be on my own for a while. Maybe you could come back . . .'

'Why don't you just go upstairs, dear? I'll wait here in case you need anything,' Esther said.

Feeling too worn down and distraught to argue, Penny nodded, and getting up from the chair she walked slowly out of the kitchen unable to think of anything beyond the way he must be feeling now.

*

An hour later Penny was curled up in a chair beside the roaring fire Esther Delaney had built in the sitting room, nursing a steaming mug of Lemsip and a handful of fresh tissues. She was calmer now, but her face was ravaged by the tears she had shed in the privacy of her room. She was still shaking, but not as badly as before, and having thrown up as violently as she had seemed, in some peculiar way, to have cleared her head. Or maybe it was the fact that the worst was now happening, that the terrible speculation and fear were at an end and knowing what she had to face had brought its own perverse sense of relief.

She looked up as Esther bustled into the room with a tray containing an ashtray, two glasses of red wine and the bottle she had poured it from.

'No, really, not for me,' Penny said, shaking her head as Esther offered her one of the glasses. 'But you carry on.'

After stoking up the fire and putting everything tidily back in place Esther settled herself in the opposite chair, while Penny gazed through the condensation on the windows at the drizzling rain and thought about David boarding the flight in London. It was almost too much to bear.

'Why was Wally with David?' she asked, pushing the words through the suffocating emotion in her throat.

Esther sucked noisily on her cigarette, then took a hasty mouthful of wine. For the moment Penny couldn't bring herself to look at her as she asked herself why she had to be sitting here with this irritating old woman whom, under any other circumstances, she would probably feel sorry for.

'He had to give statements to the lawyers and to Stirling,' Esther answered. 'I'm sure he'll tell you all about it when he comes back.'

Penny nodded. The fact that Wally, apparently, wasn't going to face any charges himself mattered to her neither one way nor the other. All that mattered was David. Then, turning to look at Esther, she felt herself soften slightly, for the compassion in Esther's eyes seemed as genuine as the love in David's voice. 'Why did you do it?' Penny asked. 'Why did you get me and Christian together when you must have known what it would do to David? But no, of course, you didn't, did you?' She sighed, remembering that David had told her that Esther hadn't known the whole story.

Esther's eyes darkened with sorrow. 'It wasn't until you'd gone off with Christian that David told me about Gabriella and Jenny and the way Christian was . . .' She stopped, flattening her lips and looking down at her drink. 'Such a terrible thing for Christian to have done to David, taking you away like that,' she muttered. 'But I promise you, my dear, that had I known what he was up to I'd have put a stop to it right away. Oh dear, I've made such a terrible mess of those boys' lives and I really should have listened a bit harder to what Billy was trying to tell me. He was talking about David, you see. He was trying to tell me about David, but I thought he meant Christian.'

Penny tensed, but she was no longer listening to Esther: she was thinking about the geomancer she had seen in Hong Kong. Feeling as ill as she had lately and with the results of her blood tests still to come, the memory of his hand closing over hers wrapped itself around her heart in a cold grip of terror.

Realizing that Esther had fallen silent, she said, 'Are you able to tell me what happened during the past two weeks? Do you know why David didn't call until now?'

'I really don't know much more than you do,' Esther said solemnly. 'Wally will be able to tell us when he gets back, I'm sure.'

'When will that be, do you know?'

'Tomorrow, I think. Maybe the next day.'

Penny took a sip of her lemon drink, then stared down

at the crackling logs in the hearth. 'Where's Christian now?' she asked.

'In Miami.'

'And Gabriella?' she said almost to herself.

When Esther didn't answer right away Penny turned to look at her and felt her heart contract with unease at the look on the old woman's face. Obviously she knew much more than she was telling.

'It's you he loves, my dear,' Esther said, her voice quaking slightly. 'You must know that, when he came after you the way he did. He knew what a risk he was taking, dear boy. He knew it would probably be the end but he did it anyway, so you can't ever doubt how much he loves you.'

'I don't,' Penny responded. 'But you didn't answer my question. Where's Gabriella now?'

Esther's face twitched; then, sighing, she looked helplessly down at her drink. 'She's with David,' she answered quietly.

Penny could feel the slow burn of jealousy and pain driving right to the very core of her. 'How long has she been with him?' she asked.

'As far as I know, ever since he went to Marseille.'

Penny's hand went to her mouth as the betrayal dug ruthlessly into her heart. 'So that's why he didn't call,' she said.

'I expect so,' Esther replied dully. 'I can't say for sure of course. But, yes, I expect so.'

Penny looked at her. 'What do you think it means?' she said. 'That Gabriella was there.'

Esther wrinkled her brow thoughtfully. 'It could mean a lot of things,' she said, 'but, now that we know the whole story, my guess is that she's been doing her own kind of deal with David while the lawyers have been doing one with the DA. But even if she is going to stand by him I'm afraid it doesn't look like it's going to do him much good.'

'Do you think that's a possibility? That she will stand by him?' Penny said, despising herself for not wanting it to be true when it could, in the end, make a difference to the sentence he received.

'Anything's possible,' Esther answered. 'But why don't you look at it this way, dear? He's just called you. He didn't go without saying goodbye or telling you how much he loves you. So nothing's changed for him on that front and in your heart you must know it. But there's a whole other agenda for him now and, whichever way you look at it, right at this moment you just can't come first.'

'No,' Penny mumbled, not liking the truth of it but knowing she had no choice but to accept it. And because she needed to voice her thoughts, she said, 'It's just . . . Well, it's just so hard to imagine what he's going through, to get any idea at all of what's really going on. I hate being in this position, feeling so shut out and useless.'

'But you're not useless, my dear. It's going to be very important now for David to know that you love him, that you're going to keep things running for him. And I shall be here to help you, of course. And you'll know soon enough what's happening to him. Though if he's surrendering himself it'll probably be because of the evidence Christian's already given against him. Or maybe because Gabriella's going to give evidence too. Oh dear, we just don't know, do we?'

'Oh God!' Penny groaned, her head falling back in despair. 'Hasn't she tormented him enough? How many pounds of flesh does she want, for God's sake?'

Esther was silent as she picked up her glass.

'Have you ever met her?' Penny asked.

Esther nodded forlornly. 'I'm afraid so,' she answered. 'Not a pleasant woman. Not pleasant at all. Dismissed me like I was a nobody. Not that I blame her, of course, but really there was no need for her to be quite so rude.

Funny thing was, Wally liked her.' She laughed briskly. 'But then the old thing likes anyone who makes him feel important and she certainly knew how to do that. Beats me why she bothered, but there it is. People think I'm just a silly old woman, but I'm not always quite so silly and I could see through Gabriella Villers as plain as I can see through glass and I think she knew it. All that one was interested in was money and, now I know everything, the power she has over David, of course. Dreadful woman, stopping him seeing his children the way she does. Still, mustn't be too down on her, must we? It might just be that she will speak up for David and he won't have to go to prison after all.'

Penny allowed her thoughts to drift for a while; then, more from a need to say something than out of any real concern, she said, 'I suppose yours and Wally's income will dry up now.'

Esther gave a nervous laugh. 'For a while, maybe,' she said. 'But David will take care of us. He'll see that we don't go without.'

Penny frowned. 'That's going to be pretty hard for him now that he doesn't have any money, isn't it?' she commented.

Esther's eyes drifted off to the window. This was obviously something she didn't want to talk about, and as she emptied the bottle into her glass Penny watched the way her hands were shaking. But before Penny could say anything Esther was already talking.

'Do tell me to mind my own business if you want to,' she said, holding her glass in front of her wine-stained lips, 'but I have to tell you, dear, that you really don't look at all well. Are you sure you're all right? Is there anything I can do?'

Penny shook her head as the knot of fear in her chest tightened. Then, again out of a need to share her feelings with someone, she said, 'My friend wants me to find out if there are any hospitals for tropical diseases nearby.'

She made a half-hearted attempt at laughter; then, hardly thinking about what she was saying or to whom she was saying it, she added, 'But to tell you the truth, Esther, I don't think I've got a tropical disease. What I think is, I'm pregnant.'

Esther's busy eyes were suddenly arrested in their sockets as she stared incredulously across the room at Penny. Then, abruptly, she started shaking her head. 'No,' she said emphatically. 'You're not pregnant. I'd know if you were pregnant.'

Penny looked at her curiously. 'How would you know?' she asked.

'I just would,' Esther answered. 'Believe me, I know these things, and you're not pregnant.'

Penny wasn't about to argue, because in her heart she didn't believe it either. 'No, you're right,' she sighed miserably. 'I've just got several doses of jet lag, some kind of delayed reaction to trauma and a touch of flu, all of which are curable.' She paused. 'But what if I were pregnant?' she said, suddenly wanting to go ahead with the fantasy.

To her surprise Esther's eyes started to sparkle. 'Well, it wouldn't be a problem, dear,' she told her. 'You'd never want for anything, you know, David would make sure of that, and I'd be here to look after you.' Then her expression started to turn oddly wistful. 'You know, I almost wish you were. That baby would be so lucky having you and David as parents.'

Penny gave a splutter of laughter. 'Wouldn't it just! With one of us so screwed up right now she doesn't know which way to turn and the other on his way to jail . . . yes, I'd call that really lucky.'

Esther smiled and, realizing that the old woman was already knitting bootees, Penny decided that to run any further with the fantasy would be less than wise. So, changing the subject, she said: 'What will you do now? Do you think you'll stay in France?'

Esther nodded, but it was clear that she was still lost in her reverie. 'Have to stay if you're pregnant,' she said. 'You can't go through it on your own and David would want to know you were being taken care of.'

'But I'm not pregnant,' Penny said abruptly.

'Ah, but you might be,' Esther persisted. 'Being sick the way you are and looking the way you do.'

'You were convinced just now that I wasn't,' Penny pointed out, trying to ignore the unsettling currents of excitement the possibility was evoking. If she were pregnant, if she really were carrying his baby . . . But no, she had to stop herself thinking that way. She wasn't pregnant and she had to be out of her mind to be sitting there hoping she was. 'No,' she said decisively. 'I can't be pregnant. It's too early for all these symptoms and . . .' Even as she said the words she could feel herself starting to freeze. But it was too late to take them back and from the look on Esther's face she could see that Esther was thinking the very thing Penny didn't want anyone ever to think: that, if she was pregnant and it was too soon for the baby to be David's, then it had to be Christian's.

As the horror turned her insides to ice the swell of nausea sent her running back to the bathroom. By the time she came out again Esther had opened another bottle of wine and was sitting crookedly back in her chair.

She waited until Penny was sitting down too. Then, fixing her with slightly unfocused eyes, she said, 'Have you missed a period, dear? You can tell me now. Have you missed a period?'

Dully, Penny nodded her head. 'I should have had one last weekend,' she answered. Then, as though Esther had asked the question, she said, 'I never once made love with Christian without using a contraceptive. David and I never used one at all.' She sighed as Esther blinked rapidly. 'But that still doesn't change the dates,' she said.

'I couldn't be suffering like this if I was only three weeks pregnant.'

'Ah, but no one pregnancy is ever the same as another,' Esther told her. 'What we need to find out is when you were ovulating, that's what we need to do. It's generally thirteen or fourteen days before your period is due and by my reckoning that was when you were with David.'

Penny forced a smile, but her eyelids were drooping and suddenly all she wanted was to sleep. Esther carried on talking for a while, but though the words were reaching her Penny couldn't find the strength to respond.

'. . . and when you're in your sixth month,' Esther was saying, 'David will have you flown out to the States so you can be near him when the baby comes. I'll come with you to look after you in the final stages and they'll probably let him out for the delivery. They do that sometimes, you know. Oh, he's going to be so happy about this, Penny.'

Penny wondered if she'd drifted off for a while, for the next thing she knew Esther was saying, 'But you're not pregnant, so you really must stop worrying. You just have to get some rest after everything you've been through. Come on now, let me take you up to bed . . .'

'Oh God, I wish David was here,' Penny heard herself mumble as Esther led her towards the stairs. 'I wish I could have gone with him. I don't even know where to contact him.'

'Shh,' Esther soothed. 'He'll be in touch, don't you worry about that. And Wally will always know how to reach him.'

'I'm not pregnant,' Penny said, the words sounding as strange in her ears as the heaviness she felt in her legs.

'No, I know,' Esther answered, pushing open the bedroom door.

Penny smiled, almost as though it was she who was

drunk, not Esther. 'I've got to keep the bed warm,' she mumbled. 'This is the bed.' And suddenly she started to cry. 'Oh, God,' she wailed, 'I'm damned well falling apart here and I promised him—'

'Shh,' Esther said softly, pulling back the covers and sitting Penny on the edge of the bed.

'I'm making such a fool of myself,' Penny sniffed, her eyelids so heavy now she could barely keep them open, 'but I feel so terrible and I might have an incurable disease and I might be pregnant . . .'

'Just you go to sleep now.' Esther smiled, easing her back against the pillows. 'Go to sleep and dream of David. He loves you, Penny, and he's going to want this baby even more than you do.'

'But what if it's not his baby?'

'Of course it is. It couldn't be anyone else's.'

'But there isn't a baby.'

'Maybe not, but if there is you really won't need to worry about a thing,' Esther whispered.

'I got to tell you, Marielle,' Stirling said, slotting documents into his briefcase, 'that you and that poxy little magazine are giving me a headache. So, for the umpteenth time, it's not in my power to hand the god-damned thing over to you because, to begin with, it's not in Villers's name and, to end with, there's no funny money involved that we can find. Now, why don't you do me a favour and pop along home and work out how you're going to get a reference out of Penny the Moon when she fires you?'

Marielle didn't even flinch. 'You made me promises,' she reminded him tightly.

Stirling was shaking his head. 'Uh-uh,' he said. 'Never any promises. All I did was get you to see things my way and, since that suited you, Marielle, you went along with it like the decent, l w-abiding citizen you are. Shame it's gonna cost you yo ir job, but hey, that's the way life goes. Win some, lose some. Looks like you lost, Marielle.' He said it with such relish, such unbridled glee, that Marielle snatched up a book and flung it at him.

Fortunately for her it missed, but he didn't look any too pleased. 'Get the hell out of here, will you,' he said, sounding more bored than annoyed. 'I got things to do and dealing with you don't figure on my agenda today.'

'Fine upstanding member of law and order you are,' she spat. 'First you renege on David; now you renege on me.'

'Wasn't me reneged on Villers,' Stirling informed her smoothly. 'I did what I could to get him the deal he wanted, but I don't run the DEA and nor do I run the District Attorney's office. And as for you, Marielle, we had no deal. Like I said before, you were just doing your duty as a law-abiding citizen. Now, unless you're of a mind to bounce around on my dick for a while, I suggest you scram.'

Marielle glared at him.

'A blow job?' he suggested.

'You bastard!' Marielle seethed. 'You used me—'

'It was mutual, Marielle,' he cut in. 'Anyway, what are you so worried about? The magazine's still there, isn't it? Could be that Penny the Moon won't want to hang around now that Villers is gone, so you might end up with what you want after all. You're sure sly enough to, even if you don't have any more brains than a daffodil's dick.'

'You can insult me all you like,' Marielle snarled, 'but I'm going to report you to your superiors. You exploited me, used me for sex, sent me out to do your dirty work . . .'

'Put a fucking sock in it, Marielle,' he yawned. 'You twitched that cute little butt of yours in my face so many times I got to feeling sorry for you – that's how comes my dick found its way into your various available orifices.' He grinned. 'Real angel of mercy, me. Don't like to see a person in distress, not if I can do anything to

534

help, and you sure looked like a person in distress to me, coming on to me the way you did. Anyway, time to go find some other poor sucker to put you out of your misery, 'cos I'm outa here in the next five minutes.'

Marielle was quiet for a moment. She knew she'd lost; in fact, if she were honest with herself she'd known it from the moment David had flown out to the Philippines to get Penny back. She'd misjudged just how strongly David felt about Penny, just like she'd misjudged her own powers of manipulation when it came to getting what she wanted out of Stirling. Had she been anyone else she might have felt embarrassed at the lamentable naïveté and preposterous belief in her own importance that had led her to think she could take on men such as Villers and Stirling, but Marielle wasn't about to give herself a hard time over that. What she wouldn't mind knowing, though, was just what Gabriella Villers had been doing in France up until the time David had given himself up. Because, if Gabriella Villers had been here for the reasons Marielle thought she had, there was every chance Penny the Moon wouldn't hang around were she ever to find out.

'What the hell's it got to do with you?' Stirling snorted when she asked.

'Just curious,' she responded with a sultry smile.

Stirling eyed her nastily. He knew only too well what was going on in that pretty little head of hers, but she was rowing the wrong boat, 'cos if he was going to tell anyone what Gabriella Villers had been doing here it would be Penny the Moon, not Marielle Descourts. He'd been toying with the idea for a couple of days now of paying Penny the Moon a visit before he left; but, on reflection, he didn't think he would. Gabriella Villers wasn't a woman to be relied on, so whatever information he gave Penny the Moon now was likely to be out of date by the time he got there, so what was the point? Sure, he might be able to put her mind at rest on a couple of things, but Villers hadn't asked him to, so why get involved? Well, hell, maybe he would, but not right now, 'cos whichever way any of them looked at this, David was going down, and he, Stirling, didn't want to do anything that might tip that wife of his over the edge at this stage of the game. Five years was the best David could hope for now, out in two, maybe three, but it was going to be a whole lot longer if Mrs Villers chose it to be.

Marielle was still looking at him and as he caught the gleam in her eye he started to grin. This woman just didn't know when she was beat – and, hell, why deprive himself of a little last-minute fun? 'You want to reconsider about that blow job?' he said.

Marielle's eyebrows went up.

Five minutes later she was back on her feet and Stirling was zipping up his fly.

'Ah! That'll be my cab,' Stirling said, looking at his watch as a car horn sounded on the jetty outside.

'Robert,' she said, drawing out his name as he snapped the locks on his suitcase, 'I'm still curious to know what Gabriella Villers was doing here in France.'

Stirling grinned. 'Then I guess you're just gonna have to stay that way, Marielle,' he said, and picking up his case, he gave her a quick pat on the bottom and left her life.

Chapter 27

For the second time Penny picked up the glass of wine in front of her, then, unable to face it, put it back on the table. She'd arrived at the Delaneys' a while ago now, but though Wally obviously knew she was waiting for news of David he seemed to be enjoying keeping her in suspense. As he chuntered on about the new stock he'd picked up in London for his antique shop Penny could see the malicious gleam in his eyes and the very sight of his gapped teeth and the ginger bristle on his chin caused her to swallow hard on the bile in her throat.

It was now Wednesday evening. Esther had said she would call the minute Wally walked in, but she hadn't, because when Penny had called just before leaving the office she'd discovered that Wally had been back more than two hours.

'How are you feeling now, dear?' Esther said, as Wally took a break from his inanities and began stuffing his new pipe.

'Much better, thank you,' Penny lied. She'd been to the doctor's again that morning to get the results of her blood tests. There was nothing wrong with her that a few days in bed wouldn't cure, he had told her.

Esther's expression was unreadable.

'You know, the last thing David told me before he got on that plane,' Wally said in his grating bark, as though continuing a conversation that had been going for some time, 'was that I had to tell you everything you wanted to know. I wasn't to hold back about anything.'

Penny looked at him and felt such hatred well up in her that it was all she could do to stop herself smashing a fist in his loathsome face. She hadn't realized until now that the antipathy between them had built to such a pitch that she could hardly bear to look at him, never mind listen to him. 'Do you know where he is now?' she said, a razor edge to her voice.

Wally shrugged. 'Being debriefed, no doubt. That's what happens when they go in, you know. Haven't heard anything since he left, though.' He paused. 'At least, not much.'

He looked so insufferably smug and was so clearly savouring the power he had over her that Penny took the decision there and then not to play his game. Yes, she wanted to know what had been going on these past two weeks, but since she now knew that Gabriella had been there she could guess at most of it; and since she'd far rather hear the details from David, even if it did mean waiting until he could get in touch again, that was what she would do.

'Well,' she said, forcing a brightness she was very far from feeling, 'I guess I'd better be heading home.'

Wally's disgruntlement was a small, but none the less rewarding, pleasure. 'Thought you wanted to know what happened,' he said irritably.

'You can tell me if you like,' Penny responded, 'but if you think you can toss it out in little morsels and expect me to grovel in gratitude for each one, then quite frankly, Wally, you can forget it.'

As his face flushed with anger she saw Esther's eyes grow wide with something akin to admiration.

'Told you before all this started,' Wally said peevishly, 'that I didn't approve. Not my fault. No good crying to me.'

'I'm not crying,' Penny said coldly. 'Neither am I here

538

by choice. It's only because you were with David before he went—'

'No good getting angry with me about that,' Wally told her. 'Fact of life now.'

'You're quite right, Wally,' she answered, picking up her bag and getting to her feet. 'It is a fact of life, but I don't think for one minute that David would have charged you with telling me anything at all if he thought you were going to treat me like this.'

'How am I treating you? I'm about to tell you, aren't I?' he grunted testily.

'Are you?' she said, actually not wanting him to go any further now for fear of what he might say about Gabriella – which, in turn, was the only reason she wasn't letting rip with what she really thought of him.

He looked at his watch. 'Got to go to Antibes,' he said. 'Tell you when I get back.'

'I won't be here when you get back,' she said, taking her coat from the back of the chair.

'OK. I'll come over in the morning,' he said, seeming for some inexplicable reason to like the idea.

'Suit yourself, Wally,' she responded.

Esther walked her to the door. 'There's something I can tell you now, dear,' she said in a whisper. 'David asked him to give you a message before he got on the plane. He said to tell you he loves you.'

Penny's heart churned. 'Thanks,' she said, looking out at the inky-black night and knowing that Esther was probably making it up in order to make her feel better. 'Will you be coming over with Wally tomorrow?' she asked.

'Probably,' Esther answered. 'Actually, I can come with you now, if you like, if you want to talk about him.'

The offer was tempting, for in truth Penny had started to dread being alone lately, but she didn't want to get into another situation with Esther and her frustrated motherhood, or even grandmotherhood, when Penny felt confused enough as it was. 'No, it's OK,' she said, smiling. 'I'm feeling pretty tired and—'

'Did you get the results of your blood tests?' Esther interrupted.

'Yes,' Penny answered.

'And did they test you for pregnancy?'

'No, I don't think so,' Penny said, and, suddenly wanting to get away, she started towards her car without even saying goodbye. To her intense frustration it wouldn't start, and since Esther wouldn't hear of her getting a taxi she had no choice then but to let Esther run her home. And of course, once they were there, Esther just had to pop in to use the toilet and almost before Penny knew it a bottle of wine was open and Esther appeared happily ensconced for the evening.

'No, not for me, thanks,' Penny said, when Esther held up the bottle to offer her some wine.

Outside, the rain was drumming a lulling beat on the kitchen windows while, inside, the Aga was giving out a sleepy, comforting warmth that was filling the air with the nostalgia of Christmas. Only ten days to go, but the thought of how David was going to spend the festive season had taken all the joy out of it for Penny. She'd been toying with the idea of flying out there to surprise him on Christmas Day, but until she discovered exactly where he was or if she would even be allowed to see him she could do nothing.

Surprisingly she and Esther fell into easy conversation, though Esther was doing most of the talking as Penny listened to the tranquillizing rhythm of her voice that was strangely nothing like the jerky, nervous voice she had come to know. She was talking about David, of course, telling Penny how right they were for each other and how very much he loved her. Whether David had ever voiced these sentiments about her to Esther Penny somehow doubted, but since he'd told her often enough how much he loved her what was the harm in listening?

And before long, without even really thinking about what was happening, she was allowing Esther to lead her back into the cosy fantasy of having his baby, something Esther was so sure he would want. Through the floating drowsiness in her mind Penny felt as though this was something she was reading in a book or watching on a screen. Esther told the story so beautifully, made it all sound so possible and preordained that Penny, feeling that same remoteness creeping over her as she'd felt so often these past few days, allowed herself to be drawn into the sublime unreality of it. She was thinking of all the many ways she could break the news to David and each one felt as tragically romantic as the next. She found it so easy to envisage all the scenarios Esther conjured that it wasn't until Esther finally got up to go that she realized what a fool she had been. Slipping out of reality like that and allowing herself to imagine those kind of things was surely the road to madness.

Wally didn't come the next day and when Penny, against her better judgement yet somehow unable to stop herself, called to speak to Esther, Jacqueline, the cleaner, told her that Esther was out. Penny left a message, but Esther didn't call back. She called again in the evening, only to be told by Wally that Esther was in bed with the flu. Penny's frustration at the way she seemed to be losing control of herself, as well as the way she was allowing the Delaneys to get to her, was building to such a pitch that, were it not for the fact they had her car and she was so sick she didn't dare to leave the house anyway, she'd have gone over there and done something she'd have probably lived to regret. Her insides ached, she had cried so much, and she so desperately wanted to get hold of Sammy that the impossibility of it was crushing her with such loneliness and despair that she wondered if she would ever feel healthy or happy again.

On Friday morning, knowing she couldn't go on like

this, she got her own cleaner to drive her to the *pharmacie*. When they returned they found her car at the gates with a brief note on the windscreen from Wally telling her he'd had her battery recharged and taken the car for a drive so it was ready to use. Not even wanting to analyse this spurious piece of kindness, for she had too much else on her mind, she drove the car up to the house, then went upstairs to her bathroom and took out the pregnancy-testing kit she had just bought.

Three minutes later she had her answer. The shock was so profound that all she could do was stare down at the two narrow blue lines. Why she should feel so shocked when she'd suspected it for days didn't make any sense, but as the fantasy pregnancy began to establish itself as a reality she could feel the true horror of it totally eclipsing the falsified joy.

She didn't know if the baby was David's and, if it wasn't, she didn't want it. But how was she ever going to know? Even if there was a way of telling and it turned out to be his, she had to be out of her mind to think he would be happy about it. Didn't he have enough to be dealing with? Wouldn't he already be suffering for what he was going to miss of his sons' lives, without having this thrown at him too? And knowing the circumstances surrounding the birth of his second son, how could she even contemplate putting him through this new torment when she didn't even know if the child was his or Christian's?

She lifted her eyes to the mirror and stared back at her ashen reflection. The very idea that Christian might have dealt him this final blow made her feel faint from the sheer brutality of a fate that could do this. How would she ever tell him? But no, she wouldn't, he would never have to know. She'd just go quietly into hospital one morning and come out again in the afternoon without anyone ever having to know.

She was about to turn away, when her eye was caught

by the test, which she'd set down on the bidet. She picked it up and stared at it again. There was no question it was positive, for the blue line couldn't have been more pronounced. It was a baby. She was carrying a baby. Then, lifting her face back to the mirror, she started to shake her head. This child wasn't Christian's, it couldn't be. She had been ovulating at the time she and David made love and they hadn't used any contraception at all, whereas she and Christian had never made love without it. So the baby had to be David's.

Without giving any thought to what she was doing, she flung open the bathroom door and raced to the phone.

'Esther,' she said breathlessly when Esther answered. 'Can I come and see you?'

'Of course you can, dear,' Esther answered. 'You come whenever you like.'

It took Penny less than ten minutes to get there. Wally was in the garden, fiddling about with the roses, and barely looked up as Penny sailed past with a quick thank you for seeing to her car.

Esther was in the kitchen, wearing a shocking-pink dress with a black fur trim on the pockets and collar. Fleetingly, as excitement tripped through her heart, it crossed Penny's mind that if Esther was going to become a grandmother she might just start dressing the part – a thought that alone should have told her she was not, at this very minute, of sound mind.

'I did a test,' Penny told her, hardly able to contain her joy, 'and it was positive.'

Esther looked at her unblinkingly.

'Didn't you hear me?' Penny said, her smile beginning to falter.

Esther's face twitched as she turned it towards the window. 'Congratulations, my dear,' she mumbled.

Penny stared at her in disbelief.

Esther didn't move.

'What do you think David will say?' Penny asked, so confused she barely knew what she was saying.

Esther's narrow shoulders gave a shrug. Then, turning back to Penny, she said, 'What are you going to do?'

Penny was so stunned she didn't know how to respond. 'Um, uh,' she said, putting a hand to her head, 'I don't know. I mean, I suppose I should tell David, but I don't know how to get hold of him.'

At that moment Wally came into the house.

'I'm going to have a baby,' Penny blurted out before she could stop herself.

Wally paused a moment in his stride, then kept on going across the kitchen. 'Hmmph,' he said.

'Penny would like to know how she can get hold of David,' Esther said tonelessly. 'Maybe, with the contacts we have—'

'Esther, you know the situation,' Wally interrupted.

'Yes, yes, of course,' Esther responded, her head going down.

Penny looked from one to the other and felt herself start to tremble with rage. But whatever the situation was she'd be damned if she was going to ask them. 'It's OK,' she said, her fists clenching at her side, 'I'm perfectly capable of finding out where David is, so please don't put yourself to the trouble. I'm leaving right now and maybe you'd like to forget I ever came.'

As she walked across the kitchen and out into the garden Esther came running after her. 'Go and see a doctor,' Esther said under her breath. 'You'll need to do that. And, I promise, it'll be all right.'

Penny shook her off.

'I'll call you as soon as I can,' Esther said as Penny slammed her car door. She said something else too, but by then Penny had already put her foot down and was speeding through the gates. The crazy, awful and unbearable part of it was that she hadn't realized until now just how much she had allowed Esther to get to her with all her perfectly painted scenarios of a pregnancy that in reality was nothing short of a nightmare.

By seven that evening Penny was sitting alone in her kitchen. She had seen the doctor and was waiting now for him to contact her to let her know the earliest date she could have her pregnancy terminated. She didn't know if she was doing the right thing, wasn't even sure that she had really come to a decision at all. She felt so traumatized by everything and so desperate to speak to Sammy that she barely knew what was in her mind.

As her eyes darted nervously about the room she was wondering if there was a way she could get a message to David, if only to wish him a Happy Christmas and let him know she was thinking of him. Pierre had disappeared at the same time as David and Penny guessed that he was probably over there in the States too, maybe facing charges of his own. To call Sylvia was out of the question when she was still recovering from her operation and, short of calling the DEA to try to get hold of Stirling, there was no one else. She looked at the clock and swiftly calculated the time difference between France and Miami. Maybe, she thought, she would at least try to find Stirling's number.

However, before she could pick up the phone the bell in the hall sounded, announcing someone's arrival at the gates.

'Hello,' Penny said into the entryphone.

'Penny, dear, it's Esther. Can I come in?'

Penny so badly wanted to say no, but right now even Esther's company was better than sitting here alone putting herself through this misery so she pushed the button to release the gates.

It took some time for Esther to come to the point of her visit, and when she finally did Penny wished to God she'd never allowed her in. It was like a nightmare with no end.

'Of course,' Esther was saying, 'I have absolutely no right to ask for your word that you won't try contacting David, but I must make you aware of what it will do to his chances of a lighter sentence if you do contact him. We've heard, through the other people who work for him and Christian, you understand,' she said, flushing, 'that Gabriella's going to stand by him and that is what is really important to him right now. I'm sure you understand that. It ought to go down well with the judge that he has a loving and secure home to go back to when he comes out of prison and two boys who need him. So if you get in touch now and tell him you're pregnant you could make things very difficult for him. I'm sure you understand that, dear.'

Penny was reeling from the cruel bluntness of Esther's words, but even worse was the heartbreaking realization that David had to be protected from her. Then she thought of the poor, unborn baby inside her . . .

'And,' Esther went on, as though reading her mind, 'as you don't really know whether or not the baby is David's . . .'

Rage suddenly gathered in Penny's eyes. 'Don't go any further with that,' she said through her teeth. 'I'd like you to leave now, Esther, and I don't want you ever to come back. But before you go you have my word that I won't contact David and I would like yours that you will never tell him I was pregnant. I use the past tense because I have decided to have an abortion.'

Esther's face paled as she looked away. Her shame at having encouraged Penny to want this baby was so evident that Penny wanted to crush her with the full might of her anger.

'If there's ever anything I can do . . .' Esther said lamely as they walked to the door. 'We're clearing out David's apartment—'

'What do you mean, *you're* clearing his apartment?' Penny cried, feeling the intrusion as though it were her own belongings that were about to be rifled by these abhorrent strangers.

'Gabriella asked us to,' Esther responded tonelessly. 'So if there's anything you might want before we send it all back to the United States . . .'

'As a matter of fact, there is,' Penny said stiffly. 'I don't have a proper photograph of David. Only one we had taken for a newspaper once. So if you find any . . .'

'I shall look out for one,' Esther assured her. 'I know there are some albums there, so if you pop by our house tomorrow you can take your pick.'

Like a fool, Penny went the next day. Esther had the photographs waiting for her. Wally was sitting in the corner, reading a newspaper. All but one of the photographs Esther was offering were of David on his wedding day. The single exception showed Gabriella standing beside him, tall and willowy and radiantly beautiful. She was wearing nothing but a sarong tied beneath the bronzed bulge of her pregnant belly.

Wally didn't look up once as, without a word, Penny put the photographs back on the table and walked out of the house. The following morning the doctor called to tell her the earliest time she could go into hospital. She almost laughed out loud. Of all the days in the year, Christmas Eve surely had to be the worst. But what difference did it make if it was Christmas Eve? She wasn't going to have the baby, so the sooner she went through with the operation the better.

'What time do I have to be there?' she asked.

'Around eight in the morning,' he answered. 'You should be able to leave by mid-afternoon. The gynaecologist would like to see you to check you over first. Can you make next Monday at four?'

'Yes,' she answered and without even saying goodbye she hung up the phone.

*

547

As Esther opened the door and walked in, peeling off her long, black gloves and unbuttoning her mink, Wally glanced up from the TV. Then, leaning forward for his gin and tonic, he said, 'Well? What happened?'

'She wouldn't let me in,' Esther answered dismally as she scooped up a glittery ball that had fallen from the Christmas tree. 'We've only two days of shopping left before Christmas, dear, and we don't have anything for our friends yet,' she reminded him.

'We'll go tomorrow,' he grunted, returning to the events of the soap opera he was watching.

Esther sat down on the edge of a chair and waited in silence until finally the credits rolled and Wally turned to look at her.

'What did she say?' he asked.

Esther shook her head as she stared blindly down at the floor. 'She wouldn't let me in,' she repeated, pulling her gloves through her fist.

'Did you offer to drive her to the clinic?'

Esther nodded. 'She said the doctor's taking her.'

Wally's bottom lip jutted forward as he sucked in his moustache. Then, eyeing Esther suspiciously, he said, 'You haven't told her anything you shouldn't have, have you, old thing?'

'No,' Esther said dully.

Wally's eyes stayed on her for a while, but when she didn't look up he turned back to the screen.

A few minutes later Esther reached for her handbag and took out her cigarettes. As she lit one, tears began to spill from her eyes.

'There, there, old thing,' Wally said gruffly, his fingers tightening around the gin and tonic. 'Pull yourself together now. I told you before, blubbing's not going to get us anywhere.'

'I'm sorry,' Esther sniffed, dabbing her cheeks with her handkerchief. 'It's just that she told me Christian used contraceptives and I don't understand why he would have done that if he can't have children. I'm so dreadfully confused about it, dear.'

Wally sighed impatiently. 'He used them, Esther, because he didn't want her to know that he couldn't have children, not when he was trying to get her to give up everything for him. You know as well as I do that it was one of the reasons his marriage broke up. And besides, young people these days have got to think about this Aids thing, what?'

'Yes, of course,' Esther said, nodding. 'It's just so awful, knowing what a dilemma she's in . . .'

'You just think about the dilemma we'll be in if we don't get that money,' Wally reminded her coldly.

'But the baby is David's,' Esther protested, fresh tears starting down her cheeks. 'She'd never have an abortion if she knew that. She loves him, Wally, and he loves her too. And think how wonderful it would be for us to have a baby to spoil . . .'

'You get that idea out of your head right now, Esther Delaney,' he barked angrily. 'That baby is nothing to do with you, nothing at all. Billy's dead and no one, not David nor Christian, nor that baby over there, can take his place. So you just pull yourself together now and stop all this nonsense. Do you hear me?'

'Yes,' Esther sobbed. 'Yes, I hear you, dear. But—'

'No buts, Esther,' he said, cutting across her. 'We have to look out for ourselves now, and with David going to prison we need the money Gabriella is offering us to make sure that baby doesn't come along. I know it's hard . . .'

'But what if David were ever to find out?' Esther wailed. 'He'd never forgive us, Wally, and I just can't bear to think—'

'He's not going to find out!' Wally seethed. 'Now, you just go and make yourself a cup of tea and settle down.'

They didn't discuss it again until much later that night when Wally took the call from Gabriella Villers asking for the latest on Penny. By the time he rang off Esther was pacing the bedroom, shaking so hard she could barely get her cigarette in her mouth.

'Now, come on, Esther,' Wally sighed, pulling her stiffly into his arms. 'She's doing this for David's own good. If it ever gets out that Penny Moon is pregnant, then you know as well as I do that it could ruin his chances of a lighter sentence. And you don't want that now, do you, old thing?'

'No,' she said hoarsely. 'No, I don't want that.'

'That's the ticket,' he said, stroking her hair. 'You just think about how much sooner he'll be coming back if we do what we can to help him. And tomorrow, you go off and treat yourself to something nice in one of those jewellers' down on the Croisette, mm?'

'Mmm.' Esther nodded. 'Do you think I should get something for Penny?'

'That would be nice,' he said, smiling. 'She'll probably need something to cheer her up a bit over Christmas.'

Esther's car was laden with shopping when she pulled up in front of their house early the following evening. On her way back from her spending spree she had driven over to Penny's villa, but once again Penny had refused to let her in. However, their brief conversation on the entryphone had told Esther what she had gone there to find out.

Smiling shakily as Jacqueline came to help her unload the car, she picked up the neatly wrapped gift she had bought for Penny and, leaving Jacqueline to continue without her, walked into the house.

Seeing how haggard she looked, Wally took her by the shoulders and led her to the sofa. Then, not wanting her to see the triumph gleaming in his eyes, he turned her face into his shoulder.

'Did you pop over to Penny's?' he asked, already knowing the answer.

Esther's body was limp. 'Yes,' she said weakly. Then, after a pause, 'It's done.'

Wally nodded. Then, deciding that the call to Gabriella to tell her where she should deposit the half million dollars she had promised for this could wait, he snuggled Esther deeper into his arms, saying, 'It's all right, old thing. It's going to be all right. Gabriella will stand by him now. His sentence won't be a long one and, you never know, maybe he won't have to go to prison at all.'

Penny was lying fully clothed on her bed, staring at nothing. Her face was bloodless and drawn; her heart, for the moment, was mercifully numb. It was raining outside and from somewhere, way in the distance, came the melodious chant of Christmas carols, or maybe it was just her imagination.

Coming back from the clinic she had seen so many children, so many expectant mothers, all flushed with the excitement of the season. Dimly she recollected Ruth putting out a hand to cover hers, but she couldn't remember whether she had responded or not. Dear Ruth. It had been so kind of her to come to the clinic to drive Penny home. Her secret would be safe with Ruth, she was sure of that. Ruth wouldn't tell Sylvia even though she was planning to visit Sylvia over Christmas and Sylvia would be sure to want to know about Penny.

Penny's eyes closed, but though they stayed that way for a long time she wasn't sleeping. In her mind she was talking to David, trying to tell him what she had done and asking him to forgive her.

An hour or more ticked by and at last the church bells that had been chiming out merrily over the hillside clanged untidily into silence, telling her that Midnight Mass was starting, that Christmas Day had begun.

Pulling herself up from the bed she went downstairs to her desk and taking a sheet of paper from the drawer she started to write David a letter she knew she would probably never send. But maybe, if she wrote it all down – explained what had happened, the way she was feeling now and the reasons why she had taken the decision she had – it would help her to come to terms with it in her mind. And maybe, should the day ever dawn when she needed to, she could give him the letter in the hope it would help him to understand.

When she reached the part where Esther Delaney had reminded her that she didn't know whose baby it was she found her thoughts beginning to stray and, turning to gaze out at the black, starry night she wondered where David was now and what kind of Christmas he would have. It would be foolish of her to hope that he might call, but in her heart she knew that she did. So much so that when the telephone suddenly rang she found herself staring at it in dread of what she was going to say.

'Hello?' she said softly into the receiver.

There was a loud hissing noise, a sudden burst of static, then Sammy's distant voice came down the line. 'Pen? Are you there, Pen?' she shouted.

'Yes, I'm here,' Penny called back. 'Where are you?'

'On a boat somewhere in the Caribbean,' Sammy answered. 'I didn't expect to find you in tonight. I was going to leave a message.'

'You're OK, are you?' Penny asked.

'Yeah! I'm just great. How are you?'

'I'm fine,' Penny answered.

'What are you doing for Christmas?'

As the emptiness of the days ahead stretched out in front of her Penny said, 'Oh, a couple of parties – you know the sort of thing.'

'You sound a bit down. Are you sure you're OK?'

'I'm sure. I miss you,' she added quietly.

'What? What was that? I didn't hear what you said.'

'I said I'm fine. It's good to hear your voice.'

'And to hear yours. I miss you and love you hundreds

552

of thousands.'

'Love you hundreds of thousands too.'

'You have a great Christmas, OK?'

'I will.' Penny smiled. 'Happy Christmas and God bless.'

'Good night, God bless,' Sammy said, sounding just as she had as a child.

Smiling through her tears, Penny replaced the receiver and turned back to her letter.

In August of the following year David was sentenced to ten years in prison. By then, knowing what Gabriella was going to do, he had severed all contact with Penny, believing it to be the only way of releasing her from her commitment to him and allowing her to get on with her life. So he had no idea that the day after she received the news, with Sammy at her side and Ruth having once again come out of retirement to step into the breach, Penny gave birth by Caesarian to a healthy, eight-pound baby girl with a veritable mop of blonde curls and her father's beautifully sleepy blue eyes.

Chapter 28

'You know, this feels really weird,' Penny laughed as she drove in through the gates of the villa. 'I mean, it's usually me doing the interviewing and I can't quite get the hang of it this way round.'

Serena Brothers, the new editor of *Starke* magazine, laughed too. She'd flown over from London the day before specifically for this interview, which was a bit of a *coup* in itself, there having been so much speculation lately about Penny Moon and what was happening over here, as well as being a nice little jaunt to the Rivieria in the middle of June. Of course, she had her boss, Sylvia Starke, to thank for it, as so many others had Sylvia to thank for their lucky breaks.

'Do you think that bit back there at the office went all right?' Penny asked, uncertainly. 'I mean, did you get what you were hoping for?'

'It was fantastic,' Serena murmured, trying to stop her mouth dropping open at the sight of the spectacular villa they were approaching. 'And so is this. Is this really where you live?'

Penny laughed. 'Yep, it's where we live. A bit on the ostentatious side, but we like it.'

'Just look at that view!' Serena groaned. 'How do you ever drag yourself away from it? And this wonderful garden. You must have an army of gardeners to keep it this way.'

'Heavens no, I do the whole thing myself,' Penny teased as she stopped the car at the front of the villa.

Serena laughed. 'You really are amazing, you know. You've achieved so much down here.'

'Not without help,' Penny said. 'Which reminds me: I've got a few things I'd like you to take back for Sylvia, if you don't mind. Nothing heavy.'

'Not a problem,' Serena answered, getting out of the little convertible Peugeot Penny was still driving around in. It was totally impractical, of course, but there was the great lumbering estate car they used for family days out.

'You know, I'm filled with admiration,' Serena went on. 'I mean, how on earth do you manage to find the time to run the magazine, write an entire book of short stories, run this house *and* bring up a little girl?'

'More help,' Penny grinned. Then, wincing as she heard the noise coming from the other side of the house, she said, 'I hope you're ready for this. It's Shana's birthday today, so things could get a bit out of hand.'

Laughing, Serena said, 'How old is she?'

'Two years and ten months,' Penny answered wryly. Then, with an ironic lift of her eyebrows that did nothing to disguise the pride, she added, 'With David as a father, I'm afraid every day is a birthday.'

'I can't wait to meet them both,' Serena said, following Penny round to the swimming pool.

'Dear God,' Penny muttered, coming to a standstill as they rounded the corner of the house. 'Will you just look at them!'

Serena was doing just that, watching in delight as the tiny girl, with white-blonde curls and a rotund little tummy, chased her father with a trifle, trying to splodge it in his face. It didn't take her long to succeed and she screamed with laughter as David scooped her up in his arms and ran back to the table, where he dipped his hand in a bowl of gooey dessert and wiped it all over her face.

'Most days are like this around here,' Penny remarked. 'You get used to it after a while.'

'Mummy!' Shana squealed, spotting Penny coming towards them.

David turned, his face and hair still thick with trifle, and, even as she burst out laughing, Penny's heart felt as if it were melting. God, she loved him so much. Then suddenly she was backing away as she caught the wicked glint in his eyes. 'No!' she cried as he and Shana started towards her. 'No, David, stop! I'm having my photograph taken in a minute.'

'But we want a kiss from Mummy, don't we, Shana?' David declared.

'David, I'm warning you . . .' Penny laughed.

'Kiss, Mummy! Kiss!' Shana cried, bouncing up and down in David's arms and clapping her hands.

'Oh no, David, please don't,' Penny wailed as he grabbed her arm. But it was too late and as his mouth came down on hers and Shana hugged them both in a wet, sticky embrace Penny couldn't stop herself responding to the brief touch of his tongue on hers.

'You wait,' she told him huskily as he let her go. 'I'll get you back for this.'

His eyes were dancing as, turning to Serena, he waited to be introduced.

'You don't have to bother shaking his hand,' Penny assured Serena as she looked at him warily. With no little relief Serena introduced herself, using a hand to shade her eyes from the sun.

'So,' David said, trying to hold Shana at bay as she rubbed her hands over his face, 'how's the star of the family doing?'

'She's doing just fine,' Serena told him, feeling something of an intruder for a moment as David's eyes lingered on Penny's.

'Your turn next,' Penny told him. 'So go and clean up. Shana, are you going to say hello to Serena?'

Shana turned and fixed Serena with stunningly blue eyes which were so like her father's that Serena felt her own blink. 'Hello, Shana,' she said, smiling.

Putting a thumb in her mouth and rubbing her head against David's so that her glossy curls mingled with his, Shana said, 'I'm a bit shy, Mummy.'

Both David and Penny burst out laughing. 'Well, that's news to me,' Penny said, giving her leg a playful squeeze. 'Now come on, be polite and say hello.'

'Hello,' Shana whispered.

'Good girl. Now off you go to the shower with Daddy.'

As Penny and Serena watched them saunter off to the shower in the pool house Serena said, 'I hope you don't mind me saying, but they're both absolutely gorgeous.'

Penny smiled. 'Yes, I think so too. Anyway, let me get you something to drink. What would you like?'

'Something cold,' Serena answered, following Penny into the kitchen.

She waited until Penny handed her an Orangina, apologizing for the baby glass, then said, 'How long has David been back now?'

'Just over a month,' Penny answered, looking up as Sammy came into the kitchen.

'I thought I heard you come in,' Sammy said, giving Penny a quick peck on the cheek. 'How's it going?'

'I wish you'd all stop asking that,' Penny groaned. 'You're letting Serena know how nervous I was.'

'She's been a right pain in the neck preparing for this interview,' Sammy told Serena. 'About time she got a taste of her own medicine, if you ask me. Anyway, I'm Sammy, Penny's sister.'

'Nice to meet you, Sammy,' Serena said, shaking Sammy's hand. 'Do you live here too?'

'God, no. I'm just passing through on my way to Italy.'

'She arrived a week ago and we can't get rid of her,' Penny smiled fondly.

'So how's the bun fight going out there?' Sammy asked. 'I came in to get out of the way.'

'I think you just got your answer,' Penny replied with a laugh as Shana gave a piercing scream, which was followed by a thunderous splash as she pushed David into the pool. 'I'm sorry,' she said to Serena; 'it's always like this around here. We're a pretty rowdy bunch, especially those two out there. But he'll clean up in a minute and come and join us. Shall we go through to the sitting room? It's a bit cooler in there.'

'This is so idyllic,' Serena sighed as they sat down on facing sofas. 'You seem so happy, all of you.'

'We are,' Penny answered, 'now. But we had to wait for it, as you know. Oh God, what's happening now?' she laughed as the yelling and screaming started up again.

Serena smiled. 'Looks like Sammy's joining in the bun fight,' she said, getting out her tape recorder. She waited for Penny to turn back, then said, 'OK, we've covered the success of *Nuance* and the new book. Anything else you'd like to add before we move on?'

'No, I don't think so,' Penny said, chewing her lips thoughtfully. 'If anything occurs to me, I'll let you know.'

Serena nodded, consulting her notepad. 'Ah, there is just one thing,' she said. 'You didn't tell me exactly how many offers from other magazines you've turned down in the last six months.'

'Only two,' Penny laughed.

'Not even tempted?' Serena asked. 'Wasn't one of them in New York?'

'Not tempted for a moment,' Penny answered. 'Mine and Shana's lives are here, and now that David's back we'll definitely be staying.'

'Meaning you were thinking of leaving at one time?'

'It crossed my mind once or twice,' Penny said, finding it incredible now to think how she'd once intended that as soon as she heard David was being released she would pack up and leave France before he came back. 'But as you can see, we're settled here now and I don't see that changing for a while.'

'Sylvia told me,' Serena went on warily, 'that you wouldn't mind answering some personal questions. Is that right?'

'Depends how personal,' Penny responded with arched brows. 'But ask away. If I don't want to answer, I won't. I imagine the same will go for David when he finally joins us.'

'OK,' Serena said, leaning over to start the tape recorder, but before she did she said, 'You obviously know that plenty of rumours have been flying ever since David came out of prison, so a lot of my questions will be either to confirm or deny them, OK?'

Penny nodded, and tucked her legs in under her, thinking that she was quite enjoying this after all.

'So,' Serena said, once the tape recorder was whirling, 'I believe that David didn't know anything about Shana until quite some time after she was born. Is that right?'

Penny nodded.

'So what made you decide to tell him?'

Smiling, Penny said, 'You mean who made me tell him. Sylvia, of course. She surprised us all with a visit when Shana was about ten months old – having been tipped off about Shana's existence by Ruth Elliot – and after taking one look at Shana she said, "if David doesn't already know about this little angel, Penny, then you must tell him. If you don't, I will." '

Serena laughed at the near-perfect imitation of Sylvia's Swiss-French accent. 'So what did you do?' she asked.

Penny let her head fall back as she felt herself returning to those long, dark, dreadful days of early pregnancy that felt so distant now it might almost have happened in another life. By her third month she had started to feel human again, but the going still hadn't been easy, for in

the one letter she had received from David he had told
her that he and Gabriella had resolved a lot of their differences and were going some way towards patching
things up, so he could make no promises for the future.
He had sounded so distant, so like a stranger, as he'd
gone on to thank her for all she had done, for her support
and for the friendship they had that he hoped would
endure. He'd included a little about his sons, telling her
that Gabriella was bringing them to see him on a regular
basis and that at last he was getting to know them,
though not, of course, under the best of circumstances.

Knowing that the letter had been read by others, perhaps even written for their eyes too, had been small
comfort when there was no way of finding out what the
truth really was. And carrying a child of her own, a child
she just knew in her heart was his, had made the coolness of his letter all the harder to bear. She'd written
back, but by the time it reached the jail he was no longer
there. He had finally got bail and was at home with
Gabriella and their children, which was where he stayed
until sentence was finally passed.

It was Stirling who had told Penny about Gabriella's
final act of treachery when she had given false evidence,
claiming that David had been involved in the importation
of heroin. Stirling's call had come just a few days after
Penny had returned home with Shana, and though she
longed to fly out to see David, who was by then in a federal prison in Florida, the baby had to come first. She'd
written to him regularly in the months that followed,
chatty, newsy letters that never made any mention of
Shana though she never once failed to tell him how much
she still loved him. He hadn't answered one of them
until . . .

Penny smiled at Serena. 'What else could I do?' she
said in answer to Serena's question. 'Sylvia would have
told him if I hadn't, and I guess she was the prompt I
needed, having come so close so many times to telling

him already. So I sent him a letter I'd written the day I so very nearly had an abortion which explained why I had decided to go through with the pregnancy and why I wasn't going to tell him about it. With it I sent another letter, telling him all about his daughter. I enclosed a photograph, which was a bit sneaky really, because I knew once he saw her he'd never be able to resist her, and then I waited. It was awful. I was so afraid of how angry he might be because I hadn't told him sooner – or worse, that he wouldn't write back at all.' Her face softened in a smile. 'Fortunately he did neither.'

'What did he do?' Serena asked.

Penny laughed. 'Well, he was pretty mad at me, bawled me out on the phone as I seem to remember, then he told me he loved me . . . Actually, don't put that bit in – it sounds mawkish and self-indulgent. He told me he wanted to see me as soon as I could get there and of course he wanted to see Shana too.' She shrugged. 'So we went.' And it was during that first visit, she was thinking to herself, that she finally learned the true extent of all the double-dealing Gabriella had done, including promising him she would stand by him if he cut all contact with Penny. Which, of course, he had, in the hope of receiving a shorter sentence, at the end of which he would return to Penny. But Gabriella's treachery, or revenge, or whatever she wanted to call it, knew no limits, for, though, David's; had ceased contact with Penny Gabriella was all the time preparing to turn state's evidence against him. And after he had been sentenced she had started divorce proceedings in the belief that it would further destroy his image as a family man, thereby reducing his chances of an early parole. What Gabriella hadn't bargained for, though, was the overcrowded prison system that needed room for more deserving cases than David's; nor for the leniency of the Appeal Court judges.

But Penny didn't go into any of that with Serena; she

561

simply moved her eyes back to hers, saying, 'And his joy when he saw us was quite something to behold. We both cried – a lot. So did Shana, but she didn't know why. After that we went to see him as often as we could . . . and now' – she waved a hand towards the garden – 'he's home.'

'And much earlier than expected?'

'Much. But he served over three years and, since they needed the space in the prison, they . . . Well, I guess you could say they deported him.'

'And Gabriella? What's happened to her?'

Penny grimaced. It had been a bad day for Gabriella when she'd discovered David was being released, but perhaps an even worse one was when she had learned of Shana's existence. It was only recently that David and Penny had heard how she'd paid Esther and Wally Delaney half a million dollars to persuade Penny the baby she was carrying was Christian's in the hope she would abort it. Oddly enough, Gabriella had told David about it herself, though whether she had ever managed to catch up with the Delaneys, who had disappeared from the face of the earth the minute they'd found out Penny was still pregnant, Penny had no idea, and nor did she care. She and David had Shana and that was all that mattered to them.

Again, Gabriella's treachery was something she didn't feel she needed to go into, so she said, in a perfectly matter-of-fact voice, 'Gabriella is about to marry someone who's richer than David ever was or probably ever will be.'

'Such faith,' he commented, coming into the room. Then, moving in behind Penny, he put his hands on her shoulders, and stooped to whisper in her ear that he'd saved the final tub of *tiramisu* for later and exactly what he expected her to do with it.

With a gurgle of laughter and a suitable blush, Penny looked across at Serena. 'You'll have to excuse him,' she

562

said. 'He always carries on as though no one else is in the room. It drives poor Sammy nuts.'

'Making up for lost time,' David responded, sitting down next to her and pushing a hand under her hair to stroke the back of her neck.

'Can I ask about your other children?' Serena said to David. 'Will you see them at all?'

'We're hoping,' he answered, 'that they might come out for the summer. Gabriella's yet to agree, but we're making some headway.'

Serena looked at him for a moment, openly appraising him. 'I have to say,' she commented, finally, 'that you appear amazingly unscathed by your experience of the American prison system.'

Penny turned to look at him, knowing that he'd show Serena nothing of the toll his experience had taken on him. That was something he discussed only with her.

'Well, that,' he said, crossing his long legs at the ankles as he put his hands behind his head, 'I can explain. You see, there are those who have a rough time and go under. Then there are those who have a rough time and survive. And then there are those who write best-selling books about it.'

Serena's eyes widened hungrily. 'You mean you've written a book?' she said, already thinking about serial rights.

'No,' David answered with a grin, causing Penny to choke back a laugh.

Serena looked vaguely baffled; then, collecting herself, she said to Penny, 'I know you've more or less answered this question, but can you just clarify for me the exact reasons why you didn't tell David about the baby straight off?'

Penny turned to look at David, then smiled as he reached out for her hand.

'Because,' David answered, knowing full well that

Serena was trying to get to the bottom of the rumour concerning Christian Mureau, 'she loves me, didn't want to add to my load, and if she ever does anything like that again I'll make damned sure she never sees or tastes another *tiramisu* in her life.'

Penny burst out laughing. 'Private joke,' she told Serena. 'And if what you're really wondering is about Christian Mureau then I think Shana herself has given you the answer, because just like Sylvia did, you only have to take one look at her to know whose she is.'

'You know,' Serena said, her eyes shining with a certain wistfulness as she looked from one to the other of them, 'I don't know when I've ever seen two people so much in love.'

David turned to look quizzically at Penny. 'Yep,' he nodded in agreement, 'she's in love all right. She's got that kind of mushy look about her, wouldn't you say?'

'You both have,' Serena laughed.

'You mean I look like that!' David cried.

Thumping him, Penny turned back to Serena and asked if there were any more questions.

'Well, just the one, I suppose,' she answered. 'Any plans to get married?'

Again David turned to Penny. 'No,' he said, 'we don't have any plans, but we could always make some. What do you say, do you want to make plans?'

Penny shrugged. 'We could.'

'Is that a yes?' he said, discreetly pressing his thumb into her palm.

'It's a yes,' she said shakily, wishing Serena was already gone.

'I guess the honeymoon's already sorted?' he said softly, still looking into Penny's eyes.

'Where else?' She smiled. 'All three of us?'

David turned to Serena. 'You planning on coming too?' he said incredulously.

'Daddy! Daddy!' Shana cried, charging into the room.

David turned and was about to swing her up in his arms when, with a delighted gurgle of laughter, she pushed the last *tiramisu* into his face.

Out of the Shadows

Susan Lewis

Since Susannah Cates' husband was sent to prison three years ago, life has been a constant struggle to provide for herself and their teenage daughter. Nothing ever seems to go right and the most she hopes for now is that nothing more will go wrong.

Worried by her mother's unhappiness, thirteen-year-old Neve decides to take matters into her own hands. And when Susannah's closest friend Patsy discovers what Neve is up to, she immediately lends her support. As their plans start to unfold they have no way of knowing what kind of fates they are stirring, all they can see is Susannah's excitement, because at last a way seems to be opening up for her to escape her bad luck.

However, the spectre of horror is all the time pacing behind the scenes and never, in all Susannah's worst nightmares, could she have imagined her happiness causing so much pain to someone she loves . . .

'Spellbinding!' *Daily Mail*

'Sad, happy, sensual and intriguing' *Woman's Own*

arrow books

Missing

Susan Lewis

It's an early autumn day like any other as Miles Avery drives his wife, Jacqueline, to the station. Nothing remarkable crops up in conversation, nor do either of them appear anything other than their normal selves. At the station, Jacqueline gets out, takes an overnight bag from the back seat, then turns towards the platforms. This is the last anyone sees of her.

Three weeks later, Miles calls the police. Enquiries are made, but there is no evidence of her boarding a train, or even entering the station. Very soon the finger of suspicion starts to turn towards Miles, and as dark secrets from the past begin to merge with those of the present, the great love he has been trying to protect is not only revealed but thrown into terrible jeopardy . . .

'A multi-faceted tear jerker' *heat*

'An irresistible blend of intrigue and passion, and the consequences of secrets and betrayal' *Woman*

arrow books

ALSO AVAILABLE IN ARROW

A French Affair

Susan Lewis

When Natalie Moore is killed in a freak accident in France her mother – the very poised and elegant Jessica – knows instinctively there is more to it. However, Natalie's father – the glamorous, high-flying Charlie – is so paralysed by the horror of losing his daughter, that he refuses even to discuss his wife's suspicions.

In the end, when their marriage is rocked by yet another terrible shock, Jessica decides to go back to France alone in search of some answers. When she gets to the idyllic vineyard in the heart of Burgundy she soon finds a great deal more than she was expecting in a love that is totally forbidden and a truth that will almost certainly devastate her life . . .

'One of the best around' *Independent on Sunday*

'Spellbinding! . . . you just keep turning the pages, with the atmosphere growing more and more intense as the story leads to its dramatic climax' *Daily Mail*

arrow books

Obsession

Susan Lewis

Corrie Browne is an ordinary girl with extraordinary ambitions. Determined to find the father she has never known, her search takes her from the quiet Suffolk village where she lives, to a new life in London, a fastpace television career – and to three people who come to dominate her life.

Luke, charismatic, blond and charming, is the only one to make Corrie feel welcome at TW TV and the only one to recognise her talent. Cristoff, an internationally famous film director, is the man who teaches her everything he knows about sex and passion. And Annelise is her boss and friend – a woman about whom Corrie knows a secret that must never be revealed. Three colleagues – all of whom are to play an important role in Corrie's search for love and success. One of whom intends Corrie's ultimate destruction.

arrow books

ALSO AVAILABLE IN ARROW

Just One More Day: A Memoir

Susan Lewis

In 1960s Bristol a family is overshadowed by tragedy . . .

While Susan, a feisty seven-year-old, is busy being brave, her mother, Eddress, is struggling for courage. Though bound by an indestructible love, their journey through a world that is darkening with tragedy is fraught with misunderstandings.

As a mother's greatest fear becomes reality, Eddress tries to deny the truth. And, faced with a wall of adult secrets, Susan creates a world that will never allow her mother to leave.

Set in a world where a fridge is a luxury, cars have starting handles, and where bingo and coupons bring in the little extras, *Just One More Day* is a deeply moving true-life account of how the spectre of death moved into Susan's family, and how hard they all tried to pretend it wasn't there.

'Susan Lewis fans know she can write compelling fiction, but not, until now, that she can write even more engrossing fact. We use the phrase honest truth too lightly: it should be reserved for books – deeply moving books – like this' Alan Coren

arrow books